RETREAT, HELL!

McDougal looked back at the men of his regiment, most of them green boys who'd never heard a shot fired in anger. The call of the bugle was no longer needed as the men raced to the battlement walls, fumbling to sling on cartridge boxes. Though only a regiment sergeant major, he took one look at the Roum lieutenant colonel who was second in command and knew that the old patrician was out of his element.

The Bantag leaped forward, shouting their deep soul-searing death cries. McDougal could see some of his own men already stepping back off the firing line, ready to flee.

Drawing his revolver, he leaped on the top of the breastworks and pointed the revolver at the advancing charge.

"Come on you bastards," he yelled with a laugh, "we're all going to die, so let's go down fighting!"

THE LOST REGIMENT

NEVER SOUND RETREAT

William R. Forstchen

A ROC BOOK

ROC
Published by the Penguin Group
Penguin Putnam Inc., 375 Hudson Street,
New York, New York 10014, U.S.A.
Penguin Books Ltd, 27 Wrights Lane,
London W8 5TZ, England
Penguin Books Australia Ltd, Ringwood,
Victoria, Australia
Penguin Books Canada Ltd, 10 Alcorn Avenue,
Toronto, Ontario, Canada M4V 3B2
Penguin Books (N.Z.) Ltd, 182–190 Wairau Road,
Auckland 10, New Zealand

Penguin Books Ltd, Registered Offices:
Harmondsworth, Middlesex, England

First published by Roc, an imprint of Dutton Signet,
a member of Penguin Putnam Inc.

First Printing, January, 1998
10 9 8 7 6 5 4 3 2

Cover art by San Julian

Printed in the United States of America

This one's for Mom and Dad, who endured and encouraged my obsession with Civil War history and took me on my first tour of eastern battlefields when I was fourteen. Little did I know until years later that Mom saved every cent she could spare for over a year in order to finance that wonderful week-long trip, which for me was a visit to sacred ground. The most treasured items in my collection are the ones Dad helped me to buy, often after a long day of prowling old antique shops to find the one relic we could afford. With their guidance and help I knew that owning a book on the Civil War was far more important than a Beatles album, and a battered old cartridge box was a possession to be sought more eagerly than the latest style in clothes. I learned through them that being a "history nerd" was, in fact, a status and position to be proud of.

This book is also for Norm Schiach, fellow collector; Tim Kindred, fellow reenactor for over twenty years; and finally for Major General J. L. Chamberlain. I think the parallels are rather obvious.

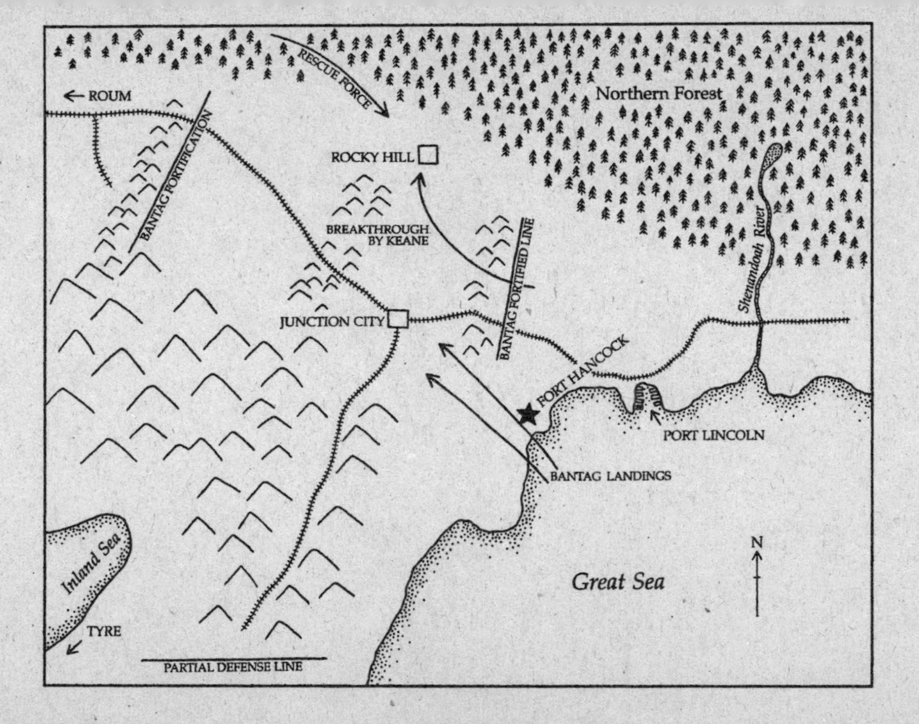
ROUM
RESCUE FORCE
Northern Forest
ROCKY HILL
BANTAG FORTIFICATION
BREAKTHROUGH BY KEANE
BANTAG FORTIFIED LINE
Shenandoah River
JUNCTION CITY
FORT HANCOCK
PORT LINCOLN
BANTAG LANDINGS
N
Great Sea
Inland Sea
TYRE
PARTIAL DEFENSE LINE

Foreword

BREECHLOADERS, WINGS, AND STEAM MOBILITY—TACTICAL AND OPERATIONAL TRANSITION IN THE CURRENT WAR AGAINST THE BANTAG HORDE

BY

LIEUTENANT COLONEL ROMULUS CLADIUS, STAFF COLLEGE, ARMY OF THE REPUBLIC

In the history of the Wars of the Republic against the various Hordes, one can observe several periods of rapid technological innovations, and the resulting impact on tactics, operational considerations, and army organization.

The men of the 35th Maine and 44th New York wrought tremendous change on the world of Valennia by their passage through the Tunnels of Light. Their arrival near Suzdal could not have been more timely, at least from the human perspective. Their social and political beliefs, formed in the legendary Civil War fought on their home world was carried to our world and became the inspiration for the people of Suzdal to rise up—first against their Boyar masters, and then against the Tugar Horde. The five hundred and fifty men lead by Colonel Keane carried as well the technological knowledge which enabled them to create the weapons of war needed to stand against the mobile horse archers of the Hordes. With this combination of political ideology and modern weapons, the people of Rus set forth to first liberate themselves and then the world. I, as a citizen of the State of Roum, shall forever be indebted to the people of Rus for this act.

Throughout the first and second wars against the Tugar and Merki Hordes, the Republic was almost always in the lead in regards to technological innovation. One of the few exceptions was the Merki application of engines to airships, but even there the legendary Chuck Ferguson managed to launch a response within a matter of weeks and reestablish balance.

It is the war against the Bantag though that has presented the first true challenge to the technical prowess of human arms. Exhausted after the bitter struggle against the Merki, the newly formed Republic failed to push the initiative by rapidly expanding eastward to bring in new allies. Some claim that the main motivation was political, for a rapid expansion and incorporation of new states would have shifted the balance of power in Congress and perhaps even the Presidency itself. I, for one, do not necessarily believe that so cynical a motive was present. An examination of the *Congressional Record* will show that this point was raised on the floor of Congress; however, the simple hard facts of economics played a far greater role.

Testimony by Secretary of the Treasury William Webster clearly showed that the Republic had the resources to either rebuild its internal rail net after the devastation of the Merki invasion or embark on building a rail line to Nippon, but it could not do both. As usual in such things, a half measure was decided upon, with some resources allocated to pushing a line as far as the Shenandoah River, five hundred miles east of Roum, but no farther. The building program requested by Colonel Keane, including the pushing of a line down the western shore of the Great Sea, was given a lower priority until such time as all the rail links within the borders of the Republic were completed. (And yes, there were political considerations here, for if one looks at the layout of congressional districts, one can see that every congressman made sure that tracks were laid within their district before signing off on expansion eastward. But such is the reality of representative government.)

So, quite simply, after years of war, the economy of the Republic was near collapse and time was needed to repair the damage of the last war before expansion could be resumed. Nevertheless, if the rail line had been aggressively pushed eastward to reach the people of Nippon before the Bantag expanded north, ten more corps of infantry could have been recruited. Even if they had been armed with the older smoothbore muskets, their additional numbers would have had a profound impact, and all the subsequent crisises most likely averted. For against an army of over twenty-two corps of infantry, any Bantag advance would have been all but impossible. But that is now a "what if." The Bantag cut us off to the east and south, and locked the people of Nippon behind their curtain as they have also locked the tens of millions of the Chin.

Therein is the crux of the problem confronting the Republic. Our dream was to liberate the world from the horror of the human-devouring Hordes. At this moment that no longer seems possible, at least within our lifetimes. For even if the Bantag are defeated, they can retreat before us, falling back far faster by horse than we can pursue by the laying of rails.

It was now realized that no society which is nomadic can ever hope to create and sustain a technologically based military system. If the Bantag had been pushed off base prior to the arrival of Ha'ark the Redeemer, the Republic would have gone on to sweep the world. Once Ha'ark was in place, and the factories created, the war between humans and the Hordes took on an entirely new dimension—it is now an arms race.

Ha'ark wisely placed his industrial base nearly a thousand miles beyond the frontier of the Republic and there, in secret, turned out weapons of war. It is interesting to note the parallel evolution of military technology on the home world of the men of the 35th Maine and that of Ha'ark. The one crucial difference, however, is the fact that Ha'ark's world appears to have been a hundred years more advanced and, due to that, he has a foreknowledge of tactical application which our own armies can only guess at.

The first warning of these changes came about due to the escape of Sergeant Major Hans Schuder and several hundred prisoners from the Bantag empire. Only at this point was it realized just how advanced this new enemy has become.

Not only has Ha'ark achieved parity in terms of infantry weapons, but he might very well have advanced beyond us in the areas of naval, air, and the new application of steam for the propulsion of ironclad artillery.

The months after the liberation of Hans Schuder have proven to be tumultuous within our ranks. The first question has always been: Where would the enemy strike? The second question confronting us is: How will he apply his technical advantages when battle is joined? Perhaps most troubling, though, is the question: What does he know about warfare that we do not know? We have pushed to the edge of our abilities over the last decade, moving from slavery to a modern army. But to Ha'ark, our efforts must seem primitive; the only thing that is restraining him is the struggle he must be waging even now to bring his own society forward to match us.

Bearing these issues in mind, I would like to suggest some of the following considerations in terms of tactical employment of infantry against the threat of Horde warriors similarly armed. . . .

Extract of report to Colonel Andrew Lawrence Keane, submitted eight weeks after the escape and rescue of Sergeant Major Hans Schuder

Chapter One

"We're hit, we're hit!"

Jack Petracci, commander of the Republic airship *Flying Cloud,* looked back to where his copilot and engineer, Feyodor, was pointing. A neat round hole had been punched into the stern of the airship just aft of the rear starboard engine. He studied the hole for several seconds. Some fabric was hanging loose, no struts were broken, controls to the tail elevators and rudder were intact and, most importantly, there was no fire.

"It's all right," Jack cried.

"No, damn it! I heard an explosion. The shell blew up inside the air hydrogen bag; we're burning!"

Jack ignored him and turned forward again. Straight ahead a Bantag airship, one of their new designs with wings, was boring straight in. Through his earphones he could hear Stefan, their top gunner, cursing wildly as he fired off another round. An explosion detonated on the enemy's wing where it was attached to the ship's airbag. A blue flash of light rippled up the side of the Bantag airship, and, within seconds, it was enveloped in flames, plummeting down, disappearing into the clouds below. That was two down, but there were still four more circling them.

Jack struggled to throw *Flying Cloud* into a steep banking turn to port, and, as the ship started to swing about, he looked downward to his left. Through a hole in the clouds he could see sunlight sparkling on the waves of the sea nearly twelve thousand feet below.

Pushing the flight stick forward, he dived again for the clouds. The advantage they had maintained over the last four months of simply being able to outclimb any opponent was finished; the damn Bantag had improved their machines yet again, and the only hope now was to duck into the clouds again and hope to shake off pursuit.

"Major Petracci!" Stefan's excited cry through the speaking tube was edged with hysteria. "We're burning!"

Jack looked back over his shoulder. Feyodor, in the aft-gunner position, was looking toward him, mouth open in a scream, pointing to the stern of the ship. Something was wrong with the underside—the fabric seemed to be rippling, sagging. At that same instant his stomach lurched. *Flying Cloud* was falling.

He pulled back on the stick. Nothing! The cables had severed.

Seconds before he had been nosing the ship over, now the stern was dropping as the rear gasbag spilled its contents in a swirling ball of fire. For a brief instant the bow surged up. From the aft end of the ship flames were racing straight at the gondola cab. Suddenly the bottom of the ship astern peeled back, erupting into a shimmering blue haze of fire.

His gaze locked on Feyodor, who stared at him wide-eyed with terror.

"Get out!" Jack screamed. "Everyone get out!"

"We're going to burn!" Feyodor cried.

Jack scrambled to the middle of the cabin. Unbolting the escape hatch, he kicked it open.

"The umbrellas Ferguson made, we've got to use them!"

"Like hell," Feyodor screamed.

"It's that or burn!"

Jack grabbed hold of Feyodor and dragged him to the hatch. The ship was dropping, bits of burning fabric swirling around the gondola. A burst of heat washed over him, and he saw the fireball racing toward them. Still connected to his speaking tube, he could hear Stefan screaming, trapped on the topside of the ship.

"Stefan! Jump, damn it, jump!"

He tore the speaking tube off and, still hanging on to Feyodor, leapt through the escape hatch. Feyodor fell and lay spread-eagled across the hatch, arms and legs still inside the ship. Dangling in the air, Jack looked up and saw the fireball explode through the cab. Feyodor instinctively pulled his hands in to cover his face. He started to fall through the hatch, and, an instant later, the two were free, Jack still clinging to his friend. They fell away from the ship, which seemed to hover in the sky above them. He let go of Feyodor and started to fumble with the fifty-pound bag strapped to his back.

There had been times when the inventor, Chuck Ferguson, had driven him damn near to distraction, but at this instant all he could do was fervently pray that this latest idea of his worked. Jack found the heavy metal ring, grabbed hold, and pulled. Nothing happened!

He looked over at Feyodor, who was tumbling end over end, a dozen feet away. His gaze shifted upward. The airship was falling, and, in spite of his terror, he felt a surge of anguish. *Flying Cloud* had carried him safely through twenty missions deep in Bantag territory, and now it was dying. To his horror he saw a small object falling away from the ship, wrapped in flames . . . it was Stefan. The boy was on fire and falling.

He turned his gaze away, refocusing on his own plight. He reached around to his back and could feel the flap on his backpack, but nothing was coming out. Cursing at Ferguson for not testing the damn idea more thoroughly, he reached over his shoulder and dug his hand into the silk fabric within as he plummeted into the clouds . . .

"Your move, Andrew."

Andrew Lawrence Keane, commander of the Armies of the Republic, stirred from his thoughts and looked over at his old friend, Dr. Emil Weiss.

"What was that?"

Weiss smiled and nodded toward the chessboard. "Your move, Andrew."

"Oh, of course." Absently he picked up his queen and moved it forward, taking Emil's bishop.

Emil shook his head. "And you the famous general." He sighed as he moved his own queen down the length of the board.

"Check and mate in one, my friend."

Andrew said nothing and just stared at the board. Normally he considered himself a fairly good chess player. Back when he was a professor of history at Bowdoin College he had taken it as a point of pride that he could beat any student who challenged him.

Andrew reached over and, with a touch of his finger, knocked over his king, thus signifying his withdrawal from the game. He looked up at the clock ticking on the wall. It was past midnight. His gaze continued to wander around the room. The map of the eastern frontier filled one entire wall, blue pins and tape marking positions of his units, red pins the suspected positions of the Bantag. He studied it intently for several minutes, Emil saying nothing.

His headquarters office was spartan, maps lining the walls, piles of documents arrayed on shelves behind his desk, a collapsible cot in the far corner opposite the woodstove. Hans Schuder, boots still on, was sprawled on the cot, slouch cap covering his face, snoring softly. Some of the men with Ferguson's team had made the cot as a special present, making sure it was long enough for Andrew's wiry six-foot-four frame. His staff made a point of trying to brighten up the office with the flowers which seemed to be part of the Rus soul, and one of his boys made sure that fresh blossoms were arranged daily in an empty vodka bottle on his desk. The blooms were alien and exotic, brilliant reds, greens, and blues, wildflowers of an alien world, their scent rich and sweet. Woodcut prints from *Gates's Illustrated Weekly* had been carefully clipped and pegged to the wall devoid of maps, scenes from the rescue of Hans, the launching of the newest ironclad on the Great Sea, and, from just last week, a picture of *Flying Cloud* on its deepest penetration into Bantag territory, having flown within sight of the factory complex where Hans had been kept prisoner.

And now Jack's gone, damn it. Standing up to stretch, Andrew walked to the door, opened it, and looked into the next room. The telegrapher was at his station . . . fast asleep, cap pulled low over his eyes to block out the glare of the kerosene lamp. Two orderlies were stretched out on the floor, one of them stirring, looking up, ready to get to his feet. Andrew motioned for him to be still and, closing the door, looked back at Emil.

"Even though it's been four days, I still half expect to see Petracci walk back in. Hard to believe we've lost him. *Flying Cloud* was the last of our airships. We're blind now."

Reaching across the table, he took the bottle of vodka from Emil's side of the board, poured himself a shot, and downed it.

"Jack, Feyodor, Stefan . . . damn all to hell."

Emil said nothing in reply. All of the news had been bad of late, the buildup of enemy shipping in their fortified port of Xi'an, the news earlier this day that the Bantag Horde had cut off Nippon, even the political side of things, with the adroit maneuvering of the human ambassadors sent by Ha'ark the Bantag leader to divide the Republic against itself.

"The fall of Nippon," Andrew sighed, leaning forward to play with the pieces on the chessboard. "They can come at us now from one of two ways. I need to know which one it is, and we're blind." As he talked he propped his king back up, then maneuvered Emil's queen and rooks.

"East around the sea," he said softly as he moved the queen off to the upper right corner of the board. In his imagination he could see the positioning. Nippon was several hundred miles to the east. If they had pushed the rail line aggressively, the way he wanted, and the hell with internal politics, they might have made it out to them in time, shipped in arms, and started building an army. The Nippon population was big enough that he could have fielded twenty divisions from their ranks within a year. With those twenty additional divisions, no Bantag army could ever have challenged them.

"Damn, if only we had pushed the rail line through to Nippon."

"If wishes were horses . . ." Emil replied. "And besides. We're not talking about the old days, when we could have thrown smoothbore muskets in their hands, trained them for a month, then lined them up and had them bang away. War is getting too damn complex now.

"The units they've let us see are still armed the old way, with bow and lance, but remember everything Hans told us. They have factories, breechloading rifles and artillery, and those damn land cruisers. Even if we had gotten to Nippon in time, we would have been hundreds of miles out on a string pulled taut and ready to snap. It might have been a repeat of the First Roum Campaign, but only worse, far worse. Cut the rail line anywhere along that three-hundred-mile stretch, and you would have been finished."

"What you're saying is that the Nippon were doomed from the start."

Emil shook his head sadly.

"It's like the classifying of the wounded I do during a battle. Those who can take care of themselves for a while, we hand them the bandages, give them a little morphine, and tell them to wait. It's deciding about the other two, who will we try and save and who do we set aside to die because they're too far gone, that still breaks my heart every time I do it."

He looked away, and yet again Andrew sensed the all-so-different side of the war that Emil, his own Kathleen, and the other doctors experienced. In spite of his loathing for it all, there were still moments that seemed to transcend the brutality and revealed to him, yet again, the inner workings of his soul.

The eternal question he had wrestled with for ten years was before him yet again . . . what am I? Though I loathe war, I know I would be somehow lost without it. All that I am now was formed in the crucible of battle. How I prayed for peace, and yet how I felt somehow incomplete when peace came, as if I was a machine of Mars, packed away but only until the bugles called again.

"It's that moment when I have to look into a boy's eyes," Emil said, interrupting his thoughts. "It's that horrible moment when I have to lie as convincingly as I can that I'll be back later to take care of him, but that there's others who are hurt far worse . . ." His voice trailed off into silence for a moment.

Andrew felt a wave of guilt for what he had just been musing about. *Gates's Illustrated Weekly* had printed hundreds of pictures of heroic struggle on the battlefields of the Republic, but they had never done one of the operating room, the battlefield that Dr. Emil Weiss fought upon. That was the other side of the equation which he had seen often enough. A man would go down by his side. There was the stunned moment of disbelief, shock in the wounded soldier's eyes, disbelief that it had finally happened, and then the fumbling at the clothes to see how bad it was. Funny, you could never really tell in those first few seconds until you actually saw the damage inflicted on your body; then you knew. A veteran, one who knew about wounds, would examine himself, and there might be a smile of relief, a sense that it was bad but he'd still make it. For the others, though, their gaze would suddenly unfocus, as if they were already seeing into the other land. And even though the doctor lied, both of them somehow knew.

He remembered his own moment, the retreat off Seminary Ridge at Gettysburg, the few survivors of the Thirty-fifth gathered round him, and then the shell all but tearing his left arm off. The last he could remember was lying on the ground, looking up at his men, the regimental flag above them fluttering in the afternoon breeze, shot-torn and wreathed in battle smoke, then a fading away into the darkness, to awake with Emil sitting by his side, breaking the news that the arm was gone forever.

"You can't save the whole world, Andrew Keane."

Andrew tried to reason with himself that his frustration was coldly pragmatic, a hundred thousand potential troops for his army lost, in large part because of the shortsightedness of the government. But no, it was far more, far more . . . the thought of the Horde riding into yet another city, the division between those who will live a little longer, and those who will go immediately to the slaughter pits. He had hoped that somehow they could push the railroad ahead of the Bantag, lay rails faster than the Horde could move, then finally swing south, cut them off, and rescue millions, tens of millions. But the Horde had been the one to do the cutting off. As long as the Bantag held the way to the east and south, all those behind them were now doomed.

He looked across the room to where Sergeant Major Hans Schuder slept. Like any old campaigner, Hans knew when to catch a nap and could drift off in seconds.

Andrew watched him affectionately. Hans had been back for four months now. The physical wounds, the bullet hole in his leg, the saber slash to his head, were healed; but he was changed.

Andrew knew sadly that the old Hans would never quite return. He had simply seen too much in his long years of captivity. Emil had even coined a term for it, "survivor's guilt," and said that many of the nearly three hundred that Hans had brought out suffered from it. Yet on Hans, the burden was heaviest. It was his decision which had triggered the breakout from the Bantag prison, and in the process knowingly condemned the thousands left behind to certain death.

"Ah now! And you won't believe who I just dragged in!"

Andrew looked back up and saw Pat O'Donald towering in the doorway, shaking the rain from his poncho. Taking off his soaked and drooping campaign hat, he pulled up a chair beside Andrew, took the bottle without asking, poured a drink into an empty glass, and downed it.

Hans stirred from his slumber and, cursing, looked up.

"You damn stupid mick, can't you keep it down?"

"Mick is it? You thick-headed Dutchman."

"Prussian by Gott," Hans snapped back.

Andrew started to smile, shaking his head, waiting for the inevitable exchange, with Hans swearing at Pat in German, and Pat lapsing into a wondrous stream of Gaelic invective. But Pat broke it off and pointed back to the door, and all in the room fell silent.

Jack Petracci stood in the doorway, grinning and standing at attention.

Andrew leapt from his chair and, with hand extended, rushed up to Jack's side.

"We thought you were dead, son. What the hell happened?"

Holding on to Jack's hand Andrew led him over to the table, motioning for him to take a seat. Behind him Andrew saw Feyodor, his hand wrapped in bandages, and gestured for him to come over as well. Jack looked longingly at the bottle, and Pat, laughing, poured out drinks for everyone. Jack took the first drink and handed it over to Feyodor, who clumsily cupped it, grimacing as he tried to wrap his hands around the mug.

"I was down at the dock watching as one of the courier ships from the blockade fleet came in," Pat announced, "and by all the saints I seen him standin' on the deck."

"We'd given you up, Petracci," Hans interjected, pulling a chair up beside Jack. "What happened?"

"They've got a new airship design," Jack whispered shakily, as the vodka hit him. "Must have kept it hidden till they made half a dozen of them. Bigger wings, two engines, one on each wing. We did our run over Xi'an and about twenty miles east, turned about to head back, and I was starting to go down low for a closer look at things. Suddenly these new ships came diving out of the clouds."

He sighed and took a long sip of his drink.

"So we started to climb. Clouds were at nine thousand; I punched through into clear sky at ten. But they came through after us and kept right on climbing. Damnedest thing, sir, not only could they match our height, they were faster. It must be those wings of theirs."

"I want sketches of them as soon as possible for Ferguson to look at," Andrew said.

More and more Andrew found that he was looking

to Ferguson as a talisman, the young inventor always able to find yet another answer to whatever the Hordes threw at them. In the last war it was the rockets, in this one it might very well be the airships and the land ironclads he was developing.

"Already made some," Jack replied, as he reached into his bedraggled tunic and pulled out a sheaf of papers, spreading them out on the table. Andrew leaned over to examine the drawings. Besides being the best pilot of the Republic, Jack had a fair hand as an illustrator as well. The ships looked sleeker, the engines mounted on the wings, and, looking at the scale line, Andrew saw that Jack estimated them at being nearly a hundred feet across. He looked over at Hans, who shook his head.

"Damn Ha'ark," Hans mumbled. "I should have shot the bastard when we met under the flag of truce. Bet this is another one of the things he brought from that world of his."

"If you'd shot him, you wouldn't be here now," Andrew replied. "I think, all things considered, the trade was worth it."

"Then what happened?" Hans asked, his face drawn with worry.

"Well, we had a running fight all the way back to the coast. I dodged down into the clouds, but they were patchy. Anytime I broke through, one of them was on me. They had at least ten ships up, six of them the newer design. Just as we cleared the coast they boxed us in. I tried to climb out, but they were on top of us. We dropped two of them, but they finally put an explosive round in our stern as I was climbing through twelve thousand feet, and *Flying Cloud* went up."

"Tell 'em about how you jumped," Pat interjected with a grin.

Jack sighed, and Andrew could detect the terror that still lingered just below the surface. Back during the rescue of Hans he had flown with Jack on *Flying Cloud*. It had been one of the most terrifying experiences of his life. He'd rather charge a battery of guns or face an onslaught of Bantag cavalry than have to go up in one of those machines again.

"Ferguson saved our lives. I thought the umbrella idea of his was insane, but we jumped anyhow—there was nothing left to do. It took a little doing to get them out of the packs on our backs, but once they popped open we floated down and landed in the sea."

"Stefan?" Emil asked quietly.

"He got out too late," Jack whispered. He closed his eyes and took another drink.

"You know what was amazing?" Feyodor said, breaking the silence. "A couple of the Bantag flyers came down through the clouds, one of them circled us as we floated down. Thought we were dead for sure, their gunner had me in his sights, and then the bastard simply waved and took off."

"Fellow pilot," Jack replied casually. "I'd have done the same."

"They're Bantag," Hans growled.

Jack looked over at him and shook his head.

"I know that, but he gave me a break, and I'll do the same if I ever see him again. But anyhow, we were lucky. Came down a couple miles off the coast. There was *Petersburg* almost right under us. When Bullfinch heard what we'd seen he transferred us over to a picketboat and had us brought straight back here."

"You know, if Ferguson was here, I think I'd kiss him," Feyodor announced, then grimaced as Emil leaned over the table and started to unwrap the bandages from his hands to examine the wounds.

"What was it that you saw?" Hans asked.

"Like I said we got about twenty miles east of Xi'an and saw a dozen trains on the line, all of them packed with troops from the look of it. But they were heading east, sir."

"You sure of that?"

"Absolutely, sir. The encampments we saw springing up around Xi'an, they were struck, the gear packed, the troops heading back east. The ships were still along the river, but there were no workers. I wanted to get down for a closer look at the sheds lining the riverbank, see if we could somehow peek inside, but that's when we got jumped."

Surprised, Andrew looked over at Hans.

"One if by land, two if by sea," he said. "This could mean they're giving up a seaborne attack."

"Jack, could they have shot you down earlier?" Hans asked.

"What do you mean?"

"They chased you for what, an hour, two hours?"

"Something like that. Why?"

"Yet they didn't get you till you were clear of the coast."

"I don't see your point, Hans."

"Nothing, son. Just wondering." Hans sighed, then he lowered his head.

Andrew stood up and went over to the map hanging on the wall. There were indications of at least thirty umens in the area of Nippon. Most of them were still armed the old way, with bows and lances, but there were units of artillery and even some mounted infantry armed with muzzle-loading rifles. One of the photographs Jack had taken on an earlier mission clearly showed rows of parked cannons in Xi'an. If Ha'ark was giving up on a seaborne assault, was he now shifting his modern units to Nippon?

Hans came up to join him.

"Are we being set up?" Hans whispered. "Did they want Jack to see the move? They must have figured we were down to the one airship. Maybe they wanted him to see it and report back."

"Then why shoot him down? They couldn't have known about the umbrellas."

"Maybe they did. Or maybe someone got carried away and shot him down against orders. Hell, he said they dodged around for eighty miles, then, just after he got over the coast, down he goes."

"Are you saying it's a trick?"

"Expect the unexpected with Ha'ark. A game within a game."

Andrew said nothing, looking over at Hans. He could sense the fear Hans carried of Ha'ark. Not a fear of meeting him on the field but rather of his cunning, his unrelenting will. Was that now blinding him? If Jack had escaped, and was then blocked the next time he returned to Xi'an, there'd be reason for suspicion. But shoot him down without word first getting back?

He stared at the map. The trouble was there was no way of knowing.

Emil had finished unwrapping Feyodor's bandages and was clucking softly as he examined the copilot's red and swollen hands.

"If they do come from the east," Andrew said, pointing at the map, "it'll be a hard fight for them. The terrain's in our favor, mostly forest, not very good ground for cavalry at all. If need be, we can fall back to the final river line on the Shenandoah—it's damn near six hundred yards across."

"They could stretch the front into the woods though," Hans replied. "Remember, this Ha'ark is different. He knows war maybe fifty, a hundred years ahead of us. They'll fight dismounted, as infantry, not like the Merki trying to maneuver a hundred thousand mounted warriors through the forest when we got flanked on the Neiper. If they had left their horses behind them, they actually would have moved faster through the forest and might have bagged you. In one of my conversations with Ha'ark he seemed to have a damn good grasp of the mistakes the Merki made."

Andrew nodded.

"So what do you think it will be?"

"Both," Hans replied. "He has the resources to fight on two fronts. Our one point of threat to him is right here, out of Port Lincoln. It's our one base on this sea from which we can mount an invasion one day. We have to take out Xi'an before he takes us out here. Whoever succeeds at that first wins the war."

"So you're convinced it's a feint, this withdrawal of his modern army from Xi'an."

Hans nodded and pointed to the ground between the eastern shore of the Inland Sea and the western shore of the Great Sea.

"We know he's moved upwards of ten umens over here. That's not enough to break the three corps we're committing to hold that front. Andrew, I think he'll strike behind us by sea. Land somewhere between here and Port Lincoln down to our front a hundred miles to the south."

"Even if it is a feint, there's still Bullfinch and the fleet in front of Xi'an."

"He's convinced he can beat the blockade fleet."

Andrew sighed and continued to gaze at the map, as he had done now for four months. The equation was simple enough. Both sides were dependent on their factories to supply the sinews of war. His own bases were more than five hundred miles to the west, starting at Roum. The Bantag factories were a thousand miles to the southeast, three hundred miles back from Xi'an. If the Bantag could seize Port Lincoln, any hope of ever striking at them was gone. The Hordes would continue to build and finally overwhelm his forces without any danger to their industrial base. Yet his own ability to leap forward and seize Xi'an was limited as well. Even if they could take Xi'an, all the land strength of the Bantag could then be marshaled against them while his own troops would be hanging six hundred miles away, dangling at the end of a seaborne supply line.

Was Ha'ark capable of striking now? Hans was pushing an equation that was a speculation built upon two assumptions, the first that the withdrawal was not real, and the second that their fleet could beat Bullfinch. It was pushing it too far.

"And now we're blind," Andrew whispered, looking back at Jack and Feyodor. Emil had fetched his medical bag and was busy dabbing Feyodor's hands with what Emil claimed was an antiseptic.

"One more flight, damn it," Andrew said, "just one more flight."

Jack heard him and looked up.

"Sorry, Jack, wasn't talking about you. Losing *Flying Cloud* wasn't your fault."

"Still feel like it was, sir," Jack replied.

"Are you sure about what you saw down there?"

"At least a dozen trains heading east, fully loaded," Feyodor interjected.

Andrew looked back at Hans.

"It'll be more than month before we get our newest airship built and can check again."

"What about our going back to Suzdal to meet with Congress and the president?" Hans asked.

Andrew hesitated for a moment. The meetings had been planned for weeks, but it'd put him nearly three days away from field headquarters. Yet there were so many things to iron out back home as well.

"We still go. The old arrangement stands. Pat, you head east. Vincent Hawthorne will stay here as chief of staff and keep an eye on the southern front. Marcus will continue to oversee the building of the fortifications and rail line in the south."

Andrew started for the door, pausing to pat Jack on the shoulder.

"Glad to have you back, Petracci. You're heading home to Rus for some leave, you can take the train with us tomorrow morning."

"Well, sir, I'd rather stay out here."

"There's nothing for you to do until we get those new airships. Take some leave, work with Ferguson on the designs and start training our new pilots."

Andrew walked out of the room and into the cool night air. From the front porch of his clapboard headquarters he looked out over the rail yard that was the main supply head serving Port Lincoln and the eastern front. Nearly a dozen trains were in the yard, off-loading supplies, the last one in for the night bringing with it a new battery and the Forty-third Roum Infantry.

The troops were filing off, moving through the

night, passing in front of his headquarters, not aware that he was standing in the shadows. Stepping to the end of the porch, he watched them head down into the town built along the bluffs above the harbor. The sound of their passing carried with it the old familiar haunting rhythm, the tramping of boots, the banging of tin-cups and canteens, the soft-spoken conversations, snatches of songs, the whispering, swirling, pulsing beat of an army moving in the night, the same rhythm that he had heard on the road to Antietam, Gettysburg, Cold Harbor and later at the Ford, Roum, and, finally, Hispania.

Wagons rumbled past, piled high with boxes of hardtack, moving toward the warehouses, followed by others bearing artillery ammunition, shoes, uniforms, barrels of salted pork, and the thousand other items that now made up his modern army in the field.

He looked overhead, the Great Wheel hovering in the sky above. Yet again it filled him with wonder. Which star, of the myriad spread out above him, was home?

How many nights had he wondered that? He smiled, remembering after the end of the Merki War, when he and Kathleen had taken a brief vacation, spending a week in an abandoned villa offered to them by Proconsul Marcus of Roum. It had only been the two of them, the children, and a few servants. At night they would walk up to a high meadow, where the grass was nearly waist high, lie down, and watch the stars. They had made a game of trying to pick out which one was the sun of earth. He could remember one night all so well, the stars coming out, Kathleen wrapped in his embrace, breathing softly and then whispering that this was home, this was their Earth, the place that was theirs forever.

And yet . . . he wondered about Maine. The oceans here were different, freshwater and warm, they lacked the delicious chill of an autumn breeze coming in off the sea, the icy fog of winter, the crystal blue days of summer that were so achingly beautiful. Funny, all that he now was he would not change, not Kathleen, the children, even the dream of the Republic he had struggled so hard to create on this nightmare world. Yet as he looked at the stars above he wished that somehow he could recapture and hold what once was, the lazy summer nights of Maine, the youthful innocence, the belief that such hopes would indeed be true.

"Thinking of Maine?"

He turned to see Hans by his side, looking up at the stars as well.

"How did you know?"

"Could tell somehow. I feel the same. A wish for peace, a place for my wife, my son to be safe. Remember that meadow we hiked to north of Augusta, back when you were a fresh young lieutenant and we marched your company for the first time?"

Andrew smiled wistfully. "Snow Pond above Augusta. Remember it well."

"It was peaceful there that day, so peaceful, the breeze rippling the water, the white clouds drifting in, the blue sky, the air cool, fresh like it was the day the Earth was born. I've dreamed of it ever since. When I was back there"—he nodded toward the south—"at night I'd dream that I could close my eyes and the years would peel back and we'd be there again and all that would happen to us was then a dream yet to be."

Andrew said nothing for a long moment. The Hans who had come back to him from the hell of the Bantag prisons was changed. He was still the same old grizzled sergeant major, that was eternal, yet now there was a tragic longing, a looking for something he feared they would never find in this world.

"We're in trouble, Hans," he finally said, and as he spoke, he continued to gaze at the sky. "When the last war ended I dreamed it was over, but it never will be, at least as long as we are alive. Maybe for our children, but not for us. It will just keep going on, and on."

Hans nodded as he reached into his pocket, fished out a plug of tobacco, and bit off a chew. He absently offered the plug to Andrew, who took a bite, then looked over at Hans and smiled. It was a ritual they had developed so many years back when they were still on Earth. In the years when Hans was a prisoner, the memory of this simple gesture could move him to tears.

"Why us, Hans?" Andrew sighed.

"Because we're here, lad, because we're here."

Chapter Two

"My Qar Qarth."

Ha'ark, grinning with delight, accepted the bow and salute of his lieutenants, Jurak and Bakkth, two of his companions who had traveled through the Tunnel of Light with him. Ha'ark Qar Qarth the Redeemer looked around at the assembled umen leaders and clan Qarths who were gathered in his golden yurt and felt a cold chill of delight. Hard to believe, even to imagine, that five years past he was but a frightened draftee, forced to join the imperial forces in the war of the False Pretender back on his home world.

Was that even me, he wondered? More a scholar than a soldier, wanting nothing of the war, driven to it because of an unfortunate encounter with the daughter of a petty judge who, to defend her honor, had later claimed that his attentions were forced rather than gladly accepted. The thought was amusing now; at least he had claimed that they were not forced and, with a wry smile, realized that the truth fell somewhere in the middle.

By the time he had been forced into the army the glorious early days of victory for the imperial side were long past, and when he had left for the depot his family offered the traditional services for the dead. It was no longer a war of honor or quarter, and the imperial armies were in retreat. Cities still loyal were under constant bombardment, and the great palace had disappeared under a rain of atomic rockets.

When he and the rest of his unit had fallen through the Tunnel of Light to this world he had thought it was the end . . . and now he was Qar Qarth.

The memory of it all caused him to laugh softly, and those around him, his clan leaders, his umen commanders and tribal Qarths started to laugh as well. They knew not why they were laughing, simply that some thought had amused their Redeemer and, therefore, was worth laughing about as well.

It was so pathetically simple to convince the barbarians of this world that he was the Redeemer of prophecy; all he needed to do was draw on some of the ancient mythology, for it was obvious that those of this world were of the clans lost when the great empire had collapsed, eons ago. The ancestors had created the portals to leap between worlds, but the knowledge of how such things functioned was lost in the wreckage of empire.

For that he was grateful—the portals were now simply a threat through which rivals might appear. In his old world he was nothing but an unwilling soldier in an unwinnable war, but here he was the Redeemer, the Qar Qarth of the Bantag Horde, and here he would forge an empire of his own making.

He was grateful, as well, for the presence of the humans, for without them as the common enemy he might never have risen to power, and without them now there would be no war to enshrine his name in glory. His thoughts lingered for a moment on Schuder. There were times when he could still reach out and touch into his soul, to feel the fear, the torment that still lingered there. Strange, he almost missed him at times. For a cattle, a human, Schuder was remarkably civilized, a good soldier, and he wished he could have bent him to his will. As Schuder had been the force behind the creation of the human armies, so he might have served here. He was certain there would be a day when he would meet Schuder once again. It would be a pleasure to share a talk with him one more time, before he was led to the feast where his brains would be devoured.

Schuder's escape had the potential of being a humiliation, but the blame had been shifted, and more than one who had opposed him had been forced to fall upon his sword in atonement for fault, real or conjured.

If Schuder had created a problem, it was that he was now forced to launch his war too soon.

He motioned for Jurak and Bakkth to join him, and together they left the yurt. As they stepped out into the evening air he took a deep breath, glad to be free of the noise and the stench of the moon feast. To try and carry on any rational conversation, while humans were slowly being roasted alive, was all but impossible.

He could see the look of displeasure on Jurak's face.

"Barbaric," Jurak growled. "I wouldn't mind it so much if they simply cut their throats first."

Ha'ark chuckled and shook his head.

"But then the shamans could not divine the future."

"Seeing the future by interpreting the howls of a creature as he's slowly cooked and his brains devoured while he's still alive is beyond belief."

"It's their way, and it serves our purpose."

Even as Jurak voiced his protest a wild piercing scream erupted from the yurt, the hysterical screams greeted seconds later by roars of approval as the shaman undoubtedly declared some favorable sign from the insane howls of the human whose legs were being plunged repeatedly into a caldron of boiling water until the flesh and muscle finally sloughed off the bones.

The night of the moon feast was young, yet from the thousands of yurts spread across the steppe, from that of the most lowly caste to the golden yurt of the Redeemer, the ritual was being repeated so that the air was alive with shrieks of agony, the cries for mercy, the anguished gasping out of life. It was considered a bad omen if the subject of the feast died too quickly, and those who could make the torment linger till the coming of dawn believed that their luck would be good for the coming month.

It was always a strange sight, in the early-morning light, when the flaps of the yurts were pulled back so that the rising light of dawn would fill the tent. The human cattle who had survived would then be brought out and those still strong enough made to stand while their skulls were cracked open and their brains devoured. The auguries were held to be especially good if the last sight of the human had was of the rising sun, for as his world went dark his spirit, primitive as it was, would wing to the everlasting sky, where he would serve forever as a slave of the departed ancestors.

And even as he died, they would tear the boiled and roasted flesh from his limbs in a frenzy of feeding, their passions aroused by the long night of ritual. A hundred thousand humans would die this night to feed the belly of his Horde. He was told that the Chin were numberless, but after four years encamped in this one region such feasting was taking its toll on their numbers. It was good that the war had started; otherwise, his subjects would have grown restless.

"You saw the destruction of the airship?" Ha'ark asked, his icy gaze fixed on Bakkth.

"Yes."

Ha'ark growled angrily.

"Part of the reason I allowed you to command the airships was so that discipline would be instilled. The pilots should all be taken out and impaled for their stupidity. The orders were to prevent it from flying too low, to attack if necessary but ensûre that it escaped."

Bakkth nervously shook his head.

"If I execute the pilots, who will we get to fly, Ha'ark? It takes months to train these primitives. I was there, and I tell you that the one who placed the shot that hit the human airship was shot down as well."

"A likely story. You're protecting someone, perhaps even yourself."

"Let is rest, Ha'ark," Jurak interjected. "Anyhow, I think we can all agree that it was remarkable luck that they had parachutes. Letting them see the maneuver, then shooting them down afterward will convince Keane that the report is true and not just a feigned movement."

Ha'ark waved aside Jurak's defense of his friend even though it was true. The elaborate deception he had conceived did have that one flaw—Keane might see it as nothing but a trick. The shooting down might be the final factor that convinced Keane to believe the report of the redeployment as true and thus set him up for the trap. If so, then the gods were yet again showing their favor. Tomorrow his own airships would push across the sea to ensure that the Yankees had no new ships ready to fly, for already the trains had been turned about, the tens of thousands of troops were returning to their barracks in Xi'an.

"Are you certain you saw them picked up?" he asked.

"I flew down personally."

Bakkth did not add that he had actually felt admiration for the human pilot who had so masterfully fought them for nearly two hours. His orders had been to direct the attack on the ship, but to do it in such a manner as to let them escape, but he could not blame his pilots too much for wanting to close with their new flying machines and test them against the human ship which had flown for months, with impunity, above them. Nor would he ever admit to the friendly wave he had offered to a skillful foe.

"And the trains?"

"As we planned. The human would have had to be blind not to see them moving east. He flew above the rail line leading back here, even dipping beneath the cloud cover for a closer look before finally turning back."

"And the concealment in Xi'an?"

"The camouflage was in place. The umens well hidden, the monitors concealed in sheds as were the land cruisers and special craft for moving them."

Ha'ark nodded as he absently fished in the pouch by his hip, pulled out a plug of tobacco, and took a chew. It reminded him yet again of Hans. What would the old sergeant say of his plan, he wondered. There would have to be, at the very least, a certain professional admiration for it all.

Hans . . . would Hans see through the elaborate deception? The trick was to convince them that the main thrust was coming to the north and east, out of the territory of the Nippon. In truth, that could very well be the place where victory would be won anyhow; twenty-five of his umens were committed to this opening move which Jurak would lead. But it had to be done slowly, to draw more and yet more of their troops into the vulnerable forward position. At the same time he wanted them to maintain a presence on the western shore of the ocean. To ensure that, eighteen umens had made the long march around the sea, crossing at the narrows hundreds of leagues to the south, and were just now moving into position to hold the Second Army of the humans between the two seas.

He could picture the two fronts as two points on the base of a triangle. All that was left was to strike the blow at the point of the triangle, thus cutting the two fronts off. That was the purpose of the strike force assembling in Xi'an, to close the trap. There, at the point of decision, would be the best of his modern weapons, his assault troops armed with breechloaders, and the precious land cruisers.

He turned away from his companions and began to pace the wooden deck in front of his yurt. Yet it was too soon, far too soon. There were only enough ships to transport three umens, thirty batteries of artillery, and twenty land cruisers. His plan had been to shatter the Yankee fleet in one surprise blow, then spring out and strike the land forces. He had toyed with the idea of delaying everything till next spring, but his fear was that in that time the Yankees could match, and perhaps even exceed, what he had already created.

With the limited transport only half his force could be moved in the first strike, and then it would be at least ten days before the second wave could be brought up. The timing of it all was so crucial. He looked back over his shoulder at Jurak. Attacking now was something Jurak had not approved of, urging that they wait till spring, when fifteen more umens could be fully armed with modern weapons, the additional transports readied, and the rail line run all the way up past Nippon so that the eastern army could be fully supplied.

Jurak could not see that audacity was needed. If they could cut off the two wings of Keane's army, the campaign might press as far as Roum before the autumn rains stopped them. Then, no matter how much the Yankees produced, come spring it would be over.

He stopped in his pacing, tormented yet again by the one key question.

"Bakkth, are you certain they landed alive and were picked up?"

"I saw their ironclad come alongside them and haul them aboard."

Ha'ark nodded and spit a stream of tobacco juice.

"Perhaps for the best then, we won't have to worry about the ship coming back, but regardless of that, I want a constant air patrol. Especially at dawn, that's usually when they came in."

"I've already ordered it, Ha'ark."

Ha'ark nodded. Of late he was becoming uncomfortable with the fact that his companions, those who had crossed through the Tunnel with him, still addressed him by his name rather than as Qar Qarth or the Redeemer. It was a familiarity that he would have to put an end to.

"Surprising they thought up the idea of parachutes," Jurak said. "Perhaps we should consider the same."

Ha'ark shook his head.

"A waste of precious silk and weight. Our machines still do not have enough power or lift, and two parachutes mean on less bomb. Besides, it is good for the pilots to realize that they either return victorious or not at all."

"A waste of good training."

"There are a thousand more volunteers waiting to replace them. Finding more pilots is not my worry, making more machines is."

That was something Jurak still did not seem to grasp fully, and that was the core of his problem. More than half a million Chin slaves labored in his mines, factories, armories. A hundred thousand worked just on the rail line he was pushing north into the territory of the Nippon, so that his supply head would be close to the front. It was the wringing of this transformation out of a barbarian world that was the real challenge. The lives of the cattle, or for that matter his own warriors, were secondary if it meant that one more airship could be created, or one more artillery piece or land cruiser, or the locomotive or ship to haul them to the place of battle.

That was the true genius of what he was creating, the dragging of a primitive fallen race into the modern age, though compared to the war he had known on the world of his birth, what he was creating here was but one step removed from barbarity. If not for the human slaves, the task would be hopeless, for no rider of the Horde would ever deem to lower himself to the task of labor. Only those of the lowest caste could be compelled to be the guards in the factories or to run the locomotives or work in the engine room of the ships. It would take a generation at least to transform that thinking. The Tugars never understood that, the Merki were just beginning to grasp it even as they went down to defeat. This would have to be different.

It would be war itself, the very reason for their own existence, that would serve as the catalyst of change. He could promise them that once the Republic was defeated, things could be as they once were, that again they could go with bow and lance on the everlasting ride about the world, harvesting the human slaves who waited to feed them. But he knew the lie of that.

The Yankees had brought an infection to this world, the disease of knowledge, bow and horse giving way to rifle and locomotive, and once the change was started it would never stop. When this war was done he would indulge them in their ritual of the eastward ride for a while, but the rail lines would follow them, linking back to the factories. Only those humans who were trained to labor would then be kept alive, all others would be put to the sword. For the secret of technology had been unlocked, and nothing could ever change it back again. Even if the Republic was completely shattered, its cities leveled, all its populace put to the sword, still the infection was there and would spread. Some humans would manage to escape, fleeing into the great northern forests, there to labor in secret. If he should ever let down his guard and allow his people to revert, twenty years hence, when they returned, it would be to face a disaster.

He knew with a grim certainty that this was a racial war for control of this world, and the only alternative to total victory was annihilation.

"I still think we should wait," Jurak said, while pensively gazing at the twilight sky.

"Why?"

"It won't be until next season that the rail line up to Nippon and on into the forest where their rail line is located is completed. Even then, there's the difference in gauges—we'll have to convert their line as we advance. Well have a logistical nightmare trying to keep our northern army supplied without that rail link. If we wait till spring, we could have another dozen monitors, a hundred landing ships, fifty or more airships, at least another ten umens converted and trained with rifles and modern artillery. Supplies to the north with a completed rail line would be ensured as well."

"And what of the humans in that time, Jurak? They adapt faster than we do. Their own railhead running down along the western shore is still vulnerable, but it won't be by next spring. They have no airships at the moment, but we can be assured that if we wait till spring, we will see dozens, with wings like ours. Remember it is an old maxim of the master Hunaga, 'If surprise is lost retreat or strike, to do neither is death.' We cannot retreat; therefore, we must strike. As it is, I fear this four-month delay; it gives us but a month, two at most, before the winter storms."

"So it begins then."

"It has to. I expect you to be at the front in the north in five days' time. Remember, you are to draw them in. I do not want a breakthrough, for if you do achieve one, they will fall back on their own rail line and retreat faster than you can advance.

"Bakkth, send airships over their base tomorrow to make sure they have no new airships ready to probe our secrets. Make sure no one flies near our point of attack, we must not let them know of our interest there."

He gazed appraisingly at his companion. Jurak's and Bakkth's personalities were ideally suited for this campaign. Unlike the umen commanders and clan Qarths, they could grasp the fact that victory could be achieved by more than a simple headlong rush.

"Draw them in. I will do the rest."

"So, you liked my umbrella idea."

Jack tried to conceal his shock at Ferguson's drawn and pale appearance as he stood up from his drafting table. Jack could see that his friend had lost weight, his cheeks were sunken, his eyes looked like two coals of darkness sinking into Chuck's skull-like visage. His skin had that almost translucent ghostly white glow typical of those in the advanced stages of consumption. Wrestling down his fear of the tuberculosis that was slowly draining the life from the Republic's master inventor, Jack came across the room, grasped Chuck's hand, and then, to his own surprise, gave him an affectionate embrace.

"You saved my bloody ass with the idea." Jack laughed, patting his friend on the shoulder, then motioning for him to sit down.

"And you said you'd never use it."

"Well, when it was that or burn to death, there really wasn't much choice. Death by fire is one hell of a good argument for jumping."

"Too bad about Stefan."

Jack nodded. In the small circle of men who wore the sky-blue uniform of the Air Corps of the Republic it was an unwritten rule never to get attached to anyone. One of the boys, whose ship never returned during the rescue effort for Hans, had calculated that from the time a pilot got his wings until he turned up missing or dead was a little less than six months—and that was during the period of semi-peace leading up to the start of the war. He had tried not to like Stefan, but the boyish enthusiasm, and his uncanny ability to nail Bantag airships, had won Jack over. And now he was dead.

Before coming to visit Chuck he had gone to see the boy's mother and given the usual lie that her son had died instantly. There was no sense in tormenting her with the truth, that her youngest child had fallen from twelve thousand feet wrapped in flames. She had given her other two boys and a husband in the last war and now all she had as comfort, and which she proudly displayed with tears in her eyes, was the personal letter from Andrew, offering his condolences.

"How's Feyodor?"

"He'll fly again."

"Bad?"

Jack nodded. "Hands, arms. Pretty shaken up as well. Swears he'll never go up again, but he will, it's in his blood."

Chuck nodded. Feyodor's brother had served as Chuck's assistant in the last war, and now headed the ordnance department back at Port Lincoln. It was the burns, as well, that drew his sympathy. His own wife had been horrifically scarred by fire.

Even as they chatted the door behind Chuck opened and Olivia Varinna Ferguson came in, carrying a steaming pot of tea and two mugs. She smiled at Jack and in spite of the scars Jack could still see her beauty radiating through.

As she poured Chuck's tea she chatted with Jack, pointing out the front page of *Gates's Illustrated Weekly* on Chuck's desk, which showed the last fight of *Flying Cloud.* It was embellished, of course, with four enemy ships going down in flames, along with a small sidebar portrait of Stefan manning his position as fire blazed up around him.

Jack looked around the room. The walls were covered with drawings of Chuck's creations, some of them from Chuck's own hand, others from *Gates*—airships, ironclads, breechloading artillery, field ambulances with coiled spring suspension, locomotives, telegraphs, and drilling rigs for oil. The office was bright, the north wall made of glass to provide Chuck with natural light for his drawings. Behind his office were the beginnings of the college which Congress had voted to fund, half a dozen clapboard buildings housing classrooms, drafting rooms, and research labs. Many of the young men were gone now, up with the army, serving in the engineering, ordnance, and technical units, but Jack could see one class at least was in session, Theodore, his copilot's brother, teaching a small group made up primarily of women.

Another coughing spasm hit, and Olivia motioned for the pilot to leave the room. Standing up, Jack walked out onto the porch of the clapboard building and gazed across the reservoir, which provided power and water for the factories below. The surface of the lake was mirror-smooth, except for the ripples caused by a flock of brightly colored geese drifting lazily along the shore. The geese kicked up, honking, as a blast of fire erupted to the west, beyond the dam, as a fresh batch of iron was poured. Jack looked to the west and the valley of the Vina River, leading down to the old town of Suzdal. Both banks of the dark stream were lined with factories, rail track, and hundreds of new homes for the workers who came from across the Republic to work in the new industries. So much of this had sprung from Chuck's mind, Jack realized. Their very survival dependent on this lonely Leonardo.

"Jack, please don't take too much of his time, he needs to sleep," Chuck's wife whispered, joining him on the porch.

"How is he? Truthfully."

She lowered her head.

"Not good," she whispered, "not good. Sometimes he's too exhausted even to cough. He has to sleep sitting up now. He needs rest Jack, months, maybe a year away from all this." She motioned back to the office and from there down toward the factories.

"He slips out of here, goes down to the factories to check on the work, the buildings filled with blast furnaces, steam, dust, and smoke. It's killing him. He has to go away."

Jack nodded, unable to say what was in his heart, that Chuck was his friend, but the republic was on the edge of a disaster, another war far more brutal than the previous two. Victory was dependent on Chuck's outthinking Ha'ark. He was taking the same risks as Andrew, Hans, right down to the lowest private on the firing line. But Chuck . . . Chuck would never be replaced.

"Hey, Jack, get back in here."

Jack looked at her, unable to say anything.

"It's Dr. Weiss's orders. He's supposed to rest during the afternoon."

"The hell with Weiss, there's work to be done," Chuck announced.

Shaking her head, she walked off the porch and back to the simple whitewashed house next to the office.

Jack went back into the office and settled down in the chair by Chuck's desk.

"So how are you really feeling?"

Chuck sighed and looked over at the grandfather clock ticking in the corner of the room.

"They say somebody with what I've got can last ten, even twenty years if they take it easy and move to a cool dry climate."

He chuckled sadly. "Rus is blazing hot in the summer, cold and damp in the winter. Great place for someone with consumption."

"But you can at least rest some more."

Chuck shook his head and laughed, then pointed at Gates's illustration.

"He got the wings on their ships, but I take it that it's all wrong."

Jack examined the engraving and nodded.

"The wings were larger and not at the center of gravity but somewhat forward. The small tail wings were farther aft. The ship was sleeker, and the ones that brought me down had a curious arrangement underneath."

"What was that?"

"Wheels, one under each wing and one astern."

Chuck nodded.

"I was thinking about that myself. From the report that you telegraphed in I was working up some estimates. The gas cells just don't seem to add up to provide enough lift. The wings are lifting surfaces, we know that, they make it more maneuverable as well in turns. I think they've put on engines damn near as good as ours; in fact I'd be willing to bet they stripped an engine off one of our downed machines and copied it. Anyhow, I think they actually have to get the thing moving forward at twenty miles an hour or more on the ground till the wings provide enough lift, then it takes off and flies."

As he talked Chuck pulled out a sheaf of drafting paper and unrolled it across his desk, using his cup of tea to hold down one side.

"By doing that they cut down on the bulk of the actual airship, there's less drag. It means they can't hover unless flying into a significant head wind, but it also means they can go a hell of a lot faster. You also mentioned that you saw what looked like flaps on the end of the wings."

Jack, reaching into his haversack, pulled out his own drawings and pointed them out.

"You said you saw the flaps moving, then the ship banked over and turned?"

"Yup. They don't turn in a flat circle; they bank over and turn." As he spoke Jack held up his hands, tilted them, and moved them through a turn.

Warming to his subject, Chuck picked up a pencil and jotted a quick sketch into the corner of his own drawings.

"That allows tighter turns. They don't just use a rudder to turn. Damn, I never thought of that. It'd be easy enough to put those flaps on our wings and run cables back to a control stick. I've been thinking about that engine on the wing arrangement as well. It cuts down drag with fuel tanks inside the wings.

"The length of the wings is rather long, how about if we tried this?" And yet again his pencil scribbled out a change in design, Jack leaning over the table, watching.

"Cut the wings in half and put one on top of the other?"

"Strange-looking I know, but with support struts going between the two wings it will make them stiffer, a biwing design. I even thought of another change." He pointed to the bow of the ship.

"Pilot up front and forward?" Jack asked.

"With the old design, the gondola car underneath, you had a 360-degree view, but it was underneath. If we put you up forward in the bow, you'd have a 360-degree view forward, up, and down. You'd also have a forward view down as you did before. We'd put a second person in what I'd call a turret directly under the wings. He'd be a gunner and could also drop bombs. We'd put a third person, a gunner, topside and aft on the tail. You'd all be hooked together by speaker hoses, and I even thought of a small access tunnel that your bomb dropper could use to get up to the forward cab. With this arrangement there isn't a blind spot on the entire ship."

"How long before we get them?"

"That's the problem." Chuck sighed. "Three weeks, maybe a month for the smaller test model, three months or more for ships with the range of *Flying Cloud*. My suggestion is that we scrap those currently under production and take the material to refit for this new design."

"That leaves us with no ships at all."

Chuck nodded. "More *Flying Cloud* models would be nothing but sitting ducks, even with the wings I was putting on. I want to take one of the smaller two-engine models, refit it, use it as a test. Then start turning out two-engine models like the Bantag's, and then some of these."

He pulled out another sheet of paper and unrolled it. Jack could feel a rush of desire, as if Chuck had unrolled a copy of one of the racy lithographs that someone had been mysteriously producing in the last couple of months and which had become so popular with the soldiers.

"Four engines, 120-foot wingspan but with only half the gas of *Flying Cloud.* I figure it can do nearly sixty miles an hour, maybe seventy. It should be able to carry half a ton of bombs six hundred miles."

"How many can you make?"

"I want sixty of the smaller ones as escorts," Chuck replied, "and twenty of these big ones by next spring."

Amazed, Jack shook his head.

"I know, seems impossible, but I think this war will be decided by airships. I don't want them fed in piecemeal. I convinced Colonel Keane on that score. Build them and unleash them all at once, have one all-out pitched battle and destroy their airship facilities on the ground. We struck a deal with the Cartha, paying a pretty penny, but with them as the middlemen we're buying every stitch of silk to be had."

"The Cartha?"

"Yeah, I know, the bastards are playing both sides."

Jack could understand the pressure they were under, the ruins of the Merki tribes hovering on their western border, the Bantag on the east. The Cartha were even supplying the Bantag with metal. Pat was calling for taking them out, or at least blockading their ports, but with the fleet stretched to its limits, literally disassembling ships from the Inland Sea fleet and shipping them by rail to the Great Sea, Bullfinch had argued that now was not the time to start a war on yet another front.

"But what about now? We're blind."

Chuck nodded. "I know but do you see any alternative? Send up the ships we're currently making, and they'd get slaughtered."

Jack realized that he should feel a sense of relief. What Chuck had told him was that he could anticipate living till next spring. As a pilot without an airship, he was out of the war. He could stay on in Suzdal, help his friend with the design work, do some test flying, and most definitely have his pick of every lovely lady in the city. And yet, the knowledge that Keane would be fighting blind a thousand miles to the east filled him with dread.

"What else do you have?"

Chuck smiled and pulled a sketchbook out of his desk and started to thumb through it.

"Wonderful how war can unleash the creative talent," he said coldly. "Improved engine design, both for your airships and for our navy. I rather like this beauty I've got here."

Jack looked at the curious sketch.

"What the hell is it?"

"I just took the design for an old Mississippi riverboat. Cut off all the gingerbread works, the way we did back on Earth during the war. There'll be a small armored top and that's it."

"All that just to carry one gun?"

"Ah, here's the beauty of it. It's a ship for landing troops straight on to a beach while under fire. That entire hold can carry two hundred men. The bow simple drops down and out they go, the steam-powered Gatling gun I've been working on providing cover from the armored turret."

Jack was reminded of a copy he had once seen of a sketchbook belonging to Leonardo da Vinci. Hastily drawn pictures filled the pages, some just rough outlines, others expanded out with greater detail. Jack took Chuck's sketchbook from his friend and leafed through it. He paused for a moment to study an artillery piece, mounted on a strange-looking carriage so that it was pointed nearly vertical; beside it stood a man who was hunched over, looking into the middle of what appeared to be a long pipe with telescopes mounted on either side.

"Range finder," Chuck announced proudly. "Simple idea. Mount two telescopes ten feet apart, have a mirror in the middle to split the image. The gunner turns a dial which ever so slowly shifts the mirrors, and when the two images merge the dial will show him how many yards it is to the target. Simple geometry of knowing a base, and the angles of the mirror gives you the height. You then cut the fuse and fire. Any airship that wanders into range is dead."

Jack nodded, turning the page. The next one he managed to figure out quickly enough since he had heard his friend talk about it. It was a ship that was almost submerged except for a small conning tower. The ship could fire something Chuck called a torpedo, which would then be guided to its target by a rubber hose through which jets of air would be used to turn the torpedo to port or starboard.

Next came the sketches of the land cruisers which were going into production. The first land ironclad company, under the command of one of Chuck's new engineering students, was even now trying out its first maneuvers with the dozen machines produced so far.

"How are these going?" Jack asked.

"Power to weight ratio is all off. At best they can only make four miles an hour, and on any type of upslope it's damn near a crawl. There's a big fight going on as well regarding how to use them. Gregory Timokin, the engineer I assigned to test them out, says they should be kept together as a strike force. The testing board is saying they should be dispersed, a couple to each corps as starters."

"And what do you think?"

"Keep them together, of course, the same way I want to see your airships learn how to fight as a unit rather than individuals. Mass; this next war will be about mass and the concentration of mass at the crucial point."

"The Bantag have sixty umens; I've heard rumors they can marshal another forty, even sixty if they coordinate with other tribes and the Merki. If it's a war of mass. They have it and we don't."

"So we outthink them, as we always have, Jack."

"I'm afraid this new leader can match us even in that. I never thought I'd see the day where their airships could fly circles around ours."

Chuck suddenly leaned forward and started to cough. His features were contorted with pain, the cough sounding like deep rumbling thunder. Gasping, he fumbled for a handkerchief and covered his mouth. Jack saw flecks of blood. Ferguson's wife was instantly through the door, kneeling by Chuck's side, looking at him anxiously until the spasm passed. Her gaze shifted to Jack, as if he was the blame for the attack.

"To bed right now."

"In a couple of minutes."

"Now!"

Chuck looked back over at Jack.

"There's not enough time for everything to be done," he whispered, still gasping for breath. "I've got to train others to do this work. It's here that the war will be won or lost." He tapped his notebook. "The new airships, the land cruisers, and heaven knows what else they have, they scare me."

"Why's that?"

"It shows me that whoever it is on the other side, this Ha'ark, he knows more than I do."

The shrill call of the pipes and the thumping rattle of the drums set Andrew's heart to pounding as the regimental bands struck up "Battle Cry of Freedom." The Thirty-fifth Maine, as befitted its privileged position as the first regiment of the Army of the Republic, led the parade through the city square of Suzdal, tattered national colors and state flag at the fore. The two flags were the most treasured of all the heirlooms of the Republic. Battle honors were inscribed in gold lettering on the red-and-white stripes of the American flag—*Antietam, Fredericksburg, Chancellorsville, Gettysburg, Wildnerness, Spotsylvania, Cold Harbor, Petersburg, the Ford, Suzdal, Roum, St. Gregory's, Potomac, Second Ford, Hispania.*

It was a belief as old as armies that the spirits of the fallen dead of a regiment, a battalion, a legion, or phalanx, forever hovered about the standard they had followed, and Andrew could sense their presence now—boys with forgotten names, who were in his company in the Cornfield and West Woods of Antietam, his own brother Johnnie lost at Gettysburg, and all the thousands who followed and stood beneath the fading silken folds, wreathed in the grey smoke of battle, facing rebel charges, the Hordes of Tugars, Merki, and now the Bantag.

As an actual fighting unit the old Thirty-fifth was in reality no more. Only a handful of those who had come through the Tunnel of Light with him still stood beneath the colors. Two-thirds of the Maine boys who boarded the transport *Ogunquit* were dead—Hispania alone had claimed nearly three-score of them. Those who still survived were now in command of regiments, brigades, divisions, and corps, or ran the government. The young flag bearer who had led the charge across the very square the regiment was parading across, William Webster, was now the secretary of the treasury. His financial genius somehow kept the Republic solvent. Gates ran the newspaper and a flourishing publishing business, Ferguson the research and college, Morrow the Agriculture Department for the supply of food.

The ranks were filled, instead, with the best the Republic had to offer, the young men of Rus, of Roum, even a few from Erin, Asgard, refugees from Cartha, and the Chin and Zulus that Hans had brought back with him out of bondage. After two years training with the Thirty-fifth they would move on to other commands as young officers—the Thirty-fifth was now the West Point of the Republic.

There was a hushed awe as the colors went past the review stand, Andrew coming to rigid attention, tears in his eyes as he saluted the treasured colors. Sergeant Major Hans Schuder rode before them, returning the salute. Hans insisted upon retaining the title of Sergeant Major, in the same way Andrew was still technically a colonel, even as they stood as the first- and second-in-command of the Armies of the Republic.

Father Casmar, the prelate of the Holy Orthodox Church of Suzdal raised his hands in blessing, the colors respectfully dipping low as they passed him. Andrew wondered what some of his old comrades from New England would think of that. The curious religion of the Rus seemed to be an amalgamation of early Orthodox Christianity with a fair smattering of pagan customs still lingering. Thus God was called Perm, the ancient Slavic pagan deity, and Jesus was Kesus.

Hans rode on, the regiment parading by in perfect step. Behind them came the First Suzdal, the original regiment of the Republic of Rus, and the reverent silence of the crowd gave way to thundering cheers, for this was truly their own. In the crowd Andrew could see many a veteran of the Old First, men with empty sleeves, or leaning on crutches, standing at attention as their cherished colors floated by. Other regiments followed, the Second and Third Suzdal, the Fifth Murom, the Seventeenth and Twenty-third Roum, which had been sent west for combined training with the Rus. All these were the reserve battalions, going to the front to join the rest of their regiments already on the line.

Some of the men were still dressed in the old white or butternut uniforms of the original armies, while newer recruits proudly wore the navy blue tunic and sky-blue trousers of the new uniform, patterned after the cherished uniform of the regiment which had led them to freedom. Black slouch caps were pulled down at a jaunty angle and rubberized ground cloths were slung over the left shoulder in the old horse-collar arrangement. Black cartridge boxes bounced on the right hip and heavy leather brogans slapped on the pavement. Trouser legs were tucked into calf-high wool socks to prevent the dust and biting insects from getting up their trousers, and, as Andrew watched them pass, he remembered the road to Gettysburg, and everything seemed to merge into an eternal oneness. He wondered, as well, how many of those marching past would soon go to join the ghosts of comrades who had marched through the June twilight so many years before and from there departed into legend.

The thought set him to wondering yet again. If this should indeed be his last campaign, what then afterward? Would his old comrades from the past—Mina, Malady, Colonel Estes, his brother John—would they be waiting upon the far shore, under the shade of the trees as Stonewall Jackson said upon his deathbed? And if they were, would they still be in the old union blue, gathered about a sparkling fire, laughing, telling the old stories and remembering glories past? If there is a heaven, he thought, might it not be Valhalla after all, a warrior's paradise, for he knew that in spite of his protestations and genuine desire for peace, war was part of his soul forever. Perhaps in such a paradise the good Lord allowed the fallen warriors to tramp the fields yet again, and to feel the shiver go down their spines as musketry rattled in the distance and the thump of artillery echoed across the heavenly sky.

Yet again he thought of Lee's famous statement at Fredericksburg, "It is good war is so terrible, else we would grow too fond of it," and he refocused his attention on the troops marching past.

Some of the regiments were still carrying the old Springfield pattern .58 caliber rifled musket, but most of the men now had three-banded Sharps breechloading rifles capable of four to five rounds a minute and lethal at six hundred yards.

Behind the line regiments came special detachments—led by the First and Second Sharpshooters Companies, the men armed with the deadly Whitworth rifle which fired a hexagonal bullet and was capable of dropping a target at three-quarters of a mile. It was with just such a gun that Jubadi of the Merki had been killed. The men of the sniper detachments gave Andrew a chilly sense. It was one thing to kill impersonally in battle, or even in the heat of passion when charging or facing a charge in turn. This was a different kind of war, a stalking, a deliberate picking out and selection of who was next to die. Even though the targets were Horde riders, it still troubled him. In their cartridge boxes they also carried a new kind of bullet, yet another of Ferguson's creations, an exploding round designed to be fired at ammunition wagons and caissons, though more than one of the snipers boasted that such a round could tear a hole bigger than a man's fist in a Bantag. As the men passed he could almost sense a cold remorselessness in them.

Behind the snipers marched the technicians of this new army: signals units, field telegraph line layers, engineers, even a pontoon bridging detachment. Most of the men in these auxiliaries units were veterans who, owing to age or injury, simply could not keep up with what was required of a rifle regiment on the line. As they passed they looked up at Andrew with the steady gaze of old comrades, and he relaxed slightly, nodding a greeting to those who stirred a memory of what had been.

Next came the new cavalry units. The supply of

horses for the army had at last been solved by the catastrophic defeat inflicted on the Merki. Tens of thousands of horses had been abandoned by the Horde as it retreated. The vast steppe area between Rus and Roum served as an ideal pasture and breeding ground, so that now there was more than enough transport for the artillery and nearly ten thousand mounts for a corps of cavalry. Many an old Boyar or patrician from before the wars had once again found a place where he felt he could fight with honor and ride proudly at the head of a troop or regiment. They most likely would never be a straight-out match for a Horde rider, and tactical doctrine emphasized fighting as dismounted infantry. But as a screen and for scouting the vast open stretches of steppe they were indispensable.

Finally the third branch of the combat arms came rumbling into the square, led by the old Forty-fourth New York Light Artillery, their four bronze Napoleons sparkling in the afternoon light. Though the weapons were obsolete when compared to the newer breechloading ten- and twenty-pounders, Pat would never hear of their retirement, insisting there was still a place for a good solid Napoleon delivering canister at close range. Thus the Forty-fourth would go off to war with its traditional weapon, and there might be a place for them yet, Andrew thought. Like the Thirty-fifth, the old Forty-fourth served as the training school for the Republic's artillery.

The program to build the newer alternating-screw breechloaders had gone nowhere near as fast as he wished. The old four-pounders with which he had first outfitted his army had long since been retired, most of them melted down to forge newer weapons. Only twelve of Ferguson's fearful brass-cartridge ten-pounders had been produced for the first of the land ironclads, while the rest of the breechloaders were still charged with a separate shell and powder bag. Many of the Parrott guns used at Hispania were still in service and would be for at least another year. The half dozen batteries were followed by the First and Second Rus Rocket Batteries, the forty rockets mounted on each wagon actually being dummy rounds since no one in his right mind would parade several hundred of the deadly and rather unpredictable weapons through the streets, where a single firecracker might set them off.

Behind the artillery and rockets came the new weapon that everyone in Suzdal was curious to see. Andrew had debated whether he should even allow it to be shown, but realized that security in this case came second to morale. Gates had broken the story of what the Bantags had, and it was time for the people to be reassured.

The piercing shriek of a steam whistle echoed across the plaza, counterpointed by a deep insistent rumbling as the first of the Republic's new land ironclads slowly turned the corner by the White House and started across the plaza. Billows of black coal-fired smoke puffed from the machine's stack, bits of soot swirling about in the sulfurous clouds. White clouds of steam shot out from underneath the machine as its six iron wheels, each of them six feet high and with rims four feet in diameter, crunched over the cobblestone pavement.

The ironclad's forward gun port was open, the ten-pound breechloading fieldpiece's muzzle protruding. The small turret on top was covered with canvas—that was one weapon Andrew did not yet want discussed—but the upper port atop the turret was open, and the commander of the ironclad, Major Gregory Timokin, stood chest high in the opening. His uniform consisted of a heavy steel helmet and chain mail covering his face and upper body to protect them from metal flakes and bolt heads which snapped off inside the machine when it was struck by bullets and artillery rounds. The young major stood with arms crossed, obviously proud of his position, and as the machine rumbled past the reviewing stand he saluted Andrew, then made the sign of the cross as they passed Father Casmar.

Andrew was pleased and somewhat amused to see the name "*Saint Malady*" emblazoned on the black armored side of the ironclad. Malady, a hard-drinking, foul-mouthed sergeant if ever there was one, had been elevated to the role of patron saint of all steam engineers after his heroic death at the siege of Suzdal, when he rammed his locomotive into an attacking column.

As the last of the units passed, Andrew finally relaxed and looked over at President Kalenka, who had stood next to him throughout the parade.

"Impressive, Andrew; they look damn good."

"But not enough."

"We have twelve corps now, over two hundred thousand men. We beat the Merki with not much more than half of that at Hispania."

Andrew knew all the figures by heart. Twelve corps active, four more forming. Of the twelve corps two were on permanent duty to the west, for out on the vast steppes beyond Cartha the remnants of the defeated Merki still lingered, raiding, eager to penetrate for a killing attack if they suspected that defenses were down. If they ever reunited, they could field fifteen—maybe even twenty—umens. Two more corps were kept as strategic reserves garrisoned at Suzdal and Roum, ready to react either east or west, depending on the threat. That left eight for the Bantag front.

Then there were the eighty batteries of artillery, one corps of cavalry, a fleet of sixteen monitors and two dozen other ships, an air corps unit, various detached units, garrison troops, home guard militia armed with old smoothbores, nearly a third of a million men under arms.

Bill Webster, head of treasury and finance, was constantly pointing out it was now simply impossible to put one more man into the front line. Nearly every fit man between eighteen and thirty was in the ranks or working in the factories. Close to 20 percent of the total population of the Republic was in uniform; not even the Union at the height of the war supported much more than 5 percent of its total population in the army at one time. The Confederacy had somehow managed to put fully 20 percent of its total population into uniform, and its economy was in a shambles by the end of the second year of fighting. Crops still had to be planted, harvests brought in, trees felled, coal and iron ore dug, uniforms and accoutrements made, track laid and repaired, telegraph wire strung, and, above all else, the daily routine of living had to go on, the raising and teaching of children, the cooking of meals, the tending to the aged, the sick, and the wounded.

The overcast skies finally opened up, as if they had been respectfully waiting for the parade to end, and a chilly rain came spattering down, with big heavy drops that set the crowd in the square scattering.

Andrew looked over at Father Casmar.

"Join us for dinner, Father?"

"Why I'd be delighted, thank you."

Andrew smiled, for he never knew a clergyman to turn down the prospect of a good home-cooked meal.

"Andrew Lawrence Keane, where's your poncho?"

Andrew looked down from the reviewing stand to see Kathleen standing beneath an umbrella, looking up at him peevishly. It still thrilled him that even after the nearly seven years they had been together the mere sight of her, the look of her green eyes, the wisp of red hair peeking out from under her bonnet, could set his heart pounding. He loved, as well, that when she was upset with him or when affection took hold, a touch of her old Irish brogue came back.

She motioned for him to join her under the umbrella, but he shook his head. There was something about an umbrella that he felt was somehow undignified; a man made do with a good slouch cap and poncho or not at all. Fortunately his orderly came up and helped Andrew throw the rubberized canvas poncho over his head. It was not army regulation, fortunately; otherwise, it would barely come to his thighs. Like all armies, the belief was that one size fit all, and his first chief quartermaster, John Mina, had decreed that ponchos were to be cut for the height of an average Rus soldier, which was five-foot-six. Fortunately there was the privilege of command and Andrew had one made to cover his lanky six-foot-four-inch frame.

John . . . and Andrew found he still missed his old friend, dead in the final day of Hispania. He had briefly transferred responsibility of logistics to Ferguson, almost a punishment, for Ferguson had often been the biggest thorn in John's side. Now it fell under Pat's control, and Pat had wisely found a team of young men to handle the responsibility for him.

Though Pat might feign the role of a hard-drinking and not-too-smart Irishman, the years of war had seasoned him into a tough and proficient commander in his own right. Beneath the roaring, swearing, drinking, and bluster, traits which endeared him to the men of his command, he was a shrewd pragmatist with the sort of common sense that seemed capable of taking the most complex of issues and reducing them to a simple answer.

Stepping down from the podium, he fell in by Kathleen's side, joined by Kal, Father Casmar, and a moment later by Hans, who trotted up, then dismounted to lead his horse.

"The boys looked splendid," Kal announced.

"The question is, how will they fight," Hans replied. "Nearly half our men did not serve in the last war, they've never stood on a skirmish line, let alone against a Horde charge."

"They'll learn," Kal said. "Same way I did back in the beginning, same way we did at Hispania."

"Different kind of fighting now," Hans continued, and he looked over sharply at Kal.

Andrew was silent. There had been a sharp debate on the floor of Congress only the day before about the nature of the war. This, at least on the surface, did not seem like the same grim war of survival back when the Merki had overrun Rus. It was distant, remote. Over 150,000 men were now deployed a thousand miles away, and yet, to date, there had been precious little fighting—a few skirmishes on the front facing Nippon, the occasional bombing of a ship by a Bantag flyer. More men were dying of disease than of wounds. It had finally been voiced, the question of whether they were really at war. The wild enthusiasm expressed when Hans had escaped was tempered now. The economy was again on a wartime footing—anything but the most essential items was scarce, food was rationed, nearly every family had someone up at the front—but there was no fighting.

Beyond that, Ha'ark had proven to be a masterful diplomat. A steady stream of human ambassadors, Chin slaves, had been coming through the lines, assuring peace with the one request that the Republic withdraw its forces from the Great Sea. Kal had been busy trying to suppress a rebellion in Congress, but one was definitely simmering. To his utter astonishment the Senate had even voted to allow a formal ambassador to journey to Rus, and he was now locked in the basement of the White House, blindfolded and under guard whenever he left the Executive Mansion. Andrew could see that Hans had endured a grueling time with the Senate; the three days of hearings, discussion of strategy, the begging for yet more appropriations had taken their toll.

Hans looked around at the crowd that was scattering as the rain increased. A smile finally creased his leathery features when a diminutive dark-skinned girl came through the press, carrying a sleeping baby in her arms. Hans nestled her in close under his arm.

"You looked so handsome today," she said in halting Rus, and Hans chuckled.

Andrew suppressed a grin, to hear Hans called handsome was indeed strange. Tamira looked over at Andrew.

"Does he have to go back tomorrow?"

Andrew nodded. "We both do, Tamira, I'm sorry."

"Soldier's wife," Kathleen announced, a touch of sadness in her voice.

They continued up the street toward the neighborhood the Union soldiers had settled into, and which had become a fairly good replication of a New England country village. There was a small town square with an octagonal band shell, a Presbyterian and a Unitarian church facing the square, even a statue to the Thirty-fifth and Forty-fourth in the middle. As they turned the corner Andrew looked affectionately at his house, a modest two-story garrison-style house, painted white. Again part of him wished that tonight he would be asleep upstairs, the children in the next room. That tomorrow he could awake, facing nothing more demanding than perhaps a lecture at the small college which had been flourishing until the start of this new war and was now all but empty, with so many of the young students and professors going back into the ranks. The only classes still open were the ones taught by Ferguson and his assistant Theodore as he struggled to pass on all that he knew about engineering, hoping to spark some young mind who could continue his work, if ever the worst should happen.

"At least one more quite dinner here at home, gentlemen," Kathleen announced, as she stepped up on the porch and closed her umbrella. "Let's forget about what is coming next."

But Andrew already sensed that the respite of a few hours was not to be, seeing an orderly from headquarters waiting on the porch. At their approach he nervously snapped to attention and handed a sealed envelop to Andrew.

With a flick of his thumb Andrew snapped the seal open and slid out the single sheet of paper. Scanning the sheet, he handed it to Kal.

"Hans, we're heading back within the hour. I knew we should have stayed at headquarters."

Hans took the message from Kal and examined it, then sadly looked over at his wife and nodded.

"Bad news?" Casmar asked.

"Vincent's reporting advanced elements of the Bantag approaching out of Nippon and against the southern front. It looks like they're going to open the ball before fall weather sets in. It's starting."

"Andrew, at least there's still time for dinner."

It was far more than dinner, Andrew knew; they'd been apart for nearly two months and were looking forward to one more night together. He could see the disappointment, but there was nothing he could say to change it now. In three days all hell could break loose.

"One hour, Kathleen." He didn't add that it would take an hour for the engineer to get steam up on his command train; otherwise, he'd be gone within ten minutes. He looked over at Hans and sensed the same thing that was in his heart—dread, but an eagerness as well to lock horns at last and get it over with.

Chapter Three

"Sir, they're pushing in, not just skirmishers anymore, but artillery and mounted infantry armed with breechloaders."

Pat O'Donald stirred from a deep sleep which had produced a most pleasant dream, carrying him back over twenty years to Ireland and a fine freckled-faced lass.

"Where?"

"We just had a patrol ride in. Claim they ran into advance riders of the Bantag early this afternoon. Their captain is outside."

"Bring him in."

Yawning he stood up and pulled on his uniform trousers. A young cavalryman, smelling of horse sweat and leather, came into his tent and saluted. Pat scanned his face, the boy was young, barely out of his teens, but already in command of a troop.

"Captain Yuri Divonovich, Troop B, Second Suzdal Mounted Rifles, reporting, sir."

"Go on, Yuri."

Yuri motioned to the map on the small table in the center of the tent and Pat came up to his side as the captain started to point out details.

"Sir, we were up near this pass here, where we'd already done some roadbed work for the railroad.

Hoped to get a good view east and south, thirty miles or more. As we crested the pass we ran smack into a Bantag mounted patrol, two hundred at least."

"Is that it?" Pat asked, feeling slightly annoyed at being dragged out of bed in the middle of the night to be told an enemy patrol was sighted thirty miles forward of their first line.

"No, sir, of course not."

Pat could sense a touch of anger in the captain's reply, and he smiled. The boy had spunk.

"All right, Captain, keep talking."

"Well, sir, they were mostly armed with bows, so we had good range on them with our Sharps. I managed to scramble up out of the pass and got to the top of the ridge. From there I could see dust plumes rising from the steppe, the entire horizon was dusty."

"Bantag cavalry?"

"Yes, sir. It was hard to tell with field glasses, lots of haze and dust, but I think I counted at least ten umen standards and what looked to be a number of horse-drawn field batteries. Like I said, sir, it was hard to see clearly, but I estimate they were ten, fifteen miles farther back. I only had a couple of minutes to watch; their patrol was making it rather hot for me, so I finally had to pull back. Just as we started to withdraw a mounted unit armed with breechloaders came up in support and gave us a time of it."

"You certain it was breechloaders?"

"Certain of it, sir." The captain took off his slouch cap and stuck his finger through a bullet hole in the crown.

Pat laughed, but the report was disturbing, a confirmation of Jack's information a week ago. Had they really shifted their modern units north, or was this just a false lead, Ha'ark throwing a few units with breechloaders forward so they would be spotted?

"Fine, Captain. Any losses?"

"Seven dead, eighteen wounded, sir, lost five horses as well. We dropped a parcel of them, but they kept on coming, chased us all night. I think we were about five miles from here when they finally reined in."

Pat nodded. He could see that the boy had experienced a bit of a fright. The whole idea of a cavalry arm was still somewhat new to the army, and like the Union cav back home, they'd have to learn their trade by fighting, and most likely take a hell of a lot of beatings from warriors born to the saddle. Being chased by Bantag, especially when one knew what would happen if wounded and captured, took nerve.

Pat turned back to his cot, reached underneath, pulled out a small bottle, and tossed it to the captain. Gratefully the young officer took a long drink.

"Thank you, sir."

Pat motioned for him to keep the bottle and turned to hunch over the map. Studying it intently, he traced in lines where Yuri had reported the enemy formation.

Andrew and Schuder were suppose to be back at Port Lincoln later in the afternoon, his reported sightings of the skirmishers the day before causing them to return to headquarters. He looked at the small clock atop his field desk. Just after one in the morning. Let the boys sleep a few more hours, then best to get them moving into the fortified lines.

Stepping out of his tent, he looked up at the stars, sparkling in the cool night sky. It was going to be a wonderful day for a fight.

* * *

Pat O'Donald squinted as he shaded his eyes and gazed eastward into the early-morning sun.

"Fine day for a battle," he announced, looking at his staff. Whistling off-key, he paced back and forth, watching as the umens of the Bantag Horde deployed across the rolling steppe, several miles distant. He could not have asked for a better field of fire. His men were dug in on a low crest line several hundred feet above the prairie, the scattering of trees which had once marched down from the high hills having all been cut to offer clear fields of fire. He knew it was just a forward position, the tip of the Republic's spear, probing into the edge of the domain that had always been, and most likely always would be, controlled by horse-mounted warriors. But behind him was the type of terrain that was ideal for what he wanted, right on back to what was now called the Shenandoah River, a 120 miles away.

The ground he would fall back on was hilly, mostly forest, broken up with small open patches of farmland tilled by descendants of the Irish, a discovery which had delighted Pat, though to his chagrin he found he could barely understand a word of the Gaelic dialect they spoke. He was trying to form a regiment of them, hoping that the grand old tradition of the Irish Brigade, complete to green flag, could be revived, but the men were woefully uncooperative when it came to army discipline, and with the war his pet project was on hold.

The only real road was what was called the Old Tugar track, the path that the Horde had once traversed in its ride around the world. A trestle bridge had been thrown across the Shenandoah and a rail line pushed up through the forest to within fifty miles of this forward position. It was a bit of a gamble putting two full corps so far forward without a railhead, with two more corps in the fallback position ten miles to the rear, but Pat had argued, and Andrew agreed, that the rough terrain all but eliminated the prospect of mounted units cutting them off. If the damn Bantag wanted a fight, they were going to have to slug their way through primeval forest, paying with blood every step of the way.

The Bantag formations approached in their old traditional checkerboard pattern, each block fifty riders across and twenty deep. It was an impressive sight, a hundred thousand at the very least he estimated, but madness on this ground.

He walked down the length of his line, carefully looking at the men deployed along the breastworks. The old veterans could easily be spotted, watching with a casual insolence, the new recruits silent and pale, or talking nervously. Sergeants paced behind the firing line, some offering words of encouragement, or cursing at the men to be silent.

Hans smiled at the stream of imprecations one of them was leveling at a shaking young boy who had fired his rifle with the enemy still almost two miles off.

Rick Schneid, commander of First Corps, rode up and snapped off a salute.

"Splendid day for a fight," Rick announced loudly so the men nearby could hear. "We'll pile the bastards up."

Pat nodded, saying nothing as Rick dismounted.

"Where's all them new weapons Hans kept talking about?" Pat asked softly. "Those bastards out there are armed with bows and lances."

"Maybe they don't have that much to go around."

"Still, keep a sharp eye open."

Even as he spoke one of Rick's staff officers shouted and pointed off to the southeast, where through a pass in the hills could be seen the sparkling of the sea. A lone Bantag airship was coming through the pass, climbing steeply.

"Well, we had to expect that," Pat announced. "Still, wish we weren't blind. Can't see for all the dust out there. Like to know what they might have hidden."

"I think the damn fools are going to charge," Rick said, and he nodded toward the front.

Two of the umens, twenty thousand riders, were spreading out, the checkerboard pattern of alternating blocks and open spaces shifting into one long open line, five ranks or more deep and several miles across. Even from two miles away, in the still morning air, he could hear the thunder of their coming, while two more umens maneuvered in heavy column formation to swing in behind them.

"Unbelievable," Pat whispered. "You'd think they would have learned."

"They might think they can simply break us."

Pat nodded. There was always that chance a panic could set in, but as he surveyed his line he knew the men would hold. He could even hear some of the sergeants and officers laughing, offering encouragement to their men. Veterans of Hispania were shaking their heads with disbelief, many of them pulling cartridges and percussion caps out of their pouches and lining them up along the breastworks so they could be reached more quickly.

Pat, as if by instinct, moved to where a battery was deployed, gunners standing at the ready. Their captain, sporting a black eye patch, stood on the parapets, telescope trained forward. The ground forward had been paced out weeks before, firing stakes topped with fluttering red pennants driven in, so the range was clearly marked.

"Case shot, three thousand yards, fifteen-second fuses!" one of them shouted, and within seconds the runners came up from the caissons, which were well dug in behind revetments thirty yards to the rear of the firing line. Breechblocks were screwed open, shells rammed in, powder bags pushed in behind them.

Pat watched the gunners carefully. He felt a wave of nostalgia for his beloved bronze Napoleons, but he had to admit that the twenty-pounders before him were about to do a devilish job at over twice the range of what he could have ever hoped for.

Farther up the line, a half mile to the north, one of the batteries opened with a salvo, the other ten batteries along the line joining in. The commander in front of him waited a few more seconds.

"Battery fire by salvo"—the battery commander stood with right arm raised high, fist clenched and then snapped it down—"FIRE!"

The four guns leapt back, the view forward instantly disappearing in a swirling cloud of smoke.

"Range twenty-eight hundred yards, fuse fourteen seconds!"

Pat, unable to contain himself, stepped forward and scrambled up on the breastworks, raising his field glasses, breathing deeply of the sulfurous black-powder smoke swirling around him.

After several seconds a swirling eddy parted and he silently counted off the interval of time. A burst of fire silently ignited directly in front of the charging line, followed almost instantly by three more detonations, two of them plowing straight into the Bantag ranks. Grinning, he looked over at the battery commander to offer his congratulations but the one-eyed captain was already back by his guns, as the metallic clang of breechblocks being slammed shut echoed.

"FIRE!"

The four guns kicked back yet again, and even while the crews scrambled to push the heavy weapons forward, the gun sergeants were pulling the breeches open. Wet sponges were run up the barrel to dampen any sparks, then the sergeants turned the elevation screws up, dropping the barrels ever so slightly lower. Hans looked forward again and saw the bursts igniting, one of them directly over the charging line, the others falling long.

Though his true desire was to stay with the gunners, he stepped back and away, walking down the top of the breastworks to get clear of the battery's smoke. Flame was igniting up and down his line as over forty guns were now in play. Out across the field he could see the enemy line relentlessly advancing, closing up the gaps in their lines as they continued to push forward.

Though they were the bloody enemy, he could not help but admire the Bantag's discipline. They continued to advance at the walk, taking the pounding, closing ranks, red-and-yellow pennants held high and defiant. Even as he watched, a shell detonated directly above a flag bearer, reducing his towering form to a bloody smear, the horse beneath the standard-bearer collapsing in a flying heap. The shredded standard wavered, started to fall, and then was instantly swept up by another Bantag.

The range closed to less than a mile and above the thundering of the guns Pat could hear the high clarion call of the narga horns, the Horde battle trumpets. Red pennants dipped, twirling in circles as their bearers broke out from the line and galloped down the front, signaling for the umens to break into a canter.

Pat heard an increasing note of urgency in the battery commander's voice and looked over his shoulder, catching the young captain's gaze. The captain stiffened, and his next command was again issued in a slow deliberate voice. Pat looked down at the riflemen, deployed nearly shoulder to shoulder behind the breastworks.

"Which regiment is this?" he asked of a lieutenant pacing behind the line.

"Third Kev, sir!"

Pat nodded. "You're good lads. Be sure to mark your targets and aim low! If they survive getting shot, send them back home as bloody eunuchs."

Some of the riflemen looked up at him and grinned nervously. He knew that this was simply not where he should be. His headquarters was nearly a mile to the rear, connected to each of the division command posts by telegraph . . . but this was where he wanted to be at this moment. His corps and division commanders were good men, they knew what to do, and, besides, he had to see this first clash to judge the mettle not only of the enemy but of his own men as well.

He paced farther down the line, to where a regiment armed with the new Sharps long rifles were deployed.

"Range is eight hundred," a captain was chanting. "Set your sights at eight hundred!"

Sergeants paced the line, checking to see that the men had properly levered up their rear sights. Nearly all the men of this regiment looked like veterans, and more than one of them was grinning with anticipation.

"Beats the bloody smoothbores we carried against the Tugars," one of them announced, looking up at Pat. "Fifty paces then!"

Hans nodded in agreement and turned to look back at the enemy line. The nargas sounded yet again, and the slow canter moved to a quicker pace. A bit too soon, he thought; the climb up the slope was going to blow their horses.

"Fourth Suzdal, volley fire present!"

Pat felt a chill course down his spine at the sound of hundreds of rifles being raised and then lowered, many of the men resting them on the top of the breastworks. He thought the range was impossibly far, a waste of ammunition, but the men were eager to try. The troops of the Ninth Kev to the right were looking over with obvious envy, for they were still armed with the older Springfields.

"Take aim . . . FIRE!"

An explosive volley erupted as nearly five hundred rifles discharged simultaneously. Smoke again obscured the field, and he leaned forward, waiting for it slowly to rise. Already the men were nearly finished reloading, breeches slapped open, paper cartridges rammed in, breeches closed, and percussion caps placed on nipples. He wished Ferguson had perfected the system which automatically slid a percussion cap in place rather than by hand, since it would increase the rate of fire. Another volley erupted farther up the line and was repeated less than ten seconds later. Pat knew that had to be the men of the Second Roum, who were carrying the even newer and highly coveted Sharps, which fired brass cartridge rounds. The cartridges were so valuable that if they held their position at the end of the day, every fired cartridge was to be picked up and sent back to Suzdal for reloading.

Just before the Fourth fired again the smoke cleared enough so that he could see a number of enemy riders had been dropped by the opening blow. Another volley slashed out, followed by shouted commands from sergeants to lever the sights down to six hundred yards.

Hans watched in silent amazement as the regiments armed with the newer weapons tore holes in the enemy line at ranges he had once only dreamed of. The charge pressed forward nevertheless, and at four hundred yards the artillery gunners switched from case to canister. The nargas sounded yet again and the Bantag line surged forward into the charge, their deep piercing screams thundering above even the roar of artillery and the rattle of musketry. The regiments armed with Springfield muzzle loaders now opened up as well, and Pat started to curse with a wild delighted abandon as his battle front, wreathed in flame and smoke, poured a rain of death into the Horde. It was impossible to see, the field ahead so obscured by smoke that battery and regiment commanders were reduced to guessing the range and shouting out commands.

From out of the smoke a single arrow fluttered past, followed an instant later by a shower of feathered shafts. One of the men below Pat pitched over backwards, flinging his arms wide, dead before he even hit the ground. Another man staggered away, cursing, hands cupped over his left eye, the shaft protruding through his clenched hands.

"Sir, will you please get down!"

Pat looked down to see an old sergeant gazing up at him angrily.

"Damn it, sir, I don't want it said you got killed right in front of me!"

Pat grinned and jumped down behind the breastworks, and even as he did so the sergeant, cursing, staggered backwards, an arrow driven clear through his left arm. Pat started up to him, but the sergeant waved him off.

"Got worse at the Ford," he growled, and, after breaking the shaft off, continued to pace the line, swearing at his men.

The enemy fire was barely effective, some of the shafts arcing high overhead to plunge a hundred yards or more behind the lines. Trained officers knew that if the enemy was within shooting range, it meant they had to be down to 250 yards or less, and ordered their men to lever their sights down and go to independent fire.

The fusillade increased to a thundering roar, and Pat stood, hands on hips, glorying in the thrill of it all. A searing explosion detonated to his right, and turning he saw one of the twenty-pounders collapsing, its crew flung into the air like broken dolls. Someone had forgotten to sponge, he thought grimly, that or a breechblock on the newfangled things had let go.

Only a few arrows were still winging in, and he looked behind the line to the fifty-foot-high signal towers erected a hundred yards to the rear. The crew atop the tower was vigorously waving a white pennant back and forth. Able to see above the smoke, they were relaying the word that the charge was broken and falling back. Cries to cease fire echoed along the line, and the silence which descended on the field was startling after the wild volleys of but a moment before.

As the firing died away Pat could hear the one sound on a battlefield that had always torn into his heart, the screams of wounded and crippled horses. Their shrieks of agony echoed beyond the smoke, which was slowly lifting. Dark forms started to show, the nearest within thirty to forty yards of the breastworks. A lone Bantag stood in the field, obviously stunned, staggering about. Half a dozen shots rang out and he collapsed. More shots erupted as men dropped enemy riders who were trying to get away on foot. He watched the executions without pity . . . if the places were reversed, far worse would be done to them.

He paced down the line. There was only a handful of wounded and dead among the regiment he had been with. Some of the men were laughing, talking excitedly. "Hey, Sarge, you had me scared to death," he heard one of them announce. "I never thought it'd be this easy!"

Pat looked over at the young soldier. The boy was right, it had been too easy . . . something was wrong.

"Sir!"

Pat turned, it was one of his orderlies.

"I just came from the signal tower. I think you should go up for a look."

"What is it?"

"I think it's best that you see."

Pat turned to look back to the east, but the smoke still clung to the ground and it was impossible to see. Farther north he could hear a renewed volley; apparently they were coming on again up there.

He trotted back to the tower, and by the time he reached the top of the fifty-foot ladder he was panting for breath. Getting too old for this kind of running around, he thought. Maybe Emil's right, should knock off the drink.

Stepping out onto the narrow platform, he nervously grasped a rail and tried not to look down from the top of the rickety structure.

Raising his glasses, he swept the field in front. The charge was streaming back to the rear, ranks broken, thousands of horses and Bantag dead and wounded littered the ground. It reminded him of Cold Harbor, when Butcher Grant had sent them in against the Reb fortifications in front of Richmond and eight thousand men had fallen in less than twenty minutes. But it was what the Bantag were moving up under the cover of the attack which held his attention, and he whistled softly.

"It's going to be an interesting day," he announced grimly.

Jurak gazed angrily at Kagga, commander of the umen of the black horse. The charge had been a wasteful folly, Kagga had insisted upon the honor of trying a traditional attack, and reluctantly, he had agreed.

"How many dead out there?" Jurak snarled. "Three thousand, five thousand?"

"They are demons," Kagga replied, head hanging low, his tunic smeared with blood as he cradled his shattered right arm.

Confused, Kagga looked back at the stricken field. "The Redeemer was right, the old days are gone. Half my umen was destroyed out there."

Kagga could not help but flinch as a shell fluttered overhead to detonate a hundred yards behind them.

"You'll most likely lose that arm," Jurak replied coolly. "Go to the healers to get it taken care of."

A battery of guns, which had wheeled into position to his right, opened up. Jurak looked across the smoke-covered field, hoping to see if the first salvo had any effect, but the ridge before them was all but invisible.

A gang of Nippon and Chin laborers ran past, heading into the battle, their human stench washing over him so that he gagged. He had left the cattle city of Eto with nearly fifty thousand of them, a good third dying on the forced march, but those who survived would now dig gun emplacements, and, as they died, fill the roasting pots.

His signals unit was nearly finished assembling the collapsible tower, and one of them was already on top, even before the final lashings were secure. Within seconds the red pennant was fluttering back and forth, Jurak looking up expectantly.

"The right wing is into the woods, sire."

Jurak nodded, turning to look down at the map, which was unrolled on the table before him.

The tower was already starting to draw enemy fire, three shells detonating fifty paces away. It would not do for him to show fear, so he tried to ignore the explosions and hissing fragments of iron as he examined the map. Two umens armed with modern weapons had gained the woods, and there would abandon their horses, except for the pack animals loaded with supplies. By early afternoon they should be on the enemy flank and start to roll it up. But that was merely the tactical focus of this assault. Five more umens had ranged sixty miles farther to the north. The approach had been quietly reconnoitered for the last month, units sent forward to penetrate the vast forest, secure the lines of advance and prevent any human patrols from approaching.

Under the cover of Jurak's frontal assault the flanking forces would move into the forest, then strike due west in a vast encircling movement. That was the master stroke which would fall when the rest of Ha'ark's plan was unleashed. Yet again, though, Jurak thought of the maxim of Hugana—"At the moment of attack all things change, the more complex your plan, the greater the change and confusion."

Ha'ark was trying to coordinate attacks on two fronts, with the surprise blow he would personally lead adding a third. This was not a modern army fighting against the False Pretender, seasoned by a generation of combat, coordinated through wireless and aircraft that could leap the length of the Great Sea in an hour. His warriors, though brave to the point of foolhardy madness, barely understood the concepts of modern war Ha'ark was trying to impose.

And yet, though the humans had started their war less than half a generation ago, they were obviously becoming masters of such things. Perhaps it was the fact that for the humans there was no alternative, the war was either victory or annihilation. Though it was the same for the Hordes, Jurak sensed that such a grim certainty was still not clear to his warriors. Humans were cattle; they deserved slaughter but were not yet fully hated and indeed feared. The Merki had not learned that until it was too late. He could only hope that his own warriors would learn it in the days to come.

He turned to look back at the ridge. Seeing the carnage the humans had wrought was proof enough of their skill. The curtain of smoke was finally breaking up as the first breeze of morning came out of the forest to the north and west. Raising his telescope he focused on the tower set in the middle of their line. A towering red giant of a man stood there. It must be the one called O'Donald, Jurak realized. He had hoped it would have been Schuder, or even one-armed Keane.

So that is my foe here. He thought back on the report. Hard-drinking and hard-driving in battle to the point of recklessness, the most popular field commander with the soldiers, master of the rearguard action when the Merki broke through into Rus. A good opponent. The trick now was to draw him out.

Jurak saw Pat raise his field glasses and sensed that the human was looking straight at him. Jurak raised his hand in salute and was startled when seconds later the gesture was mockingly returned.

You've won the first round, Jurak thought. Let us see what comes next.

Returning Vincent Hawthorne's salute, Andrew stepped off the train and started for his headquarters, Hans falling in by his side.

"What's the latest, Vincent?"

"O'Donald reports heavy fighting since dawn, sir."

"What's the pattern of attack?" Hans asked.

"Curious, sir, according to Pat."

Reaching the door into the clapboard building which served as army headquarters, Andrew acknowledged the salute of the sentries and stepped inside. There was a sense of barely controlled excitement as all heads turned to watch him. Half a dozen telegraphers were hunched over in their booths, stacks of paper piled up around them from incoming and outgoing messages. Self-important staff officers scurried about or stood before the maps lining the wall, examining the red and blue pins denoting where troops were deployed, the men posing as if the weight of the campaign rested on their shoulders.

Andrew followed Vincent's lead to the map showing the eastern front.

"So far they've faced two charges, the first one right after dawn, the second one an hour ago."

Andrew looked at the clock on the wall; it was shortly after three in the afternoon.

"Describe the attacks," Hans interjected.

"First one was in the same old way. Two umens in line, followed by two in column to provide fire support."

"Weapons?"

"Bows and lances. Pat said they must have piled up at least five thousand casualties within twenty minutes. We lost less than a hundred. Reports of some of their units gaining the flank and fighting in the woods, but nothing serious yet."

"Then what?"

"They moved up at least ten thousand slaves to start digging gun positions a mile out."

"What did Pat do?" Andrew asked quietly.

"He claimed that to save on ammunition they held fire."

Andrew nodded and looked over at Hans. Orders were that if human slaves were used they had to be fired upon. It had always been a bitter choice, but there was no other way, for if they didn't, the Horde would finally wind up using them as shields when they came in for the attack.

"I'd've done the same," Hans finally replied. "It's a devil moving artillery ammunition fifty miles up that road past the railhead, might as well save it to kill Bantag."

"Then what?" Andrew pressed, deciding to let pass the decision by Pat to disobey standing orders.

"They moved their artillery up to sixteen hundred yards shortly after noon and opened up with close to a hundred guns. It's been generally an artillery battle since," Vincent said.

"I bet Pat's enjoying that," Hans added with a grim smile.

"The second charge?"

"Limited, half an umen on foot and another mounted umen struck the northern part of the line. This time they were armed with rifles and got up to within one hundred yards before breaking."

"Any problems?"

"Just got the latest report from Pat a few minutes ago, sir. He said that one, maybe two umens armed with rifles are in the woods to the north and moving to flank. He'll abandon the line just before dusk and pull back into the woods to the next position."

Vincent handed over copies of all the reports which had been filed since dawn, and Andrew browsed through them, then motioned for Vincent and Hans to follow him and retired into his private office and closed the door. Going over to his desk, he sat down and spent several minutes quietly reading the telegrams. It was strange to be running a battle over two hundred miles behind the front line. The whole scale of this fight was proving to be somewhat daunting to him, with more than sixty thousand troops deployed to the east, and a local reserve of a corps at Port Lincoln while several more corps were deployed nearly two hundred miles to the south.

He found himself longing for the days when it had simply been a regiment, the left and right flank of his entire responsibility within sight; where orders could be delivered in seconds, and in an ultimate sense there was someone above him who would make all the hard choices.

He passed the reports over to Hans as he finished reading them, then fixed his gaze on the map hanging behind his desk.

"He went through a hell of a lot of artillery ammunition," Hans finally said, breaking the silence.

"The breechloaders can fire twice as fast and have double the range, we expected that."

"Ten thousand rounds Andrew, that's over 150 caisson loads. We'll be digging into our reserve stockpiles within a week at that rate."

"Once we're into the forest it'll slack off," Andrew replied.

"No land cruisers though," Hans said. "Most of the units armed with older weapons; that's curious."

Andrew nodded. Ten umens clearly identified, and it looked like yet more coming in. Was this the main attack?

"Vincent, what's the latest from Bullfinch?"

"We didn't get a courier ship in today, sir. Last report was the one you saw from yesterday."

Andrew looked back at Hans. "What do you think?"

"Well at least it's started. There's one of two possibilities on the eastern front. Either it's an attack to draw our attention, or once they push us back from the edge of the steppe they'll bring up everything they have. Maybe two units armed with breech-loading rifles identified so far. My estimate is they have at least ten, maybe twelve or thirteen. Once they've pushed Pat back, if it's the main attack, they'll move them up."

"And?"

"It's a diversion."

"Why do you think that?"

"Logistics, Andrew. Before they cut off Nippon we knew that if they were working on a rail line at all in that direction, it was at least two hundred miles back from what would be the front. When I was a prisoner we were making rails in the factories and they had to be going someplace, since the line to Xi'an was completed, so I figured it was for a northern track. But even if they were up to laying a mile of track a day, they'd still be two hundred or more miles short of what has started as the front line. If they did attack that way, they'd face the same problem the Tugars and Merki faced when they hit us from the west, and that was funneling everything they had through one road in the forest while all the time we were falling back on our base of supplies."

"But it's the only way to get at us," Hawthorne interjected, "at least as long as we control the sea. The force coming up between the two oceans is even farther from supplies. As long as we blockade Xi'an and patrol farther south, there's no way they'll get supplies out to either front."

"But will we?" Hans asked. "We know they were building ships, and we've been blind for two weeks now. So there's no telling what they've marshaled at Xi'an."

Andrew could sense the slightest tone of accusation in Hans's voice. Ever since Hans was rescued he had been pressing for a cutting-out raid back on Xi'an, volunteering to lead it himself in order to destroy the construction yards and ships anchored there. Of course the idea was suicidal, throwing an ill-trained force eighty miles up a river into what was a fortified camp of the enemy. There simply weren't enough ships or trained men to do the job. Bullfinch had successfully pressed for the creation of a marine division, but it'd be a year before such a unit was ready for action.

"So you think there'll be a second blow then?" Andrew replied.

Andrew half listened as Hans and Vincent launched into a debate and looked back again at the map, though after studying it for so many long months it was etched into his memory.

Andrew finally turned to look back at Hans.

"I want you down on the southern front by tomorrow," Andrew said.

"I thought Marcus would be in charge there?"

Andrew nodded. "I've changed my mind. The assignment was made before we got you back. I want experience. Marcus is damn good on a straight defense, but we might need some flexible thinking there if what you're worried about comes to pass."

"He might be upset with this, sir," Vincent announced. "Most of the units down there are Roum."

"He's a soldier," Andrew said, "and a damn good one at that. He'll understand, and besides, Tenth Corps is in reserve in Roum. I'll want him to supervise bringing them up if things get hot."

Hans grinned.

"You seem happy about this, Hans."

"I want Ha'ark, and I half suspect that's where he'll turn up."

Ha'ark the Redeemer stirred in his sleep and sat up. Strange, the image was so clear. Again it was

Schuder walking in his dreams, but this time it was as if Schuder was seeking him out rather than the other way around. Good, if that was what the human wanted, he would provide for it.

Standing, he stretched and stepped out into the moonlight. The guards who flanked his yurt were instantly alert, weapons snapping into place, and he saw his staff, who had been up through the night overseeing the deployment, waiting expectantly, ready to dash off and fulfill his slightest whim. He motioned for them to be still, to leave him alone, and he walked off toward the low rise of ground that looked out over the sea.

A gentle cooling breeze was blowing down from the north, the first harbinger of the autumn. How he loathed this climate, missing the bracing snow-laden air of home. Perhaps when this war was done he would move his capital northward into what had once been the Tugar realms, thus escaping the hot desert winds and dank tropical forests of the south.

A strange ocean this, he thought, no salt, the birds different, no crashing surf. Several miles out he could see the line of Yankee ships riding at anchor for the night, silhouetted by the light of the twin moons, not having moved since sunset. Perfect.

To his left, coming down into the bay, yet still invisible to the ships at sea, was the vanguard of his flotilla. Already the first of his surprises should be moving into position, ready to strike just before the first light of dawn. One of his staff approached and stood respectfully to one side.

"What is it?"

"My Qar Qarth. You ordered me to awake you when the signal was received that the first attack ships had deployed."

Ha'ark looked down again toward the sea and saw a bobbing flicker of light flashing on and off.

"My Qar Qarth, the pilot boat is reporting they are in position."

"Fine, you did your job. Now fetch me something warm to drink."

The officer bowed and disappeared back into the night, to return a moment later with a heavy mug of steaming tea. Ha'ark sipped at it, accepting as well a cold joint of meat. In the moments since he had awakened he could sense a rising of the light. Those gathered around the smoldering fire by his tent were now visible as shadows. The eastern horizon was beginning to discolor into a deep indigo purple. Directly overhead the Wheel was no longer a sparkling brilliance, its light fading.

Ha'ark turned to look down at the harbor. The beetlelike ships were slowly moving toward the outer bar. He knew that though he could clearly see them from his position, the Yankee ships would not be able to see their smoke rising above the spit of land enclosing the bay, but in another few minutes the light would increase enough to make them visible. The deployment was slow. All his ironclads should have been past the bar, but it was too late for that. If he delayed any longer, the first surprise would be lost.

"Signal the attack," Ha'ark announced.

Chapter Four

"Sir, there's a light flickering up on the bluffs."

Admiral Oliver Bullfinch nodded.

"Already seen it, ensign."

"Think it means something, sir?"

Bullfinch did not reply. The ensign should know better than to ask a question of an admiral, but he could not bring himself to come down too hard on the boy, for only half a dozen years ago he had been an ensign himself.

The eastern sky was just beginning to lighten. In a few more minutes it would be time to order the picketboat in for a closer look at the harbor on the other side of the bluff. This was always the most worrisome moment of their watch. If a sally was coming out, it would be now, the enemy ships moving down into the bay during the night. Beyond that the bastards might have run some of their galleys out under cover of darkness to lay a few torpedoes or even attempt a boarding raid.

Bullfinch turned his attention to the lookout, who was posted on the catwalk which spanned between the twin smokestacks aft.

"Any sign of airships?"

"No, sir, nothing yet."

That, at least was a relief. A wooden picketboat

had been lost to them shortly after Hans was rescued, and two more damaged. The airship gunners were already up on the deck, manning the light two-pounder breechloaders which were used to keep the airships away, and as he paced the top of *Petersburg*'s gun housing he nodded to the men who had been silhouetted by moonlight only minutes before but were now becoming visible in the pale light of early dawn.

He returned his attention to the light up on the bluff. It was still winking on and off in a rhythmic pattern, obviously a signal, but to what?

Down below on the gundeck he could hear the ringing of the bell signaling the end of the midnight-to-dawn watch. In a few minutes the ship would come to life, boiler pressure brought up again, gun ports thrown open to air the ship, breakfast served, then a cautious run into the edge of the enemy torpedo field for another long tedious day of waiting and hoping that something, anything, would happen to break the boredom. There were times when he actually envied Pat, Vincent, and the others for the excitement they were most likely enjoying. Everyone talked of the Battle of Hispania, but few noted his own campaign in support of the Cartha when they rebelled against the Merki and then held back a foray by the Bantag. Without that action, the victory at Hispania might very well have been a hollow one. Except for the rescue of Hans, he had seen no action since, only endless months of patrolling.

He walked over to the ensign. In a few more minutes it would be time to signal the other five ironclads of the fleet to start moving back in closer to shore. The ensign's back was turned, and as Bullfinch approached, the boy looked over at him and pointed off toward the starboard bow.

"Sir, what is that?"

Bullfinch looked to where the boy was pointing but saw nothing.

"There, sir. Looks like a log; there's some water breaking around it."

"I still don't see it."

Though he would not admit it, he feared that the vision in his remaining eye was starting to slip a bit. Maybe it was time to go to Emil and see about glasses, though he hoped that wouldn't be necessary. Glasses would certainly ruin the dashing look that his black eye patch created and which made him easily recognizable to the fine young ladies when he was in port. Having to wear a monocle would certainly ruin the effect.

"There's something out there, sir, I'm convinced of it."

The ensign started down the length of the upper deck, still pointing to starboard, and Bullfinch followed. One of the antiairship gunners was now pointing as well. Bullfinch stopped, straining to look, and at that instant a flash of light burst across the ocean.

Startled, he turned to his right as a boiling cloud of fire erupted from the ironclad *Constellation.* Stunned, Bullfinch watched as the fireball expanded and a deep, rolling thunderclap washed over him. The light began to subside, and Bullfinch heard the ensign shouting, grabbing hold of his sleeve, still pointing.

Time seemed to distort and move in slow motion. He was still mesmerized by the sight of the ironclad blowing up, wondering if it had been an infernal machine that the Bantag had laid during the night to drift into his line. He shifted his gaze back to where the ensign was pointing. There was something out there. At first glance, in the dying light of the exploding ironclad, it looked like a pole or log jutting out of the water, a thin rippling wave washing out to either side. It was moving, but moving against the breeze, coming straight at them.

A second explosion ripped through the *Constellation*, this one even more violent than the first . . . The magazine was going, Bullfinch realized. The flash of the explosion illuminated the ocean, and he could see that the pole was still coming toward them . . . and was mounted on top of a dark round object which just barely jutted out of the water.

The *Hunley*. It was like the Confederate submersible ship *Hunley*. He spared a quick glance back at the *Constellation*—the second explosion had broken the back of the ironclad, bow and stern rising out of the water, the sound of the explosion washing over him. Debris was raining down, shells from the magazine detonating in the air.

Bullfinch realized that only a score of seconds had transpired since the ensign had first pointed out the strange object, and already it had drawn twenty, perhaps thirty yards closer.

"Beat to quarters!" Bullfinch roared as he turned and raced toward the bridge. "Ensign, get a crew forward, cut the anchor!"

The deck was still illuminated by the explosions wracking the dying ship as another light flared up. Sickened, Bullfinch saw that one of his wooden picketboats was exploding. How many of the damn things did the bastards have?

Scrambling up the ladder to the exposed flying bridge, he shouted for the helmsman to signal the engine room for full speed astern. His executive officer came up out of the hatchway from below, shirtless and barefoot.

"Get the guns cleared below and order the antiairship gunners starboard to start shooting at that submersible!"

"What, sir?"

"The pole, that pole out there!" Bullfinch roared. "It's a periscope for an underwater ship. They're hitting our fleet with them!"

"Sir!"

Bullfinch looked up to the lookout, perched twenty feet above him.

"I think I see puffs of smoke from behind the bluff, looks like it might be from ships coming out."

Bullfinch spared a quick glance to shore but could see nothing, his vision still dazzled from the explosions wracking *Constellation* and the picketboat.

The first of the antiairship guns opened up, and Bullfinch, who had momentarily lost sight of the periscope, saw where the geyser from the shell kicked up. The shot had missed it by a dozen yards. The target was so damn small, he realized, a thin pole maybe half a foot across and ten feet high, and then what looked to be a small rounded dome maybe three feet across and only a foot or so out of the water. It most likely had a spar torpedo mounted on a pole twenty or more feet forward. A minute, maybe a minute and a half, Bullfinch realized, his stomach knotting with fear.

The other three antiairship guns on the starboard side fired, plumes of spray erupting to either side of the submersible, but it continued to bore straight in. The deck lurched beneath his feet as the anchor line parted. A speaking tube whistled next to him, and he uncorked it.

"Engine room here. Don't have much steam up but getting under way now, sir!"

"Hurry, damn it, give it everything you've got, engines full astern."

Bullfinch looked back at the periscope. Maybe eighty yards.

"Helm hard aport!"

"Helm hard aport it is, sir."

He could feel the first shuddering bite of the paddle wheel as it slowly started to turn, the steam pressure barely enough to gain purchase against the weight of the wheel and the resistance of the water. *Petersburg* ever so slowly started to back up. On the gun deck below he could hear shouted commands as gun hatches were flung open and crews strained to run their pieces out, but he knew with a grim certainty that they could never bring their guns to bear in time.

The first gunner to fire on the topside antiairship gun had finished reloading, his assistant slamming the breechblock shut and stepping back. The gunner sighted down the barrel and squeezed the trigger. The gun kicked back on its friction slider, the water erupting just forward of the periscope.

It was now less than fifty yards away, and Bullfinch realized that given the probable length of the submersible and the spar torpedo, the weapon was most likely less than thirty yards away.

The helm was beginning to answer, *Petersburg* drawing away from the enemy, but the submersible was still gaining.

The other three guns fired again, one of the rounds detonating halfway up the side of the periscope. A triumphal shout went up from the crew, and for an instant Bullfinch thought they were saved, but then saw that it was still continuing to bore in. It was down to twenty yards, then ten . . . he felt a faint jarring blow.

Time seemed to stretch into an eternity. Did the weapon have a percussion head, or was it fired from inside the submersible by a trigger? He waited, holding his breath, and as *Petersburg* continued to back up, he could almost sense the damn thing banging against the side of his ship . . . but still nothing happened.

Ever so slowly the submersible seemed to rise out of the water, and Bullfinch could see that a hole had been drilled in the vessel. The shot he thought had struck too far forward had, in fact, punched clean through into the hull.

The ship, which Bullfinch thought looked to be nothing more than a boiler with the ends covered over, rose lazily, wallowing on its port side. A hatch just aft of the periscope mount popped open and a Bantag tried to scramble out. One of the antiairship guns fired, nearly tearing him in half. The submersible slipped back beneath the water and disappeared.

Amazed that they had survived, Bullfinch started to turn to his exec, ready to express relief, when another flash of light flared up. Sickened, he watched as *Saint Gregory*, a heavy monitor and the newest addition to his fleet, exploded.

He turned away with head lowered. He had allowed the enemy to catch him by surprise. Ferguson had talked about submersibles, and was even testing one, but never had he thought that the Bantag would have leapt ahead of them with such a thing.

"I can see them now!" the lookout cried. "Sir, the

first ship, it's a damn big thing. Looks like a monitor! Also see three, make that four airships coming up from the east, southeast."

Bullfinch turned to his executive officer.

"Petronius. Get a boat crew. I want you to get over to the picketboat"—he hesitated for an instant, scanning to see which of his light wooden ships was closest—"*Defiant.* Then you are to get the hell out of here at best possible speed and make for Port Lincoln. You are to report everything you see here. Now get going!"

The exec hesitated.

"Damn it, Petronius. We're going into a hell of a fight, and I've already lost a third of my ironclads. I want someone to get out with a warning now, before it's too late."

He turned back to look at his bridge crew.

"Signal the fleet," Bullfinch announced. "Form on the flagship, we're going in."

Chomping on the butt of a cigar, Pat O'Donald wondered if this was how Grant felt during the Battle of the Wilderness. That had been one fight the Forty-fourth New York had sat out, for there was simply nothing to shoot at in the dense forest. Deployed to the rear at the burned-out ruins of the Chancellor House, he had spent the battle with a precious bottle of rye watching the smoke rise out of the tangled jungle where 150,000 infantry fought it out.

It was the same now, artillery deployed to the rear, his infantry spread out in an arc, right flank on the sea, left flank curving back through five miles of forest anchoring his left on a broad stretch of bogs and swamp. It had been going on since dawn, and so far the bastards on the other side had been getting the worst of it, charging against well-dug-in troops.

If this is the way the Horde wanted to fight its war then so be it. He estimated they were trading casualties at four, even five to one. At this rate, by the time they fell back to the Shenandoah, there wouldn't be a Bantag left standing.

Looking up he saw an enemy airship circling several thousand feet above. Damn, if only we had a few of those, I'd know what was really going on behind their lines, he thought with bitter frustration. There was still no telling just how strong this punch was. Were there forty or more umens backed up into the steppe, or was this the ploy that Hans kept insisting it was?

A steady rain of leaves and small branches kept raining down around him, plucked from the trees by Bantag fire that was too high. A renewed roar of volley fire erupted to his left, and he cocked an ear toward the thunder, gauging the sound. It was the new Sharps, rapid fire. Must mean another charge, and even above the thunder he could hear the throaty roar of the Bantag as they closed in. He waited. No sense in getting excited about it yet. The sustained thunder rippled down the length of the line until it was directly in front of him. All of Ninth Corps was being hit. He could see his staff looking around in an agitated manner. Spitting out the butt of the cigar, he fished in his breast pocket for another, pulled it out, and lit it, working hard to display an outward calm.

"Relax, gentlemen," he said, while puffing the new cigar to life. "The day's only started."

"Hard astarboard!"

Squinting through the narrow view slit of the armored bridge, Bullfinch tried to see through the clouds of smoke obscuring the ocean. As *Petersburg* slowly pivoted, he caught a momentary glimpse of *Ironsides,* flames pouring out of her gun ports, yet still the ship fought, turning to ram the Bantag ironclad on its port side.

A thundering jar rang through his ship, followed a second later by high, piercing screams. Pulling open the hatch which led down to the main gun deck, he stuck his head below. Another shot had blown clear through the starboard side of his ship. Men twisted in agony, torn apart in the shower of iron and wooden splinters. It was the third shot to pierce their side.

He closed the hatch, trying to block out the horror of what he had just seen, and returned to commanding what was left of his fleet.

"Damn it all to hell, I can't see anything!" Reaching up, he popped open the hatch to the unprotected flying bridge.

"Sir!"

He ignored the protests and scrambled up the ladder and out into the open, grateful for the cooling breeze after having spent five sweat-drenched hours locked up inside the armored command bridge. A rifle bullet snicked past, and, looking toward the monitor which they were aiming for, he saw several Bantag snipers arrayed along the top of the gunhouse. Answering fire came from his own contingent of marines firing out of the gunports and the Bantag dropped. Going to the starboard side, he leaned over the railing of the flying bridge and was horrified to see the damage inflicted on his beloved ship. The entire side was shredded, pieces of armor buckled and bent at right angles. He turned away to scan the rest of the battle. *Roum* was still in the fight, as was the turreted ironclad *Fredericksburg.*

Another bullet snapped past, plucking at the coattails of his uniform. Cursing, he ducked low and looked back to port. *Ironsides* was down at the bow and listing heavily. Two Bantag ironclads were off its stern, both of them pouring in a broadside at nearly the same instant. *Ironsides* visibly shuddered from the blows. It seemed to hang in the balance, then ever so slowly rolled up on its port side. Its propeller was still turning as it continued to go over, men scrambling out of the gun ports. An instant later the ship disappeared in a thunderclap explosion. Sickened, Bullfinch lowered his gaze, ignoring the snap of a bullet striking the deck by his feet, half-wishing the damn thing had hit him.

Petersburg lurched beneath his feet, the entire ship recoiling as the massive hundred-pound Parrott gun forward fired on the Bantag ship a hundred yards ahead. The shot struck directly amidships, and he had the grim satisfaction of seeing some damage done as the solid bolt sliced through the enemy armor and plowed into the interior of the ship. He looked around at the battle. Three ironclads left—the enemy had lost three, but there were still eight in action. The two that had finished off *Ironsides* were now turning toward him, looking like ugly black beetles crawling across the sea. If his ships had one advantage in this fiasco, it was better engines. They had speed, and that was it.

From the corner of his eye he saw the gun ports of the enemy ship directly ahead swing open, and he flung himself down on the deck. An instant later the broadside of four guns fired. A shower of sparks and debris erupted around him as the heavy bolts slammed into the side of his ship. From the renewed screams and curses below he knew at least one of them had again penetrated.

"Sir!"

One of his bridge crew was sticking his head up from the armored bridge below. "They've dismounted the forward Parrott, sir!"

"Damn all to hell!"

He stood back up, scrambled down below, and looked over at his signal officer. His voice tightened. He could not believe what he was about to do, but there was nothing left.

"Signal the fleet. Disengage, withdraw to the north," he whispered.

The crew looked at him, stunned.

"Damn it, do it now! We're beaten. We've got to save what's left!"

Feeling somewhat dizzy, Hans Schuder walked up the gangplank, grateful to be off the damn courier ship which had brought him from Port Lincoln. Crews were already busy behind him off-loading crates of ammunition for the twenty-pounder guns.

It was a hell of a way to supply the southern front, Hans thought. Move everything by train to Port Lincoln, unload the trains, load the supplies into one of the four light steamers that moved back and forth between Port Lincoln and Brunswick, unload the boats at Brunswick, load up the wagons then haul the supplies and distribute them along the 130-mile front. There had been talk of trying to build a port facility on the eastern shore of the Inland Sea, but the effort would have required a massive dredging operation and the cutting of a road over the Green Mountains, which ran like a jagged spine from the northeast, up nearly to Junction City and for several hundred miles to the southwest. The rail line, which they had been promised by Congress over a year ago, was still forty miles short of the defensive position, slowing inching its way over the mountains behind him.

The harbor area had the feel of barely controlled insanity that was typical of any supply head. Drivers swore at their teams, cracking whips, arguing with each other as they maneuvered through the foul, muddy streets. Crates of supplies were piled up haphazardly along the dock; bored guards stood about, leaning on their weapons, not caring much about anything other than when their watch was finished; harassed young officers ran back and forth all looking so self-important, as only a quartermaster officer could look. He could sense that the trail of youngsters on his own staff were looking around disdainfully, hoping that Hans would explode and start some solid chewing out, but at the moment all he wanted to do was get to his headquarters, a long twenty-mile ride away.

He sifted through the dispatches which had been handed to him before the ship even properly tied off. Pat was still holding out at the first fallback line, and the battle had been raging since dawn. News from Bullfinch nearly three days old, indicated nothing new. The troubling fact was a strong push by several umens up along the western coast of the Great Sea. Patrols had come in this morning indicating they were less than fifty miles out and closing. It could mean that by this time tomorrow action would be joined on his front.

Three umens . . . again he felt blind. There was no telling just how many Pat was facing, though he now claimed that twelve umens had been identified. It could still be a ruse. Three now to the south here. That would be the forward screen, pushing the pickets back, masking what might be coming from behind.

This war was taking on a scope he had never imagined possible, fighting on diverse fronts over five hundred miles apart. Something was not yet in place, he could sense that. Ha'ark still had something waiting, but there was nothing that could be done about that until the Bantag leader showed his hand.

Tomorrow he would order troops forward to engage the advancing units. Might as well take them as far forward as possible. After all, it was always a game of forcing them to trade lives for land. The more land they were forced to take by frontal attacks, the more we'll bleed them white.

And yet . . . He sensed that Ha'ark knew this game three moves before they were even made. The campaign, so far, was going as they assumed it would. Attack on two fronts, but we hold the key to that. We have the ocean, we can shift back and forth by rail while they are separated. Ha'ark would never be so foolish as to run his war that way. There had to be another part to this puzzle . . . but what was it?

"Your ship is ready, my Qarth."

Ha'ark walked own the gangplank to board the battle-scarred ironclad. As he stepped on board he could see the grins of delight of his warriors. There was a time when they had felt dishonored for having their horses taken away, to be replaced by a thing of iron, steam, and smoke. But today they had tasted victory, and that had changed everything.

"We are honored by your presence, our Qar Qarth."

Ha'ark acknowledged the salute.

"I am honored to be among you. You have done well today."

He could see the effect his words had. There was a time when so many of them had viewed him with, at best, wary caution. He was, at least by outward appearance, the fulfillment of prophecy, the Redeemer sent to save the race in its hour of crisis, but there had yet to be a true testing by blood. This triumph, this making of Yankee engines which could then defeat the humans, had now, in the minds of those who fought at sea, become proof of that prophecy.

As the ship cast off he walked up to the bow, signaling to his guards that he wanted to be alone. In the twilight it seemed as if the water of the harbor had disappeared, to be replaced with iron, steel, wood, and sinew. After the victory of the morning the vast flotilla had come down the final bend of the river, and the sight of his creation filled him with awe. More than five hundred galleys, powered by a hundred thousand Chin cattle, would transport three umens of troops into battle, then return to pick up three more. More than a hundred Chin sailing ships would transport thirty batteries of artillery, twenty mortar batteries, and the thousands of tons of food, supplies, and ammunition needed by his army. Six of his ironclads were already ranging far forward, driving back any surviving Yankee ships so that no prying eyes might see, while overhead ranged ten of his airships. As the paddle wheel of his flagship churned the water astern to foam, he looked aft. The towlines were taut, the ship straining, and then, ever so slowly, it lurched forward. The first barge started to move, followed seconds later by the second, third, and fourth. It was cumbersome and slow but they were moving at last. The other five steamships were already moving, each of them pulling a string of barges as well, the barges which contained his guarantee of victory.

Chapter Five

Pat O'Donald looked at the report just handed to him by a sweat-drenched courier.

"It's from McMurtry," Pat announced as he handed it over to Rick Schneid.

"Wandering Folk in the forest report dismounted Bantag on flank, twenty miles north of the farthest outposts. Should I deploy farther north?" Rick read.

"What do you make of it?" Pat asked.

"We've got scouts a good fifteen miles out on the flank who have seen nothing. These Wandering Folk, I don't trust them. They won't fight with us on our side, they just hide. Why would they help us now?"

The battery behind them opened with a salvo, and Pat watched as shots impacted a mile down the road, scattering a mounted unit. The smoke of the guns hung heavy in the gloomy forest. A gust of wind whipped through the trees overhead, carrying with it a plume of smoke and ash. The day before, the woods north of the road had caught fire and were still burning.

"Did you talk to any of these people?" Pat asked, looking over at the courier.

The courier shook his head. "No, sir. I believe General McMurtry talked with them, though. I was simply given this dispatch and ordered to get it down to you."

Tom McMurtry was a good man, Pat thought, part of his old battery, coming up through the ranks to command a division in Schneid's corps. He was now on the extreme left, ten miles away. But damn it, the report was vague.

Pat sat back down at his field desk and unrolled the well-worn map. They had fallen back twenty-five miles in the last three days, pulling out in late afternoon. The units which had fought leapfrogged back through the two corps which had fallen back the day before. This would give the units a day to rest and refit before becoming the front line again. The positions had been surveyed months before, fields of fire cleared, earthern forts and breastworks already dug. So far it had been a lovely killing match, almost too damn simple. Once pressure built up too much on the flanks all he had to do was pull out, fall back, and make them pay again.

But what was this report of a flanking force farther out? He looked at the courier.

"Were you there when McMurtry talked with them?"

"Like I said, sir, I'm not sure if he talked with them. I did see a couple of them at headquarters," the orderly replied. "They're a queer lot; never could trust them."

And damn frustrating as well, Pat thought. There were tens of thousands of them living in the northern forest, descendants of those who had fled generations ago into the woods rather than submit to the demands of the Hordes. Those humans who stayed behind had been mandated by their Horde masters to hunt them down. The old prejudice, no matter how illogical, still held, and there was barely a man in the army who thought the Wanderers to be worthy of consideration. Many half feared that they might even be possessed by demons.

Andrew, over Kal's misgivings, had sent repeated entreaties to them to join in the rebellion, and always there had been a refusal, a desire simply to be left out of the war. Pat could maybe see their point. They had survived for hundreds of years by going far enough north to avoid the Hordes, and most likely believed that the rebellion would end in the same way any other attempt at throwing off the yoke of the Hordes had ended, in total annihilation. Yet if ever they were needed, it was now.

Was this an accurate report, he wondered, or was it a trick, a Bantag slave sent in to lure a detachment deeper into the forest, where it might be cut off. If there was a weakness to the defensive lines, Pat realized, it was the northern flank. The damn forest was all but impenetrable, but if they were successful in getting an umen or two far enough north, then swinging around, it might mean getting cut off.

"We can't ignore it," Rick said, leaning over to point at the map where McMurtry had sketched in the reported location.

"So damn little to go on. Damn telegraph."

The line up to the left flank had repeatedly failed, and Pat was tempted to let fly with a stream of imprecations. But now was not the time. Andrew had lectured him often enough on that. The worse it got, the calmer he had to appear if he was to run an army. Once he got excited it'd race down through the ranks and unsteady even the lowest private. Andrew could play that role for him before, but now he had four corps under his direct control and had to act the part himself.

"Rick. Pull a battalion of the cav attached to your corps. Order it north, if need be to the north pole. I want this checked out now."

He looked up at the sun which was just clearing the trees to the east. It was going to be a hot day, he could sense that already, made worse by the fires and the fighting in the woods. By noon the boys would be suffering.

An inner voice was whispering a warning to him, to leapfrog back to where Third and Eleventh Corps were dug in ten miles to the rear. That would put them within ten miles of the railhead in case they had to get out fast.

He looked back at the map. But this was such lovely ground, a straight north–south ridgeline rising five hundred feet out of the valley below. Firing lanes cut, we could pile up twenty, thirty thousand of the bastards down there and not take a scratch. There was no position this good short of the Shenandoah River. Orders were to bleed them white, and besides, he hated to give up ground without a fight.

"Are we pulling back?" Rick asked.

Pat pulled another cigar out, bit off the end, and stoked it to a bright red glow. The roar of battle forward redoubled, and he could see the swirling clouds of smoke rising out of the forest ahead.

"Good ground here; let's make them pay for it."

"Sir! *Petersburg* is coming in!"

Andrew looked up from the pile of reports spread across his desk. Even though Vincent was his chief of staff and had unlimited access, part of him wanted to offer a rebuke for the way he had burst into the office. And then the full import of what Vincent was saying hit him.

"*Petersburg?* What the hell is it doing here?"

"It looks all shot to hell, just came out of the fog a few minutes ago."

Andrew was out from behind his desk in an instant, heading for the door. The last of the morning mist coming off the ocean was dissolving into long, wispy streamers. At any other time or place he would have been out watching the sunrise for mornings like this. Fog breaking up over the sea as the first light of dawn hit so reminded him of home.

His stomach knotted as he saw the ironclad, sides blackened and flame-scorched, drawing into the bay. He knew he should wait in his office—it was undignified as commander to go running down to the dock just because a ship was coming in—but he was drawn nevertheless, struggling to keep his pace down to a calm walk. It was obvious that word had already spread through the port. Soldiers were pouring out of warehouses, shading their eyes to look down to where the irconlad was coming in. Even the crews in the rail yard had stopped work and were heading to the wharves.

"She's flying an admiral's pennant, sir. If Bullfinch is back, we've lost the blockade," Hawthorne said anxiously. Andrew knew it was best not to reply, for to do so would betray his own fears.

He lost sight of the ship for a moment as he walked between two long rows of warehouses. He could hear the men inside shouting that he was passing by. A quick glance over his shoulder revealed that hundreds of men were now following him, anxious to hear the news.

"Andrew!"

From out of a side street Emil came up, puffing hard, and fell in beside him.

"Saw it from the hospital window; I have the ambulances coming to take off the casualties."

Andrew nodded, saying nothing. As he turned the corner around the last of the warehouses *Petersburg* stood plainly in view, water foaming beneath its stern as the ship backed engines to ease its way up against the dock. Several hoses snaked out of open gun ports, water pulsing out from pumps working below.

He slowed for a moment. The entire starboard side of the ship was a shambles. He quickly counted five holes that had been driven clean through the armor siding.

"My God, sir," Hawthorne whispered, "they cut her to ribbons."

Cries of astonishment rippled through the crowd as they pushed forward to look at the wreckage of the Eastern Fleet's flagship. The bent and mangled side hatch door opened, and the deck crew streamed out, scrambling along the side of the ship, catching lines tossed from the wharf.

A vent of steam escaped as the engine shut down and the ship gently bumped against the dock. Men lining the wharf were besieging the deck crew with questions. Andrew looked over at Vincent, and a nod was all that was necessary. Vincent scrambled onto the top of a piling, drew his revolver, and fired it into the air. Instantly all eyes were on him.

"All right, you damn bastards!" he roared. "You're behaving like a mob of schoolgirls. Now get the hell back to work."

The men looked at him wide-eyed. In the background the clang of an ambulance bell sounded as a white, canvas-covered wagon turned onto the main street leading to the dock.

"Listen, men," Vincent continued, softening his tone. "It's obvious they've had a fight here. Now clear away so we can get your wounded comrades to the hospital. I promise you we'll send a messenger with news around to all the units once we find out what's happened. We've got to stay calm. So get back to work; there's a job to be done."

The men, talking excitedly, reluctantly broke away from the wharf and started back up the hill, leaping aside as the first of half a dozen ambulances pulled up at the edge of the dock. The deck crew threw a gangplank across and the first stretcher came out, carrying a man who had lost both legs just above the knees.

He was in a daze, blinking in the light. Andrew stepped aside and for an instant the wounded sailor was looking at him. Andrew reached out and touched him lightly on the shoulder.

"You're home now, son," he whispered. The sailor tried to say something, but Emil was shouldering Andrew aside, placing a hand on the sailor's forehead, and urging the stretcher bearers on.

Andrew watched in silence, hiding his emotions as the stream of wounded were unloaded, men missing limbs, faces scorched and blackened, blood-soaked bandages wrapped over the gaping wounds torn into their bodies by shell and flying splinters. The walking wounded came next, hobbling down the gangplank, some of them trying to salute, but Andrew just motioned them on.

Finally Bullfinch appeared, hesitating as he reached the edge of the gangplank as if he was a schoolboy returning home with a report of his failure.

Andrew motioned for him to join him, returning his salute as he stepped onto the dock. Together they started to walk down to the far end of the wharf.

"We lost, sir," Bullfinch finally said, his voice thick with emotion. Andrew looked down at the diminutive admiral, who, like Hawthorne, was only twenty-seven.

"Tell me about it." Andrew listened in silence as his admiral described the disaster.

"I'm sorry, sir," Bullfinch finished, and as he choked out the words he finally broke down, lowering his head. Andrew put a hand on his shoulder, knowing the anguish, remembering his own failure when Third Corps was cut off, the debacle of the retreat back to the Neiper, and his dread of having to face Kal.

He looked at the ruins of *Petersburg*, and the full import of what it signified finally started to sink in. Ha'ark had jumped the level of technology, making ships and guns that could not only match, but exceed human output. The uneasy foreboding that had haunted him was coming to pass—Ha'ark was no longer imitating, he was leaping ahead. Ferguson could run all his calculations, they could upgrade their guns, their armor, and maybe for the moment regain balance, but the distinct advantage the Republic had maintained ever since the wars began, that they could count on superior weapons, was finished. He could sense that in the men who had stood by the dock. For years they had fought, bled, and died, first with smoothbores, then with rifled muskets, and now breechloaders, knowing they would have the edge. The damage to *Petersburg* was grim evidence that it might never be the same again.

Yet that was a question looking months, even

years, into the future. It was what this victory implied for the moment that he had to focus on.

"Sir, I sent my executive officer ahead to tell you. Didn't you know?"

Andrew shook his head. "This is the first word we've received."

"My god," Bullfinch gasped. "I saw airships heading north—they must have sunk *Defiant*. I thought you'd have at least a day's warning."

"Of what?"

"My other ships? Haven't any reported in, sir?"

"You're the first ship we've seen in days."

Bullfinch looked as if he had been struck a mortal blow.

"We got separated during the night. *Roum* was listing heavily, falling behind. Their airships were over us nearly constantly, dropping bombs. Sir, they could be up here by late afternoon."

"You mean they've broken the blockade?"

"It's more than that, sir. As we were heading north our lookout reported a flotilla coming down the river into the bay."

"Flotilla?"

"He said it looked like dozens, maybe a hundred or more ships. They knocked the door down, sir; they have the sea and can go where they damn well please."

Andrew looked over at Vincent.

"The land cruisers," Vincent said. "Sir, it's the only way they could ever bring them into action. They must be planning a landing."

"But where?"

"They could hit the Shenandoah River and cut off Pat," Bullfinch whispered. "It's navigable right up to the railroad bridge."

Andrew suddenly felt as if his stomach was on fire. Wearily he sat down on one of the pilings, his gaze fixed on *Petersburg.*

The bastards have the sea; they can hit us anywhere. But where? Where would Ha'ark hit them? Pat, Hans, or here?

Or all three . . . Ha'ark would do the audacious, the master stroke. Andrew felt a wave of self-reproach, of bitter anger. He had been lured out, it was why Ha'ark had waited so long, even after the mask was pulled off, revealing his intentions. Lure the army to the end of the line, then in one blow slam the back door shut.

"He'll hit us near Fort Hancock," Andrew said softly. "They must have mapped this before we even got there. He cast this plan in his mind a year, two, even three years ago. Take Fort Hancock, drive ten miles to the northwest, cut the rail and both fronts at Junction City, where the line branches to the south. Hold there, and then simply let the land forces on both fronts grind us down when we run out of supplies."

"The logistical support though," Bullfinch interjected. "We talked about this before. There's no real harbor at Hancock, there's a fort there with thirty-pound Parrott guns . . ." Then his voice trailed off at the cold realization that thirty-pound Parrotts were useless against Ha'ark's ironclads.

"If his ironclads can tear *Petersburg* up, they'll most certainly pound the fort into submission," Vincent snapped.

"Vincent, what do we have at Hancock?" Andrew asked.

"Sir, only one regiment, the Third Roum Heavy

Artillery. Garrison troops, older men, disabled veterans."

One day's, warning, Andrew thought bitterly, one day and we could have a division, two divisions waiting for him, tear him apart right on the beach if he tried to land.

"Vincent, how many trains are in the yard right now?"

"Fifteen, I think, sir. There's another twenty up on the Shenandoah, and ten, maybe twelve down on the southern front."

"I want the line cleared of all traffic coming east from Roum past Junction City. Get that signal out right now. You're to take two divisions of Fifth Corps, run them up to Fort Hancock now. Get them there. If you get there ahead of the bastards, start digging in, meet them on the beaches. I'll alert Marcus back in Roum to release Tenth Corps and move it up to support. I'll hold one division here in case they go for a landing here or to the east. We can make up another brigade from the men in the supply units."

"What about Hans and Pat?"

What to do there? They had to be alerted, but should he order a pullout right now? Twenty trainloads to move a corps, and that meant abandoning a fair part of their supplies. Pull back the four corps under Pat, the three under Hans. Once that started rolling, it would be impossible to stop. And there was the chance, still the chance, that the lookout was wrong, that all Ha'ark had on the sea was eight or so ironclads and some lighter support ships. But he never would have made the effort to build them unless he wanted to use the sea for offensive operations.

Everything now was tied to a single ribbon of

track. Ten corps, over two hundred thousand men, thousands of tons of supplies, all of it to be moved on two strips of iron. It was always the inherent weakness in this new type of war, everything in the end was tied to a twin ribbon of iron that could so easily be cut.

What do to? First priority was to move to try and hold Fort Hancock. There was only a single regiment of garrison troops there, a battery of thirty-pound rifles, muzzle loaders from the last war. Useless against what Ha'ark might have. Get Vincent moving, then see where the blow hits and figure the next step from there.

"I want the first train moving within the hour, Vincent. I'm counting on you. Now get moving!"

There was the slightest flicker of a smile. The boy had what he wanted again, a field command. Saluting, he turned and ran, calling for his orderlies, who had been waiting at a respectful distance to follow him.

"Can *Petersburg* fight?" Andrew asked, shifting his attention back to Bullfinch, who had stood silent, head lowered.

"I lost half my crew, sir. We not only have to repair the damage, we have to add more armor, another three inches at least. The added weight, sir . . ." His voice trailed off, and he sadly shook his head.

"No, sir. She's finished."

"Then strip the guns out. We're going to need them here. If we have time, pull the armor off as well and be prepared to scuttle her."

Startled, Bullfinch could not reply.

"I'm sending you back to Roum, Mr. Bullfinch."

"Roum, sir? The fighting's here," he hesitated. "Are you relieving me of command, sir?"

Andrew tried to laugh, but the chuckle sounded false, hollow. "Lincoln once said that if he fired every general who lost a battle he wouldn't have anyone left.

"I'm not sure of this yet, Bullfinch, but you might be needed more there in a couple of days. I want you to get on the first train heading out to Junction City. Take your staff with you. If that's where Ha'ark hits, then get yourself back to Roum."

"Sir, if you're relieving me of command, just tell me, sir, straight out."

Andrew stood up and smiled.

"It's not victory that defines us, son, it's how we handle defeat. You've only started to fight in this war. Now get on that train, I'll forward your orders out later."

"Sir . . ." he tried to look Andrew in the eyes, but couldn't, lowering his head.

"You did the best you could. Now let's get ready for what comes next. Take your staff and get out of here."

Bullfinch finally looked up.

"Thank you, sir. I won't let you down."

Saluting, he departed, following Hawthorne. Once again Andrew sat down on the piling, his gaze wandering to the ship.

"We're in it this time, aren't we."

Emil approached him, ready if need be to withdraw if Andrew indicated.

"How bad is it?" he asked.

Andrew stirred.

"Emil, it might be worse than the Potomac."

Emil sighed and sat down on a piling across from Andrew.

"Those poor boys in that boat. Never could understand why anyone would be crazy enough to join the navy. Samual Johnson was right."

"What was that?" Andrew replied absently.

"Samuel Johnson. Said a ship was like a prison, with the added factor that you could drown. The wounds some of those boys had. Ghastly." He shook his head sadly. "Damn all wars."

Andrew said nothing, still staring at the ship as if it represented the shattering of all that he had planned and hoped for.

"Andrew, we've got twelve hundred wounded up in the hospital, just arrived from the eastern front. Should I get them out?"

Another factor he suddenly realized. If they were about to be cut off, what of the wounded, a train that could haul two hundred stretcher cases could move two regiments instead. But if they were cut off?

"One train, the serious cases. We need to get Fifth Corps in position first. I'll release two more trains to you if they hit us where I think they will, so you can get the rest out."

"I better get back to the hospital."

"Fine, Emil. I'll keep you posted."

"Andrew?"

He looked up into his old friend's eyes as Emil stood up and came to his side.

"You haven't lost yet," Emil said quietly, and then, with hands tucked into the pockets of his jacket, he walked away.

Haven't lost yet.

All he felt now was numbness. A wondering if he had gone to the well one too many times. Ten damn years of this, dear God, he thought, ten damn years, and it never seems to end.

Again there was the dream, the memory of Maine,

to escape back to another time, another place of peace, tranquillity. Once it had just been a company, then a regiment. From there to a corps, an army, now armies, and always the same, a right decision brought victory, but even then, at such moments there was the fresh-turned earth, the sightless eyes gazing at the heavens, the harvest of death.

Johnnie. How old would Johnnie be now, the baby brother dead at Gettysburg. Same age as Hawthorne and Bullfinch? No, my God, a year older than them. Hard to imagine that, the dead innocent boy might have lived to become the cold proficient killer like Hawthorne, or the shaken, frightened admiral who could never believe in the prospect of defeat and now confronted it in all its horror.

More stretchers were coming off *Petersburg,* but these did not require a rush to an ambulance, but rather the slow walk to the graveyard on the edge of town, where hundreds of dead from this new campaign were already being laid to rest. The army was so organized in its grim business that the graves were already dug.

How many have died under my command, he wondered . . . The price of victory? A hundred thousand? No, more likely two hundred thousand by now. Every day yet more dead, and now the lives of two hundred thousand more hung in the balance.

Strange, he could remember the stories about Grant and Sherman . . . how when Sherman came to understand the full enormity of what would be required to win that his nerves broke and he went home, hiding for months in his house, unwilling to return to face the task until finally ordered back. And Grant, the damn butcher who could send men into the slaughter of Cold Harbor, but supposedly became ill at the sight of blood, and could not even eat a piece of meat unless it was cooked clean through.

He could sense his men looking at him, solitary, sitting alone on the end of the pier, lost in thought, staring at the ship. What show do I have to put on for them now? Confidence, always the game; let them see you fearless, confident. There was a time, he knew, when he could play it so well. At Fredericksburg, during the charge on Mayre's Heights, turning his back to the enemy fire, walking backwards, shouting encouragement, yet terrified of the bullet he was convinced would strike between the shoulder blades. Or pacing the line at Gettysburg after Colonel Estes went down and he took command. Even at Hispania, when all seemed lost, waiting in the line with his men for the final charge. This was different now. The fighting hundreds of miles away, no heat of the moment, no frightful grim joy of battle to sweep one up and thus transport a commander to fight beyond his own fears.

But this situation was different. To be truly alone, to confront one's own fears in silence. To calculate and recalculate, always knowing that in those grim calculations a mistake meant two hundred thousand dead, a war lost, the dream destroyed, and in the most intimate sense, Kathleen and the children dead as well.

He felt as if his knees had gone to jelly as a surge of fear tore into his heart. Kathleen, the children. Yet again the enormity of it all reduced to the simplest terms, the survival of those whom he loved the most.

He finally looked away from the ship and saw them, the staff, the youngsters who but a short time before were peasants in the fields, craftsmen in shops, some of them even the sons of Boyars and patricians, now wearing Union blue, waiting for him to decide.

Wearily he stood up and he could sense their anticipation, ready to spring forward to fulfill his orders, hoping, praying for that moment of distinction, of glory that would make their names, their memories shine.

Glory . . . such a strange concept. How I dreamed of it myself, how I still believe in it. Yet it masks the grim reality, that in the end we are doing a butcher's job. Both sides, a butcher's job, and we mask it with banners, uniforms, honor, and glory. For to believe otherwise leads in the end to madness, and in this war, the baring of one's own neck to the butcher of the other side.

He approached them, slowing to step around the bodies that were being unloaded from *Petersburg*. Without a word he motioned for his staff to follow and slowly walked back up the hill to wait for what would come next.

Leaning back in the saddle, Hans silently cursed all horses. It was one thing to go galloping after the Commanche when one was thirty-five, but chasing the damn Horde when one was pushing into the mid-fifties was something else. And the damnable horses were simply too big, size of Clydesdales back home, he thought, as he drew his left up out of the stirrup and rubbed the old wound, which was aching. Uncorking his canteen, he took a swig of water, swished it around, and spit it out, clearing the dust, then soaked his bandanna and wiped the grime from his face and the back of his neck. A troop of cavalry trotted past, pushing on to the next pass, where a flurry of rifle fire marked the forward line as a dismounted regiment worked its way up to the crest. A battery of ten-pounders to his left opened up, firing high to drop shells over the ridge onto the road beyond. Raising his field glasses, he watched the forward signal unit, which, with a flutter of flags, was passing back word to the battery as to its accuracy. Apparently the range was good because the battery set to with a will.

Looking to the next ridge, he felt a swelling of pride at the sight of a full corps of infantry deploying, skirmishers to the fore, regiments in column, moving at the double time. A wounded horse whinnied pitifully to his right, and Hans turned about and rode up to the beast, which was lying on its side, its forelegs broken. A Bantag rider was sprawled in front of him, neck broken from the fall. Damn stupid charge, Hans thought, coming across the valley like that. Hundreds of them littered the field, a troop of his own cavalry now riding among them, doing the grim work of dispatching the crippled survivors. Hans drew his pistol, aimed it at the horse's head, and squeezed the trigger. So damn strange, he always felt far more pity for the animals caught in war. Maybe it was their innocence of all this.

A courier on a lathered horse, lashing the animal hard, galloped up to Hans, reining in hard to stop.

"Suppose they countercharged right now?" Hans barked, even as the courier handed over a message.

"Sir?"

"Suppose those bastards countercharge. You wouldn't get a mile before your animal broke down and you got left behind. Take better care of him."

"Sir. This is from the forward telegraph station. It just came in."

Hans unfolded the message, scanned it, then

folded it up and put it in his pocket. Pulling out a pad of notepaper, he jotted off a quick note and handed it back to the courier.

"Get this back, but son, take it easy, we have a long day ahead of us yet."

"Yes, sir!" The boy saluted, reining his horse around. He started to dig in his spurs and, aware of Hans's critical gaze, relented and simply urged his mount up to a slow canter.

The battery that had been shelling the road was starting to limber up, ready to move forward, and Hans trotted over to their commander.

"Send the battery back, Captain."

"Sir? We've got them on the run, sir."

"Actually, Captain," Hans said grimly, "it's the other way around."

"Pat, we've just lost our telegraph connection to Port Lincoln," Schneid announced as he handed over the dispatch.

Swearing, Pat looked up at the Bantag airship that was droning lazily overhead, just outside of antiairship range.

"Bet it was that bastard up there."

"Another one, about twenty miles short of the Shenandoah, swooped down, cut off a couple hundred feet of wire, then took off again. But that's not the worst of it."

"Go on. It's been bad enough today already."

He was still mulling over the latest message from Andrew, reporting the breakdown of the blockade. It was something, so far, he had only shared with Rick; no sense in triggering a panic. And besides, even if the bastards were going to try something on him, lookouts on the high hills facing the sea would see the fleet hours before it came in.

"We just got a report in from McMurtry—the telegraph line is up again. Indications of a strong Bantag force moving behind our flank. Nothing sighted yet, but the forest about twenty miles north was all cut to hell with tracks. The patrol ran into a skirmishing screen and can't get farther in."

"So them Wandering People were right," Pat said quietly.

The gunfire to forward had slackened somewhat; the bastards were most likely taking a breather before trying again. Casualties had been light, fewer than five hundred so far today and at least, eight maybe ten times that number for them.

Hans was right; there was more, far more. The flanking force, how much? A umen? Even that could play hell if they fell on the bridge over the Shenandoah. Wouldn't be well supplied though—whatever they could carry—but enough to put up one day's good fight. No, if they were going to go through all that trouble, it would be three, maybe even five or six umens. And what would one day accomplish if they were flanking me here? Lose a corps, maybe half my force cutting out.

There was something more afoot. Far more. They want me to hold this position, that's it. They want me here, while they continue to swing all the way into my rear. Audacious, damn them, but it'll hit thin air if we can get out in time.

"Rick, start pulling out now. Alert Eleventh Corps to stay awake on their left; we'll be falling back on them before evening."

"We're getting out?"

"That's right."

"How far, Pat?"

"I think right back to the Shenandoah. Me bunions hurt, Schneid. They always hurt just before somethin' bad's about to happen. So get the lads moving."

"Colonel, will you look at that!"

Colonel Arnett, Thirty-third Roum, of the First Brigade, First Division, Eleventh Corps had felt uncomfortable all day. He was, he realized, on the extreme left of the line. Granted, it was the reserve fallback position, and the battle being fought by First and Ninth Corps was eight miles up ahead. Strange, not a sound of the conflict could be heard, though if one put his hand to the ground, he could feel the land shivering from the battery fire. From the lookout tower the woods on the horizon were wrapped in smoke so that it seemed as if one was gazing into the fiery pit of Hades.

He looked to where the private was pointing. A few rabbits were bounding out of the woods, followed by what passed for deer on this world, gray shaggy things with a wide spread of antlers. More and yet more animals came bounding out of the forest to his left, running in panic. Flights of birds soared out of the woods, darting madly between the trees.

Funny, it reminded him of something, but what?

A single rifle cracked, followed by two more shots. One of the pickets out of the edge of the woods surrounding the fort was shouting something. Some of the men lining the breastworks were laughing at the sight of all the animals running through the clearing and were raising their weapons, looking at Arnett and waiting for permission to take a shot at dinner.

"Sir!"

It was Sergeant McDougal. He was one of the few men who had come through with the old Forty-fourth and never managed to reach a commission, just plain drunkenness and disorderly behavior always kept relegating him back down to the ranks. Even being a sergeant was almost more than he could handle.

"What now, McDougal?"

"Chancellorsville, sir! Chancellorsville!"

"What the hell are you talking about . . ." And then the realization hit. The regiments flanked by Stonewall Jackson at Chancellorsville reported the same things just before the Rebs hit, animals bounding panic-stricken out of the forest . . . fleeing ahead of the mile-wide line of the Confederate attack.

"Bugler, sound assembly!" Arnett roared, and it was the last command he ever gave as, an instant later, a sniper bullet smashed into his forehead.

McDougal caught the colonel as he fell, saw that he was dead, and dropped him. McDougal took a quick look around. The Thirty-third was well dug in on a low hilltop. Though drunk, he still knew how to fight, and, running to the parapet wall, he saw the black-clad host storming out of the forest and into the cleared firing lanes cut around the position. Bullets snicked through the air above him, a geyser of dirt erupting from the battlement wall by his side.

Laughing, he looked back at the men of his regiment, most of them green boys who'd never heard a shot fired in anger. The call of the bugle was no longer needed as the men raced to the battlement walls, fumbling to sling on cartridge boxes. Though only a regimental sergeant major, he took one look at the Roum lieutenant colonel who was second-in-command and knew that the old patrician was out of his element.

The Bantag leapt forward, shouting their deep soul-searching death cries. McDougal could see some of his own men already stepping back off the firing line, ready to flee.

Drawing his revolver, he leapt on top of the breastworks and, laughing, pointed the revolver at the advancing charge.

"Stand and fight, you sons of bitches," he roared. "We're all going to die, so let's go down fighting!"

Whipping his horse, Vincent Hawthorne urged it into one final desperate surge. He could see the messenger coming down off the crest a mile ahead, galloping hard, and the urgency of the rider already told him what he had dreaded to hear, though the thumping of the guns in the distance was indication enough of what was happening.

Overhead one of the damn airships was moving lazily to the southeast, toward the ocean. Even as he watched it, there was a puff of smoke, and several seconds later he heard the scream of the light shell as it came in and detonated fifty yards away. He continued to urge his horse forward, finally reining in as the messenger approached, motioning for him to swing around and ride alongside. The messenger turned his horse about and fell in on Vincent's flank.

"They're coming!" he shouted.

Even as the messenger screamed his warning Vincent reached the crest of the hill and reined in hard.

Fort Hancock, which guarded the narrow harbor two miles beyond, was wreathed in smoke. Flashes of light told him that the fort's guns were still firing, but he knew already there was precious little the fort's thirty-pounders could do against the forces arrayed before it.

Sighing, he looked back across the open prairie he had just crossed. The first regiments of infantry were visible in the distance, four, maybe five miles away. Another two hours before they'd be up, and by then it would be far too late.

"Sir, did you get our last message? We got no reply, the line went dead. I was told to come look for you."

"No. I saw where the telegraph wire's been cut as I came up," Vincent replied. "Damn airships."

"It's hell down there," the messenger said. "They've got some damn big guns."

Through the eddies of smoke he could see a half dozen ironclads sitting almost stationary less than a hundred yards offshore, pouring their shot into the fort. He had expected to see that, but it was what was going on along the shore a couple of miles south of the bay that filled him with awe . . . and fear.

Chapter Six

If ever he had felt a moment of triumph, it was here, at this moment. Ha'ark wished that others, who had known him before, could see him thus, those who had scoffed at him, those who had felt themselves his betters because of their blood, and not because of what they had accomplished as he had now accomplished.

The galley he was in raced toward the rocky beach, maneuvering at the last second to slow its forward movement. It was a point of honor that he must be first, so that the legend would be fed, to grow in its telling. As the boat slid up onto the beach it stopped with a sudden lurch, and, losing his balance, he fell forward off the boat, landing on his hands and knees on the muddy shore.

He could hear the gasps, the cries of some that an ill omen had occurred. His mind raced and then, smiling, he dug down into the mud with his hands, and stood up, holding his arms high.

"See, my warriors!" he roared. "I seize this world with both hands!"

A wild triumphal roar erupted, and the warriors, eager to join him, leapt from the sides of the boat, into the muddy water, wading ashore. Casting the dirt down he turned to struggle up the slippery ledge to the high firm ground beyond, hiding his delight as some of his soldiers scrambled to pick up as a lucky talisman the mud he had dropped.

Dozens of boats beached to either side of him, each one disgorging eighty warriors, who raced up onto the open ground and began to spread out in open order, pushing a line forward toward the low ridgeline beyond. The airship overhead had already signaled that the nearest forces were still an hour or more away. Surprise had been nearly complete. His greatest fear had been that Keane would have received enough warning to block him. He did not yet have the ships that could land directly on a defended beach, and all his plans would have been for naught.

To his right, just beyond artillery range, the enemy fort was still under attack. Maybe the fools would be stupid enough to try and stay, for if they lingered much longer, his ground troops would cut off their escape and thus acquire rations for the evening.

More and yet more ships came in, disgorging their regiments, while one of the precious flat-bottomed steamships edged its way to shore, dropped a forward ramp, and the first battery of artillery was pushed ashore. Hundreds of warriors, armed with picks and shovels, were busy cutting a road through the ledge, and within minutes the battery was up off the beach, horses hitched to the caissons and then lashed forward.

Raising his field glasses, he could see a small cluster of riders on the far ridge. Was it Hans?

He focused in on them. No; if it was Hans, he would know. There would be that sense of defiance, that damnable defiance. If he could sense anything from this one, it was fear. Good, very good.

Two airships came in low over the hills and, running with the breeze, swept over the ocean, then turned into the wind. Dripping down, they approached one of the galleys, from which a small red balloon was flying. The first airship passed over the galley, snagging the balloon, and it soared up, cans of fuel dangling from the end of the line, which was quickly hauled up. The second airship moved into position, another balloon went up, to be snagged as well. The warriors around him watched the show with awe and looked with admiration at Ha'ark. Yet again he had shown them a new thing, a way of keeping the flying machines above them for yet more hours. It was so simple, Ha'ark thought, and yet so wondrous to them. Once their position was secured a station would be established and the airships landed.

His attention now shifted to the center of all his plans. A steamship moved in close to shore, and, as its whistle sounded, the towline astern of the ship was cast off. The four barges behind slowed to a stop. Galleys moved in on either side of the barges, lines were cast over, and the ungainly craft towed slowly the last hundred yards to the beach, galleys and barges sliding up onto the muddy shore.

The bow of the first barge dropped forward. Puffs of smoke swirled up in a black cloud, and, with its whistle shrieking, the first land cruiser edged off the barge, its great wheels sinking deep into the mud. Troops carrying heavy planks leapt from the galleys and ran up in front of the cruiser, throwing the boards down in front of the machine. He held his breath, waiting. The land cruiser edged forward, the middle drive wheels leaving the barge. The boards underneath cracked under the weight, sinking. The machine remained stationary for a moment, steam and smoke pouring out of it, and then ever so slowly it edged forward, heading toward the opening cut in the ledge. The land cruiser reared up as its front wheels dug into the embankment. It rose higher, and yet higher, its forward gun pointing to the heavens. Wheels spinning, it seemed to hang in midair, then cleared the ledge, slamming down onto the hard ground of the open steppe.

The driver held the whistle down in triumph, the high, piercing shriek sending a shiver down Ha'ark's spine. Farther down the beach the second cruiser was ashore, then a third, and a fourth. Whistles shrieking, they slowly started forward, infantry companies spreading out before the advance, artillery batteries falling in beside the cruisers.

The chant started somewhere forward, and in an instant swept the length of the line . . . "Ha . . . ark, Ha . . . ark, Ha . . . ark!"

Grinning, Ha'ark waited as an orderly brought his horse. Mounting, he cantered over to the nearest land cruiser and, leaping from his mount, scrambled on top of the machine. Ha'ark motioned to the rifle in its scabbard, and an orderly drew it out and tossed it to him. He held it aloft, the sunlight rippling along the burnished barrel. Warriors who but short years ago would have charged with swords drawn, now held bayonet-tipped rifles aloft in reply.

"Ha . . . ark! Ha . . . ark! Ha . . . ark!"

Smiling, he looked back toward the rider on the hill.

"Ha . . . ark!"

The words floated in the late-afternoon air as Vincent lowered his field glasses. So that was him.

He tried to focus his thoughts, knowing all that Hans had told him. There were some of the Horde that could somehow sense the minds of others. Hans believed in it; so did Andrew. He now felt it as well, a probing, a taunting, a show of irresistible force that in his heart Vincent knew he could not stop.

Looking back down at the fort, he was horrified to see a column of men breaking out of the western sally port, running. They had waited too long. Bantag skirmishers were already deploying on their flank, pouring fire in.

He focused his glasses on one of them, watching as the Bantag fired, levered his breech open, slid a cartridge in, slammed the breech shut, capped the nipple, and aimed. Sharps pattern rifles, just like ours. Four, maybe five rounds a minute. He lowered his glasses and saw men dropping. The Bantag were good shots, hitting at two and three hundred yards. The knot of men thinned out, the strongest surging forward, running in panic.

The black-uniformed Bantag warriors charged, their long strides closing the gap at a frightening speed. The panicked regiment shied away, turning to the north, but there was no safety there, only a downhill run to the bay.

The messenger beside him was cursing, crying. Vincent ignored him. Looking back across the prairie, he saw a battery of guns, twenty-pounders, racing forward, still almost a mile away. Can we make the stand here, Vincent wondered, or should we pull back? Some of his staff was now gathered around him, looking in wide-eyed wonder at the army deploying from the beach.

Vincent turned and started barking out orders.

"Get that battery up here now! Then detail off the two closest regiments armed with Sharps to open out into a skirmish line and come forward." Vincent pointed at one of his men, and the orderly saluted and galloped off.

He pointed at the next one in line. "Get back to General Gordon, tell him to hold the rest of the division on the ridge behind us, and dig in! Then I want a message sent back to General Keane."

Vincent motioned for a message pad. Fishing a pencil out of his breast pocket, he jotted down a quick note—"Sir. The main invasion has hit here at Fort Hancock. Estimate two umens armed with modern weapons. Supported by eight ironclads, several hundred other ships. At least twenty land cruisers like one Hans described. Will try to delay them, await your orders."

After he signed his name he passed the dispatch over. "Ride like hell!"

Taking his field glasses up, he focused on the fort. Cursing softly, he watched as the last of the garrison was slaughtered. One of the Bantag, as if sensing that he was watching, held a man aloft by his hair while laughing and looking straight up at Vincent. With a flourish of his blade he sliced the man's throat, then lapped at the blood as it cascaded out.

Bitter cursing erupted around Vincent.

"They panicked and broke," Vincent said coldly. "They should have held the fort; we might have been able to get them out."

He knew that wasn't true, but at least they would have taken down more of the bastards before they died. The last knot of men were finally cornered down on the beach. Sickened, Vincent watched as some of them turned their weapons on themselves rather than face the final horror. The Bantag were butchering the corpses, hacking off limbs and strapping the dangling arms and legs to their backpacks before moving on, the action reminding him of his own men tying a dead chicken or a slab of freshly butchered pork to their belts in anticipation of dinner.

The battery was drawing closer. He could hear the shouts of the drivers, the major in command reining in beside Vincent and snapping off a salute. The major looked toward the valley below where the invasion force was fanning out and starting to advance, his jaw dropping in amazement.

"Major. Deploy right here! Aim for the nearest land cruiser."

"What, sir?"

"The land locomotive. The black thing down there belching smoke, damn it!"

Still mounted, Vincent waited impatiently as the first gun came up the slope, its crew cursing, shouting, urging the tired horses on for a final burst of effort. The first gun skidded around, its crew jumping off the caisson, those who had come up on foot, gasping for breath after the final run.

The team outriders urged the horses back down the slope once the gun was unhitched, placing the caisson behind the slope to protect it from direct fire. One of the gunners flipped the lid of the caisson open, looked back at the gun sergeant, and waited for orders. The rest of the gun crew maneuvered their weapon into position, the sergeant working the elevation screw down.

The major of the battery looked over at Vincent and pointed at one of the land cruisers, which was wreathed in a black cloud of smoke. Vincent nodded.

"Solid shot!"

The command was passed down to the sergeant, who shouted to the loader at the caisson. The loader pulled out a bolt, his assistant hoisting out a wooden box containing the powder bag. The lid of the box was torn off and the bag slid out. The two ran to the gun as the sergeant stepped clear. The round was shoved into the breech, the powder bag going in behind it, and the breech was slammed shut and the primer set.

The battery commander was already dismounted, standing by the gun, carefully studying the land cruiser with his binoculars.

"Range twenty-eight hundred yards!"

Vincent could not help but smile as the sergeant stepped away from the gun and, shading his eyes, studied the target for a moment before nodding in agreement with his young commander's estimate of range. Moving back behind his gun, the sergeant cursed the crew soundly as two men, holding the prolonge pole jutting from the back of the gun trail, moved the weapon slightly to the right. Two men on each of the wheels strained to pivot the gun until the sergeant, with a shout, held up both arms straight overhead, signaling that he was satisfied with how the weapon was aimed.

Stepping back from the gun, he picked up the lanyard, ignoring the crew of the next three guns, which were swinging into position on his right.

"Stand clear!"

The gun crew stepped away from the wheels and trail.

The sergeant jerked the lanyard. With an explosive roar the gun leapt back, a ten-foot tongue of flame erupting from the muzzle as the twenty-pound bolt burst clear of the barrel and thundered downrange. Vincent fixed his attention on the land cruiser, counting off the seconds. A plume of dust erupted fifty yards to the left. Not bad for a first shot, he thought, but the major, obviously embarrassed, roared at the crew as they swabbed the bore and reloaded. The second and third guns joined in, followed a minute later by the fourth gun of the battery.

Plumes of dust erupted around the land cruiser, one of the solid bolts striking a Bantag infantryman, who simply disintegrated in a spray of blood.

The range closed to just over two thousand yards, and still the land cruiser advanced. Bantag infantry swarmed forward, and Vincent looked anxiously over his shoulder. A long line of skirmishers, advancing at the double quick, were coming up the slope behind him, the first of the men, panting for breath, coming up to Vincent's side and saluting.

"Colonel Petrovic, sir, Seventh Kev reporting!"

"Colonel, you see your targets. Try and keep their infantry back."

The colonel looked wide-eyed at the host deploying before them, nodded grimly, then, shouting orders, urged his men forward. A bullet fluttered by overhead. Surprised, Vincent looked back across the field and saw that some of the Bantag skirmishers were already opening up at nearly a thousand yards. Either it was damn stupid or they really believed they could hit something, and for an instant he wondered if some of them were armed with Whitworth sniper guns.

He fixed his attention on the land cruiser on which Ha'ark had been riding, hoping that the bastard was foolish enough still to be aboard. He was still there!

There was usually a sniper attached to each regiment and with luck they might be able to drop him now. He saw the distinctive green uniform of the regimental sniper and shouted for him to come over.

As the sniper came up and saluted Vincent looked back, but Ha'ark was gone.

Damn, did he know what I wanted to do? Vincent wondered. He saw a white horse, galloping along the line, just out of range.

"We hit it!"

Vincent turned his attention back to the land cruiser the battery had been shooting at as a spray of dust and fragments erupted from its forward armor. The machine kept moving . . . another round hit, there was an explosion of sparks, and he held his breath. The cruiser continued on, and a groan went up from the battery . . . the twenty-pound bolt had barely dented the shield.

The battery commander looked over at him.

"Pour it on; let it get closer and pour it on!"

"Sir, should we consider pulling back?"

Vincent looked over at one of his staff, who was nervously pointing to their left flank. The Bantag who had annihilated the regiment in the fort were working their way up the slope, edging around to the north. Down in the narrow bay one of the ironclads was moving in. Its forward gun erupted, and seconds later a heavy shot screamed overhead, the round exploding a half mile behind them.

"A few more minutes. We have to find out if we can punch a hole in those damn machines down there."

The skirmishers of the Seventh Kev were opening up, their rear sights levered up so that their weapons were angled high. Puffs of dust were kicking up as the Bantag skirmishers found their range and the whip-crack sound of bullets echoed around Vincent. An orderly moved his horse in front of Vincent, the boy looking scared even as he tried to play the hero, shielding his commander with his own body.

Vincent was about to chide him when a look of startled surprise filled the boy's features. He pitched forward, the back of his head gone.

Vincent leaned forward to him, blood and brains splattering across his uniform. Staff gathered around Vincent, taking the body from him. Vincent tried to act unperturbed. The boy had taken the bullet for him . . . and he didn't even know his name.

Several more shots hit the land cruiser, ricocheting off. The machine disappeared behind a cloud of smoke as it finally fired back. A round screamed in, detonating twenty yards forward of the number one gun, shell fragments whistling over the crew.

A battery which had been moving up behind the land cruiser deployed—Bantag crews unhitching their weapons, swinging them into position. Vincent, field glasses raised, carefully studied them. They moved quickly, obviously well practiced, not like the Merki gunners who were unsure of their weapons and how to use them. In less than a minute the first gun opened fire, followed seconds later by the other three. Two of the shots were short by fifty yards or more, the third screamed overhead, but the fourth plowed into the ground directly under the number three gun, exploding, shattering a wheel and wiping out half the crew.

Alongside the battery a wagon drew up, and half a dozen Bantag jumped out, unloading what looked to be pipes. Curious he watched them as the pipes were pointed to the sky, a bipod stand placed just under the muzzle.

Were they rocket launchers? The crew disappeared from view for a moment as smoke from the battery obscured them. The rifle fire of the Seventh Kev was picking up in tempo, and his mount, nervous, was shying back and forth so that it was hard to keep his field glasses trained on the crew by the wagon.

"Sir!"

He tore his attention away to where several of his staff were now pointing. The flanking force on the left was nearly to the crest, while off to the right, a half mile down the line, several companies of Bantag were moving at the double. Vincent looked back and saw that the second regiment armed with Sharps was still coming up, a half mile away, while on the distant ridgeline, his remaining regiments and second battery were deploying out.

"All right, sound the retreat," Vincent announced. "It's time to get the hell out of here."

The battery commander was down by his number three gun, shouting for the spare wheel to be unlashed from the battery limber wagon.

"Forget the gun, Major!" Vincent shouted. "Get your wounded loaded up and get the hell out!"

The Bantag down in the valley, as if sensing the pullout, were up, racing forward, hoping to trigger a panic. The men of the Seventh Kev, however, knew their business. Odd-numbered men stood up and sprinted to the rear, deploying back a hundred yards, then turned about. The even-numbered men waited, their colonel watching, as the remaining three guns of the battery were hitched up, drivers lashing the teams into a gallop.

A final volley was fired and the even-numbered men stood up and started for the rear. A strange whistling sound hummed overhead. An explosion erupted twenty yards behind Vincent, followed seconds later by three more. In less than ten seconds another four more explosions detonated along the ridge, catching several men of the Seventh as they pulled back.

Vincent fixed his attention back on the Bantag with the pipes. Mortars . . . the damn things were some new kind of mortar, he realized. He watched as one of the crew held what looked to be a shell over the barrel, dropped it in, then snatched his hand away. A second later a jet of flame erupted from the barrel. Seconds later the loader repeated it again. How the hell did the damn thing work?

"Damn it, sir! Let's go!"

One of his staff, leaning over, was grabbing hold of his reins, pulling his horse around. Vincent wanted to explode at him, but realized he was doing his job. He had killed one of his staff already by foolishly exposing himself.

He spared one final glance at the land cruiser. Its forward shield was scored from half a dozen hits, but still it came on. Bursts of smoke boiled out of its low smokestack; Bantag infantry to either side were moving along at a walk. The damn thing was slow-moving, but it seemed invincible.

Mortar rounds bracketed Vincent, and he could not help but flinch as pieces of shrapnel shrieked past him. As he turned his mount away he sensed something, and, looking over his shoulder, he again saw the white horse, Ha'ark was standing tall in the stirrups, rifle held high in a sardonic salute. Vincent was tempted to reply with a rude gesture. No, not that, he realized. Act professional. Standing in his stirrups, he snapped off a salute, then spurred his mount down the slope, smarting with humiliation at the jeering cries of the Bantag warriors behind him.

* * *

Furious, Andrew turned on his staff.

"Damn all to hell! I want to know what the hell is going on!"

The completely unnerved major who was in charge of the headquarters signals company stood before Andrew, barely able to conceal his fear.

"Sir. Telegraph lines are down in both directions. Like I told you before, sir, we have repair crews out, but as quick as we fix one break, their damn airships swoop down and cut the line somewhere else."

Andrew wanted to tear into the officer with frustrated rage. Everything had descended into chaos; he could sense the mounting panic on the part of his staff. From the window which looked out on the rail yard he could see the madness setting in, men racing back and forth, officers shouting, cursing, rushing to load two batteries on board a train which had just backed into the siding while an infantry officer, gestating wildly, was obviously arguing that his unit should have the train instead.

The major stood before him, waiting for the explosion. From the corner of his eye he saw Emil leaning against the doorsill, and to Andrew's utter amazement, the old doctor had a cigar in his mouth. The mere sight of Emil acting in a way he had always preached against startled Andrew. Emil gave a subtle nod for Andrew to join him.

"Just get the damn thing fixed!" Andrew snapped, and he stormed out of the office, joining Emil on the front porch.

"You're losing control," Emil said calmly.

"I don't need to hear this now, doctor," Andrew snapped. "I've got three different armies out there, and I've lost touch with all of them!"

"And three damn good generals running them," Emil replied softly, putting his hand on Andrew's shoulder, leading him off the porch and out of earshot of the staff inside the building.

Taking the cigar from his mouth he offered it to Andrew, and struck a light for him. Andrew puffed it to life.

"And your glasses are dirty," Emil announced, shaking his head. Reaching up, he took the glasses off. It was one of those annoying little things Andrew found a one-armed man simply had a hard time doing, and at home he usually relied on Kathleen to clean his glasses for him.

Emil pulled out a handkerchief, rubbed the lenses clean and, in a fatherly fashion, helped Andrew put them back on.

"There, that's better."

Andrew took a deep drag on the cigar, inhaled the smoke, and blew it out noisily.

"Pat and Hans both got the message that something was up before the lines went dead."

"But it's not knowing what they're doing that's driving me insane," Andrew replied, taking another deep pull on the cigar so that for a moment he felt light-headed, his heart racing.

"They'll do the right thing."

"I've never commanded like this before," Andrew said. "Before I was almost always there; I could see what was happening; I could sense the battle, the feel of how the men were taking it, what the other side was doing and, more importantly, about to do. They only caught me off guard once, when I lost Hans and Third Corps on the Potomac. It's like that now, only worse."

"That was four years ago, Andrew. It's all different

now. A different war, and you'll have to get used to it. Things will play out the same at this moment whether you're there or not. Right now, you're just going to have to wait."

Andrew muttered a curse under his breath.

"Something you were never really all that good at," Emil said with a smile.

He blocked Emil out for a moment, his attention fixed on the harbor. *Fredericksburg* had come limping in shortly before noon, listing heavily, with a report of having fought a duel with one of the Bantag ironclads covering the fleet. They had sunk the enemy ship but were forced to pull back when three more ironclads came about and started to close in. The ship's crews on *Petersburg* and *Fredericksburg* were hard at work, hoisting the guns out, and one of the fifty-pounders was already being dragged up the hill by a team of twenty horses, its firepower to be added to the earthen fortress guarding the harbor entrance. Out on the horizon a thin plume of smoke marked where one of the enemy ships had already taken up station.

Amazingly, everything was now reversed. Our port blockaded, what was going on just over the horizon a blank slate. He had never quite realized until now just how crucial sea power was in all of this. Bullfinch had talked incessantly about it, that it would be sea power that decided this war, but it had never fully registered until this moment. Ha'ark could strike anywhere, at will, with the additional advantage of controlling the air. He thought of the new monitor taking shape down in the shipyard. It might have matched the enemy but was now simply a hunk of worthless iron which they would most likely have to blow up.

"Feeling better?"

"Damn it, Emil, don't talk to me like I'm a child."

"I'm your doctor, Andrew. I have a license that allows me to get away with it."

Andrew looked over at his friend and sighed.

"I don't know what to do next, Emil. I'm blinded, cut off. I simply don't know what to do."

"First off, it's chaos back there." Emil nodded toward the rail yard.

"Take command right there for starters, Andrew. Ship up what you can and trust that Marcus will bring up Tenth Corps from Roum. One of two things will happen in the next day—either we hold at Hancock or we lose it and lose Junction City and the rail line is cut. If that happens, then what?"

Andrew nodded. The enormity of losing the main junction was frightening. Hans would have to pull back over the Green Mountains. If the Bantag gained the passes ahead of him, Hans would be trapped in the mountains with no hope of escape. Pat was a little better off—there were more than enough trains to move him back quickly. But to what? At best a fighting withdrawal to retake Junction City. Even if we retake it, they'll have jumped the front hundreds of miles closer to home. They'll have the logistical advantage of a port at their backs and wide-open terrain to maneuver in. We'll most likely have to fall back all the way to Roum, and if that happens, they'll eventually outproduce us and win.

One thing at a time, he realized. Get the support up to Vincent and trust that Hans and Pat know what to do.

The thought almost made him smile. Hell, it was Hans who had taught him the business, and it was

Pat who pulled off the masterful retreat from the Neiper and then held the center at Hispania.

"All right, Emil, point made," Andrew conceded.

Emil nodded, and then, reaching up, he took the cigar and tossed it on the ground.

"Bad for your health, Andrew."

Andrew smiled.

"Emil, I'm going up to Junction City. Perhaps the line is still open from there to Hans and back to Roum. Stay here, get the wounded ready to ship out. If we get contact back with Pat, order him to abandon the front, get his men across the Shenandoah, and be ready to pull all the way back to here."

"Yes, sir."

Without another word Andrew turned and walked back into his headquarters, quietly calling for his staff to get ready to move.

Emil watched him go. When he knew that Andrew was no longer in view he fished another cigar out of his pocket, lit it, and strolled way.

A volley of rifle fire slashed through the trees, a hail of small branches and leaves dropping around Pat as he reined in his horse and leaned over to shout at the sergeant who was leading a knot of men off the firing line.

"Sergeant, where the hell are you going!" Pat roared.

"Sir, I'm taking my regiment back for a rest, sir!"

Pat looked at the weary, powder-blackened face.

"Sean McDougal?"

"That it is, Pat."

Pat studied him warily, getting set to roar into a good chewing out. He looked at the weary men, less than a score, standing around their sergeant, who had a shot-torn standard over his shoulder.

"Regiment you say?"

"Damn Thirty-third Roum, Pattie."

"You've been drinking again, McDougal."

"You're damn right, you son of a bitch. Do ya have a problem with it?" McDougal announced defiantly.

"Where's the rest of your men?"

McDougal shook his head. "Them's it, Pattie, them's it."

Another volley crashed through the forest and Pat could not help but flinch as a rifle bullet slapped into a tree less than a foot away, spraying him with sap and splinters of bark.

McDougal grinned.

Pat looked over at one of his staff.

"Thirty-third Roum was supposed to be on the extreme left of the line, sir."

The deep, booming roar of a Bantag charge erupted from the forest. The volley line forward, less than fifty yards away, redoubled its fire. Part of the line sagged back, a knot of Bantag breaking clean through. A reserve company sprinted forward, bayonets lowered, and a vicious hand-to-hand struggle ensued.

McDougal watched the fight with the exhausted disinterest of someone who was completely fought out.

"McDougal, what the hell happened back there?" Pat nodded to the north.

"We was caught with our pants down, we was. They came roaring in on the flank. I sez to the colonel, I sez, it was just like Chancellorsville, and then he bought it. None of the lads who were dressed up like officers knew what to do, so I figured Sean, me boy, it's a good day to take command of a regiment."

Without even bothering to look for approval he slipped a bottle out of his haversack, uncorked it, drained the last drop, then threw the bottle against a tree.

"We held the fort for an hour, ran out of ammunition for the four guns. Them hairy bastards had these queer weapons they did, pipes that fired shells, like a cohorn mortar it was. They brought up several of them and started tearing the inside of the fort apart. A charge finally broke over the west wall of the fort—the west wall mind you—behind us. So I gathered what boys that were left and fought me way through."

Behind them the last of the breakthrough was sealed off while at the same time the line began to fall back. To the west Pat could sense that the attack was lapping over the line yet again. It was time to retreat. The problem was there wasn't much room left to go, another mile and they'd be back on the rail line, with First and Ninth Corps still strung out on the road behind them with at least twenty umens of the Horde pressing in from the east.

"A tight spot we're in, Pattie! A tight spot it is!"

Pat could not help but grin as the realization came to him of what McDougal had just pulled off. He had already heard that the fort on the northern edge of Eleventh Corps line had taken the full brunt of the flanking attack and stopped it cold for nearly an hour, allowing the rest of Eleventh Corps to shift its deployment in time to avoid getting rolled up. Some of the regiments farther down the line had broken, but the Thirty-third held its post damn near to the last man. Maybe it was because they had no other place to go, or maybe it was McDougal. He sensed it was a bit of both, and he could only wonder how the old drunk had managed to get his men through three miles of forest teeming with battle-crazed Bantag.

"Get to the rear, Sean. You've done enough for today."

"Right I have, damn it," McDougal growled. Turning to his men, he bellowed out a command, and the young Roum soldiers shouldered their rifles and, forming up, marched to the rear, Pat falling behind them as the last of the skirmishers pulling back from the Bantag onslaught fell in around him.

"Bastard should get the Medal of Honor," Pat announced to his staff. "Problem is he'd pawn it for a bottle later on."

A bullet zipped past so close that Pat felt the air stir near his cheek. Turning in his saddle, he saw a Bantag skirmisher coming out of the smoke-choked forest, loading his rifle on the run. Pat drew his revolver, fired three rounds, and finally dropped him. More shadows came out of the forest, and, spurring his mount, while ducking to avoid the low-hanging branches, he dodged around the trees and passed through the line where the retreating ranks had reformed. It was good ground, sloping down to the north, the trees thick enough that two men could hide behind them. Seconds after he passed through the line a volley erupted, the explosive roar sending a shiver down his spine.

From out of the forest he could hear the Bantag charge coming in. Turning his mount about he started riding slowly down the line, shouting encouragement as the boys poured it on. A battery of ten-pounders, which had been worked up through a narrow forest path, deployed out, the infantry in front of the guns scattering to either side as the commander shouted for them to clear a lane. Pat reined in behind the gun and roared with delight as the four pieces slammed a load of double canister into the woods, tearing the bark from trees, knocking down branches, and breaking the enemy charge.

"General!"

Pat saw Schneid, whom he had left in command of the withdrawal, coming through the forest.

"How is it going?" Pat shouted.

"They smell victory and are closing in fast. Lost a couple of batteries in the tangle on the road. I ordered my men to stop short of the station and hold. We've started loading the wounded on the trains, but a lot of the boys are going to have to walk out."

Another charge was beginning to build, and Pat's horse kicked up when a rifle ball clipped its left ear.

"Sir, it's rather hot here!" Rick shouted. "Shouldn't you get back where you belong?"

Pat ignored him as a renewed charge surged out of the woods. Kicking his horse into a canter, he trotted down the line, waving his hat and shouting for his men to hold.

"Keep moving, keep moving!" Vincent roared. "If you drop behind, you're dinner for those bastards!"

Edging his horse up against a knot of soldiers who were staggering across the open steppe, he used the flat of his sword, slapping several of them across the back. They looked up at him angrily.

"Damn it, they're closing in! Keep moving!"

In the gathering twilight he looked to the south, where a column of Bantag infantry was moving at the double, racing to outflank them yet again. The men around him staggered on, barely increasing their pace.

An artillery round thundered past, detonating on the slope ahead, dropping several men. Less than a half mile behind, Bantag land cruisers crept forward at a slow yet relentless pace, the infantry moving with them, dashing forward a few paces, kneeling to fire, then pausing to reload as the next wave of skirmishers swept past them.

On the slope ahead he knew that fresh troops were waiting, Second Division, Fifth Corps, which had come up in the late afternoon and deployed just in front of Junction City. One of the men he had been urging on silently collapsed to his hands and knees, gasping, blood pouring out of his mouth. His comrades paused to try and pick him up.

"He's finished," Vincent shouted. "You'll have to leave him."

A sergeant looked up angrily at Vincent.

"Damn it, sir, the Seventh doesn't leave its dead or wounded behind."

"Give him to me," Vincent snapped, and they passed the dying soldier up. Holding him tight, Vincent spurred his horse up the slope, and felt the body he was carrying go limp. Reaching the crest he passed through the line and let the body slip to the ground.

The men of Second Division had been digging in since arriving at the position so that a shallow trench, a foot or so deep, was cut into the steppe, sod and dirt piled up forward. The exhausted survivors of First Division, which had fought a running ten-mile retreat throughout the afternoon, were lying on the reverse slope, draining canteens of water which their comrades from Second Division had passed over to them.

Sensing what was coming, Vincent passed orders for the division to continue its retreat toward the fortifications surrounding the town. Watching the men stand up to continue their retreat, he saw a train coming into town from the northeast, its whistle echoing in the distance, flatcars loaded with infantry and a battery of guns.

Vincent dismounted, handed his trembling horse off to an orderly, and walked up to the crest of the ridge. All along the forward slope exhausted stragglers of First Division were staggering up the slope. The Bantag farther down broke into a charge, their long-legged stride taking them up the hill at a frightening speed. The men of Second Division were screaming at their comrades to clear the way.

The charge pushed some of the men from First Division forward in a final desperate run to safety, others simply collapsed, or turned about, ready to trade their lives.

"At two hundred yards volley fire present!" The cry, issued by the division commander, raced down the line.

Vincent said nothing, bracing himself.

"Take aim!"

Those men still forward started to fling themselves to ground.

"Fire!"

The brilliant glare of rifle fire slashed down the half mile of front. More than one member of First Division, too slow to get down, was swept away by the fire. The forward line of Bantag skirmishers disappeared in the smoke.

"At one hundred yards volley fire present!"

Survivors forward got up and continued to race toward the line. Vincent knew the division commander was deliberately holding to volley fire to try to give them a chance to get in between rounds. The Bantag seemed to know it as well; the charging wave raced forward, and, as the rifles lining the ridge were raised, then pointed downhill, they hit the ground, hugging the earth.

Vincent cursed. The bastards were trained, in fact trained too well in modern tactics. The Merki and Tugars, screaming like maniacs, would have simply continued to swarm in. The volley exploded and the Bantag were up again running full out.

"Independent fire at will!"

The battery deployed to Vincent's right, which had been deliberately aiming high, engaging a Bantag battery which was deploying on the next ridge a mile away, was now cranking down its barrels, the commander screaming for double canister.

The first scattering of shots erupted when the charge was less than fifty yards away. The fastest of the Bantag crashed into the lines, slashing left and right with their bayonet-tipped rifles.

An explosive roar erupted along the line, those few survivors forward crushed under by the rifle fire or the charge closing in behind them. The four guns of the battery fired with some of the Bantag almost to the very muzzles of the guns, fragments of bodies sweeping back twenty yards or more. Riflemen from a supporting company stood up, charging in around the guns, driving back the last of the attackers.

The Bantag charge disintegrated, falling back. Vincent watched the withdrawal, saying nothing. It had been an impetuous attack, pushed in with the hope that they could break through on the coattails of the retreating survivors of First Division. Second Division held its fire as the Bantag pulled back down the hill, and the few men who had escaped them stood up and staggered the last few yards to safety.

The division commander came up to Vincent's side.

"That wasn't too rough, sir."

"It's only started." He motioned toward the next ridgeline. Several batteries were already deploying, and the dark silhouettes of the first of the land cruisers came into view.

Fortunately the damned things only move at little better than two miles an hour, Vincent thought. Any faster and they would have bagged us all. But they were monstrous, relentless, coming forward with a blind mechanical will that mere flesh and courage could not resist.

The battery commander was ordering his guns laid to engage the first of the cruisers, but Vincent shouted for him to aim at their batteries instead.

The men of Second Division, seeing the cruisers for the first time, looked nervously back and forth at each other, while survivors of First Division, who had formed up on the line to continue the fight, cursed, telling their comrades that nothing would stop them.

The forward wave of Bantag skirmishers had retreated to the bottom of the shallow valley which separated the two ridges, ducking behind the embankment of a meandering stream for cover. Puffs of smoke erupted, one of the gunners with the battery doubling over and collapsing.

Fire reopened along the line as some of the men concentrated on keeping the Bantag skirmishers in the valley suppressed, while others raised their sights on the advancing waves coming down from the opposite slopes. Mortar fire rained down along the line, the Bantag gunners quickly bracketing the trench, driving the men to ground. The line of land cruisers continued its relentless advance, sparks flying from the armor as rifle fire bounced off.

"So that's their new weapon."

Vincent turned, amazed, as he stiffened to attention and saluted.

"You look like you've had a rough day, Hawthorne."

"Nearly 50 percent lost from First Division, sir. I never should have pushed them that far forward."

"You didn't know what they had. I'd have done the same to try and relieve the fort."

Bullets fluttered past the two as Andrew raised his field glasses and studied the line of land cruisers.

"Just like Hans described them. How'd the twenty-pounders do against them?"

"We let them close to two hundred yards, and the rounds still bounced off," Vincent announced sadly. "I'm sorry, sir, we lost the entire battery I ordered up. One in the first skirmish, the other three when I tried to make a stand."

Andrew nodded, saying nothing. It was a gamble Vincent had to take.

"So we won't stop them here."

"No, sir, just slow things down a bit."

Andrew looked back to the northwest, toward Junction City. In the dim light of evening he could see a railroad crew working to off-load the two heavy thirty-pound and one fifty-pound muzzle loaders he had brought from Port Lincoln. A team of horses was already hooked to one of the guns and moving through the main street of the depot, heading east, to position the gun in the earthen fortress outside of town. He looked back at the land cruisers, judging their speed.

It'd be dark by the time the cruisers reached town. Would Ha'ark press the attack? Undoubtedly. Ha'ark must realize that in twelve hours he might be able to bring up thousands of reinforcements from three different directions.

Vincent had bought enough time to bring the heavy guns up; there was no sense in risking the men in their current position any longer.

"That's him!" Vincent announced.

On the next ridgeline Andrew could see a white horse standing out in the twilight. Raising his field glasses, he studied the rider intently. Ha'ark slowed, turning his mount, and raised his field glasses as well.

Curious, Andrew thought. Same as the Merki Qar Qarth Tamuka, the projection of thought. He felt as if this one, as well, was looking into his mind, a vague sense of presence which had troubled him a number of times over the last few months becoming crystal clear at last. This one was different, lacking the primitive rage of Tamuka. There was, instead, a clear, calculating coldness, as if, in some ways, he was looking at a mirror of himself.

He felt as if he were on a stage, that he had to act, to project something. But what? And he knew even as he cast through his thoughts that this one was probing, sensing all. Show nothing, he realized, reveal nothing at all, neither rage nor fear. Strange how different this was. With Tamuka it was a matching of rage, of primal hatreds; here it was a matching of thought, of intellect, as if all that was happening was like moves on a chessboard, point and counterpoint, a planning of moves, a grasping of the shifting plans of the other, and then a recasting of coldly calculated plans yet again.

You won this opening move, Andrew thought. There was no sense in trying to conceal that.

Andrew lowered his field glasses, and the bond snapped.

"Come on, Vincent," he said calmly. "Let's get the boys back into the fortress line. It's going to be a long night."

The more complex the plan, the quicker it will fail, Jurak thought yet again as he rode through the smoke-choked forest, his horse gingerly stepping around the piles of dead, shying nervously as a human, gasping with pain, rolled over and started to raise a revolver. Half a dozen shots from his staff flung the man back down. Passing a casualty station, he tried to ignore the piles of limbs, the low moans of the wounded, and the stench of the funeral pyres.

It had cost too much, far too much already, fifty thousand dead and wounded and today was supposed to be the end of it, the closing of the door behind the humans. But the Qarth commander of his flanking attack could not resist the fight. He had to attack where the reserves were, rather than swing but half a day's march farther out. Rather than crash through to the road, sever all retreat, then fight a defensive holding action, he had attacked the enemy reserves instead. Granted, he had hurt them, but the claims that their entire corps had been destroyed was foolishness, a lie to cover his mistake.

Ha'ark would have had him executed for his stupidity and most likely would have when the time came, but he had resolved that problem by getting himself killed leading a final desperate charge.

Farther up the road the roar of battle continued, even though night had fallen and most of the warriors had stopped advancing, fearing the night spirits of the forest more than Yankee weapons. But the Yankees did not fear such things and were fighting to squeeze the last of their men out of the trap that should have been so firmly shut.

They were bloodied though, crippled and in retreat. But it was not total victory, and he was not pleased.

"Sir, we've lost all touch with Junction City; the telegraph line was cut this morning by an airship. As fast as we'd repair a break, a new one was cut."

Unable to suppress a groan, Hans Schuder eased out of the saddle and slipped to the ground next to the table where the field telegraph was set up. The captain in charge was tracing out the cuts on the map, talking excitedly, his features ghostlike in the glare of the kerosene lamp.

"When was the last report and from where?"

"A train taking our wounded to Junction City stopped ten miles short of the town just before dusk. The crew reported a large number of Bantag infantry moving toward the track and clearly visible fighting around the town. The engineer backed the train out. The report just came in."

Sighing, Hans settled down stiffly onto a stool next to the table. Cursing, he rubbed his backside, wondering why anyone would be fool enough to like horses. The captain looked at him, then reached into his haversack and pulled out a flask. Grateful, Hans took a long sip and passed it back.

"Any word from Colonel Keane?"

"Only this, sir. The line was up for a few minutes

just before four o'clock, then went down again for good."

The captain passed Hans the telegram, and he held it close to the light, squinting to read the roughly printed Cyrillic lettering. Damn, we should have taught these people English or German, he thought, rather than the other way around. The language problem was proving to be difficult now that more than half the troops were from Roum and insisted on using Latin. He finally passed it over to the captain to read.

"Hans. Am moving to Junction City. First reports indicate heavy force landing at Fort Hancock with a dozen or more land cruisers. I believe . . ." The captain looked up from the sheet of paper. "The line went dead there, sir."

Believe, believe what? Hans thought. So now what? Sighing, he leaned back, rubbing his eyes. From the south he could hear a scattering of rifle fire, punctuated by the occasional boom of a fieldpiece. We're twenty miles forward of our defensive line. Nearly forty miles from there back to the railhead, then two hundred miles up to Junction City. By this time tomorrow the Bantag could be twenty, thirty miles up that line, tearing up track.

"How many trains do we have at the railhead?" Hans asked.

The captain shuffled through some papers. "Ten, sir."

Ten trains for three corps. It was starting to look like the Third Corps debacle all over again. Eight, maybe ten umens pushing us from the south. Ha'ark between us and the other forces at Junction City. Even if Andrew holds the town, Ha'ark could push south, tearing up track, then close in on me from behind blocking the passes through the Green Mountains. But if I close in on him, he can always withdraw to the coast, maybe even leapfrog and land somewhere else.

It didn't look good, not good at all.

"Well, Captain," Hans said wearily, "we've got our heads in the noose and a bare arse sticking up waiting to get kicked."

The captain said nothing.

Ha'ark will expect me to fall back, Hans realized. In fact, he's begging me to. So do what he doesn't expect and do it now.

Hans finally looked at the captain and smiled. "Come on, son, you've got a busy night ahead of you."

"We press the attack," Ha'ark snarled. "We press it."

Angrily he paced back and forth in front of his commanders, pointing toward the city, which was clearly illuminated in the valley below. Even as he spoke the shriek of a distant train whistle echoed across the valley.

"I know the warriors are tired, they have fought superbly, but the plan was to seize that junction by nightfall. It is now two hours past the sun setting, and they still own it!"

"My Qar Qarth, it is night," a voice whispered in the dark.

"Of course it is night!"

"We have never fought at night, my Qar Qarth."

"Damn all," Ha'ark roared. He turned, his gaze fixing on the commander of the land cruisers.

"You, at least, will lead the land cruisers into the attack, will you not?"

The commander of the cruisers looked around sardonically at the others. "Of course, my Qar Qarth," he replied formally, the flicker of a smile creasing his features. "My warriors are not cowards."

Ha'ark whirled back on the others, some of them gazing with outright hatred at the cruiser commander for uttering the foulest of insults.

"We trained to fight at night, though you did not believe we would. These spirits you fear will scoff at you, the same way they now scoff at the Merki and the Tugars for losing to the human scum."

He stopped, staring at each in turn.

"We move at once. Those of you who do not follow are cowards!"

Chapter Seven

The high, shrill cry of the steam whistles sent a shiver down Andrew's spine, the cry echoing from where plumes of sparks marked the advance of the land cruisers moving toward Junction City.

He could sense the edge of panic from the troops deployed along the wall of the earthen fort guarding the eastern approach into town. A volley erupted from the two bastions flanking the tracks heading south out of town, sparkles of light snapped from the fields beyond, marking where Bantag skirmishers were advancing.

"Get some flares up," Andrew announced. The rocket-launching team deployed in the middle of the fort sent the first flare aloft. Bursting, the flare slowly began to descend, suspended beneath a small parachute. Rifle fire crackled along the line as men started to pick off the line of Bantag skirmishers caught in the glare. Flares erupted all along the line, showing that the Horde was attacking in force, coming in from the east, southeast, and south. An attacking column was already across the rail line farther south, moving at the double to envelop the town from the west.

"I'm going to make a try at it, sir!"

Andrew looked back to the ensign and his ship's

crew that had come up with the fifty-pounder taken from *Petersburg*.

Seconds later the gun ignited with a roar, kicking back half a dozen yards, the gout of flame blinding Andrew. The crew swarmed around its gun, a score of infantrymen joining in to help manhandle it back into position. The shell detonated directly in front of the land cruiser that was bearing down on the fort.

One of the thirty-pounders deployed into the next bastion fired, its round striking the front armor of a cruiser. A hot white glare of sparks erupted, a ragged cheer going up from the men around Andrew, until the next flare revealed the machine was still lumbering forward.

Pacing nervously back and forth, Vincent at his side, he watched as the row of machines slowly closed in. The land cruisers started to return fire, shells detonating along the battlement walls.

At six hundred yards the third shot fired by the fifty-pounder struck squarely on the front armor of the machine coming straight at them. Again there was the explosive flare of light as the shell detonated . . . and still the machine came on.

"Sir, let's try to enfilade the one farther down the line!" Vincent shouted, pointing to one of the machines that was inexorably closing in on the southern bastion. "Maybe the side armor isn't as thick."

Andrew nodded, and Vincent sprinted over to the gun crew, pointing out their new target. Cursing and shouting the crew heaved its gun around, the ensign looking over at Andrew.

"More than double the range again, sir."

"Try it!"

The first shell plowed a furrow just forward of the cruiser. Rifle fire was crackling all along the battlement line, Bantag skirmishers pressing in close, picking off two of the rammers working to reload the heavy gun.

Andrew stood beside the piece, watching, taking all in. The four land cruisers approaching straight toward the fort were now less than three hundred yards away, switching from shell to canister, the shrieking rounds swirling over the fortress wall while rifle bullets crackled past.

The fifty-pounder kicked back yet again, followed an instant later by a flash of sparks on the side of the land cruiser. A plume of steam and smoke erupted from the machine which seemed to lift into the air as a series of explosions detonated inside the cruiser, tearing it apart.

Wild cheering swept the battlement walls, the ensign urging his men to train their gun on the next cruiser.

Andrew turned to Vincent.

"Sound the retreat. Send up the signal."

Vincent nodded, disappearing into the shadows, and as the first notes of the bugle call sounded, the ensign turned in surprise toward his commander.

"We got one of the bastards," he shouted. "Why retreat now?"

Andrew pointed to where four advancing land cruisers were down to less than two hundred yards.

"You'll get off one more shot before they're over us!" Andrew shouted, trying to be heard above the cacophonous roar of rifle fire, the detonation of shells, and the crumping thump of mortar shells that were beginning to rain down into the fort.

"Spike your gun, and let's get out of here."

Four rockets soared straight up, green flares igniting, the prearranged signal to begin the retreat.

Vincent came up to Andrew's side, leading a horse, and Andrew clumsily swung into the saddle, heading for the fortress sally port.

By the light of the flares to the south he saw that the Bantag column that had crossed the rail line was continuing to move to the west.

"They're flanking outward," Andrew shouted, "most likely moving to cut the rail line west of town."

Infantry poured out of the fort heading back toward the town, and in the darkness behind them came the triumphal roaring of the Bantag host.

Bugle calls to the south marked where the defenders of the southern bastion were pulling out as well and by the light of a final flare he saw a land cruiser creep up the side of the fortress, then crash down inside, a swarm of Bantag following behind it.

Troops moved past Andrew at the double, officers shouting the names of regiments to rally in their stragglers. From the rail yard on the north side of town train whistles shrieked. In the hours since the landing half a dozen trains had come up from the west, dumping off their supplies and troops twenty miles to the west, where a reserve line was already being dug. The trains were then rushed to Junction City, allowing Andrew to evacuate the two divisions of Fifth Corps to the west, while keeping the trains he had used earlier in the day for moving Pat's troops back from the Shenandoah.

Fires erupted along the rows of warehouses as hundreds of tons of rations, uniforms, medical supplies, limber wagons, bridging equipment, and millions of rounds of ammunition were put to the torch.

Andrew rode down the street, reining in for a moment as a firefight flared up when an advance company of Bantag somehow managed to break into the center of the town and were quickly swarmed under. There was a sense of panic in the air, but most of the men of Fifth Corps were veterans, and though frightened, knew what to do, officers and sergeants urging the men back toward the rail yard.

A clanging of bells caused Andrew to draw his mount over to the side of the road as half a dozen ambulances galloped past, the wagons filled with the seriously wounded.

Reaching the rail yard, he turned to look back at the town, which was engulfed with flames. Fighting raged on the main street as the last of the men from the south bastion provided a rear guard, holding back the Bantag skirmishers pushing in. He had counted on all coordination on the Bantag side breaking down, and so far his bet was working. Ha'ark should have worked more units around from the south to close in on the lightly held line to the west. There was a scattering of skirmish fire from that direction, but so far no major push, and the rail lines to the northwest and northeast were still open.

A shell passed overhead, detonating on the far side of the rail yard. Looking back to the southeast, he saw another flash of light, a gun on one of the land cruisers. Several more shots followed, one of them exploding in the rail yard, knocking down half a dozen men who were moving toward one of the trains. If a lucky shot should knock out a locomotive now, the retreat could still turn into a disaster.

Edging his horse through the crowd, he urged the men to hurry, ordering a battery crew to pull the breechblocks off their ten-pounders and abandon the guns.

The first train, loaded with wounded, lurched out of the depot, switching to the main line heading north and from there west, back to Roum. A second train followed as soon as the switch was cleared; survivors of First Division Fifth Corps piled on board.

The blocking force down in the burning town was buckling, the unit leapfrogging back a dozen yards, passing through a deployed line, which fired a volley, then fell back in turn. The third and fourth trains started out of the station, shells detonating on either side, shrapnel tearing into a cluster of men piled aboard an open flatcar.

"Vincent, you're heading out on the next train," Andrew shouted.

"Sir?"

"You heard me, son. I'm sending you west."

"Sir, I thought I was going back in to Port Lincoln, and you'd head west to coordinate the fight."

Andrew smiled and, reaching over, put his hand on Vincent's shoulder.

"I'd be a hell of a commander leaving Pat and the boys back in the pocket."

Vincent looked at him, and Andrew was pleased that Vincent offered no argument based on sentimentality or loyalty. He saw the logic of it and simply nodded his head.

Andrew pulled a slip of paper out of his pocket and passed it over.

"These are your orders and authorization on my part to assume command of all forces to the west of the breakthrough. I wrote them out earlier."

"So you were planning this all along?"

"But of course."

They hunched low as a shell exploded less than a dozen yards away, blood spraying over the two from one of Vincent's staff, who was decapitated by the round.

"I don't know how Hans will react, but I think he'll make the right move. If so, put Bullfinch in charge. Set up that blocking force with Tenth Corps and the men you get out of here. As soon as I get Pat's forces back from the Shenandoah and reorganized, I'll try to break out. Do you understand that?"

"Yes, sir."

"You're in charge over there. I'm counting on you to hold it all together. There's bound to be panic." He had to shout the last words as the fifth train thundered past them, whistle shrieking. A steady hum of bullets whistled overhead as the Bantag closed the ring, the forces to the east reaching the edge of the burning town, then pushing northward to sever the rail line heading back east.

Vincent reached over and took Andrew's hand.

"I'll see you in a week, sir!"

"Get going, son, and tell Kathleen . . ." The words trailed off. What the hell could he tell her. He tried to force a smile, then shook his head.

"Your train," Andrew said, nodding as the whistle of the sixth train sounded, signaling that it was pulling out.

Vincent slid down off his horse. He looked at the animal for a moment, patted it on the muzzle, then drew his revolver. Andrew looked away as Vincent shot the beast rather than let it fall into the hands of the enemy.

Dashing to the train, he leapt up onto the engine cab as, with wheels spinning, it started out of the station. The ring closing around the depot was now barely two hundred yards across. Andrew dismounted and started to draw his revolver. He looked into the eyes of the horse which had carried him, grateful that his beloved Mercury was still back at Port Lincoln.

Shaking his head he turned and walked away, letting the horse go, shouting for his staff to follow. Reaching the cab of the last train, he climbed on board and looked back out at the closing circle. This was going to be a near thing. The rocket signal crew was waiting on the first flatcar.

"All right, send them up!" he shouted.

Half a dozen rockets soared into the air, detonating over the two trains waiting for the last units to pull in. A final volley erupted along the contracting line, the men turning and running. The engineer behind Andrew eased the throttle in, the train lurching forward. Men scrambled along the sides of the flatcars, leaping up, turning to help injured comrades while others, reloading their weapons stood up, firing over their heads. Looking back down the street he saw a land cruiser lumbering into view, turning slowly to bring its gun to bear.

The land cruiser's gun fired straight up the street. An instant later a shuddering blow shook the train. Andrew was startled when someone slammed into him, and he fell back into the wood tender as a burst of steam exploded around him.

"Stay down!" The voice was high-pitched, filled with fear, and he felt a body on top of him. Covering his face with his hand, he felt a wash of heat as the steam from the boiler washed over him.

Someone grabbed him by the shoulder, pulling him. The world went dark for an instant and he felt a surge of fear, wondering if he was blind, until he realized that a blanket had been thrown over his head. He felt arms wrapping around his legs and he fell out of the cab, more hands grabbing hold of him, dragging him back from the engine. The blanket was pulled off and he looked up, still unable to see, his glasses covered with steam.

"Sir, sir, are you all right?"

Unable to reply, he could only nod.

"Get him out of here!" he heard someone scream.

Trying to shout a protest that he could still walk, his words were ignored as half a dozen men grabbed hold of him and started to run. He heard a hoarse, howling scream—a Bantag war cry. Something banged into the knot of men carrying him, pistol shots rang out, hands wrapped around his waist, fell away. The crowd around him surged forward again, running hard, racing to catch up to the next train which was pulling out of the station.

"It's Keane, it's Keane!" The cry was repeated over the shouts, screams, yells, the crackling of rifle fire, pistol shots, grunts of pain, and the rising ululation of the Bantag Horde pressing in around them.

He heard the shriek of a train whistle, the rumbling clang of train wheels nearby, and suddenly he was lifted, other hands reaching out to grab him and an instant later he felt the vibration of the train wheels beneath him as the last car shifted through a switch.

"I'm all right, damn it!" he roared, and the men holding on to him let go. Wiping his jacket sleeve across his glasses while they were still on, he looked back. Several of his staff, who had been carrying him, were staggering alongside the car.

More than a hundred men, having jumped off the disabled train, now surged around the back of the last train out of Junction City as it slowly started to pick up speed.

Andrew went down on his knees, reaching out,

grabbing one of his orderlies by the hand, pulling him up. Horrified, he realized that the boy's skin was peeling off as he jerked him on board. Dimly he could see the boy's scalded face and realized that the boy was screaming.

Rifle fire was erupting on all sides, men running by the side of the train, staggering, dropping, and seconds later disappearing into the dark horde that was in pursuit.

Andrew, still kneeling, reached back out, grabbing someone by the shoulder. The soldier lost his footing, fell, and Andrew felt as if he was going to slip off the flatcar. Other hands reached out, grabbing the soldier, hoisting him on board . . . and then suddenly there was no longer anyone running alongside.

A man standing above Andrew grunted, doubled over, and pitched headfirst off the car. Someone else collapsed over Andrew, screaming, his rifle going over the side. Rifle fire was sweeping the car from three directions. Andrew tried to stand up but two men were instantly on top of him, swearing, holding him down, one of them falling silent an instant later, his blood splattering over Andrew's face.

Clearing the yard and the final switch which turned the train northeast and back toward Port Lincoln, they continued to pick up speed. Several shells shrieked in, one of them exploding directly overhead so that more men on the car went down.

Rifle fire continued to snap past, faring up again as the train thundered past an advance element of Bantag who had tried to sprint over the hills northeast of town and back down to the track ahead of the train. Finally they were clear, and Andrew regained to his feet.

Horrified, he looked around. Nearly every man on

the flat car was dead or wounded. To his amazement the boy on his staff whom he had pulled on board was by his side, strips of his skin dangling from his hands.

"Sir, are you all right?" he asked.

Andrew motioned for him to sit down.

"You scared the hell out of us, sir. We didn't think we'd get you out."

"Just be still, son."

The boy was obviously in shock, and Andrew eased him back down onto the flatcar bed. The boy's face was swelling, his breathing labored.

"Feels funny inside, sir," he gasped. "Think I breathed in the steam. Feels funny inside."

"Just lie still."

For the first time Andrew realized that he had indeed been scalded, his hand ached, the left side of his face swollen and tender.

The boy started to shake, and Andrew drew him into his grasp, cradled the boy's head against his chest, and held him, crying silently as the boy slipped away into silence . . . and the train continued eastward into the night.

Ignoring the warnings of his staff that the exploding ammunition made the town dangerous, Ha'ark walked up the main street of the town, guards nervously clustered around him, holding shields aloft to ward off the debris pelting down around them.

The heat from the fires was intense, and he pulled his cloak about his face to shield himself.

He had hoped to capture the place intact, it would have supplied his army for days, perhaps even weeks. Now he would be forced to rely on ships making the long run back to Xi'an. Reaching the stalled locomotive he looked around at the slaughter, nodding approvingly. Several hundred dead at least, his warriors already butchering the dead. A few wounded, still alive, were bound together, looking about in terror. Ha'ark approached them.

"I'll spare the life of any of you that will talk," he said slowly, stumbling over the Rus words.

One of the humans, who looked to be not much older than a boy, wearing what Ha'ark recognized as a handsomely cut uniform, glared defiance.

He fixed the young soldier with his gaze and could sense the terror.

"Did Keane escape?"

A flicker of a smile showed, and the soldier spit on the ground.

"He'll have your head on a spike," the soldier snapped. "Of course he got out, but he'll be back. And Schuder will come up from the south, and together they'll finish you."

Ha'ark shook his head.

"Tell me about Keane, and I'll spare your life."

"Go to hell, you son of a bitch," the boy cried, trying to sound brave but his voice nearly breaking in terror.

Ha'ark turned away, ignoring the screams as his warriors hacked the survivors apart.

He walked along the side of the train, stopping before the locomotive. Scalded bodies lay alongside the engine, and, stepping over them, he examined the machine. It was an admirable piece of work, obviously far more powerful than his own. The lines of the machine were clean, the brasswork sparkling, such a contrast to the roughly built equipment he had.

A low, throbbing rumble sounded from the other

side of the still-smoking ruins, and walking around the front of the train, he watched as a land cruiser rolled forward. If only the things were faster, he thought, we could have overrun them, cut off all escape.

And yet, he could not complain. Only one machine had been destroyed in battle. Five more had broken down in the advance, and two were mired in a streambed. He still had nineteen, and in ten days another twenty-four would be brought from Xi'an.

That would be the question now. Could supplies and reinforcements be moved in quickly enough to expand their hold at this crucial juncture? His airships would have a base here by the end of tomorrow and then range outward, destroying bridges, landing warriors to keep cutting the telegraph lines. With control of the air, at least we'll be able to keep them blind as to our strength and deployment.

And Schuder was to the south—the boy had revealed that crucial bit of information. We have most of their army cut off; the drive now was to box them in and annihilate the two wings Keane had so foolishly thrown forward.

Grinning with delight, he turned back to watch as the town burned.

Hand stuffed into his pocket, President Kalenka walked out of the war office, head lowered against the cold, driving rain.

"Kal?"

He tried to smile as Kathleen approached, umbrella tilted down against the gale, offering him a little protection from the storm.

"A lot of rumors were sweeping through the hospital; I had to find out."

"The army's cut off." He sighed, reaching up to clutch the brim of his stovepipe hat as an eddy of wind swept across the plaza. Though it was late, well after midnight, a small crowd of women stood before the doors to *Gates's Illustrated Weekly*. A large chalkboard was displayed in the window, where one of Gates's employees posted the latest news as it came in. The last bulletin, posted at midnight, simply stated that the telegraph lines were still down. A large map of the front hung in another window, with a red line tracing the landing and attack of Ha'ark's army against Junction City. At the sight of Kal walking nearby, the crowd broke away from the newspaper and pushed in around him, shouting for news.

Kal shook his head.

"All we know is that there's heavy fighting near Junction City, Fifth Corps was engaged."

"Is it true the armies are cut off now?" someone cried.

Kal stood silent for a moment, then finally nodded.

"Neighbors, there's nothing you can do standing here in the rain. Please go home where you'll be safe and pray for our boys. I can assure you, we'll get them out."

"Your son-in-law got out, though," an angry woman shouted. "You made sure of that."

Kal turned slowly to face his accuser, a towering woman who stood defiant, arms folded across her chest.

Kal walked up to her and took off his hat.

"I have three boys with Schuder, lost two in the last war," she snapped. "But it seems yours are taken care of."

"Madam," he began softly, "my son-in-law was

ordered out by Keane. I had nothing to do with that."

He nodded to where Kathleen stood. "Her husband ordered him out while he stayed behind with his men."

"I don't even know why the hell we're fighting now," came the bitter reply. "It's on the other side of the world. Those heathen said they'd leave us alone if we stayed away. Why are you sending our boys out to die like this? Haven't we paid enough already?"

A murmur of agreement echoed in the crowd.

"Because if we don't fight them there," Kathleen interrupted, "it will be here yet again. Do you want Suzdal once again to be a battlefield?"

"All I know is my boys are lost. I don't give a damn about those Nippon people, or anyone else. I just want my boys back. Ain't that what that Bantag Qarth said, that if we left them alone, they'd leave us alone?" As she blurted out the last words, her voice started to break.

Kathleen reached out to put a consoling hand on the woman's shoulder, but the woman stepped back, shaking off the gentle touch.

"End this damn war. Just bring our boys home and end it."

There was a murmur of assent from the crowd.

"It wouldn't stop with that," Kal tried to reason. "Friends, we already argued that in Congress and realized it won't stop. This Bantag devil will come for us all if we don't fight him out on the border. It's fight him there, or on our doorsteps; there is no other choice."

"Let the Roum fight them, then. We protected

them twice; let them do it now and keep our boys here."

The woman turned and faced Kathleen.

"Ever since you folks came, there's been nothing but war. If you'd kept your noses out of our business, we would have lost far less, and the Tugar devils and the others would be gone now."

The crowd fell silent at her words. Stunned, Kathleen was unable to reply.

Kal stood silent in the driving rain, hat in hand, looking up at the angry woman.

"I'll pray for your boys tonight," he said softly. "It's late, let's go home."

He put his hat back on and, turning, left the crowd, which broke into loud arguments among themselves. Kathleen fell in by his side.

Kal looked at her.

"Are you all right?"

"In a way she's right, you know." Kathleen sighed. "More than half your people have died in the wars. It would have been one in ten if there had been no rebellion."

Kal angrily shook his head. "Would you choose slavery and the Pit rather than our freedom?"

"Such a cost, though," Kathleen whispered.

He could see the weary look of exhaustion in her eyes. The first of the serious casualties from the front had arrived this morning by hospital train, and she had been working on them all day.

"There's an old saying Andrew taught me," Kal offered. "Victory has a thousand fathers, while defeat is always an orphan."

"Have we been defeated?"

He said nothing, silently crossing himself as he walked in front of the cathedral. Pausing, he turned and walked up the steps of the church and, taking off his hat, stepped inside, Kathleen following.

The midnight service was in progress, Metropolitan Casmar leading the service. Crossing herself and genuflecting to the altar, Kathleen stepped to the back wall, standing by Kal's side.

She looked over at him, unable to voice her fears. Her years with Andrew had taught her much about what some called the art of war. On many an evening she would join Andrew in his upstairs office and he would ramble out his thoughts, his plans, his fears—the elaborate game of move and countermove. She could even remember his consideration of this prospect, of Ha'ark breaking the blockade and trying to land behind one of the two armies on the eastern or southern front, but he had never seriously considered a loss of control of the sea, let alone an outright seizure of the main junction linking both fronts to the west.

Hans had repeatedly warned of that, to expect the unexpected, and now it had come to pass.

She knew the question was who could bring the most force to bear on that point. If Ha'ark could dig in and stay supplied, the two armies would be worn down in bloody frontal assaults. Finally out of ammunition and rations, they would be destroyed. Then nothing could stop Ha'ark from a straight-on advance to Roum . . . and from there to Suzdal and the ending of the dream.

"You know," Kal whispered, "I was approached by several senators this evening. They asked that I consider an envoy to Ha'ark. Let our armies go, and we'll pull back to Roum and concede the rest."

"Merciful God in heaven," Kathleen hissed, and

then remembered where she was and quickly crossed herself. "Are they mad?"

"It was one thing to fight it out here, on our doorstep, as you said. Most of the people who look at that map in Gates's window don't even understand what it is they are looking at, it's nothing but meaningless lines and scribbles. All they see are trains disappearing east into the unknown."

"And you?" Kathleen asked.

Kal lowered his head. "There are times I wonder."

"Damn it all, Kal," Kathleen snapped angrily, "I can't believe that four short months ago people were screaming for war after Hans came back, and now this? From the beginning we knew the wars were for all or nothing, that there was no compromise."

"We finally made an arrangement with the Tugars; they have forsaken their old ways, and are gone."

"After we defeated them. There is no other choice."

"How many boys died in your hospital today? How many amputations have you performed?"

She looked at him coldly, and he lowered his gaze, remembering that she had once performed an amputation on him, and saved his life.

"Andrew went back into the trap not to be a hero and die. He went back to get his comrades out, and he expects you to do everything possible to help get them out. He would rather die than surrender to Ha'ark."

"How many will die, though?"

"Perhaps all of us," Kathleen snapped, "and I'll poison my own children before I allow them to be slaves the way you once were."

Suddenly ashamed, she looked up to realize that she had almost shouted the last words, interrupting the service. Casmar stood at the altar, looking at her, the congregation silent.

He turned back to the altar, finishing the closing prayers, Kathleen lowering her head in prayer as well. As the service finished Casmar turned away from the altar and stepped down to face the congregation, holding his hands up, motioning for them to stay.

"A final prayer, my friends," he announced, and those heading to the door stopped.

"A prayer for victory, for there is no substitute for that in this world. This war might rage for years, and we must face that now and make the sacrifices necessary, even our own lives, for to do otherwise means death for our children."

There was a stirring in the group, some looking back again at Kal and Kathleen.

"And another thing. This shall be my last service here, for tomorrow I shall go up to where the fighting is and, if need be, carry a rifle with the boys who fight. I have hidden behind my robes too long. Our friend, our liberator, Andrew Keane is trapped behind enemy lines, and I shall not rest until he and all our boys who are with him are safe."

Making the sign of blessing, he lowered his head, returned to the altar, and went down on his knees.

Stunned, Kathleen passed through the congregation as it headed toward the door, Kal following her. Though she knew it was forbidden, she stepped up to the altar anyhow, and placed her hand on Casmar's shoulder. He looked up at her, startled, then smiled.

"Thank you," she whispered.

"I've heard the talk," he said, coming to his feet. "It is the least I can do."

His gaze shifted to Kal.

"I have never made a political suggestion before, but I feel compelled to do so now."

"And that is?"

"It would be uncivilized to send back the heads of the Chin ambassadors, they are but trapped in this as well. But tomorrow morning, when the marketplace is filled with people, I would make quite a show of escorting them down to the first train heading east, blindfolded, humiliated, making it very clear"—he paused, looked at the altar, and smiled—"making it very clear they can go to hell."

Kal laughed softly.

"That certainly is a piece of advice."

"You need a little bracing, my friend. You cannot go to the front, though I know you want to. I can. Perhaps it might embarrass some of our fat senators who've been crying peace to go as well."

"If you got hurt though, or killed, Your Holiness."

Casmar smiled. "I think the robes of a martyr in a holy war might fit me rather well. You can hire that young Rublev to do a painting of me. I think I'd rather enjoy that."

"Casmar, you're getting a little old for this," Kal chided.

"No older than Hans Schuder. Now you two go and get some rest, I have a little packing to do."

Blessing the two of them, he retreated into the sacristy.

Kathleen genuflected to the altar and left the church. There was still a crowd gathered outside, some on the far side of the square, waiting for a new report from Gates's, others by the church as word spread of Casmar's announcement. Several women came forward, nodding their respect to Kathleen and

Kal, saying they were praying for Andrew. She could only nod as she took Kal by the arm and headed across the square, not even bothering to put her umbrella up. The rain was cold, refreshing, hiding her tears.

"So we're in a fix here," Hans said, pointing to the map spread out on the lowered back gate of an artillery forge wagon. His three corps commanders and six of his nine division commanders were gathered around. He looked at each of them in turn, Bates of Second Corps and Watley of the Seventh were both Thirty-fifth Maine men, while Flavius of the Eighth was from Roum. His division commanders were a mix from the old Union Army, Rus and Roum as well. Ketswana, his comrade from the prison and escape, stood by his side, listening carefully.

With the stub of a pencil, Hans traced out the extent of Ha'ark's breakthrough in the north and the suspected positions of the umens pressing up from the south.

In the minutes since they had gathered together there was no longer a need for the kerosene light, the sky to the east brightening with the dawn, though the western horizon was dark with clouds that threatened to bring rain by midday.

Hans sipped the scalding hot tea from his battered tin field cup and munched on a piece of hardtack with a slab of salt pork on top.

"Well, how many of you are for breaking out to the north?"

"Only way I can see it," Bates announced. Using the cigar he had been chewing on, the corps commander traced out the route through the mountains. "Set up a blocking force on our defensive line. Fall back to our base of supplies, then cut our way north, put pressure on that bastard. O'Donald and his four corps must be pressing back from the east; they'll be bringing up reserves from the west; we'll have him in a three-way vise; we'll be reunited within a week."

"That last report said he had maybe three, four umens at most," Watley interjected.

Hans nodded, saying nothing, looking around at the other officers. He had trained all of them, some as far back as the drill field in front of the state capital building in Augusta, others before Suzdal and Roum.

Hans looked over at Ketswana.

"What do you think?"

Ketswana shook his head.

"Go this way," he said, and with his finger he traced a line to the south and west.

Several of the officers chuckled tolerantly at what they thought was the opinion of an amateur, but Hans's steely gaze stilled their voices.

A rumble of rifle fire echoed up the valley, and the group turned to look. A dismounted line of Bantag skirmishers was probing in. Over at the telegraph station, set up under an awning, the key started to clatter, while off to the southwest there came the hollow thump of artillery.

Hans sat waiting patiently, munching on his hardtack while an argument about Ketswana's suggestion broke out. The telegrapher edged through the crowd and handed Hans the message, the group falling silent.

"Report from water tank number twenty-five," Hans announced, and motioned toward the map. The tank was twenty-five miles south of Junction City, where the open steppe started to give way toward the successive series of ridges forming the Green Mountains.

"Station shutting down. Bantag land cruiser and three regiments of Bantag infantry approaching."

Hans put the message down next to the map.

"Boys, if we head north, do you know what will happen? There'll be a dozen passes we'll have to fight through. Bates, Watley, you remember the march to Antietam?"

The two nodded. The others in the group looked at the two and back to Hans respectfully. The Battle of Antietam, the first action of the Thirty-fifth Maine, was the stuff of legends, and those few who had been with the Thirty-fifth from the beginning still spoke of it with awe.

"Turner Gap. We was in reserve for that and saw the Iron Brigade go in. You saw it, so did I. A few Reb regiments held up the entire army for the better part of the day before we pushed them out. Boys, it'll be the same thing here. If I was Ha'ark, I'd move as quick as I could, throw half an umen up into the mountains, and lock us in tight."

"Don't we have anything holding the passes?"

"Some garrison troops, old men guarding bridges. It'd be a day, two days before we could throw any type of sufficient force up there. We're talking about Ha'ark's elite troops coming on against old men, disabled veterans, rear-line troops. They'll have the passes for ten miles into the mountains by tonight, and thirty miles by tomorrow."

The group was silent as he traced the rail line and its twisting, curving path through the mountains out on the map.

"So, we try and hold along our defensive line while pushing a corps north? How long did we actually think we'd hold them up out here before having to fall back?"

"A week," Bates ventured.

Hans snorted with disdain. "If we had managed to get the railroad built all the way up to our defensive positions, then run a parallel track the length of the line to move troops back and forth, and on top of that had six corps, maybe we could have stopped them out here. Our supply head is forty miles back and there won't be any more supplies coming our way. If we hold this position for three days, I'll be amazed; then the squeeze starts. Remember, our plan was to abandon this line if pressed and then hold in the mountains. The problem is our rear has been compromised, they can bottle us up, and we starve."

Hans continued to trace out the lines as he talked.

"Three corps falling back, pressed by a hundred thousand Bantag from the south while we try and cut our way north. Let's say we do cut through. The Bantag won't leave a scrap of track from anything they've taken, every bridge will be blown. Granted we'll slow the bastards down pursuing us, but they'll be weaving through every pass they can find along a 150-mile front while we're withdrawing. Gentlemen, Ha'ark has put us in a trap."

Hans sighed and leaned over the map, his whitened knuckles bearing down on it.

"We'll be trapped in the mountains from both sides, supplies running out, and they can finish us off at their leisure."

"What about Pat's army, or troops coming up from Roum?" Bates asked.

"Even if Pat can break through," Hans replied wearily, "he'll be forced to drive westward, to try and break through toward Roum. Trying to link up with us won't solve anything other than to put both of us into the trap. Remember, interior lines. Ha'ark can pivot and turn, facing each threat as it develops."

Hans traced out the lines on the map again. "Pat pivots south toward us, Ha'ark cuts him off from Roum. Pat drives toward Roum, Ha'ark can still keep us in the bottle."

"But if we go south, that takes the pressure off Ha'ark," Flavius interjected. "By going north, we'll force him to divert some of his strength to block us."

Hans nodded and took another sip of tea, raising his head to look at the skirmish, which was broadening out across the valley. A mounted Bantag unit of regimental strength came up out of a curtain of ground fog, facing a scathing volley from a dug-in line of infantry.

"True. But again, remember the Antietam campaign, South Mountain. One damn Reb division dug in at the passes tied up most of the Army of the Potomac for an entire day. All Ha'ark needs to do is divert four or five thousand troops, and we'll bleed ourselves while being the diversion you talked about. Gentlemen, this army is not a diversion. My goal is to save as much of it as possible so it can fight again."

A gentle gust of wind, damp and cooling, swirled through the encampment from the west. Hans raised his head, sniffing the wind. It reminded him of days out on the prairie, the first scent of rain coming down out of the Rockies after endless days of scorching heat.

"And there is one final thing to consider here. Retreating is exactly what Ha'ark expects us to do, what he wants us to do, and damn him, that is exactly why we will not do it."

He looked back over at Ketswana, who nodded in agreement.

"We'll continue to retreat today, as if heading back into our defensive lines. At the same time I want all supplies that can be moved loaded up. We should be back to our defensive lines by late afternoon, and the men are to get some rest. As soon as it gets dark we begin to shift everything west, abandoning the line as we go. The following morning we break out toward the southwest."

"Back out in the open?" Flavius asked.

"Exactly." He traced a line on the map, following the Green Mountains southwestward to where they finally dropped down to the sea.

"We make for Tyre."

"That's a Cartha town; they're neutral, sir," Bates said.

"It's the only port city on the east coast of the Inland Sea that our ships can get into. We take Tyre, and the hell with their so-called neutrality."

"They'll cut us off." Bates drew a line straight across the map from where the Bantag umens were advancing. "Pin us against the mountains."

Hans pointed toward the western sky.

"We'll have rain today, maybe even tomorrow. With luck, it'll keep their damn airships down.

"We'll form up tight, square formation, supplies, wounded in the middle, each corps its own square. And then we just move, take Tyre, and get picked up."

"By who?"

Hans smiled. "Bullfinch will get something there. He pulled me out before; he'll do it again."

"My God, sir, you're talking about evacuating three corps, nearly fifty thousand men."

"Actually closer to forty thousand. Bates, I'm detaching you and one of your divisions to head up into the mountains. Act as if you're trying to break through; it should throw Ha'ark off for a while. You'll disperse out, raise hell, bushwhack. They might even detach some of their units to pursue you. In fact, I suspect Ha'ark is counting on the umens in front of us to be the force to strengthen him. We, however, will draw them in the opposite direction, away from the main fight."

"Our pickup, sir?"

Hans smiled sadly.

"I can't promise that, son. Fight as long as you can, then break into small units and head for the coast. I'll try and get some light ships in to pick you up."

Bates nodded.

"I won't leave you up there, Bates. We need to throw Ha'ark off, make him think there's some force coming up, and that's your job. Throw him off, then head west."

"But Bullfinch, sir?"

"He'll be there. I sent half a dozen mounted couriers north last night with the message for a pickup."

The roar of skirmish fire was building into long, sustained volleys, and the division forward was beginning to leapfrog back, men moving at the double. Just forward of where Hans was holding his meeting, a battery deployed opened up, lobbing its shells over the retreating line.

"Gentlemen, that's our plan. We've got a lot to do today. I'll have your orders drawn up. Now get moving."

He studied the group as they saluted. He could see that most of them were not convinced, shocked by his unorthodox move. As the assembly broke up, officers calling for their staffs, who had been watching quietly at the edge of the circle, Hans looked over at Ketswana.

"They don't like it, my friend." Ketswana said.

"They don't have to. Just as long as they do it."

"This message you sent."

Hans motioned Ketswana to draw closer.

"We won't know if it got through till we get to Tyre. If the ships are there, the message got through. If not . . ." He shrugged his shoulders.

Ketswana shook his head and laughed.

"I always knew you were a madman."

"That's why we'll win."

Andrew was off the train before it had even come to a full stop. Word had already been sent up from the telegraph station twenty miles west of Port Lincoln and a long row of ambulances was waiting. Emil pushed his way through the crowd of stretcher bearers, grabbed hold of Andrew, and guided him up to the porch of the station.

"Emil, I'm all right."

"Like hell you are," Emil snapped, forcing him to sit down. He took off Andrew's glasses, examining his eyes, then put his ear to Andrew's chest.

"Breathe deeply."

Andrew did as ordered, knowing he wouldn't escape until Emil was satisfied.

Next he took Andrew's hand, and, for the first time, Andrew muttered a protest, wincing as Emil ordered him to flex it.

Opening his black medical bag he pulled out a jar of ointment and smeared it on Andrew's face and hand. He started to bandage the hand, Andrew protesting that he needed it to write.

"Get someone to take dictation. You were lucky, Andrew, damn lucky."

Andrew told him about the sacrifice of his staff, first to protect him from the exploding boiler, then the rush to the next train.

"Stanisloff, Kal's nephew, is dead." Andrew sighed.

Emil paused in his work and looked back at the flatcar, where more than twenty bodies were stretched out.

"He saved my life. I think he's the one who knocked me down and covered me when the boiler burst."

Andrew leaned back and closed his eyes, struggling for control. It was one thing to break down in the dark, another to do it now, the sense of panic hanging in the air, thick and palatable as the scent of death.

"Oh God," Andrew whispered. "How many have died like that for me?"

"It's not just you, Keane," Emil said softly while snipping off the end of the bandage. "It's the Republic, it's winning this war. That's what he died for. He couldn't get us out; you can. That's what he died for. So you can get all of us out."

"Thank you for the guilt, good doctor."

Emil patted him on the shoulder. "Anytime it's necessary, Andrew, anytime."

"What's happening with Pat?"

"Telegraph line just came backup. Near thing, almost got flanked, but managed to pull back to their depot. The first trains are coming returning with the wounded."

He paused. "Hell of a fight for him yesterday. Half of Eleventh Corps overrun. Five thousand dead and wounded."

A booming explosion erupted, shattering the windowpanes behind Andrew, a geyser of dirt soaring up less than a hundred feet away, just behind the last car of the train.

"What the hell?" Andrew shouted, standing up.

"Just their damn ironclads," Emil announced. "Put a few shells in the hospital a half hour ago. Most of their shooting is damn poor though."

"Ironclads here?"

"Apparently moved up during the night. The hundred-pound Parrott is keeping them back, though; just an annoyance more than anything else at the moment."

Andrew stood up and walked to the side of the station. Shading his eyes from the early-morning light, he looked out to sea and saw four ships lying a couple of miles offshore. A jet of smoke erupted from one and long seconds later a tower of water shot up a couple of hundred yards short of what was left of *Petersburg*.

"They think she's still worth something, so that's where most of the fire's been directed."

Andrew stood silent, still not quite able to grasp that in twenty-four hours so much had been reversed.

Emil joined him, offering a flask of vodka.

"You haven't slept. Take a drink, and let me give you something for the pain. You need some rest."

Andrew looked down at Emil and shook his head.

"Is there anything you can actually do at this moment?" Emil asked.

"We have to deploy toward Junction City, try and

slow them down, save as much of the line as possible."

"Rest first, Andrew. There'll be time enough later. Let some others do the worrying for a little while. I'll see to it."

Andrew felt a moment of surprise as he lay down on the cot in his office, surprised that he had, in fact, agreed to Emil's orders, and then there was nothing but silence and the nightmare of a boy dying in his arms.

Chapter Eight

"My God, Vincent, you look like hell."

Vincent Hawthorne smiled as he pulled up a chair by Ferguson's desk and sat down.

"Two days and nights on one of your trains will do it to you."

Vincent looked at his old friend closely. Ferguson seemed to have slipped even more since their last meeting; there was an almost translucent glow to his skin, a pale ghostly quality that he knew was typical of consumption victims.

Taking off his rain-soaked campaign hat and poncho, Vincent sighed with relief, gladly accepting the mug of hot tea Chuck offered.

"I have to be at the White House in an hour, but I wanted to see you first. It's actually the main reason I came all the way back here."

"I'm flattered."

Vincent smiled.

"You might not appreciate what I need and the timetable to deliver it."

"Something to stop the land cruisers."

"Exactly. Look, I took notes of everything I saw out there. Ranges we fired at, effect of weapons. I also know the reports on our own land ironclads. We're faster, but they'll kill our machines in a head-on attack." As he spoke he pulled a pad of paper out of his haversack and laid it on Chuck's desk.

"What's the latest? I've been locked up in here," Chuck asked absently, thumbing through Vincent's notes.

"Marcus is moving Tenth Corps up, reinforcing the survivors of Fifth Corps who are digging in west of Junction City. Ha'ark moved about eight miles west, then stopped, holding a ridgeline and the pass facing where First and Second Divisions of Fifth Corps dug in. He hasn't pushed any farther since."

"Why?"

"I think he's stretched. Burned up a lot of munitions taking Junction City, and pushing a frontal attack will cost too much. My bet is he has enough reserve supplies for one damn good fight, and he's waiting for reinforcements and additional supplies to come up first. Then he'll broaden his hold to the west and really lock the door shut on Andrew, Pat, and Hans."

Chuck laughed softly.

"So the Quaker guns I recommended scared him off from attacking?"

Vincent nodded uncomfortably. Any reference to his own Quaker upbringing, even unintentional, triggered a sense of guilt for the pacifist heritage he had abandoned in favor of war.

"We've got forty logs, painted black, with just their fake barrels exposed, the rest concealed inside covered bombproofs so their flyers can't see them from above. Damn, it's the same trick the Rebs used at Manassas. Never thought it'd work, but I could see Ha'ark studying our position and immediately afterward they started to dig in rather than attack."

"What about Andrew and Hans?"

"Not a word since we lost Junction City."

"They'll find a way out."

"Are you so certain of that?" Vincent asked quietly.

"And you aren't?"

"Between us?"

Ferguson nodded.

"It doesn't look good. Junction City was our major supply depot. We had it there to shift equipment either east or south as needed. Chuck, we lost enough ammunition and rations to keep half a dozen corps in the field for a month. We lost the equal of all the ammunition expended at Hispania. Pat and Hans have enough with them for four, maybe five days of sustained action, then it's going to get tight. If there's going to be a breakthrough, it's got to come from our side, not theirs."

"And you want me to figure out how to smash their land cruisers in how long?"

"It'll take a week to move up all of Tenth Corps and the men from Sixth Corps that were stripping off the western front. Then I'll attack, and I damn well better break through."

"Seven days?"

"It has to be then or never."

"Why?"

"Ha'ark landed three days ago but hasn't pushed out," Vincent said, pausing to drain the rest of his tea and gratefully accepting another cup from the small samovar by Chuck's desk.

"So far Ha'ark's army at Junction City is just a blocking force—there's not enough strength there yet for a hard-hitting offensive strike against dug-in positions. I saw the fleet. He had about a dozen steamships besides his ironclads. The rest were sailing ships and galleys. Four days to get back to Xi'an for the galleys, maybe five. This blasted weather's been god-sent for keeping their airships down, but it gave them a stern wind for back home. A day to load up, then five days back. If we haven't rolled him back and made a breakthrough, he'll have four more umens landing in seven or eight days, all with modern equipment. Maybe some more land cruisers, too, maybe even a locomotive engine and some rolling stock so they can start using our rail line as well."

"And then he can turn and crush Andrew or Hans while holding you back," Chuck sighed.

Vincent nodded.

"I'm going back in three days, Chuck. Figure something out by then and give it to me."

"You're asking the impossible."

"And you've always come through before."

Stifling a cough, Chuck looked down at the notes and scanned them again.

"Come back tomorrow," he said wearily. "I've already had some ideas in the works. You sure the numbers you've got here are accurate? The reason I'm asking is that I can figure out the kinetic energy of a fifty-pound bolt hitting at the range you specified, but if the range is off, even by fifty yards, what I cook up might not work."

"I sacrificed a hell of a lot of men to make sure I got it right."

Chuck stared at the papers as if he could sense the blood that had been spilled to get them to him.

"Tomorrow; come back tomorrow."

Sighing, he leaned forward, struggling to cough, and Vincent could see he was too exhausted even to clear his lungs anymore.

"Chuck, I wish I didn't have to do this to you,"

Vincent whispered, putting his arm around his friend's shoulder, "but if you can't solve this one, we might lose it all."

"Pat, how are you?"

Pat turned about and saw Andrew approaching. He started to salute, then, ignoring all protocol, he went up to Andrew and slapped him on the shoulder, drawing back a bit when Andrew winced from the pain.

"You know, Andrew Lawrence Keane, you look like you've been to hell and back."

"Something like that."

"Why half your face's pink as a baby's arse."

Andrew tried to smile, but the pain of it stopped him.

"The hand?"

"Lost some skin. Emil's making me keep the bandage on, said I might lose it to infection if I don't, then where the hell would I be."

"Retired on pension, me bucko, no hands to hold a glass with, frightening thought."

Andrew had seen more than one veteran like that, and the thought had frightened him enough to obey Emil's orders to keep the sterilized bandage on, in spite of the difficulty and discomfort.

"How's it going? I thought I'd come up to see."

Pat pointed back to the bridge across the Shenandoah. On the far side, there was a continual roar of musketry, while batteries lining the riverbank to their left poured a stream of fire into the woods on the eastern shore a quarter mile away.

A battery of ten-pounders came onto the far end of the bridge, moving slowly as it rattled along the narrow-planked siding that ran alongside the track.

"Here comes the last train," Pat announced.

From out of the forest a plume of smoke showed, the train edging onto the bridge, pulling a dozen flatcars piled high with rails that had been torn up during the retreat, with wounded and dead riding on top of the piles of iron.

"Except for Eleventh Corps getting overrun, we haven't left any dead for the bastards," Pat announced coldly.

Four shells arced in from the forest, dropping into the river on either side of the bridge, followed a moment later by four more. The battery nearest to Andrew shifted its fire, ranging into the woods, probing for where the enemy battery was most likely deployed on the road.

A signal rocket rose up from the opposite bank, bursting high over the river.

"Now pour it on!" Pat roared.

A column of blue-clad troops appeared on the far end of the bridge, moving at the double, a final line of skirmishers closing in behind them, moving backwards, faces still turned toward the advancing Horde. When the back of the column was barely fifty yards out onto the bridge, the red banner of a Bantag umen appeared at the edge of the woods, a concentration of warriors filtering out of the trees along the riverbank. Showers of arrows and a scattering of rifle fire erupted from the eastern shore.

A dozen batteries lining the side of the river to Andrew's left opened up in a thundering salvo, exploding shells blanketing the far bank, while men armed with Sharps rifles and the detachments of snipers carrying Whitworths added to the covering fire. Nevertheless, men in the retreating column dropped by the dozens, their comrades slowing down to pick up their casualties as they pulled back.

"Come on, damn it, come on," Pat roared.

The column reached the middle of the bridge, the smoke hanging thick along the riverbank so that it was all but impossible to see the far shore.

"They're rushing the bridge!" an observer posted in a signal tower shouted.

A break in the smoke allowed Andrew to catch a glimpse of the far shore. A column of Bantag were coming forward at the run. The retreating regiment was now three-quarters of the way across. Pat paced back and forth, cursing, shouting for the men to keep moving.

A volley of shells screamed in from the opposite shore, one of them hitting the signal tower, knocking the log structure over, a second shell striking and dismounting a ten-pound Parrott muzzle-loading cannon sited beside the tower.

Pat strode back to his command bunker, Andrew following. An engineering officer came to attention at their approach and saluted nervously.

"You ready?"

"Yes, sir."

The retreating column still had a hundred yards to go, and Pat continued to swear as the unit, colors still held high, lurched forward. A knot of men rose up out of the battlements flanking the bridge and dashed out, crouched low, reaching the column and grabbing hold of the wounded, helping to drag them back.

More fire started to come down as the Bantag maneuvered additional batteries into place on the far shore, the river valley echoing with the ever-increasing thunder of the cannonade.

The head of the retreating column reached the safety of the west bank, the formation breaking up as men leapt into the protection of the trenches. The last of them finally got across, and the bridge was cleared, except for the advancing mass of Bantag.

"Now watch this!" Pat announced with a grin, and he nodded to the engineering officer, who knelt, picked up a wire, and touched it to a galvanic battery.

An instant later an explosion erupted in the middle of the bridge, just ahead of the advancing Bantag. Planks from the bridge soared up, plunging down into the river, but only part of the roadway was blown. Startled, Andrew looked over at Pat.

"All right, sound the retreat!" Pat shouted.

Bugles echoed along the line of entrenchments. Batteries fell silent, groups of men got up out of the trenches and started to run.

"Pat?" Andrew asked, stunned that they were abandoning the position.

"Just a moment, Andrew, in a moment."

The westerly breeze blew the smoke clear of the bank and in a couple of minutes the far shore was visible. The advancing column of Bantag had stalled in the middle of the bridge and then came the spine-chilling braying of nargas signaling an attack. A roaring column of Bantag stormed onto the bridge, charging at the double.

"Keep falling back!" Pat shouted. More men poured out of the trenches, running for the rear. A battery was hooked up to caissons and began to pull out of the line.

"Pat, what the hell are you doing?" Andrew cried. "We can still hold them here!"

Pat grinned, shaking his head. "A few more seconds, Andrew."

The forward column of Bantag already out on the middle of the bridge stood and began to surge forward, squeezing around the destroyed section of bridging by leaping over to the side of the bridge carrying the train tracks. The bridge for nearly two hundred yards of its length was packed with the dark-uniformed Horde, who were screaming wildly.

The head of the column was down to less than 150 yards from the western shore. A scattering of rifle fire from men still in the trenches was cutting into them, but as quickly as a warrior dropped another leapt forward, gaining five or ten more feet, while on the eastern end of the bridge the pressure continued to build as yet more warriors swarmed onto the bridge.

"All right, give it to them!" Pat roared.

The engineering officer picked up a second wire and touched it to the battery.

An explosion started on the eastern bank, dropping a section, then raced down the entire length of the bridge. Pilings were sheared in half, crossbeams exploded into splinters, the deck of the bridge erupted into flames as barrels of kerosene and benzene strapped directly under the bridge flooring burst into fireballs that soared heavenward.

To Andrew it seemed as if a thousand voices were joined together in a single cry of terror and unspeakable pain. Even though they were the enemy, he felt a surge of pity as the attacking column was consumed in fire as they plummeted into the river, burning, crushed by tree-sized timbers, or blown apart by the force of the explosions.

Pat, roaring like a demon gone berserk, jumped up

and down, slapping the engineer on the back, while from out of the woods where the "panic-stricken" men had run, there came a wild, gleeful cheering, the men coming out of the woods, whooping and hollering as if a great practical joke had been played.

All firing from the Bantag side ceased for a moment as the roar of the explosion echoed across the river valley. Hundreds of bodies littered the river. The few who survived the explosion cried pitifully for help, and snipers along the bank opened up on them so that geysers of water snapped around their bobbing forms until the foaming water turned pink.

On the road leading to the bridge a dark column ground to a halt, and stood, dumbstruck by the destruction. The guns along the western shore, which had fallen silent, fired as if triggered by a single hand, sweeping down scores of Bantag as the far shore disappeared again in a blanket of exploding shells.

"Effective but rather perverse," Andrew announced.

"Isn't it though. Figured the beggars would come on like that, so we cooked up a little surprise to egg them on. A thousand—I reckon we got us a thousand cooked sons of bitches out there."

"Damn how we hate each other," Andrew whispered.

"They'd have done the same to us, Andrew. Only worse."

"I know, damn them."

"They thought they had us on the run. This will make them move more cautiously."

The shelling from the far shore resumed and Pat ducked low, motioning Andrew to follow him into his dugout.

"I think it's safe to say that little show deserves a

drink," Pat announced. Andrew looked at him with a raised eyebrow.

"Andrew, me darlin', I've fought a withdrawal for ten days and nights, been flanked twice, and got out with me breeches still on. I think I deserve this, and so do you."

Andrew smiled and motioned for him to pass a cup over.

"To Vincent Hawthorne," Pat announced.

"Why him?"

" 'Cause if we're going to get our asses out of here, that laddie better do his job."

Andrew could not help but laugh as he raised his glass of vodka and downed it.

"So how long before they're across?" Andrew asked.

"Already are, thirty miles north of here. No way we could stop them all along the river above the falls—too damn many fords. Was hoping the rain would just keep coming and bring the river up to a flood. What about the trains?"

"Enough to move Eleventh Corps out by early afternoon and Third tomorrow morning. Two days later we'll get the rest of you out."

Pat nodded, not bothering to ask for approval as he poured another drink for himself.

"Any word from Hans? Is he moving north?"

"Nothing." Andrew sighed. "We're all on our own."

A scattering of dust sifted down as a shell impacted on top of the bunker.

"In five days we need to counterattack," Andrew said, looking at the layer of dust that had collected on the top of his drink. Swirling the cup around, he gulped the rest down anyhow.

"Three days, Pat, I want Third and Eleventh up in position for a breakout against Ha'ark, and First and Ninth corps coming in behind them. It's all or nothing; otherwise, we'll never get through."

He could only hope that Hans realized the same thing and knew that such a thought was foolish. If anyone was going to get out, it would be Hans.

Filled with a cold bitter rage, Jurak watched as the bodies in the river were slowly carried away by the current, some of them rolling end over end in the water, others sinking, disappearing into the muddy depths. Up until this time the war against the humans was, to him, like any other war. You had objectives you fought for, you advanced, and you killed rather than be killed. Unlike Ha'ark, he had never really hated them or even feared them, until this moment.

It was a war of annihilation. Nothing less would satisfy him than the death and the devouring of the red-haired commander who had stood on the other side of the river, capering with joy as his warriors were burned alive, standing beside one-armed Keane, who had so obviously planned the murderous, dishonorable deaths.

"I want the airships up now, not tomorrow, now!" Ha'ark, barely able to contain his rage, stared coldly at Bakkth, his airship commander.

"Sire, you can rage all you want, but it is a question of the winds. The storm of the last three days smashed four of our ships on the ground. We have no hangars for them here." As he spoke he pointed to the shallow valley east of Junction City.

The wreckage of four of his precious ships lay in

twisted heaps. Two of the remaining six airships that came north had sustained lesser damage, one with a wing sheared off.

"I have no news of what Schuder's army is doing in the south," Ha'ark snapped. "Only conflicting reports. The news I'm getting from Jurak on the eastern front must come by sea and is more than a day old by the time it arrives. I don't know if my reinforcements are coming up or how much strength the humans have deployed to the west. And you dare to tell me you don't want to risk flying?"

"Ha'ark, we could lose all of them on takeoff. The wind is blowing across the valley, not down it. These are not all-weather jets from our home world, Ha'ark, they're lighter-than-air ships with wings slapped on them. It takes several minutes just to get them up to speed, and in that time they'll be slammed into the other side of the valley."

"You selected it as the place for your aerodrome."

"Because it was the most sheltered place I could find at the moment. The Yankees were not so considerate as to leave an airship base for us in all this wreckage."

Ha'ark stared coldly at his old companion, sensing the slightest note of rebuke in his tone.

"Fly now. First ship south to find out what Schuder is doing, the second and third west to see what they are deploying and then to push on and cut telegraph lines and destroy bridges, fourth to Jurak so I know if they have crossed the river yet or not."

Bakkth could see that there was no hope of arguing. Nodding, he started back to where his pilots waited expectantly.

"You don't go first, Bakkth," Ha'ark announced.

"I'm the best pilot of the lot; if I don't make it, then do me a favor and keep the others on the ground."

There was a time when he felt Bakkth was almost a friend, back before the Tunnel of Light. He nodded in agreement, suddenly filled with a desire to have one of his companions from the other world simply disappear. For after all, Bakkth knew him from the before time, he knew the secrets, the weaknesses, and would never fully accept the remade Ha'ark who was now the "Redeemer."

Ground crews, which had come up with the invasion fleet, had already heated the engines up with the hope that the wind would abate. Waving for his crew, Bakkth trotted over to his airship and climbed into the pilot's chair, followed by his observer. He motioned for the tail gunner to stand back.

Ha'ark wanted to order him into the ship anyway, there was always the chance that Keane might very well have new airships moving up, but decided to defer to Bakkth's judgment. The saved weight might be the crucial difference.

With both engines turning over and revving up, the ground crew untied the cables holding the airship, a dozen of them moving to the upwind side to hold on to the wing.

Bakkth slammed the throttles forward, the low whir of the engines shifting upward into a steady high-pitched hum. The airship lumbered down the valley, the ground crew trotting alongside the upwind wing, holding on to it in order to prevent the airship from tipping up.

Ha'ark watched, feeling as if he was witnessing something from ancient history rather than his own world as the ungainly craft slowly continued down the valley, laboriously gaining speed. The slowest of the ground crew started to fall behind, letting go of the wing. Bakkth waved from the cockpit and the rest of the crew released, the wing began to tilt up from the crosswind, but Bakkth had enough forward velocity so that the aileron provided sufficient counterthrust. The airship crept off the ground, Bakkth feeding in full rudder, but even as he turned the crosswind started to drive the ship across the narrow valley.

Ha'ark held his breath as the ship barely cleared the downwind ridgeline, skimming over the top of the hills. The second ship started off, the same routine repeated, but as it cleared the ground the upwind wing soared up, the downwind wing tearing into the turf. The ship rolled over onto its side and plowed into the ground. The airbag tore open followed by a flash of blue fire. Seconds later the two bombs on board detonated with a thunderclap roar.

Ha'ark looked up and saw that Bakkth, crabbing into the wind, was heading south toward the mountains, which barely showed on the horizon in the clear morning air.

"My Qar Qarth."

It was the commander of the ground crew, down on his knees, ready to accept punishment for the destruction of yet another ship.

"Get the next one up," Ha'ark snarled. "I need to know what is happening to the west as well!"

With a flourish of his cape he stalked away. Fumbling in the pouch dangling from his belt, he pulled out a plug of tobacco and bit off a chew. He had rendered his opponents blind, cutting them off, but now he was equally blind. There was fighting in the passes to the south, reports of sighting the guidons of two different corps and the blue flag with golden chevrons, the flag of Schuder, pressing their way through the passes. Yet he sensed something amiss there.

Would Hans be so obliging as to come into the trap, or would he suspect that if the schedule worked as planned, that half an umen armed with modern weapons and ten land cruisers would soon land behind him?

Then there was Keane to the east. A prisoner had revealed that before dying, that Keane had gone back into the trap. Why? He should have sent his young assistant in and he himself should have gone west to organize the breakout. Strange and troubling.

Ha'ark paced in silence. Three more days and the additional umens would be up. Then there would be the strike force available to crush Keane, then Hans, and from there to march in triumph on Roum and Suzdal beyond. For with two-thirds of their army destroyed, the Horde would be impossible to resist.

Sergeant Major Hans Schuder bit off a chew of tobacco and, standing up in his stirrups, made no pretense of concealing the part of his anatomy that was hurting the most as he rubbed his backside.

A rifle ball fluttered past. Ignoring the shot, he spit out a stream of tobacco juice.

"Hell of a march, Ketswana," he growled, offering the plug to his friend, who was walking beside him. Ketswana bit off a chew and nodded in agreement as his powerful jaws started to work on the plug.

"Now remember, don't swallow it this time, damn it. You look ridiculous when you puke."

The staff around them chuckled but fell silent at Ketswana's threatening gaze.

A colonel from the forward part of the massive

corps-sized square broke away from the line and trotted back to Hans.

"Skirmishers report they're building up in a gully up ahead."

"Well, let the bastards come on," Hans announced. More than two hours back he had seen dark columns dismounting ahead of them, the warriors appearing to leap into the ground, while their horses were driven to the rear.

Still standing in the stirrups, he raised his field glasses to study the ground around him. The mountains to the west blocked the moisture coming in off the Inland Sea so that the land reminded him of the Texas panhandle and high prairie east of the Rockies. Some rain had come from the storm of the last three days so that the parched grass seemed to explode back to life. The knee-high prairie grass was an ocean of green, wavery in the strong breeze coming out of the west. To the east, half a mile away, was the block formation of Seventh Corps. Each side of the block was made up of a brigade, with two brigades in reserve in the center. The men marched in columns of fours, the front and rear of the block moving forward in two double ranks spaced ten yards apart, so that the formation was a square nearly six hundred yards to a side.

It was cumbersome and slow-moving; they were making barely a mile and a half an hour, but no cavalry could ever hope to break through as long as the men held. Between his block, made up of Second Corps, and that of Seventh Corps, marched Eighth Corps, a half mile to the rear. If any of the three blocks ran into problems, the other two could turn and move to support.

He had once read that Marshal Ney did the same

thing during the French retreat from Moscow, moving his corps in square in the final days of the retreat to the Niemen, thus holding off the hordes of Cossacks swarming around him. So far, it was working here as well, though if the Bantag ever managed to get four or five batteries in front of them, there'd be hell to pay. His own artillery was only carrying the ammunition available in its caissons, enough for one hard hour of fighting, and then that was it.

Turning his attention forward, he saw thousands of riderless horses half a mile beyond the gully, lone warriors trailing ropes attached to the reins of six to eight mounts. He studied them for a moment. It was impossible to count but there had to be at least an umen dismounted and deployed into the gully a quarter mile ahead.

A steady patter of fire was erupting forward, the skirmishers moving two hundred yards ahead of the square, stopping, kneeling in the grass, firing, reloading and then sprinting forward half a dozen yards before firing again. Puffs of smoke rippled from the gully, not enough to indicate that a Bantag formation fully armed with rifles was waiting, but enough to cause damage nevertheless.

Men started to drop from the forward line, and Hans looked away as regimental surgeons were forced to make a horrible decision. If the man could keep up, he was allowed to rest in one of the precious ambulances while the wound was bandaged over, but if it was too serious, a dose of morphine was administered, someone helped the soldier to reload his weapon, and he was left behind with half a dozen rounds of ammunition. Throughout the three long days of marching they had so far endured, the worst part was looking back to where a distant line of Bantag trailed them. There would be occasional puffs of smoke as a wounded man with still enough fight in him would take down one or two of his foes before being finished off.

As for the wounded who were unconscious when left behind . . . Hans did not even want to think about that. Once, when fighting the Comanche in Texas, he had killed a gut-shot comrade rather than leave him to the tender mercies of Indians who were almost as good as the Bantag when it came to inflicting torture. It still haunted him.

As he surveyed his lines he could see where more than one knot of soldiers were hiding a wounded comrade, dragging him along. So far he had turned a blind eye, but if the main body of the Bantag came up, he knew what he would have to order everyone to do . . . march on your own or die.

More puffs of smoke erupted from the gully. Studying the line, he could see Bantag arms rising over the edge of the gully, moving rhythmically up and down . . . Good, the ones carrying rifles were only armed with muzzle loaders rather than rapid-fire breechloaders.

A minié ball buzzed past Hans, smacking into a supply wagon moving behind him. Sitting back down in the saddle, he urged his mount forward, cantering up to the forward line. The men continued their relentless advance, a steady eighty yards a minute. Blades of grass shot up in the air as bullets hummed in low through the grass, and Hans did not know whether to laugh or swear at a young private who was taking deliberately high steps as if he could dance over the bullets plowing across the prairie.

Officers moved back and forth behind their regiments, some shouting for the men to keep moving, others, the older hands, calmly praising the men, urging them forward as much by as example as by command.

A soldier in front of Hans collapsed into the grass, cursing, holding his stomach. The line continued on. He looked up as Hans rode past and then at the medical orderlies who would decide his fate. Grim-faced, he struggled back to his feet and staggered back into the line, clutching himself with one hand, but still holding on to his rifle.

The forward advance swept through the line of skirmishers, who rejoined the ranks. At a shouted command from the division commander the front two ranks brought their rifles down from shoulder arms to charge bayonets, the blades flashing in the sunlight, the forward line of the column now bristling with a hedgerow of steel. Looking over to where the Seventh Corps was advancing toward the gully, he saw the same display and felt a ripple of pride at the precision of their movements, as if they were advancing on parade.

A dark wall suddenly rose up from out of the gully along a front of nearly a quarter mile, an instant later the sound of thousands of bows being discharged rolled over the square, and the advance slowed, men instinctively looking up. From the corner of his eye Hans saw the shadow of the steel-tipped rain racing across the prairie, blocking out the sun. The arrows seemed to hover overhead, then came whistling down, smashing into the square. Scores of men fell, screaming and cursing.

He was tempted to order the forward line into a charge, but from farther up along the gully to his right and in the ground between his formation and Seventh Corps, a line of mounted warriors surged out of the gully, looking like wraiths rising up out of the earth, screaming their death chants. If he charged forward, the square would be broken open by the thousands of mounted warriors swarming in on either flank, but if he continued to move at the same pace, the arrow volleys would tear his square apart.

"Bugler! Sound double time!" Hans roared.

The bugler next to him raised the call, which was picked up and echoed by the other buglers in the square, officers responded, shouting for the square to pick up its pace. Hans looked anxiously about, oblivious to the second volley of arrows thundering down around him. Sections of the line bulged, spread out, gaps opening up between regiments. The mounted warriors on his right flank continued to pour out of the gully, urging their horses into a charge.

Masterful, he realized, force us to stop in the open, then get swept by the concealed fire in the gully.

"Keep moving!" Hans roared. Spurring his mount forward he pushed through the line, raising his carbine high, Ketswana beside him screaming with maniacal glee.

Hans galloped down the front of the line, pointing toward the gully, shouting, urging the slow-moving charge forward.

The gully was less than a hundred yards away, sections of his line, unable to take the strain of the double-time advance, broke into an all-out charge. Hans turned his mount about, trying to recall them, but could see it was too late, as the entire line burst forward. At nearly the same instant the Bantag charge on his right swept in, most of them going down from well-timed volleys delivered at thirty yards or less, but part of the enemy attack lapped in around the gap created by the forward part of the square breaking forward.

"Bugler. Signal the reserve units!"

Hans turned and saw the riderless horse following him. Ketswana was still beside him, though, shouting something, but Hans could not hear him. He spurred his mount back toward the center of the square, dodging around a Bantag warrior who came straight at him, blade hissing over Hans's head. Ketswana leapt onto the back of the Bantag's horse and cut the warrior's throat, sending him tumbling from the saddle.

One of the reserve companies was already rushing forward to seal the gap and try to cover the right flank of the advancing charge. Shouting, Hans fell in by their side as they rushed forward at the double. Directly ahead a thunderous volley erupted, as the charge swept up to the edge of the gully, delivering fire down into the mass of Bantag at nearly point-blank range. The Bantag, however, did not give, firing their bows back, arrows striking with such force that they were driven clean through a man's body.

A cannon detonated to his right, and, surprised, Hans saw where a battery, acting without orders, had ventured out from the back end of the square, deployed, and was firing canister into the flank of the mounted charge, sweeping down dozens of warriors. Working feverishly the gun crews tore open the breeches, slammed in tins of canister, powder bags, closed the breeches, and fired again, shattering a line of Bantag who tried to turn to meet them.

The break in the line seemed to waver as if ready to peel back in on itself as thousands of Bantag surged around the flank, but the disciplined wall held, front two ranks presenting bayonets, while the rear two ranks fired into the milling swarm at nearly point-blank range.

The front line still held to the edge of the gully, pouring a devastating fire straight down into the thousands of archers. Bantag warriors tried to surge forward and up, but were beaten back down. One desperate Bantag lunge made it up to the lip of the gully, cracking the line open for a moment. Wounded, screaming soldiers were dragged down into the gully, where they were torn apart. A reserve regiment dashed forward, sealing the hole, while a battery swung about, dismounted their guns, then pushed them forward right up to the firing line. Hans trotted up behind the guns, cheering the crews on as elevation screws were cranked up, depressing the barrels down. Breeches were popped open and double loads of canister slammed in. Nearly half the crews were dead or wounded within seconds, and then the four guns recoiled, spraying nearly a thousand iron balls into the dense-packed ranks of the Bantag below. To Hans it seemed as if a giant's hand had smashed through the Horde, picking warriors up, tearing their bodies to shreds, and flinging them to the far side of the narrow ravine. There was a moment of stunned silence in the gully, the gunners, helped now by infantrymen who had cast aside their rifles, rolled the guns up again while breeches were popped open and fresh charges slammed in, gunnery sergeants screaming for the men to forget about swabbing the barrels before reloading.

As a powder charge was slammed into the second gun in line, a hot spark in the barrel ignited the round, a blast of fire blowing out the back of the gun, tearing the arm off the loader. The other three guns fired again, and the surviving Bantag in front of the battery broke and started to scramble up the opposite slope of the ravine.

Wild, hysterical cheering erupted along the line as the enraged men of Second Corps grimly set to work, slaughtering the Bantag on the opposite side of the ravine less than a dozen yards away. The three guns were rolled up yet again, turned now to fire down the length of the ravine in either direction. The opposite slope became nearly impassable as desperate warriors tried to claw their way out over the bodies of the dead and dying who were tumbling back on top of them. Hans heard another salvo of artillery and saw where a second battery had deployed on the left flank just outside the square and was sweeping the gully in the open stretch toward where Seventh Corps was engaged in the same desperate struggle. In the hole created by the battery in front of Hans his own infantry now started to slide down into the ravine, slashing at the wounded with bayonets, then turning to pour in a flanking fire while the artillery above them continued to tear into the now panic-stricken mob.

Hans wanted to shout for the battery commander to cease fire out of fear of hitting their comrades in the ravine when he saw some gunners loop a heavy rope around the trail of one of the guns. As men from one of the infantry units grabbed hold of the rope, the gun crew pushed their piece up over the lip of the gully. The gun skidded down into the ravine, dragging the infantry with it as it slid down the blood-soaked slope, crushing the bodies of the Bantag underneath its iron-shod wheels.

The crew leapt down, picked up the trail, and swung the gun about, screaming for the infantry who were widening the breach to fall back.

At point-blank range the load of double canister poured straight into the flank of the Bantag still trapped in the now-open grave. This final blow triggered a panic, warriors down the entire length of the line breaking, clawing up the slope to get out of the way, hundreds of them falling back as volley fire was delivered at point-blank range. Hans drew back from the line and looked over to where Seventh Corps was fighting, his chest tightening when he saw that part of the square was breaking in, a dark stream of mounted warriors pouring into the breach.

Another one of his batteries was outside the protection of the square, deployed and firing case shot to try to break up the attack on their comrades in Seventh Corps. More artillery fire opened, and he saw where several batteries from Eighth Corps, which had been marching half a mile to the rear, had galloped forward and unlimbered in order to sweep the ground between the Second and Seventh.

The forward part of Seventh Corps line was recoiling from the edge of the ravine, and dark shadows of arrow volleys soared up to come arcing down into the middle of the square.

Hans looked forward again. The Bantag they had been facing were still fleeing in panic, rifle fire continuing to sweep them as they ran across the open prairie. Standing in his stirrups he could see where the cavalry charge to his right had broken and was falling back as well.

He edged over to the battery commander.

"Good work!" he roared. "Now turn your guns about, hammer the bastards in front of Seventh Corps!"

Turning about, he caught the eye of a colonel in

command of one of the reserve regiments. The officer ran up and saluted.

"Get your men deployed on either side of this ravine, then drive toward Seventh Corps. You've got to flank the bastards out there."

The colonel, grinning, held his sword aloft, shouting for his regiment to follow. As the colors swept past Hans saw they were the old Fifth Suzdal, the regiment Hawthorne had once commanded.

"Bugler, I need a bugler!"

A boy, face blackened with powder smoke, ran up to Hans's side.

"Sound halt!"

The command was picked up and echoed across the square. Hans stood tall in his stirrups, hoping that his division and brigade commanders could see him. He pointed his carbine toward Seventh Corps.

"At the double time!" he roared.

The square, which had been advancing southwest, turned, and started toward their beleaguered comrades to the east. Hans wanted to order a charge, but knew the formation would never hold. Though they had soundly thrashed the umen deployed in front of them, there were still enough mounted warriors to the west who could prove to be a problem.

At least five minutes, Hans thought, before we can relieve Seventh Corps, and he chafed at the slowness of the advance, watching as the men of the Fifth Suzdal sprinted forward, pausing to fire a volley into the gully, driving the Bantag who were still concealed farther back, then moving forward again. The batteries from Eighth Corps, masked by his own advance, limbered up and pushed obliquely into the closing space between the two formations, while the main body of Eighth Corps relentlessly moved toward the other flank of the collapsing square.

Sickened, Hans watched as the entire forward edge of Seventh Corps was swarmed under by the Bantag charging up out of the ravine, the exposed lines to either side curling back toward the center in a desperate bid to reestablish a line.

An explosion ripped across the face of the square, throwing the Bantag charge back into the ravine.

"That's the stuff!" Hans roared. "Use the artillery on them, damn it!"

Whatley apparently had deployed his five batteries in the center of the square. The Bantag charge seemed to disappear as salvo after salvo slammed into their advance, grinding it to a halt.

Fifth Suzdal was less than a hundred yards away from the engagement, with Bantag pouring up out of the ravine that was becoming a death trap for them as well. To Hans's amazement, a lone gun, drivers lashing the straining horses, clattered by on the opposite side of the ravine, the piece that had been manhandled down into the gully only minutes before. The gun crew swung out alongside Fifth Suzdal, unlimbered, and began to spray canister into the Bantag who were pulling back, triggering them into flight as well.

His own square was now less than two hundred yards away, hemming in the Bantag cavalry who had been cutting into Seventh Corps' western flank, so that the mounted warriors were now caught between two walls of fire, while the guns from Eighth Corps sealed off the box.

Within seconds the enemy attack disintegrated. Some of the warriors tried to charge the guns, but were mowed down by a well-timed salvo delivered at less than fifty yards. Others turned to try and ride back down into the ravine and scramble up the other side, but the clutter of bodies was so thick that the horses balked and their riders were slaughtered.

Wild cheering erupted from Second Corps as it pressed its attack in. As the wave of Bantag withdrew the line of fieldpieces of Seventh Corps swept the retreat, finally switching from canister to case shot. Some of the gunners raised their sights, plowing shot into the packed horses, which were being held for the surviving warriors who had fought dismounted. For one warrior to hold a string of six to eight frightened horses was nearly impossible and after half a dozen volleys the herd was running in panic, scattering in every direction.

Hans watched the panic and was tempted to call upon the three regiments of mounted infantry. If they swept forward, they could slaughter thousands of the scattered, leaderless Bantag fleeing on foot, but a quick look to either flank showed where formations still mounted were rallying. If he sent his mounted units in now, they might get caught up in the frenzy, go too far, and be cut off. And besides, the horses would be needed for something else.

As the thunderous roar died away Hans slumped back in his saddle. Riding up to the edge of the ditch he felt a surge of pity for the hundreds of horses trapped in the carnage, many of them still alive, thrashing in agony, or crying piteously. Individual rifle shots rippled along the line as the surviving Bantag and their crippled mounts were dispatched.

Breaking clear of his square, Hans trotted over to Seventh Corps, relieved to see Ketswana emerging from the thinned ranks of Fifth Suzdal and followed by his ever-diminishing band of Zulu warriors.

"Not in my wildest dreams did I imagine killing Bantag like this!" Ketswana roared.

The ground in front of Seventh Corps, up to the edge of the gully, was carpeted with blue-clad bodies, dead and dying Bantag heaped on top of them, casualties of the final counterattack.

Hans edged his mount to the edge of the square and, unable to ride farther because of the carnage, dismounted.

"Whatley, where is he?" Hans asked, spotting a stunned colonel who was bent double, gasping for breath.

The colonel looked up at him, wide-eyed, and shook his head.

Hans moved into the square, stepping aside as Ketswana raised his revolver and shot a Bantag who was feebly trying to raise his blade to cut at Hans.

Spotting a corps guidon he moved toward it, cursing himself for the act of dispatching his own guidon north with Bates, hoping that it might fool some Bantag scouts into believing he was with the northern feint. It made it damn difficult now to be spotted.

Lying on the ground beside the guidon was Jack Whatley, pipe clenched between his teeth, clutching what was left of his right leg, which was shattered just below the knee.

"How is it, Jack?'

"Hurts like hell, worse than the one I took at Gettysburg."

"Just rest easy, Jack."

"Hans, shouldn't we stop here for the day? The boys just had one hell of a fight. Worst than Spotsylvania, almost as bad as Hispania. They need a break."

Hans shook his head.

"It's just past noon, Jack. Six hours of daylight left. We can make another ten miles. Maybe get ahead of what's coming up behind us."

"We're going to lose a lot of boys doing this, sir. A day here and we might be able to patch some of them up enough to move."

Hans said nothing, knowing that Jack was not talking about himself.

Silently he looked around at the shambles of the corps.

Three, maybe four thousand dead and wounded in the few furious moments of the battle, maybe another five hundred to a thousand in my own square.

Rifle fire still rippled from the flanks and forward, where skirmishers were again deploying. Though they had shattered maybe two umens in the fight, there were thousands of warriors left, some of them still running, but many were forming up again just beyond artillery range.

Going over to a limber wagon, he climbed up and raised his field glasses, sweeping the horizon, focusing in on the northeast. It was hard to tell, it was almost as if he sensed rather than actually saw a dark line on the horizon. Twenty, maybe twenty-five miles? How many?

Hans climbed down.

Hans sighed and knelt by Jack, putting his hand on his shoulder.

"I'm sorry, Jack," he whispered. "They need a field hospital and Dr. Weiss, and we don't have either. There's more of the bastards closing in from the northeast. We have to keep moving."

"Good God, Hans, you're talking about leaving a thousand or more men behind."

Hans sighed. "If a man can hang on to a horse,

we'll dismount half our mounted units, but he has to be able to ride."

He hesitated for a moment. "You can take my horse."

Jack grimaced as one of his staff tightened a tourniquet above the shattered knee.

"Don't think so, Hans."

Hans knew his friend would reject the offer. He was tempted to take him anyhow. Jack was a damn good corps commander, a month in a hospital and he could be back in the fight. But the hospital was still over a hundred miles away by land, then five hundred by ship. And there was the cruel bottom line, that if he made an exemption for Jack, what would be said by the hundreds left behind—that rank did have its privileges. This was the Army of the Republic, and officers, no matter how high up, had to share the rations, the wet ground, the filth, and the risks faced by the lowest of privates. If it ever became different, the Republic would never be quite the same.

"I'm thinking about forty thousand men, Jack."

"I know, Hans, fate of the game. I'd do the same."

Hans looked back toward the ravine.

"Twenty rounds for each man who stays behind. Maybe they can buy us some time. This is a hell of a position for men with rifles."

As the columns headed out Hans struggled with the wish simply to move ahead.

"Keep them moving," Hans snapped to his staff. Reining his mount around, he trotted to the back of the square, the men in the ranks looking up at him, knowing what he was doing, and parting to let him pass.

The column slowly pushed on as he headed back to the ravine. The air was thick with the smell of blood and torn bodies. Bantag corpses had been dragged out and piled up along either bank to act not only as a barrier, but also as a taunt.

Hans got off his horse and walked up to the edge of the ravine and knelt. Fishing in his pocket for a plug of tobacco, he held it out.

"Care for a chew, Jack?"

Jack smiled and shook his head.

"Got my pipe, Hans, never could stand chewing, bad for the teeth. How your wife allows you to kiss her is beyond me."

Whatley tried to smile, hiding the pain coursing through his body.

"Anything you want me to take back to . . ." he paused.

"Olga," Jack quickly slipped in, covering for the fact that Hans could not remember Jack's wife's name. He shook his head. "Don't believe in that farewell-letter routine. Too melodramatic, my friend. She'll know I was thinking of her."

"Anything I can do?"

"Well, if you could arrange for a new leg, that would be a fine place to start."

Hans lowered his head. "Jack, I just wanted . . ."

"No need to explain, Hans, I know. I'd do the same if things were different. You've got to get the rest of the boys out."

Hans nodded. Raising his head, he looked down the length of the ravine. Nearly a thousand men were waiting for the final act. Most of them were silent, a few moaning or crying softly. Hans forced himself to look into their eyes. He saw rage and bitterness in some but what was worse was understanding on the part of so many, a forced smile of encouragement, nods of recognition from faces that he knew from other fields of strife.

He slowly stood up and raised his field glasses, looking again to the northeast. There was definitely something there. The rain of the previous three days kept the dust down; otherwise, he could have spotted them from forty, even fifty miles away, but they were there and coming on, most likely reaching here by dark.

Hans knelt again and lowered his head to whisper.

"It won't be long, Jack. Three hours, maybe four. They'll see the carnage and come on hard, wanting revenge."

"Long way from Antietam, isn't it?" Jack sighed. "Gettysburg, took one in the chest there, thought I would die for sure, but I came back, remember?"

Hans nodded, saying nothing.

"Funny, survive all that, only to die in this stinking ditch on a damn world Lord knows how many billions of miles from home. Damn, wish I could just see Vassalboro one more time. Take a canoe and fish on Webber Pond in the evening."

"Maybe you will after this," Hans whispered, patting his friend on the shoulder.

"Getting religious on me, Hans?"

"No, just a thought. Maybe we go where we really want to go after it's over."

"Like to believe that, Hans, but don't know if I can"—he chuckled sadly—"but hell, I guess I'll know soon enough."

Hands trembling, he fished in his haversack, pulled out a tin of matches, and relit his pipe.

"Watch your flanks as well," Hans said, and he nodded toward a scattering of mounted Bantag who hovered just beyond rifle range, having re-formed after their defeat. "They'll be looking for vengeance. Most likely wait, though, until their friends come up with reinforcements."

"Let 'em try. There's one of them I'd love to see again." Whatley absently patted his shattered knee.

Hans looked down at the dozens of unconscious men lying along the sides of the ravine.

"Don't worry, I know what to do for them," Jack said, and his composure wavered for a moment. "Hell of a war, damn it. At least the Rebs would give ya a drink, and patch you up the way they did me at Gettysburg. Not this. Just don't like the idea I'm going to be dinner for them bastards."

He forced a smile through his tears.

"Hope some bastard chokes on me."

Hans, unable to speak, patted his friend on the arm and stood.

"God be with you, Hans Schuder."

"And with you."

Hans climbed back into the saddle, snapped off a salute, and reined his mount around, glad that no one could see his tears.

Chapter Nine

Vincent could see that Ferguson was nervous as he slowly paced back and forth behind the land ironclad and battery of guns while waiting for Kal to arrive. Jack Petracci, who had just finished the first demonstration flight of the two-engine short-range airship, strode over to join them.

"Good machine there, Chuck," Petracci announced. "Handles well, sharper turns."

"Still not fast enough," Chuck replied. "I want my new engine design on it before you go back out to fight."

Jack nodded, and the two started into a technical conversation which quickly lost Vincent. Figuring it was best to leave them alone, he edged over to where Gates and one of his artists were busy sketching the scene for the paper. Vincent, smiling, motioned for the sketch pad, and the artist handed it over. Vincent leafed through it. The artist had a good sense of detail; the new biwing design for the airship was rendered to perfection, and a close-up front view of the land ironclad, though roughly drawn, was sketched with the crew standing next to machine so that scale was clearly shown.

"I have some bad news for you, Gates," Vincent announced.

"What's that?"

Vincent tore the sheets of paper off the pad the artist was working on, crumpled them up, and tossed them on the ground.

"This is a military secret and will stay that way."

"Come on, Vincent, you can't do that."

"As acting commander on this front, I've just done it," Vincent said with a smile. "If these damn things work, there's no way we want any details in the paper, ever."

"Damn it, Vincent, everyone in Suzdal knows about the machines. Hell, they're made right here. I've got to report something."

Gates smiled as if he had suddenly drawn a trump card. "And besides, the colonel gave me permission to print some pictures just before he left for the front."

"All right, all right," Vincent replied, nodding toward the land ironclad. "But I want to see your drawings distorted, make it bigger, guns sticking out in every direction, and no details about armor."

"Vincent, aren't we getting a bit too nervous about all this?"

"Gates, how many thousands of our comrades died back on Earth because of the loudmouthed press I can't even begin to imagine."

"Listen, Vincent, you didn't even join the regiment until damn near the end of things, so don't pull that 'comrade' line on me. I was with the Thirty-fifth from the beginning; you weren't."

Vincent did not react to the taunt—he knew that more than one of the "old hands" resented his rapid rise over them in the race for promotion.

"You're right, Gates, but I am in charge here now. This Ha'ark can read, and a week from now your paper will be in some soldier's haversack up at the front." He didn't add in the details, the thought of a field of dead, the Bantag butchering them, and a copy of the paper being carried to Ha'ark.

Gates stood silent for a moment, then reluctantly nodded.

"You can be the most reasonable newspaper man I've ever met," Vincent said with a smile.

A carriage came over the crest of the hill behind them, and Vincent snapped to attention, the battery gunners, land ironclad crew, and Chuck following suit. Kal, putting his stovepipe hat on, stepped down from the carriage, and walked up to Chuck, shaking his hand.

"So you think you have something, do you?"

"Yes, sir, but you know how these things go. They work until you try them for real, so I hope you understand if it goes wrong."

"I saw the airship flying on my way over here."

"Still some problems, but it should be ready to go in a few more weeks."

"I want it now," Vincent interjected. "It leaves on the trains heading out later today."

Chuck looked over at Jack Petracci, who was walking back to his airship and shouting orders to the ground crew.

"Vincent, it hasn't been shaken down yet. That was the first flight."

"There's no telling how it might help us. I want it up at the front."

"Jack will scream bloody murder; the ship isn't ready for combat."

"We're in a crisis of the worst kind here. He'll understand."

"What about our other miracles?" Kal asked, nodding toward the firing range and cutting the argument short.

Vincent looked over at Jack, wondering if his abrupt order had just been a death sentence for one of his oldest friends with the regiment. He pushed the thought aside; there was no time now for such sentiments. Airships were needed if his plan was to work, and that meant Jack had to fly, whether the machine was ready or not.

"Ready for you to watch, sir," Chuck announced and, leading the way, he took the visitors over to the ironclad crew.

"Sir, you remember my assistant, Gregory Timokin?" Chuck said, nodding toward the ironclad commander who stood at rigid attention.

"Your father, blessed be his memory, and I were old friends," Kal said warmly, extending his hand.

"I know, sir. Father used to tell me stories about the two of you back in the old Boyar Ivor's court."

Kal smiled and leaned forward. "I hope you're not repeating some of them."

"I wouldn't dare, sir."

Kal laughed as he stepped back from Gregory to examine the ironclad.

"Is this ready to fight?"

"We just finished the changes on the drive system, sir. It's ready."

Kal motioned that he wanted to step inside the machine, and Gregory leapt forward to open the side door. The president, removing his hat, bent low and scrambled through the hatch, Gregory, Chuck, and Vincent going in behind him.

Vincent felt a sense of uneasiness as Gregory slammed the hatch shut, as if the doorway into a tomb was being sealed behind them. Though it was still early morning, the air chilly and dry after the storm of the last three days, the inside of the machine was already uncomfortably hot, laden with the scent of steam, oil, grease, and coal.

The boiler filled most of the aft end of the machine, the heat from the firebox and the glow through the open firebox door giving the interior of the machine a hellish feeling. The forward gun, a cartridge-loading ten-pounder occupied the space toward the front.

Chuck leaned over, features pale, and, clasping a pink-tinged handkerchief over his mouth, started to cough.

"Chuck, get out of here right now," Kal ordered.

Without waiting for a reply, Vincent, who was grateful for an excuse to get out of the machine, took Chuck by the arm and forced him to the door, leading him back out.

Sitting down on the ground, Chuck gasped for breath, Vincent kneeling by his side.

"After we ship out today you can take it easy for a while Chuck."

"A long rest, that's what I need," Chuck whispered, his breath rattling, coming in short gasps.

Vincent watched him intently, not expressing his fears as his old friend leaned forward, coughing, spitting up blood.

"Once Timokin gets his command in battle, make sure the machines stay together," Chuck whispered. "Don't split them up. Still don't like idea of you taking our new flyer up, we lose the element of surprise. Wanted them massed as well."

Sighing, he fell silent, looking down at the ground.

"Wish I could go up to the front with you, find out what happens."

"I'll make sure you get the full reports."

Chuck looked at him wanly and smiled.

"We'll see," he whispered, and struggled back to his feet as Kal, perspiration streaming down his face, emerged from the ironclad.

"Frightful machine," Kal announced. "Now let's see how you plan to stop them hairy devils."

Chuck slowly walked over to a limber wagon, motioning for a gunner to open the lid.

"Give me a solid shot, then load."

Chuck took the ten-pound bolt, walked back to Kal, and handed it to him.

"Standard ten-pound shot, sir, wrought iron."

Behind him the gun crew slammed the round into the breach, followed by a powder bag. Vincent knew that the lieutenant in command of the piece had been nervously sighting and resighting it, but he checked it once again after the interrupted screw breech was slammed shut.

"The first target we'll shoot at is three inches of armor," Chuck announced, "what we think they have mounted on the front of their land cruisers. Notice, sir, that it's mounted vertically, no deflection."

"I suggest, gentlemen, we get behind some cover." Ferguson motioned for the group to get behind a freshly raised breastwork.

The gun kicked back, followed an instant later by a bell-like clang and shower of sparks, a piece of the shell arcing back over the heads of the observers. Vincent had his field glasses trained on the shield, already knowing what he would see. There was a deep dent, but it had held.

The second shot, aimed at a shield angled back to simulate the front of the land cruiser, did even less damage, the bolt skidding up the side in a shower of sparks.

Two more guns, twenty-pounders, were now brought into play. The round cracked the vertically mounted shield but, like the lighter ten-pound round, skidded off the angled siding.

"A twenty-pounder might shake them up at two hundred yards," Chuck announced, "if the round strikes at a right angle. Any type of deflection over ten degrees or so and again there's a problem."

Chuck looked over at Vincent, who realized that his friend needed help since he was short of breath and going into a coughing spasm.

"The one I saw us knock out," Vincent interrupted, "was hit by a fifty-pound muzzle-loading Parrott at approximately three hundred and fifty to four hundred yards, hitting the side armor. The problem is the rate of fire of a fifty-pound muzzle loader is, at best, a round every two minutes, and that's with a crack crew. Unfortunately, the only fifty-pounders we have are mounted on the ironclads, some of our fixed fortifications, or the armored trains. There's not a single field unit in the army. The only reason we had that piece in action was that we stripped it off a ship and moved it by rail. Remember, we are talking about a piece that weighs over six tons. It is simply not usable except in a fixed position."

"In other words, useless for offensive actions," Kal interjected.

"Yes, sir. In a field action, if we let a land ironclad get to under two hundred yards before we can damage it, they've won. Their riflemen will decimate the gun crews at that range and they know that tactic. We might knock out one ironclad, but before our gun crew could reload, the surviving ironclads will be inside our lines. It was hell near our fieldpieces, made worse by the ironclad gunners pouring canister in on us. Our gun crews were ripped to shreds."

"So what is the answer, Chuck?" Kal asked.

Chuck looked back nervously at the ten-pounder gun crew and nodded.

"Load it up," he gasped.

The loader ran up from the caisson, cradling what looked like a white shell with a dark base, and slid it into the breech.

"Let's try for the sloped armor," Ferguson announced. The lieutenant commanding the piece nodded and brought the gun to bear on the target, stepped back, and looked at Chuck. Vincent trained his field glasses on the armor, holding steady as the gun fired.

Again there was a flash of light, and, to his amazement, as the flash and puff of smoke disappeared, he saw a hole drilled clean through the armor.

He looked back at Chuck, who was grinning nervously.

"What the hell was that?" Vincent asked.

Chuck led the group over to the limber wagon and motioned for the loader to bring out a round. Vincent took it, noticing a needlelike point at the top of the round, which then disappeared into a casing of what seemed to be papier-mâché.

"What the hell is this?" Vincent asked.

"It's made of spring steel, the best we've got. The problem with the old shells are they're made of wrought iron and shatter on impact. They're also too broad. I wanted a narrow point of impact, all the kinetic energy of the shell focused at a single point."

"It looks like an arrow," Kal said, taking the bolt from Vincent.

"Well, it sort of is, sir. We had some shells back

on Earth called Schenkl rounds. They had a papier-mâché section designed to engage the rifling. The papier-mâché disintegrated as the shell left the barrel. It set me to thinking. On this shell here I have a lead plate that rests on the back of the round to absorb the explosive charge, the papier-mâché sets the shell spinning as it goes down the barrel, then it peels away. The fins on the steel bolt keep the round on track, and it punches clean through. Actually, I'm not sure, but I think it melts when it hits the armor and then burns through it, spraying the inside with molten fragments."

"Range?" Vincent asked.

"Ten-pounder, sloping armor or deflection shots out to two hundred yards, twenty-pounder to three hundred. Straight-in shots on vertical armor, the ten-pounder will nail it at over three hundred and fifty yards, the twenty-pounder at five hundred."

"Damn good," Vincent cried. "Not what I'd hoped for, but pretty damn close."

"Well, it's the best I could come up with for now. We're going to use up a hell of a lot of good spring steel—it'll cut into our rifle production and a few other things—but I could have several hundred rounds ready to go in less than forty-eight hours. The molds are already made, and the crews standing by to start pouring."

"And you just thought this up overnight?" Kal asked, incredulous.

Chuck shrugged his shoulders. "Well, sir, ever since Hans came back with the report, I've been toying around a bit. Vincent here finally came back with the figures I needed, and so I thought I'd give it a try."

Kal shook his head.

"Amazing how war brings this out in us."

"What's that, sir?" Chuck asked.

"Our creative ability to kill."

Chuck didn't know how to react, but Kal put him at ease, patting him on the shoulder. "We'd all be dead if it weren't for you, Ferguson. Keep thinking up better ways to stop them."

"What I'm trying to do, sir," Chuck replied.

"Now, I've orders from your wife, you ride back in the carriage, no bouncing around on a limber wagon. Get aboard, son," Kal said, urging Chuck over to the carriage and helping him up. Kal looked at Vincent and motioned for him to take a walk, and the young commander fell in by his father-in-law's side.

"Think it will work?"

"Chuck said it, sir. One thing to test it, another thing in the field. It increases our range, but still not out as far as I'd like. Their riflemen can still pepper our artillery, or they can hold back and shell us with those new mortars of theirs. I think the tactic is to hold these new artillery bolts till they get close, then knock out as many of their machines as possible in the first few minutes before Ha'ark catches on."

"Once he realizes it," Kal replied, "he'll use the same thing on us."

"Undoubtedly," Chuck replied, "or beef up his armor—any number of responses. It'll work once, then that's it. The other problem is we could go through three hundred rounds in a couple of minutes. I'll most likely allot them to the best gun crews and make sure they're in the right place at the right time. That and place some of the rounds with our own land ironclads if we can rig them up with brass cartridge loads in time."

Their walk had carried them downrange, and Vincent stepped around the back of the armor plate and examined the hole.

"Hell for anyone inside a machine when this busts through," Vincent announced. "Whether it's boiling steel or still solid, it will bang around inside, tearing you to ribbons."

"That's the general idea, isn't it," Kal replied coldly.

"Something like that."

"By the way, there's additional news," Kal said. "It just came in over the wire."

"What?" Vincent asked nervously. Every moment he spent away from the front was an agony, his fear being that Marcus might try to engage before Vincent brought up the rest of the reserves and the dozen land ironclads.

"It's Hans."

"What?"

"He's not moving north. A courier broke through to Marcus this morning. Two arrows in him; he died within minutes after delivering the message. Hans is moving south, pushing to the end of the Green Mountain range and the shore of the Inland Sea. He aims to take Tyre."

Vincent looked at Kal, incredulous.

"Tyre?"

"Makes a hell of a problem it does," Kal said wearily. "The Cartha ambassadors made it clear that if we even cross into their territory, it's war."

"Damn them; they should be fighting alongside us."

"I can understand Hamilcar's position, son. Merki on one side, Bantag on the other."

"Same as us."

"But they can't hold out, while we can. If they don't respond to Hans's move with a declaration of war, the Merki or Bantag will attack and occupy them. Hans's taking Tyre means war on another front."

"The hell with them. Hans made the right move," Vincent announced, delighted with the news.

"I'll keep the word from the Cartha ambassador; hopefully they won't know until we've all ready gotten him out," Kal replied.

"Another sea rescue?"

"Something like that. I've sent for Bullfinch to meet with us to plan it out."

Vincent shook his head, then started to laugh.

"It's just like him. I should have thought of that. I feared he was being driven north. Breaking through to Andrew and Pat is one thing, but even then, Ha'ark could have kept Hans bottled up. This puts a whole different light on it."

Kal looked at him, confused. "I thought this was madness."

"It's genius, Father, pure genius," Vincent replied, dropping the formal sir in his excitement. "He's most likely sent some detachments north to confuse Ha'ark, then lit out in the other direction, what they'd least expect. The only damn problem is that most of the coast is inaccessible except for Tyre. It's a hell of march, 150 miles or more, fighting most of the way, but if he can get down to where the mountains end, Bullfinch can pick him up."

"Fifty thousand men?"

Vincent looked at Kal and shook his head.

"Make it ten, twenty at best," he said quietly. "Maybe twenty-five thousand. It'll take all the shipping we and Roum have, but you better start getting the ships down there now!"

"What I feared." As he spoke he looked back at Chuck, who was sitting hunched over in the carriage.

"He's slipping again."

"I know. Damn it, Father, send him away now. The climate above Roum might be better for him, maybe that villa Marcus loaned to Colonel Keane after the last war ended. He needs absolute quiet, bed rest, no worries."

"Chuck not worry?" Kal laughed, and shook his head.

"I know, I know, but we're losing him. Once we head up to the front, get him out of this city. The air here is getting worse all the time." As he spoke he motioned north, to where the factories lining the Vina River were pumping out dark plumes of smoke.

"Strange how you Yankees have changed our land," Kal replied. "As a boy I used to play in the meadows along that same river. Now it's brick, iron, shrieking whistles, a whole new city rising up that will soon be even bigger than Suzdal. Was it that way back in your Maine?"

"Getting that way. Price of progress, of freedom I guess."

A shower of sparks soared up from the ironworks as a batch of molten iron roared out of a furnace. A door in the gunworks swung open, a small switching locomotive emerging, whistle shrieking, pulling a flatcar upon which rested a freshly cast fifty-pound rifled Parrott gun, ready to be shipped to the front.

"This all came from his mind," Vincent said, "the tools of our freedom and our change. Perm save us if we lose him now."

"Perm save us even if we win," Kal replied softly.

"I'm starting to fear that the world is changing beyond anything I ever imagined."

"Fifty thousand men?" Bullfinch gasped, slamming down his mug of vodka so that it spilled across his desk and onto the deck of his cabin.

"That was how many he started with," Vincent said. "Five thousand more deployed north to try and throw Ha'ark off, muck things up a bit. You'll have to sweep the coast and try to pull them off as well."

Bullfinch shook his head and drained off what was left of his drink.

"A bit too much of that lately, Admiral," Vincent said.

"Now don't try and pull your Quaker temperance act on me," Bullfinch snapped. "I remember when you got pretty deep into the bottle yourself."

"So you lost a battle. Who hasn't around here."

"I might have lost the war," Bullfinch grumbled, staring into his mug.

"Maybe you did," Vincent replied coolly.

Startled, Bullfinch looked up.

"If you're expecting sympathy, go someplace else. I have a war to run here."

"Thanks a lot, Vincent."

"Maybe you did lose the war, getting caught by surprise off the bay like that. You should have been farther back."

"Damn it, don't you think I've fought it out a thousand times in my mind? Ferguson was working on a submersible, even said we should worry about Ha'ark doing the same. I didn't think they'd come on like that. And punching through our armor—I should have thought of that as well. I got too cocky."

"So, can you change it?"

"No, damn all to hell."

"I lost count of the number of men I've used up," Vincent said, his voice distant. "Defense of Roum, Hispania. A week ago, I ran a battery up to Fort Hancock, knowing they were going to get cut to ribbons, just so I could watch their land ironclads, observe their tactics, how much punishment the machines could take."

He paused and looked out the open gunport of Bullfinch's cabin to the flame-scorched walls of Suzdal, which still bore the scars from the Tugar and Merki Wars.

"I did a calculation," Vincent continued, his voice distant, almost dreamy. "Trade a hundred, two hundred lives to test Ha'ark's new machines, see how he fought, find out what he could do.

"Then there was this boy, on my staff, didn't even know his name . . ." His voice trailed off.

He sat in silence, listening to the gentle lapping of the river against the ironclad's hull, feeling the sway of the ship as a monitor, under full steam, passed down the river, its bow wave and wake rocking Bullfinch's flagship, *The Republic,* in its mooring.

"Make those kinds of calculations every day. Is this worth one life or ten thousand. Will I trade a regiment or a division for this piece of ground which the day after will be worthless steppe again."

He looked back over at Bullfinch.

"You made the same calculations and lost."

"Scared to death it will happen again, Vincent. God, when I saw two of my ships go up, and then the pounding, splinters slicing the deck, men cut in half, and there wasn't anything I could do to hit back."

He started to pour another drink and stopped, looking up guiltily at Vincent.

"Now another rescue, not a thousand like we tried with Hans the first time, but fifty thousand. He's starting to make a habit of this kind of thing."

"Figure on twenty, maybe thirty, if at all," Vincent replied. "He might have stolen a march on them, but they're mounted and he ain't. The last fifty miles or so will be hell. No way to take the wounded, fighting every step of the way. Make it twenty thousand."

"Vincent, I've got ten ironclads here, twenty-five other ships. All of Suzdal and Roum combined might have another hundred merchant ships and some old galleys, we might be able to squeeze out twenty, but it will be rough."

"When are you leaving?"

"*Chesapeake* is already on her way," Bullfinch said, nodding toward the monitor which had just passed. "I'll sail later today. I've telegraphed Roum and told them to be ready to have all their ships rendezvous with us in three days. But damn all, it still might not be enough."

"If so, you might have to leave someone behind," Vincent said coldly.

"And you know Hans will stay this time if that's the case. Poor old Gregory had to trick him last time."

"I know," Vincent replied. "Look, Bullfinch, we'll worry about that when the time comes. I need those corps and will need them badly. As fast as you pull those people off, get them to Roum. If we don't get Pat and Andrew out, we'll need every man we can get to form a fallback position."

"And if we don't get Pat, Andrew, and the men with them out?" Bullfinch asked.

Vincent sighed. "I guess I'm in command, and we lose the war. Ha'ark will be in Roum before winter. Same stands true even if we do get them out, but don't get Hans's men out, there'll be no reserves. As it is, I'm stripping all of Sixth Corps off the western frontier. That will give me three and a half corps to try and pull this rescue off. I'm leaving later today. Fourth Corps is already in Roum, the last elements of Sixth Corps leave with me, along with the land ironclads and Petracci's airship."

"And if the Merki come back in from the west?"

Vincent shook his head and chuckled.

"We'll be fighting on the banks of the Neiper once again, with your monitors all that's left to stop them."

"We're in the shit, aren't we?"

Vincent chuckled sadly. "Most definitely my friend, most definitely."

Andrew stepped back as the courier reined in his mount, mud spraying up around the horse.

"Their flanking column's two miles out, sir. General McMurtry is asking permission to disengage."

Andrew nodded. "Tell him we'll meet at the rendezvous this evening."

"Yes, sir!" The courier tugged his horse around and, kicking up yet more mud, galloped back up the road leading into the woods to the north.

"Don't know if this damn rain is heaven-sent or a devil's curse," Emil shouted, trying to be heard above the shrieking of a train whistle as it lurched out of the Port Lincoln train station, pulling twenty flatcars loaded down with six batteries, the gunners huddled under shelter halves tied off around fieldpieces and limber wagons in a vain attempt to block out the driving rain.

Trotting alongside the track, the horses for the batteries were being led west, more than one of them carrying a footsore infantryman riding bareback and hanging on for dear life.

"You really should take the train, Andrew," Emil said, continuing the argument he had been pressing earlier. "Don't hold much with this theory that getting wet makes you sick, but you've been pressing yourself pretty damn hard."

"No room for Mercury on the trains, doctor," Andrew said, nodding to his mount, "and he won't let anyone else ride him. Besides, Pat's up forward now. I think I'll tag along with the boys pulling back."

"You don't have to set any examples here, Andrew."

Andrew smiled. "But I do, doctor, I do. No one's getting left behind, we have trains to get them out, at least till the final rush, and I want to make sure it stays that way."

A gust of wind swirled across the Port Lincoln rail yard, and in spite of the driving rain, sparks danced around Andrew from the piles of supplies burning by a siding, the air thick with the smell of smoke and kerosene.

The whistle of the last train in the station shrieked, the engineer leaning out of the cab and waving to Emil.

"Get aboard now, Emil. I'll see you in three days."

"Take care, Andrew. Be careful and don't do anything stupid."

"Me, dear doctor?"

"You're a walking violation of the law of averages, Keane. Don't go rolling the dice again."

Andrew laughed and patted Emil on the shoulder as the old physician climbed up into the command car, which was crammed with the serious cases from the hospital.

A distant rattle of musketry echoed from the woods. Looking up, Andrew gauged the sound.

Stepping back from the train, he waved to the engineer. Pulling down on the whistle, the engineer eased in the steam, the wheels spun, grabbed hold, and, with a lurch, the train started down the track and out onto the main line. As the boxcars loaded with wounded and the last of the infantry from the rear guard drifted past, Andrew stood at attention, returning their salutes.

Stepping away from the track he looked down toward the sea. The spectacle had an apocalyptic quality to it that held Andrew's attention. The warehouses, which had been fired earlier in the day, were now smoldering ruins, clouds of steam and smoke blanketing the side of the hill, rolling black clouds swirled up from the hospital, while in the harbor explosions erupted, flashing bright in the gloom as what was left of *Petersburg* and *Fredericksburg* blew apart. The Bantag blockade ships had moved in closer, and, as he watched the shadowy beetlelike forms of the ships, another broadside erupted, shells arcing overhead to explode in the woods beyond.

"Damn poor shooting," Andrew said disdainfully, now that the worry of a lucky hit on one of the trains was over. Looking to the east, he could see dark forms moving on the far side of the ravine . . . forward skirmishers of the Bantag host advancing up the road. A flash of light detonated as one of the riders triggered a mine, the distant boom of the hundred-pound shell echoing a dozen seconds later.

"Well, it's all over," Andrew announced. "No sense in hanging around. Let's get the hell out of here."

One of the boys on his staff nodded toward the door of the headquarters. Andrew stepped back into the building for a final look around. There was a scattering of papers on the floor, the door into his room in the back open, the clock still ticking, the wall map, marked with pins and tape showing the ever-tightening pocket they were in, still hung on the far wall.

"Go ahead, Vasili," Andrew said.

The boy could not help but let the flicker of a smile appear as Andrew walked out. Upending a five-gallon can of kerosene, the boy emptied the contents out, flinging the can into Andrew's office. Pulling out a match, he flicked it to life with his fingernail, lit a newspaper, then tossed it on the floor, stepping back out.

"Enjoy yourself?" Andrew asked.

Embarrassed, the boy looked around.

"It's all right," Andrew said. "It's almost like burning down your school."

The boy nodded, ashamed to admit his incendiary fantasies.

Swinging up onto Mercury, Andrew grimaced at the clammy feel of the wet saddle soaking through his trousers. Pulling his slouch cap down low, rain beading off the brim, he led the way along the track, pausing for a moment to look behind him as flames licked out the doorway of his headquarters.

Another volley erupted from the woods to the north, this time closer. A fieldpiece clattered out of the forest, drivers lashing the horses, the caisson and gun bouncing into the air as they went over the tracks. A troop of cavalry followed. Mounted infantry appeared along the flank to the north, filtering out through the trees, weaving their way through the cluttered streets, their horses shying nervously as they dodged around the smoldering ruins of the town.

"Colonel Keane?"

Andrew barely recognized the commander of the Third Suzdal Mounted Rifles as he reined in. The young officer, the son of an old Boyar, was covered from head to foot in mud, an ugly gash creasing his face from forehead to jaw, blood mixing with the mud.

"You all right?" Andrew asked.

"Bastards shot my horse out from under me. Had to kill one of them to get a new mount."

Andrew looked at the horse and saw that the saddle and trappings were Bantag. He wondered if his young officer had checked to see what was in the ration bag behind the saddle and thought it best for now not to mention it.

"Just a little shaken, sir. I think we better get a move on. They might be spreading out ahead of us again."

"Lead the way then," Andrew said.

The cavalry officer swayed in the saddle, his guidon bearer reaching out to steady him.

Cursing, the officer shrugged off the help and urged his horse up to a canter. A rifle ball fluttered past, followed by two more, and, looking back toward the flaming town, Andrew saw several Bantag riders emerge from the smoke. Horsemen around Andrew turned, raising carbines and firing, dropping one of the skirmishers into the muddy street as the other two pulled back into the smoke.

As they continued down the track more men emerged, pulling out of the forest to gallop down the road, deploying after several hundred yards to form a screen. Crossing over a low rise, Andrew could see the last train out receding into the distance. Sparing the time for one final glance at Port Lincoln, he saw that what was left of the town was already in enemy hands.

There goes a year's worth of building and planning, Andrew thought sadly. A fleet gone, supplies to keep an army in the field for weeks, a hundred miles of rail, and nearly three thousand dead. He turned Mercury about and continued westward toward Ha'ark.

"Damn all, I wish I was going with you." Chuck Ferguson sighed, pulling his collar in tight against the wind-driven rain whipping around the station platform. The latest storm had swirled up in the afternoon and by evening had turned into a bitter-cold downpour. A wracking cough seized Chuck, and Vincent looked over anxiously at Jack Petracci, who was holding up an umbrella to try to shelter the young inventor.

"You think Andrew would be crazy enough to allow you within a hundred miles of a battlefield?" Vincent replied.

"Just, well, maybe there are better ways of going than this," Chuck said weakly.

"The hell with that," Vincent snapped back angrily. "For starters, wandering around out here in the rain is just courting trouble. Now get the hell back into the station."

Chuck, ignoring the warning, stepped past him and started to walk down the length of flatcars, looking up at the artillery crews who stirred and came to their feet at his approach.

"Remember, you can kill at over three hundred, but try and let the range close to two hundred yards, boys. Try to avoid deflection, aim 'em straight in. And keep those shells dry; otherwise, the papier-mâché will melt off."

Vincent turned away, knowing it was senseless to argue, and walked up to Kal, who stood in silence, watching the loading of the last three trains, which were taking a division of Sixth Corps to the eastern front.

"They're tough men," Vincent announced, "mostly veterans, hardened by being out on the western frontier. They'll do well."

"Do you really think you'll get them all out?" Kal asked.

"Not all of them, Father. Some, not all."

"We're bleeding ourselves white out there." Kal sighed.

"You know, if you start to waver, if you fall for anything that Ha'ark is feeding you, it's over."

Kal looked past Vincent and gave a friendly wave to a company of infantry who were marching past, several of the men obviously friends of Kal's from long ago, replying with ribald jests about the infamous tavern owner's wife.

"So few of my friends left now," Kal continued. "Try to keep them alive a bit longer."

"I'll try my best."

"You know, I was thinking about it this morning, when I couldn't sleep. I got up and walked about the White House. Remember when it was the palace of Boyar Ivor?"

"I remember. I was part of the company that escorted Andrew the first time we paid a visit here."

"Ivor wasn't such a bad old character. I think he half wanted to make some sort of agreement with you folks; just there was always the Tugars. Funny, I look back on that time when I was just another damn peasant, surviving by telling bad jokes and singing songs off-key, the palace fool. It wasn't such a bad time then in a way."

Vincent looked at him with a worried expression.

"I look at us now. Our whole society has become a machine of war. I sometimes wonder if we could even survive without war. It's like we're addicted to it, like those poor wounded veterans who've become morphine addicts. And here we go again."

Kal gestured toward the Suzdal rail yard. Crates of supplies lined the track, waiting to be loaded aboard when the trains that had moved Fourth Corps earlier in the week returned. One of the trains had five double-length cars on it, the Republic's answer to Ha'ark's land cruisers, the machines covered with tarps, the mechanics who had been working on them for weeks gathered around Chuck, who had wandered over for a final inspection. With the wind from the west, Vincent could hear the low mournful whistle of a steamboat heading down the river, pulling a dozen empty barges, puffs of smoke showing on the far side of the city.

The old earthen fortress line around the city was showing signs of disrepair, rivulets of muddy water eroding the sides in the downpour. Something to remember there, Vincent thought, get work crews out on them. Even if it's women and children, the Merki could always raid now that the frontier has been all but abandoned.

Vincent pulled out his pocket watch, checked it, and looked over at the stationmaster, who nodded in agreement.

"Time to get going," Vincent announced.

The ritual had been played out so many times that he found he really didn't feel anything from it anymore. Tanya and the children were back at the White House. She had learned long ago that tearful farewells at the station were not within his range of emotions.

He extended his hand to Kal, who clasped it warmly, drawing Vincent into the traditional Rus embrace and kiss, which he accepted woodenly.

"Take care, my son."

Vincent stepped back and saluted formally. From the corner of his eye he saw a women coming through the press, and Vincent walked up to her.

"Mrs. Keane, you shouldn't be out here like this."

She forced a smile.

"Well, Vincent, I've decided I'm going with you. The hospital here is in fine shape. I'm needed more at the front."

"Ma'am, the colonel wouldn't appreciate that."

"Frankly, Vincent, I don't care what the colonel thinks. It's my duty as well, and I'm going. I'll be on the hospital train going back later tonight."

Vincent could see that there was no sense in arguing. Her decision was a logical one. As head of the hospital system now that Emil was trapped behind the lines, it was her duty to be forward.

"Vincent. You know Andrew's always counted on you," she said softly.

"I know."

"No, that's not how I wanted to say it. Of course he knows you'll do everything to get those boys out, and him along with them. It's just, don't lose sight of things out there."

"Ma'am?"

"You're almost too good at what you do. Take Pat. He's a loudmouthed Irish bruiser, and Jesus knows I love him for it, like my da in many ways. Yet even in the thick of it, he always thinks of his men above everything else, how to spare one more life. Do you understand what I'm trying to say?"

Vincent stood silent and lowered his head, leaning forward slightly as a gust of icy wind whipped around him.

Stepping forward, she kissed him on the forehead. "Bring as many back as you can."

Unable to reply, he stepped back and, to her embarrassment, saluted her as well.

"All aboard!" The cry echoed down the station platform. Soldiers, rifles slung over shoulders, hurriedly said their final good-byes, clusters of families gathered around them in the pouring rain. Train whistles shrieked as Vincent moved through the press and ascended the narrow iron steps into his command car. Swinging the door open, he saw the men and officers of his headquarters company looking toward him, and he motioned for them to stand at ease.

Walking the length of the car, he slipped into the small private compartment and slid the door shut. Taking off his rain-soaked poncho and hat, he settled down and looked out the window.

Kal was still standing in the rain, hat off, raised in a salute. A band, standing under the protection of the station porch, was playing "Battle Cry of Freedom," sounding tinny and distant. The train lurched and eased out of the station, rumbling through the maze of tracks onto the main line, slowly gathering speed as it crossed over the bridge spanning the Vina. Looking up the valley, he saw the earthen dam for the reservoir, the factories below the dam belching dark clouds of smoke as the forges turned out yet more locomotives, rails, cannons, rifles, and shells. In the years since the Merki War a whole new city had sprung up around the works, rows of brick houses going up on the surrounding hills, spreading across the open ground where the Tugar Horde had once camped during the siege.

The dam stirred memories of the act he had performed, which had saved Suzdal, and the tens of thousands of Tugars who had died as a result. There was a time when the killing had frozen his heart. Then there was the moment when, as Weiss later put it, he had a breakdown of nerves as a result. And now? Funny, there was nothing but the war and for now, that was enough.

"Damn cold for this time of year."

Hans Schuder didn't even bother to reply as a battery commander squatted next to him, extending his hands to warm them on the flickering fire. The rifle fire along the picket line on the south side of the square flashed silently, the reports drowned out by the driving rain and rolling booms of thunder rumbling across the night sky.

Hans looked at the exhausted men around him, huddled in dark bunches around the flame, rain dripping from hats, a few of them curled up in the mud, so exhausted they were fast asleep in spite of the wet and cold.

"Bantag don't like it much either," the commander continued. "Just before dark, when they charged us, you could see their arrows had no punch. One hit me here"—he pointed to his chest—"barely nicked me. Guess it makes their bowstrings stretch or something like that. Lucky for me, I guess. Hell, had two of them things dug out of my leg—one at Hispania, the other at the Ford."

Hans grunted, too weary to reply.

"How much farther, sir?"

"Farther?"

"To, you know, we get to the coast and get picked up?"

"Honestly, son, I don't really know."

The artilleryman looked up at Hans, and Hans realized that the boy was the battery commander who had pushed his guns up into the gully two days ago.

"Four, maybe five days," Hans continued. "We're more than halfway there."

The commander sighed and absently kicked at the edge of the smoldering fire with the toe of his boot.

"Damn, thought we'd be closer by now. The mountains are getting lower on our right."

"We've got to get down to where the plains reach the sea and there's a harbor. That means Tyre," Hans said, knowing he had to say something. One moment of irresolve or a display of despair on his part could ripple through the ranks like a plague.

"Why not try and force some of the passes right over there?" The artilleryman nodded to the ridgeline, which showed up for an instant in a flash of lightning.

"They're blocked, all blocked. We get caught there, break our formations up, and we're trapped. Out here, we're keeping them back. We'll get through."

The rain slackened for a moment and Hans could hear the low rumbling growl of the Bantag nargas, echoing in the night. They had taken to blowing the horns all night long, most likely to try to keep his men awake and unnerve them. At this point, though, no one seemed to really care anymore.

Groaning as he stood up Hans slowly stretched, cursing the rheumatism and the ache of the old wounds. Walking through the mud, he passed encampments of the reserve regiments in the center of the square. A few of them had managed to keep fires going, but most were in the dark, men sleeping in clusters around the regimental flags, which had been planted in the ground to mark their positions. Another flash of lightning revealed the southern line of the square, and he strode toward it. Men were sprawled out on the ground, some under shelter halves, or grouped under caissons and ammunition wagons—half the regiment supposedly awake, while the other half slept. Farther forward, a hundred yards out, he could see the occasional flash of a rifle, where a picket fired to keep back Bantag probes. The old Horde fear of night action seemed to be dropping away the farther south he pushed, and, in spite of the storm, there had been half a dozen flare-ups during the night.

A rifle bullet snapped past, humming like an angry bee and nicked the brim of his hat. Instinctively, he ducked low and chuckled. After all this, he thought grimly, to get killed by an unaimed shot fired in the middle of the night. He stood back up again, surprised that his knees actually felt a little weak after the scare.

"Hans, you all right?"

"Fine, Ketswana, fine," Hans replied, a bit embarrassed.

"Thought it hit you for a second, scared me." Ketswana came up to Hans's side, deliberately standing in front of him, while half a dozen Zulus of Hans's headquarters company spread out around them.

"Just had a report a few of the bastards actually slipped clear into our lines a few minutes ago. You never know who's out there," and even as Ketswana spoke one of his men raised his rifle and fired into the dark. Another rifle bullet whistled by, passing between Hans and his friend.

Hans nodded and turned back toward the center of the square, no sense in risking lives.

He looked over at Ketswana and realized that, in spite of the storm, he could make out his friend's features. Dawn must be approaching.

"Pass the word, time to get up. I want to get moving before full light—we've got another long day ahead of us."

Cursing violently, Ha'ark the Redeemer paced along the wharf, watching as the ironclad, moving slowly as it plowed through the whitecaps, turned into the narrow harbor. Once clear of the storm-lashed sea, the ship leapt forward up the narrow cove for the last quarter mile, then slowed as its engines reversed. Even before the squat black vessel was tied off, Jurak was through the hatch and at Ha'ark's side.

"You're late," Ha'ark snarled. "Everything, everyone is late."

"The weather, Ha'ark. You can plan everything else, but you cannot plan for this." Jurak pointed to the heavens, where dark, low, rolling clouds raced overhead.

"It should be easing up later today," Jurak continued, and, even as he spoke, a shaft of sunlight poked through the clouds to the east for a brief instant before disappearing again as a cold shower lashed across the harbor.

"It still gives them the advantage. They're moving by rail and we are not. The weather doesn't matter to them. Keane is most likely a full day's march ahead of you."

Jurak nodded. "I have half an umen, mounted troops, pressing fairly close, but he did manage to get ahead of us."

"By how much?"

"Two days."

"Damn all, how!" Ha'ark roared.

"We had to fight through 150 miles of forest after crossing the river, and there's only one real road and the railroad bed to move our horses on. I still have seven umens all the way back out in the steppe waiting to deploy. It's a quagmire. I'm pushing artillery forward as fast as I can, and that's making it even worse. There's ten and twelve horses now to a single piece."

"What about the rail line?"

"Weeks before we get that running again. Every bridge is blown, track torn up. We didn't capture any engines or rolling stock."

Jurak stood before Ha'ark as if waiting for an explosion.

"The plan was for you to flank them and cut them off."

"Ha'ark, I moved as planned and attacked as planned but their red-haired devil, this other commander of Keane's, kept one step ahead. He's a masterful foe. I understand he's the one who fought the retreat from the Merki. He learned his lessons well."

"I'm disappointed in you," Ha'ark growled. "If

you were not my companion from before, I'd have your head."

"You may take it at any time," Jurak replied defiantly. The standoff continued for several long seconds. Ha'ark looked back at his staff, glad they had not heard the exchange, for if they had, Jurak would have to die.

"You press too far," Ha'ark hissed.

"I have sustained sixty thousand casualties in this campaign. It's like ancient history in our hospitals, Ha'ark. I've seen warriors get their limbs hacked off without anesthesia, gangrene is running rampant. I'm losing some of my best-trained soldiers to mere scratches."

"The Bantag know no different," Ha'ark replied. "It is different for you and me."

"That doesn't change what's happening to the warriors I'm responsible for. It's like stories we read in school about the wars of the Second Empire. They die like flies, and by all the gods the stench of it can be smelled for miles. Nothing we saw in our war back home comes even close to this barbarity."

"This is home," Ha'ark snapped. "We are never going back to the old world. This is home; this is our empire."

"At least you still say 'ours,' " Jurak said.

"If you wish to challenge, go ahead."

Jurak shook his head.

"No, I never wanted it the way you do. I'm more than happy to be second, that way I do not bear the responsibility so heavily upon my soul."

"If you want to leave this fight, you're free to do so."

"No, not that either," and his voice was soft, hollow. "I've come to hate them now, maybe even more than you. You received my report about what happened on the bridge."

"You were a fool to press so many in like that, the trap was so obvious."

"The blood of my warriors was up. I could not stop them. It was murderous, no honor in that killing"—Jurak looked away—"murderous bastards."

Ha'ark smiled.

"Now you are finally seeing what I saw. This is not some petty dynastic struggle, two princes fighting over a province, a hill, a filth-encrusted village where we died and then, when it's finished, they drink together again and trade stories of the game they played over our bodies. This is a war of annihilation, and in such war there is no honor, no glory."

Ha'ark indicated his staff.

"We feed such tales to them. I give one of them a bauble, a title, and the others rush out eager to risk death so they too can be thus honored. It has always been with such things that armies are led.

"And because of such things, I will announce your campaign a glorious victory, though you know the truth of that."

Even as he spoke Ha'ark made a show of patting Jurak on the shoulder so that their staffs nodded, Jurak's with obvious relief that their commander had not fallen and they along with him.

"And what of the other campaigns?" Jurak asked hurriedly, struggling to contain his annoyance at Ha'ark's display of approval.

"The first of the steamships will be up late today," Ha'ark replied, and again his anger started to flare. "Two days late."

"The weather Ha'ark, the weather. You're dealing with low-pressure steamships, not oil-fired high-pressure turbine engines. Any kind of sea, and they're down to a crawl."

"The front to the south?"

"Schuder," Ha'ark snarled. "I can't get any accurate report on where he is. Bakkth in his airship claimed he saw elements of their army pushing north. I have a full umen engaged in the passes. There are reports Schuder is with them, then other reports of part of their army moving away, to the south."

Jurak nodded. "It'd be like him to do the unexpected. How big is this force to the south?"

"I'm not sure. Bakkth never got that far south."

"And what are you going to do?"

"As originally planned. I've detailed one umen of rifles and ten land cruisers to land down the coast."

"Wouldn't they serve better here?"

"The force against Schuder was nearly all mounted bows and no artillery. It took sixty days of riding just to position them. I want more modern equipment brought to bear wherever he is. There'll be enough coming here in the next two days to secure this position. Blocking forces on the ridge to the west of the junction and to the east. With the reinforcements coming, we should hold while you move to crush them from behind."

Jurak nodded wearily.

"I'll try."

"I want the attack pressed no later than tomorrow. Even now Keane is deploying to the east of me. At least two of their umens are moving into attack position. On the other front Bakkth reports nearly thirty trains coming from the west, loaded with troops, artillery, and—I suspect—land cruisers."

"They have them?" Jurak asked, incredulous.

"And why shouldn't they. It's been nearly five moons since Schuder escaped. That's precisely why I wanted to press this attack now. Bakkth reported seeing five flatcars covered with tarps, same way we move ours. They'll be up by late today. We need to press the attack now."

"Ha'ark, I've tried to explain to you, it's chaos."

"It's chaos for them, too, damn it! I have only three umens here. One covering the east, one the west, the other the south. Tomorrow I should have at least three more and by late tomorrow, twenty more land cruisers. If I can hold my position and force them to attack frontally, we'll slaughter them by the tens of thousands, but you must bring your force up to attack the rear of Keane's line now. We must put the pressure on him, force him to attack head-on."

"Ha'ark, my warriors are exhausted."

"So are theirs. It is a matter of will now. We must break their will. Bring them up, damn it! Bring them up. Keane is in that pocket and I want his head. Once he is dead, they'll crumble. We must crush him tomorrow!"

Chapter Ten

"He's picked his positions well," Andrew said as he swept the next ridge line with his field glasses.

"Aye, damn bugger, looks like bloody Cold Harbor. You'd think he studied under Lee."

Andrew nodded as he focused on the outer line. The Bantag were well dug in, the forward trench an ugly swath of black earth zigzagging across the open fields. In front of the trenches abatis were in place, while farther up the slope, behind the front line, was a second line of fortifications, earthen forts spaced every half mile, the dark snouts of artillery pieces projecting out of embrasures.

Where the railroad line had once passed, only the roadbed was left, the crossties and track torn up, the material used to strengthen the Bantag defensive line.

"It looks like this all the way from the sea right up into the forest," Pat announced. "Six miles of it."

"Any land cruisers?"

"We've seen smoke plumes down toward where Junction City is." He pointed off to the southwest. "My guess is they're holding them in reserve, ready to shift in whatever direction we try to attack. The problem is we had a patrol by the sea just report back in. They could see where Fort Hancock was and said there's dozens of ships coming in even now."

"His second wave up from Xi'an."

"That's what I figured as well."

"Another three, maybe four umens," Andrew whispered, remembering the old ratio that an attacking force, hitting a fortified line needed odds of at least four to one in their favor at the point of attack in order to have any hope of success, and even then one could count on losing a quarter to a third of the assaulting column. If Ha'ark managed to bring three more umens in, there was no hope of their getting through, and the swarm closing in from behind would tear them apart.

Andrew sniffed the air and looked over at Pat. Pat said nothing, merely pointing across the shallow valley to where a plume of smoke was rising. Andrew focused on the smoke and swore softly. A dozen bodies were suspended from a wooden tripod, dangling head down, while several Bantag were tending a fire, an impaled human body slowly turning on a spit.

"Bastards started doing that yesterday, as soon as we got here and began deploying. Tossed a few shells at them to stir things up, but as soon as they see one of our guns fire, they dive into a bombproof and come back out laughing. Wrong thing for them to do; it's just getting the boys' blood up for some killing."

Andrew nodded, looking toward his own line, which was dug in along the crest line, the men resting behind a shallow wall of breastworks which had been thrown up during the night. Most of the men were behaving like veterans, grabbing sleep whenever there was a chance. The few that were awake sat in quiet groups around smoldering fires, frying up some salt pork, drying out clothes, or cleaning their weapons. He could see they were worn, nearly two weeks of hard campaigning had taken a toll, uniforms were filthy, tattered, an occasional elbow or knee showing. He could sense an almost professional detachment on their part, and it was now impossible to distinguish between the veterans of Hispania and the new recruits who had joined the ranks since.

"Look like we did coming out of the Wilderness," Pat said, and his comment again conjured the worst of memories.

"And before Cold Harbor," Andrew replied. "We were never the same after Cold Harbor, and that's what Ha'ark's offering us over there, another Cold Harbor."

Still looking over at the Bantag lines, Andrew strolled along the crest, glad that the driving rain of the last three days had finally abated. A cold breeze was coming down from the northwest, driving the last wisps of clouds before it, the sky overhead a canopy of crystal blue. The narrow stream in the valley below was still swollen and muddy, but he could see where, in the last few hours, it was already starting to recede.

"How deep?" Andrew asked.

"Fordable in most places," Pat replied.

Andrew sighed, again training his field glasses on the enemy line. The same view, he thought, that the Merki saw when they came up on us at Hispania, forward line of entrenchments, heavier fortifications farther up the slope with artillery. And now it's us doing the attacking.

"Any chance around the flank?" Andrew asked.

Pat shook his head.

"They picked their spot well. Get into the forest, it's a tangle in there. Must have been a big fire swept through there twenty, thirty years ago, mad jumble of fallen trees, second growth springing up, precious few trails. We could push infantry through, but our wounded, the wagons." He shook his head.

"I managed to get a few scouts up around the flank, and they say it'd be a ten-mile march, single file in places, before we could even deploy. The head of that stream comes out of a stretch of bogs. A few regiments of infantry up there could play hell with us."

"So it's straight in then," Andrew sighed.

"Looks that way."

Andrew nodded, feeling trapped into a maneuver he never dreamed he'd be forced to commit to. By this time tomorrow the Bantag pushing up from behind would be pressing in. If he was not out of the pocket by then, it was over. He might be able to hold for two, three days, but all the time more and yet more of their eastern army would press forward while his own precious supply of ammunition was expended.

"When do we attack, Andrew?"

"Three tomorrow morning."

"A night attack. It'll be chaos."

"For both sides. It's our only chance, our only chance."

Feeling as if every bone in his body had been shaken loose by the thousand-mile train ride, Major General Vincent Hawthorne stepped down from the train, accepting he salute of the honor guard drawn up by the side of the track.

Stepping away from the guard, he looked up the track. A line of a dozen trains, over a half mile long, was up ahead, troops piling out of boxcars, artillery crews cursing and struggling with makeshift ramps pushed up against flatcars in order to maneuver their fieldpieces off.

"Vincent!"

Hawthorne turned, smiling, as Marcus rushed up, slapping him on the shoulder. The Roum general seemed to be such an anachronism, still wearing the old traditional breastplate armor, leather kilt and sandals, short sword strapped to his left hip, but on his right hip was a holster for a modern revolver, and a Sharps carbine was slung over his shoulder.

"How is it here?" Vincent asked, following Marcus to where their mounts waited. Suppressing a groan, Vincent swung up into the saddle.

"Madness," Marcus said with a chuckle. "Had a bit of a flare-up this morning, probing attack, but we held."

"Wanted to see if they could push us back. Must mean he's getting reinforcements in."

"What I thought."

"Any land cruisers?"

"None; he's keeping them hidden."

Vincent trotted alongside the track, weaving his way around columns of troops as they formed up under their colors.

"Wish we had a few days to get these men rested," Vincent said as he passed a regiment from Sixth Corps, the men struggling to help unload half a dozen boxcars stacked with wooden cases filled with small-arms ammunition. "Some of these boys have been on trains for damn near a week."

The dull thump of an artillery round detonating erupted on the ridge ahead, followed seconds later by three more exploding down the side of the slope.

"Must see the smoke from all the trains," Marcus said.

"Any flyers?"

"Too much wind, just one early this morning. Nothing since."

Vincent edged his mount around a tent city that was going up alongside the track, green crosses painted on the canvas to mark them as the hospital clearing area. A rail crew was busy on the far side of the makeshift hospital, laying a section of track for a new siding.

Coming to a low rise, he slowed for a moment to look back, the sight filling him with awe. More trains were coming in from the west, streams of smoke and steam whipping ahead of them, driven by the chilled wind. All the way back to the horizon they kept on coming, carrying a corps and a half of reinforcements, supplies and the precious special weapons of Ferguson.

Yet again he thought of Lee's famous quote, and, looking over at Marcus, he smiled. "It's good war is so terrible, else we would grow too fond of it."

"I just want to get Andrew and the rest out of this trap and get the hell out of here."

Vincent urged his mount forward dropping back toward the tracks and then up the long gentle slope past where men of Fifth and Tenth Corps had been digging in for over a week. Riding through the sally port of an earthen fort dominating the ridge, he dismounted and climbed to the top of a signal tower that rose thirty feet high in the middle of the parade ground. Marcus followed him up. Taking a pair of field glasses offered by one of the signalmen, he scanned the enemy lines.

He whistled softly as he looked across the open prairie.

"The bastard's been busy," Marcus said.

Vincent nodded, looking for any sign of a weak point along the triple line of entrenchments facing him. He carefully scanned the line, hope fading with the realization that the line of fortifications was cunningly laid, with interlocking fields of fire so that any point of attack would be enfiladed by earthen forts dug in along the distant heights. Raising his glasses, he scanned the far horizon. On a distant ridge he could just barely make out a dark zigzag line of earthworks.

"Are those the opposite lines facing Colonel Keane?"

"Yes, sir," the signalman replied. "You can just make out their fortifications along the ridge. The ground drops down from there, so we can't see beyond, but we did see signs of smoke earlier today. We think they were from trains, but we couldn't be sure."

"Ha'ark's land cruisers?"

"Seen half a dozen earlier today deploying behind their lines directly ahead, nothing else."

"Junction City, anything there?"

The signalman pointed toward the southeast. "Can't see where the town was, sir, the hills block it, but we did see smoke, like from engines."

The signalman leaned over the railing, squinting, then pointed.

"There, sir."

Vincent trained field glasses on where the signalman was pointing, slowly scanning back and forth. A wavery puff of smoke appeared for an instant, then he lost it. He braced his elbows on the wooden railing and found the smoke again. He started to count and after several minutes lowered the binoculars.

"Twenty, at least twenty of them coming up." He sighed.

"I counted twenty-four, sir," the signalman added softly.

Vincent looked to the west, where his own troops were still unloading, realizing that the smoke from the trains must be clearly visible to Ha'ark.

"Marcus, he knows we're going to attack," Vincent said. "We have to attack, damn it, and he's bringing the cruisers up to meet us."

He silently scanned the lines, counting the red pennants of Bantag regiments fluttering in the breeze, his attention focusing on the north.

"I reviewed your plan for the breakout," Vincent said. "It's damn good."

"Thank you, sir, I know," Marcus said, and Vincent looked over at the Roum general, who was twice his age. A flicker of a smile was on Marcus's features. There had been a time when he had been in terrified awe of this man who seemed like a legend from the time of the Caesars. The fact that Marcus had undoubtedly wanted Vincent's approval of the plan momentarily caught him off guard.

"Your Tenth Corps, with what's left of Fifth Corps in reserve, should continue to hold the line here. Sixth Corps will spearhead the attack, followed by Fourth Corps."

"I disagree with that," Marcus replied. "They're rested. Let Roum have the honor of this attack."

"If we pull them off the line, even after dark, Ha'ark might guess our plans. Please, Marcus, we'll need Tenth Corps to cover this front," he hesitated, "especially if things go wrong. The pride of Roum aside, we both know Sixth Corps is a veteran unit and there are half a dozen Roum regiments serving with it, Marcus."

Marcus said nothing for a moment.

"I'll agree to Tenth Corps in reserve and holding the position here, but I lead the attack. I've studied the ground, I know the plan."

Vincent again shifted his attention to the position in front, and, to Marcus's obvious surprise, nodded in agreement.

"You lead the flanking attack, I'll command from here," Vincent announced.

Marcus studied Vincent carefully.

"Why? I thought you'd put up an argument over that point."

"There's still one piece to this puzzle," Vincent replied absently, then fell silent as he focused his thoughts.

One more piece to make it work. The question was, what was Andrew preparing to do? He pondered the possible alternatives. Andrew's men would be exhausted after weeks of unrelenting combat. Their supply of ammunition would be limited. Andrew would most likely go for an attack straight in, there was no hope of a flanking maneuver through the forest; if he tried that, all the wagons loaded with his wounded would be left behind. He'll attack, maybe as early as tonight, and Vincent's attention fixed itself on that thought as he continued to examine the enemy line.

Our own attack won't be ready until tomorrow morning, Vincent realized. Until then, Ha'ark's attention has to be focused, not only away from our own flanking attack, but from Andrew as well. As he contemplated what had to be done, he felt a dark coldness in his soul at the price that would have to be paid.

It's just as I suspected, Ha'ark thought as he scanned the opposite line, shading his eyes against the late-afternoon sun. The reports had been coming in for an hour or more that an attack was building. An artillery round fluttered overhead, detonating with a thunderclap roar, spraying the air around him with fragments. Ignoring the screams of pain of one of his staff, whose arm had been torn off, he continued to study the line. Heavy planks were being laid across the top of their breastworks, another battery was moving into position, the crew unlimbering their guns on open ground, and now some troops were moving out of their trenches, running down the slope with axes, cutting aside the sharpened stakes blocking the way.

The damn fools were going to attack frontally.

Grinning, he slipped his field glasses back into their carrying case and waited.

"Just remember you're the best damn bloody regiments in the whole bloody army!" Vincent roared as he cantered the length of the column.

Dismounting, he turned his horse over to an orderly. A regimental band was playing "Gary Owen" the sound of it striking him as such a bizarre incongruity, an Irish drinking song, adopted by the cavalry serving in the Army of the Potomac, and somehow transported here, to this time and place, the tune picked up by the pipers recruited from the descendants of Irish who now served in the ranks, such a strange completion of a circle, he thought.

Drawing his saber he walked up to where the shot-torn standards of Second Division, Fifth Corps stood, the flag bearer looking at him nervously.

"Scared, son?" Vincent asked softly.

"Honestly, sir," the young soldier replied. "Scared to death."

"It'll be over soon enough, just stay with me, that's all I ask."

A horseman galloped to the front of the column and reined in beside Vincent.

"Marcus, what the hell are you doing here?" Vincent snapped.

Marcus motioned for Vincent to step away from the flag bearer and division staff.

"Damn all, Vincent, don't do this," Marcus asked, a note of pleading in his voice. "It's suicide."

"We have to fix his attention, convince Ha'ark our attacks will come straight in here."

"There's got to be a better way than this."

"Got any suggestions, then?" He motioned to the east.

"Ha'ark's obviously getting reinforcements in. We have to convince him that the full weight of our attack is coming in right here. That way his reserves will be here, and not waiting for you when you lead Sixth Corps in tomorrow morning."

Vincent looked at the column behind him . . . veterans of Hispania, and the disaster in front of Junction City. They were eager now for revenge, their blood up to the point that the all-but-certain annihilation that awaited them was not fully registering.

"We need a diversion, Marcus, and this is it, a diversion to hold Ha'ark's attention here. And, by God, if I'm going to order this attack, I'm going in with it."

Marcus fell silent and lowered his head.

"You're holding up the attack. Now get back to your post, damn it. You know what to do later."

"Don't go in like this, Vincent. Your job is to direct it from the rear. Damn all, you know Andrew would relieve you if he knew what you were doing."

Vincent slowly shook his head.

"I'm ordering this division into almost certain annihilation. I'm not going to stand behind the lines and watch it. These boys have to believe this attack is meant to carry the day, and that means I go with them. And Ha'ark—I'm willing to bet he's just on the other side of this hill. I want him to know it as well, that I'm here."

"You're committing suicide."

"If you had to order this, would you stay behind?"

"That's not the point, Vincent."

"It is the point, damn you, Marcus. Now get the hell back to your post."

"Let me do it."

"General Marcus Graca, get back to your damn post!" Vincent barked out the order so that it echoed along the line.

Startled, Marcus looked at the men drawn up in solid lines before him.

Raising his hand, he gave the old traditional Roum salute to Vincent, then saluted the colors behind him.

"May the gods be with you, Hawthorne." Tears in his eyes, he reached down, took Vincent's hand, then, spurring his mount, he galloped down the line, standing in his stirrups, clenched fist raised in salute, a cheer erupting down the line.

Vincent looked back at the line and held his sword aloft.

"For the Republic!" he roared, and pointed his sword toward the crest of the ridge. Turning about he started forward, massed drummers behind him picking up the beat.

Second Division, Fifth Corps, in spite of its casualties at the battle of Junction City, presenting a battle front nearly a quarter mile across and six ranks deep, started forward. Along the crest line, a hundred yards ahead, the massed batteries redoubled their effort, eighty guns pouring a near-continual stream of fire against the enemy position fifteen hundred yards away.

As Vincent reached the crest the guns fell silent, crews by their steaming-hot pieces, many with hats off, standing in reverent silence as the thirty-five hundred men of the division passed through their ranks and scrambled over the wooden footbridges laid down across the trenches. Formation broke down for a moment as men scrambled over the trenches, up over the breastworks, then weaved their way through the abatis. The first shells from the Bantag artillery and mortars started to fall, and Vincent stood silent, drawn sword resting on his shoulder as he waited for the division to dress ranks as if on parade. Skirmishers darted past him, moving at the double time down the slope, pushing several hundred yards ahead of the advance, and already there was a scattering of rifle fire as Bantag in forward positions opened up on them.

Seeing that the ranks had re-formed, Vincent raised his sword and again pointed toward the enemy position. Turning about, he set the pace, marching at a hundred and ten yards a minute . . . fourteen minutes to cross the valley of death.

As they passed down the slope the artillery behind him opened up again, shells screaming overhead, geysers of dirt erupting along the enemy earthworks.

Looking to his left and right he saw the line coming steadily on, wavering at points where men had to scramble around a hillock or tangles of brush, but then forming up again.

Smoke started to obscure the field, most of the Bantag artillery shooting high, but the mortar fire acquired the range and stayed with them as they advanced, the piercing whistle of the shells coming down, explosions crumping, men going down, ranks dressing to the center as holes were punched in the line.

A shell detonated to his right, spraying him with dirt. His guidon bearer dropped, screaming, clutching the stump where his right leg had been severed at the knee. A corporal burst from the ranks, tossing his rifle aside, and scooped up the colors. Rifle fire erupted, skirmishers darting forward, reloading on the run, following the dark forms of Bantag moving back up the slope, withdrawing into their main lines.

Reaching the bottom of the valley, he leapt down the muddy bank of the stream which divided the field between Bantag and human lines, the cold water coming up to his thighs. A body of a Bantag bobbed in the middle of the stream; a human skirmisher, clutching his stomach, was curled up on the opposite shore, looking at Vincent, wide-eyed. Scrambling up the muddy bank Vincent paused to look back as the first two ranks plunged into the stream, colors held high, bayonets gleaming red in the late-afternoon sunlight.

The lines plunged through the stream, geysers of water erupting as a salvo of mortar shells plunged in. Hitting the eastern embankment, men clawed their way up the muddy slope. The ridgeline disappeared in a cloud of yellow-grey smoke as the Bantag infantry opened fire. Dozens of men tumbled backwards into the stream, cursing, screaming.

"Who's with me?" Vincent screamed. "Who's with me?"

Holding his sword high, he started forward, moving at the double.

"They're insane!" Ha'ark cried, watching as the human waves struggled over the stream and, breaking into a slow run, started up the slope.

His riflemen were firing as fast as they could reload, popping breeches open, slamming in cartridges which many had laid out on the breastworks in front of their positions. Behind him, a mortar team concealed on the reverse slope loaded rounds as fast as they could be brought up from the caissons, the shots whistling overhead to slash down into the advancing lines, the gun commanders, adjusting the barrels higher and yet higher after every three to four shots.

It was difficult to see the humans as smoke from the explosions bracketing their lines rolled up the slope on the western breeze.

Ha'ark looked up at an observer positioned atop a tower that was fortified with sandbags.

"Any land cruisers?"

The observer, shading his eyes against the sun, scanned the lines.

"I thought I saw something, my Qarth, by the railroad track pass, but it's not moving forward!" The observer started to raise his field glasses to examine the position once again, then jerked backwards, the glasses shattering, his face exploding as a shell detonated on the tower.

What are they waiting for? Ha'ark wondered. Suicide to send unsupported infantry in like this.

The smoke parted for an instant, and he saw a gold-embossed flag moving forward, up the slope, an officer beside the flag, waving his sword, urging the human waves on.

Was this Hawthorne?

As he considered the thought the human looked up, as if gazing straight at him, and there was the sense of a cold, deadly hatred that was startling. This one was coming to kill him, he could feel that, an intensity of belief and hatred that felt more Bantag than human.

Vincent stood still for a moment, focusing his thoughts, driving all else out of his soul.

"I'm coming for you, you son of a bitch," Vincent snarled. "It's here, it's all here. It's not to save Andrew; it's to kill you."

The second flag bearer went down by Vincent's side. Scooping up the colors, he held them aloft. The first two ranks of his charge were disintegrating under the blasts of canister and scathing rifle fire. Men staggered past him, bent low, as if advancing into a gale. A drummer boy ran past, tears streaming down his face, mechanically beating his drum, which was shattered and hanging in tatters on his bloody thigh. He saw an old man cradling a young boy, crying, then collapsing as a round struck him in the chest. A sergeant ran past, screaming obscenities, urging the line forward, and disappeared into the smoke.

Looking back through the smoke he saw the rear ranks of his charge fording the stream; rifle fire, which was passing high over the heads of the front ranks, was plunging into the ranks farther to the rear. The distant slope was covered with blue-clad forms, a carpet of bodies stretching all the way back to where the artillery continued to work, firing in support of the advancing charge.

Men around him were wavering, slowing down, some of them raising their rifles to return fire.

"Keep moving!" Vincent roared. "Charge boys, charge!"

Waving his guidon, he started forward again at the run, holding the colors high.

A quavering scream rose up from the ranks, bayonets poised forward, all formation breaking down, the division sweeping up the slope at the run. The ground ahead seemed to stretch into an eternity, wisps of smoke swirling around him. A soldier sprinted past, screaming, the sound of his voice lost in the roar of battle. An explosion of blood erupted from his back; mechanically, the soldier continued for half a dozen more steps before he fell. Vincent leapt over his body, pressing on, no longer even aware if anyone was following. The smoke parted again, a Bantag was kneeling before him, blocking a path through a line of sharpened stakes, raising his rifle. An explosion erupted next to Vincent; the Bantag fell over. The soldier who had shot him, screamed in triumph as he rushed up and pinned the Bantag to the ground with his bayonet. The soldier flipped over an instant later as a spray of canister tore across the field.

Reaching the narrow path through the rows of sharpened stakes, Vincent slowed, turning to look back. A knot of men pushed up around him, beating at the stakes with rifle butts, knocking them aside, pushing through, casualties falling, some of the men tumbling onto the sharp points, shrieking, writhing as they were impaled.

Vincent could sense the charge disintegrating on the barricade, men piling up, falling, screaming, survivors going to ground, huddled behind bodies, rising up to fire, then ducking back down.

"Keep going!" Vincent roared. "Come on, keep going!"

Holding the colors aloft he started to push through the abatis, turning to look back at his men.

He didn't feel any pain, only a numbing blow as the rifle ball smashed into his right hip and cut crosswise through his body. His knees buckled. He slammed the staff of his guidon down, bracing himself against it, while driving his sword point into the ground with his other hand.

Locking his arms, he held himself up, looking back at his men. The world about him seemed to shift, everything slowing down, focusing in on details . . . one of his staff, openmouthed, screaming, coming toward him, then collapsing, a soldier standing, firing his rifle, fumbling at his cartridge box, a drummer boy sitting on the ground, hands clasped over a bloody face, an hysterical sergeant clutching the body of a comrade and shrieking, a lone soldier, standing, laughing taking deliberate aim, firing, then reloading, untouched in the storm of steel.

Men drifted past him, wide-eyed, madness contorting their features, pushing around him, collapsing, coming up, going forward again.

There was no pain. He looked down and saw that his mud-stained trousers were red, blood trickling out of his boots. Funny, he thought, where is it coming from?

He looked back up . . . the world was distant . . . unfocused, as if he was gazing through his field glasses from the wrong end. Not even aware that he was falling, he slowly sagged to his knees and pitched forward into the mud.

"Get him! Get him!"

Ha'ark, pointing his scimitar, urged his warriors up out of the trenches, sending them forward into the smoke. Hand-to-hand fighting erupted as his warriors surged down the slope, human soldiers coming up to meet them, firing rifles at point-blank range, clubbing muskets or coming in low with bayonets raised to impale the foes towering above them.

He could see a knot of humans gathering around the prone form, tearing the flag from the staff and using it as a litter, dragging him back. As quickly as one dropped, another leapt forward to pick up the bundle.

One of his warriors reached the group, cutting down two of the bearers before being clubbed down and pinned to the ground with a bayonet. Smoke swirled around, obscuring the fight, and he could sense that they were getting away.

Cursing, he slammed his fist down on the parapet.

Rifle fire continued to blaze along the line, smoke blanketing the ground around him. The attack had lurched to a halt, the survivors clinging to their forward position, crouched behind bodies or abatis which had been torn down and piled up into barricades. Artillery pieces in the earthen forts along his line had depressed their muzzles and, in some cases, were switching to shell, plowing shot in low, striking the frail barriers and scattering them like stacks of matchwood.

The light was starting to drop away, and, gazing to the west, he saw the rim of the sun sinking behind the hills, silhouetting another line forming up as if ready to go into the assault. The fire from their batteries continued unabated, some of the shots falling short to plow into their own men.

The ferocity of the attack was startling, a grim madness which he sensed was an act of wild desperation. He had what they wanted—Keane bottled up on the other side of his position—and they would bleed themselves white to get him out . . . it was precisely as he desired.

It was going to be here, a straight assault right in, following the line of their railroad tracks eastward. Moving through the trench, he reached a covered way which zigzagged up the slope and then down into the rear, his staff following.

Once over the crest the trench emerged into clear ground, where a dozen of his land cruisers were drawn up, wisps of smoke pouring from their smokestacks.

In the twilight he could see the railroad junction and beyond, on the southern horizon the slow-moving line of land cruisers coming up as reinforcements.

Ha'ark motioned his staff to gather around him.

"It will be here. They will assault through the night. We keep the cruisers in reserve."

As he started to pass orders for the night's deployment he walked to where the land cruisers were deployed. Most of the machines were barely functioning. The movement from the coast and the week of deployment in the field had overtaxed their feeble engines and they were already cannibalizing parts from a half dozen of the machines to keep the rest moving.

So damn primitive, he thought, but still there should be enough in them for one more fight. Let the fools bleed themselves white here, then in the morning unleash the land cruisers, shatter their line here, then pivot back on Keane.

"All reinforcements to here," Ha'ark announced. "Here's where they have the line of supplies. Keane will wait for a breakthrough. By tomorrow night Jurak will be up on the other side. Then we can finish them as well."

"My Qarth, all reinforcements?"

Ha'ark hesitated for a moment but the image of Hawthorne held him. He was the commander on this flank. That he led the attack himself showed his desperation. Shells from the bombardment by the humans continued to scream overhead, shrieking down into the valley below, scattering his rear-echelon units. The rate of fire amazed him, hundreds of rounds bursting every minute. They were trying to isolate this section for a breakthrough.

"They'll press through the night. It's here," Ha'ark announced.

"My God, Vincent, my God, why?"

Through the haze of pain he could barely see her, leaning over the stretch.

"Andrew would have." The effort even to speak caused him to gasp in agony, the pain redoubling to a level he did not believe possible as two orderlies took him by the shoulders and another two by his feet, lifting him onto the table.

He could hear Kathleen barking orders, but the words were unintelligible.

Turning his head he saw the tent filled to overflowing, casualties lying on the dirt floor, waiting their turn.

"Kathleen."

"Here, Vincent, I'm here." She turned back, her

face covered with a gauze mask, the kerosene lamp hanging above her head blinding, so that it looked as if she were wreathed in a halo.

"Them first, them first."

"This time rank gets a privilege," she said in English. "This is going to hurt for a moment, then you'll be under."

"I'm dying; save the others."

"You're dying and will die if I don't get in there now and stop the bleeding."

He felt something tugging at his leg and, lifting his head, saw two orderlies cutting his trousers off. He stifled a cry as they peeled back the blood-soaked pants. He felt a wave of embarrassment at his nakedness as Kathleen walked around to the side where the bullet had entered. She leaned over, then ran her hand across his stomach and groin, pushing down, trying to feel the bullet and the extent of damage.

A wave of red-hot fire erupted, a scream escaping him. She looked up, her eyes filled with pity.

"I'm sorry, Vincent. I know it hurts. Now tell me which hurts more."

She pressed down across his stomach, probing, watching his expression. Moaning, he gasped for breath, grateful when an orderly wiped the sweat from his eyes.

"How is he?"

Kathleen looked up just as Vincent saw Marcus standing on the other side of the table.

"You're not washed, get out of here now!" Kathleen barked.

"A moment," Vincent whispered. "Marcus."

"Here, Vincent."

"How bad?"

Marcus hesitated.

"How bad, damn it?"

"The division was cut to ribbons. They managed to get a foothold in the outer trench on the right and are still holding it. I've moved another brigade up to support."

"That's all I wanted," Vincent whispered. "And the Bantag? Are they biting?"

"Putting reinforcements in the line. Report just came in of a battery pulled from the edge of the woods where we plan to attack at dawn."

"You know what to do."

Marcus nodded.

"Out! Now!" Kathleen shouted, and two orderlies came up to Marcus.

"The only one that outranks her here is Death," Vincent whispered.

"Vincent?"

He wasn't sure if he had passed out or not, but Marcus was gone, Kathleen standing over him, leaning, her face almost touching his.

"Ma'am?"

"You're going to sleep now."

"Tanya, the children."

"Don't worry."

"You know what to do if . . ."

He could feel her lips on his forehead, kissing him gently, as if she was his mother tucking him in. Tears blinded him as the memory formed, wondering where she was, wishing she was here to make the pain and the fear go away.

"I will, now go to sleep."

A strange smell engulfed him, strange, sickly-sweet. He could see her, so far away now . . . floating like an angel.

* * *

As she cut inward, an assistant holding the flaps of flesh back, she tried not to think of who it was she was working on. How many hundreds, thousands she had cut into, she could no longer remember. But this one was different, still almost a boy in her eyes. If it had been anyone else, she would have whispered words of reassurance, had an assistant administer a shot of morphine, then placed him quietly in the tent at the rear of the hospital, which even now was filled nearly to overflowing. She could save six, maybe ten others in the time she would spend here, and as she cut in deeper and saw all the damage, a moan of despair escaped her.

Chapter Eleven

Streaks of fire burst on the western horizon, and even from twenty miles away Andrew heard the distant rumble of artillery carried on the westerly breeze.

"Pat, what the hell is Vincent doing over there?" Andrew asked.

"Diversion I think . . . I hope."

"One hell of a fight going on there," Emil interjected. "God, I hope that boy isn't doing a frontal assault."

Andrew said nothing, Emil expressing his worst fear. Would Vincent, out of desperation, throw his force in like that. The battle, which had started just before sunset, had been raging for hours. The boy had most likely seen the slowly moving column of smoke moving up toward where Junction City was located, just before sunset. Ha'ark was being reinforced, could that have pushed Vincent into an attack?

Only twenty miles, twenty damn miles, but it was as good as a thousand as far as knowing what was really going on. There was nothing to do about that now, Andrew realized. He had to stay focused on what was directly ahead.

Andrew stood silent, watching, sensing more than seeing the columns of men around him. All equipment had been muffled, tin cups thrown away, canteens wrapped with strips of cloth, rifles double-checked by sergeants to make sure percussion caps were removed so that no gun could be fired accidentally.

A scattering of rifle fire was popping up and down the line, skirmishers ordered to fire every few minutes, whether they saw anything or not, an occasional flare going up as if the line was nervous, expecting an enemy attack. But they were under orders not to let the rate of fire build up as a signal that a major assault was about to be unleashed.

"It's time, Andrew," Pat announced, breaking the silence.

"Give the order."

Three flares rose in quick succession just behind Andrew, tracing fire into the sky, two bursting green, the third one red. Half a dozen more flares were launched out toward the enemy position to make it look like they were simply checking to make sure no attack was coming in.

Whispered commands echoed behind him, and the first column brushed past to his right. He felt as if they were making far too much noise, curses echoing as a man tripped and fell, a comrade treading on his hand. On the left a rifle fired, followed instantly by a cry of pain, in spite of all the precautions someone had managed to go in carrying a loaded weapon, then accidentally discharged it.

Andrew looked anxiously toward the Bantag line, expecting at any second that it would erupt in a curtain of fire . . . but there was nothing, except the popping of the skirmishers down in the valley.

The column continued to plod past, wave after wave of men. The old familiar smell of an army wafted around Andrew . . . leather, horse, filth, the cloying sweaty stench of men who had not bathed in weeks and were now perspiring with fear. It was a trigger which set his heart beating faster.

A brilliant explosion erupted on the horizon and, for an instant, Andrew feared that the distant light would somehow reveal the columns moving down into the valley.

The telegraph key in the command bunker started to tap, the sound of it startling Andrew. After a minute it stopped, the telegrapher poking his head out from behind the curtain of ponchos that had been erected to hide the position.

"Message from the rear guard, sir. They're pulling in now. Report the Bantag line quiet on their side."

"So far so good," Pat announced.

"Once the shooting starts, it's bound to stir them up, though."

"They won't push in till after dawn. They're scared to death of the mines, and the caltrops will slow them down even more."

"Cruel way to treat horses." Pat sighed. "Never did like them devilish things."

"We better get moving; nothing more we can do here. Emil, once you get the word, you're going to have to move fast, remember that."

"We're ready to go, Andrew."

"Pat, don't do anything stupid. Otherwise, I'll have to come back for you."

Pat laughed softly and patted Andrew on the arm. "Last thing I want is to be a dinner guest for those filthy buggers. I'll be along, right behind the good doctor here."

Andrew whispered a command to his horse, and, with a gentle tap of Andrew's heels, Mercury moved forward and to the left, down to the railroad track where the first engine in line waited. Andrew's heart began to race. If the Bantag had second-guessed him, it'd all be over in a matter of minutes, their artillery tearing his advancing columns to shreds. Everything was based on one damn assumption, that they would not expect him to concentrate and throw everything he had into a single arrow point launched in the middle of the night.

Waiting next to the engine, he looked back to the east, where the first of the two moons was breaking the horizon. The light was most likely silhouetting the crest, and he wondered if the Bantag could see the movement of troops coming over the ridge.

A single cannon discharged on the opposite side of the valley, flashing silently. Long seconds later the boom rolled across the field. Another cannon fired, then half a dozen, the flashes of light revealing a dark swarming mass of men clawing up the side of the earthen fort which dominated the Bantag line.

"That's it, we're on the fort!" Andrew shouted. "Now go!"

The engineer standing in the cab above him pulled back on his throttle, the wheels of the train spinning, sparks flying. Mercury shied away even as Andrew urged him forward. Andrew started down into the valley, riding alongside the track. More flashes erupted ahead. At last there came the sound of cheering, thousands of men, screaming in rage, fear, the tension of the long hours of waiting broken at last.

The flash of the guns revealed the long, serpentine columns stretching all the way from the Bantag lines, down into the valley and back up toward the jumping-off place for the attack. Riding alongside the track, Andrew could see a red lantern flare to life, a signalman marking the midpoint in the valley where the ruined trestle spanning the narrow stream once stood. The engineer was already applying the brakes, sparks hissing out, and for a brief instant Andrew feared that he had put too much speed on the train and that it would plunge into the creek.

An artillery round thundered overhead, followed seconds later by half a dozen more rounds, the Bantag gunners drawn by the shower of sparks.

The train halted, and Andrew waited, holding his breath.

The first streak of fire rose from the flatcar behind the engine. Less than a second later the second rocket shrieked into the heavens, and in an instant the entire battery of eight hundred rockets, mounted on a dozen flatcars thundered to life, the gunners leaping from the cars and running in every direction.

Andrew watched in awe as night became day, the rockets soaring upward, the first six carloads pre-aimed to thunder down behind the enemy lines, the next three angled to strike beyond the left flank of the breakthrough, the other three to hit on the right flank. He could only pray that his engineers had accurately measured the distance from the middle of the valley to a point beyond where the breakthrough was occurring. He didn't really expect that the weapon would do all that much damage against an entrenched enemy. His only hope was that it would scare the hell out of them, and perhaps even trigger a panic in the same way it had terrified the Merki at Hispania. If so, it'd buy precious moments of time to widen the breach and secure the flanks, so that the ambulances and three thousand men detailed to carry the wounded could get through, followed by Pat and the rear guard.

An explosion rocked the next-to-last car, and Andrew flinched as half a dozen rockets skidded out at a right angle to the train, bouncing and shrieking past him so that Mercury panicked, rearing and nearly unseating him. One of them plowed into the rear of an advancing column of men and detonated.

Other rockets soared off at wild angles, some going straight up, others streaking off to the rear, but the vast majority winged out toward their targets, hovering in the night sky, trailing plumes of white-hot sparks, then shrieking down.

Hundreds of explosions erupted behind the Bantag line and along the flanks. To his horror Andrew saw where his advancing column on the flank left of the attack had obviously veered off course, a score or more of rockets raining down into their lines, but the close bombardment smothered an earthen fort blocking their advance, and, in the glow of fire, he saw the charge surging forward.

"Sir, better get the hell out of here!"

Andrew looked down and saw the engineer and his two firemen, looking up anxiously.

"Smashed the safety valve shut; she'll let go any second now!"

Andrew nodded his thanks and left the men in the darkness, urging Mercury across the stream, barely aware of his staff following in his wake. Going up the slope, he passed a scattering of casualties and just as he reached the outer edge of the Bantag abatis and entanglements an explosion detonated behind him, the engine boiler tearing apart.

Reaching the first entrenchment he passed a knot of dead and dying Bantag, human bodies piled up around them. Leaping the trench, he continued up the slope passing men cut off from their commands in the confusion, his staff shouting for them to keep moving west and rejoin the first unit they found.

Rifle fire thundered straight ahead and to his right as he passed through the second line. To his surprise the enemy position had been empty but as he approached the third line he had to zigzag back and forth to find a path where Mercury could get through the tangle of bodies.

As he crested the hill the valley beyond came into view. Fighting flared all around him. In the darkness it was hard to judge, but he sensed that his column was already a half mile in past the enemy lines.

"Signal rocket!" Andrew shouted.

Several of his staff dismounted and seconds later a green flare soared up, followed at thirty-second intervals by half a dozen more flares, informing Emil it was time to get the wagons loaded with the wounded moving.

"Colonel Keane?"

A mounted shadow came out of the dark, and drew up beside him.

"McMurtry, sir."

"Where's Schneid?"

"Don't know, sir. I think up forward; I saw the rocket and thought I should report in."

"How are we doing?"

"Clean through, sir," the division commander cried excitedly. "Caught the bastards napping, damn near into the first trench before they knew it. Second trench was empty."

"I saw that," Andrew replied, and the intelligence confirming the fact made him nervous. Ha'ark had somewhere around thirty thousand. Maybe five thousand diverted to the south, ten on either flank, a thousand warriors per mile of front, but dug in. Had he pulled back a reserve? If so, come dawn he'd have an organized force ready to strike back. That was the damnable thing about a night battle, and all that he could count on now was that Ha'ark was as confused as he was. For if he wasn't, come dawn, the trap would collapse in around him.

"Detail some of your men off here," Andrew said. "Get them filling in the trenches so we can get the ambulances through. Build some fires to mark your position."

"Yes, sir."

Andrew watched for a moment, realizing that in this action, his ability of command now only extended as far as he could see, which wasn't more than a few dozen feet. He'd have to trust to the training of his men and their desperation to break through, and the confusion of the Bantag who, even now, had to be reorganizing to strike back.

Startled by the ferocity of the rocket bombardment erupting on the horizon, Ha'ark waited impatiently for the telegrapher to find out what was happening to the east.

"Line is still down, my lord," was the only information he received as the long minutes passed.

The attack in front of his position had died out, but the humans still held sections of the first trench line. Bodies brought in revealed hat patches indicating there were elements of two different human umens attacking his line.

The reserves. What to do with the reserves that even now were marching up from the junction. They had been ordered to come straight here in anticipation of yet more frontal assaults. Now this new attack on the other front. Confused, Ha'ark stared at the eastern horizon, not sure what to do.

Refusing to dismount, Marcus followed the line of skirmishers as they moved, phantomlike, through the forest, flitting from tree to tree, the ghostlike quality of the advance enhanced by the ground fog rising in the early dawn. From half a dozen miles to the south came the dull thump of artillery, still firing along the central front.

He could sense more than see the solid wall of men moving behind him, two full corps advancing in columns through the marshy ground, the men reeling with exhaustion from the difficult night march into the forest, a regiment of cavalry before them, their riders bending low in their saddles as they ducked to clear low-hanging branches. A rifle cracked in front, shattering the silence, a flurry of shots erupting, the skirmishers before him darting into the fog. Deep-throated cries of alarm erupted from the woods—they were into the enemy lines.

Marcus nodded to the officer riding beside him.

"Go!"

A bugle sounded, and, with a wild shout the cavalry regiment spurred their mounts forward, officers drawing sabers, enlisted men holding revolvers high as they plunged through the woods, skidding around trees, leaping over fallen trunks.

Marcus followed, fire erupting ahead, bullets snapping through the branches around him. He rode down into a mist-shrouded hollow, skirting the edge of a bog where half a dozen riders were trapped, several of them dead, sprawled in the stagnant water. For a moment he feared that his plan was the height of tactical folly, that the whole thing was an exercise in madness, and doing, as Hans kept saying, the unexpected, was leading to ruin.

"The last thing they're expecting is a cavalry charge through the woods at dawn," he had argued, when laying out the details of his plan to Vincent. "It goes against all doctrine, and Ha'ark understands tactical doctrine. We smash in where they least expect us, in the way they least expect."

Marcus dodged his way around a tangled mass of half a dozen horses and troopers, all of them dead from a blast of canister. Then out of the fog and smoke he saw the Bantag line, a breastwork half a dozen feet high, made out of logs, tangled branches piled up as a barrier in front. Riderless horses by the dozens stood before the breastworks and for an instant Marcus feared that all his men had been shot down. But then he saw a cavalry guidon fluttering atop the breastworks. Dismounting, he pushed his way through the sharpened stakes and scrambled up over the side of the breastworks. Troopers were deployed along the line, firing into the smoke, some of them already climbing out and rushing forward. The trench was littered with dead Bantag, many of them obviously caught totally unprepared, clusters of them lying around still-smoking fires.

A cheer erupted behind him, and, looking back, he saw the forward edge of an infantry column coming out of the smoke, the front ranks wielding axes. Crashing into the abatis, they started to cut their way through, while lines of men snaked their way through the entanglements, scrambled over the breastworks, and pushed forward, linking up with the cavalrymen for the rush on the second line.

Rifle fire was intensifying, reports of artillery thundered through the woods, and in the rapidly rising light he could see the shadowy outlines of an earthen fort, men charging up the forward edge, dozens dropping from the enfilading fire of a well-placed artillery piece. Bantag gunners struggled to reload their piece but started to drop as riflemen around Marcus poured in a concentrated fire. The flow of infantry swarming around Marcus increased dramatically as engineering troops smashed lanes through the entanglements.

A regimental flag appeared atop the fort in the second line, went down, then went back up again. Wild cheering erupted, picked up by the men surging past Marcus.

A bugle sounded forward, the recall for the cavalry, and even as the infantry continued to surge forward, troopers began to return through the smoke.

Marcus grabbed a sergeant, bleeding from a scalp wound, as he came back over the breastworks.

"How is it up there?" Marcus asked, struggling to speak Rus.

The sergeant, realizing who was before him, snapped to attention, saluted, and broke into a grin.

"Caught them napping, we did. Some of us were into their second line before they even knew it. They're running, sir. Damn, they're running."

Grinning, Marcus dismissed the sergeant, who pushed his way through the swarm of infantry, bawling curses, shouting for his troop to re-form and mount up.

Marcus followed him and, sighting his staff, reclaimed his horse, reined his mount around, and edged through the flow of infantry. More reports filtered in from excited couriers, the breakthrough of Second Division, Sixth Corps was already angling down to the edge of the forest, the Bantag line rolling back.

"Stripped his reserves to the center, thank the gods," Marcus announced. The realization of that fact eased the guilt that had been torturing him through the night that Vincent's attack might have been worse than useless.

Passing out of the advancing lines, he rode for several hundred yards, drawn at last by the sound of men cursing, shouting. Coming up over a low brush-covered ridge, he emerged onto a narrow road. A cavalry man on foot whirled about, nervously raising his carbine, aiming at Marcus then sheepishly lowered his gun.

"Sorry, sir, we just had a bunch of them hit us." The trooper nodded toward several dozen Bantag and human bodies piled by the side of the road.

"The bridge?"

The trooper pointed up the road and Marcus urged his mount into a trot, weaving his way around a company of engineering troops, who were moving at the double, carrying rough-cut planks. A wagon was in the middle of the road, piled high with lumber. He moved around it, then reined up short as the narrow forest path sloped down sharply into a boggy stream. Mud-splattered infantry were deployed on the far side of the stream, holding the Bantag breastworks that had covered the approach, having swept in from along the opposite shore.

A squat, bald-headed officer, cigar clamped firmly in his mouth, stood by the edge of the marsh, pouring out an unending stream of obscenities in English as his regiment of engineering troops struggled with a pontoon boat in midstream, the men up to their shoulders in the brown murky water, stringing out anchor lines back to the shore. Before the boat was even in place a crew of thirty men hoisted a heavy oak beam onto their shoulders and started into the stream. As the forward edge of the beam reached the edge of the boat it was laid down on the gunwale and dropped into place, a heavy iron bolt dropped through a precut hole, securing the beam to the boat. Back onshore, where the other end of the beam now rested, engineers hooked iron cables around the butt and ran the cables back into the forest, wrapping them around the nearest tree.

Marcus dismounted and walked up to the officer, who paused in his nonstop swearing and saluted.

"Stream is wider than I was told," the officer announced in barely understandable Rus.

"How long will it take?"

"You damn stupid sons of bitches, cinch up that anchor line. Yes, you, damn it!" the officer roared, then turned back to Marcus.

"Half hour, sir, be ready in half an hour. Be careful, sir, still some of them bastards in the woods on the far shore."

Even as he spoke the warning a rifle shot cracked and the officer spun around, grabbing his arm, cursing even louder than before.

Infantry on the far shore opened fire, men sprinting along the riverbank, seconds later flushing out the Bantag sniper, his body sliding down the opposite bank and into the mud.

Holding his arm the officer went back to work, blood seeping out between his fingers.

Marcus turned away from the bridge and looked back up the narrow, muddy track which passed for a road. The path was jammed with wagons carrying the bridging supplies, men unloading planks and heaving them onto the ground to corduroy the approach to the bridge. Infantry streamed past on either side of the path, jumping into the stream to ford across, rifles and cartridge boxes held high over their heads, emerging on the other side, an unending river of troops surging forward to widen the breach in the enemy line. Engineering troops on the far shore attacked the breastworks with axes, picks, and shovels, clearing away the barricade.

The second stringer was laid out to the boat, followed within minutes by two more stringers which barely reached to the opposite shore. An unending line of men now raced from the wagons, carrying oak planks, which were thrown down across the stringers, bolts dropped in on either side, locking the planks to the stringers.

A telegraph crew came along the side of the road, stringing out wire, hammering spikes into tree trunks, hooking a glass insulator onto the end of each spike, wrapping the copper strand around the insulator, then moving forward. Couriers snaked through the woods, coming in with reports to Marcus, each dispatch filling him with a sense of elation. The breakthrough was continuing to spread out, infantry already moving out of the hills and onto the edge of the open steppe, reporting only light resistance.

With the telegraph hooked in, the signal company went into operation, reestablishing the link to Tenth Corps and the rail line. Marcus hovered anxiously, watching as the signals from the center came in, the operator first writing them down in Rus, a liaison on his staff then translating them into Latin. So far it seemed to be working. The barrage at the center was continuing, but ammunition was beginning to run short. In twelve hours the massed batteries had burned up nearly a quarter of all the artillery ammunition reserves of the entire Republic, and nearly all the ten- and twenty-pounder rounds which had been brought forward.

"Sir."

Marcus looked up to see the Yankee engineering officer standing before him, features pinched and pale.

"Bring 'em up, sir. It's ready."

With a sigh, the officer sat on the ground, looking around weakly, cigar still clamped in mouth.

Teamsters, cursing and shouting, with whips cracking, drove their wagons forward. Marcus watched as the first wagon went over the bridge, observing how the pontoon boat sank as it went over, engineers swarming around the wagon as it went up the opposite bank, leaning into the wheels to help it get up the steep slope. Wagon after wagon passed, clearing the road.

Finally, he heard them coming, the hope of the entire offensive. Stepping to the side of the road he saw the black monster appear out of the last wisps of fog that was breaking up as the day grew warmer.

The heavy iron wheels of the land ironclad rumbled over the corduroy trail, smoke puffing out of its stack, its six heavy, iron wheels creaking and groaning.

Marcus looked at the machine in awe. It was smaller than the Bantag machines he had observed. Like the Bantag machine, its main gun projected out of a gun port which could be slammed shut between shots. A small rounded turret sat atop the boxlike machine, a tarp covering the gun port, the ironclad's commander sitting atop the turret, snapping a salute off to Marcus as they slowly rumbled past. *Saint Mal-*

ady was emblazoned in Cyrillic on the side of the machine. The portal where the ironclad driver sat was wide-open, the driver leaning out, looking at the bridge ahead with obvious anxiety.

The machine started down the slope and everyone seemed to freeze in place, watching tensely as the ironclad started to skid until it slammed into the first plank of the bridge. The bridge surged from the impact, the entire structure groaning and shaking so that for an instant Marcus thought it had been snapped free of its moorings.

The ironclad stood motionless. Smoke puffed out, and Marcus looked up, wondering if the swirling column would be visible above the trees. The entire ironclad shook as the rear wheels began to spin, grinding against the corduroy roadbed, a log kicking up behind the machine. Suddenly it lurched free and started up on the bridge, which immediately sank under the weight.

The pontoon boat bobbed down as the forward two wheels of the ironclad crept onto the span, followed several seconds later by the middle wheels and then the rear drive wheels. As the ironclad crept toward the middle of the span the boat continued to sink until, finally, there were only a few inches of clearance between the gunwale and the water as the ironclad reached the middle of the bridge.

Pushing on it reached the far shore, the boat bobbing back up. With smoke belching from its stack, the machine crept up the opposite shore, crested the bank, and pushed on.

A cheer erupted from the engineers, Marcus joining in, finding it hard to believe that all of this had been planned by Ferguson and Vincent nearly a week ago and a thousand miles away.

Marcus went over to where he had left the commander of the engineering regiment, eager to offer his congratulations. The man was lying on the ground, as if asleep, a young lieutenant sitting by his side, tears in his eyes.

The lieutenant looked up at Marcus.

"He's dead, sir."

Stunned, Marcus looked down at the body.

"The wound; it wasn't that bad."

"His heart, sir. Dr. Weiss told him to be careful. I guess it was his heart."

Marcus looked up as a horse-drawn wagon, loaded with coal, went over the bridge, following the ironclad with a precious load of fuel.

Behind it came a battery of ten-pounders and then the next ironclad crept onto the bridge and crossed.

He turned back to the lieutenant.

"Send up the signal rockets; we have to let Keane know."

The boy drew away from his fallen commander and went to where some of his men had erected three vertical launch tubes, shouting for them to fire.

Seconds later the rockets rose, describing an arc through the narrow opening in the forest canopy cut by the stream, three red bursts igniting more than a thousand feet in the air.

"Every five minutes," Marcus shouted.

Getting on his horse and motioning for his staff to follow, he crossed the bridge, falling in behind the advancing column.

It was going easily, almost too easily. He was hanging nearly eight miles north of the rail line with only a thin screen of infantry occupying the line back toward where Tenth Corps was positioned. The question now was, what would Ha'ark do?

* * *

Feyodor sprinted across the field to join Jack, who was anxiously hovering next to the gas generator. They had finally started filling the airship with hydrogen an hour before dawn. The stench of sulfuric acid, which was used to cook the zinc oxide in order to make hydrogen, hung heavy in the air.

The portable hydrogen generator sat in the middle of an open field. A cordon of unarmed infantry formed a circle a hundred yards wide around the airship and gas generator to keep any curious onlookers back, onlookers who might stupidly strike a match. At least the morning was damp. He hated filling a ship on a clear dry morning, when the chance for static electricity was higher.

The first two bags of the airship were filled. A ground-crew member was on top of the ship, carefully looking for any leaks, but the other two bags inside the gas cylinder were only half-filled. The crew was preparing to charge the second lead-lined tank with acid, the men moving cautiously as they unloaded the five-gallon bottles of acid from their packing cases. The acid was then poured into a hundred-gallon tank attached to the side of a lead-lined box a dozen feet long, and a half dozen feet wide by four feet high. The box was filled with zinc shavings. Once the tank was filled and the box sealed shut, a valve would be opened to allow the acid to pour into the zinc-filled box. Hoses attached to the top of the box snaked toward the airship, and Jack anxiously paced along the hoses, waiting, knowing he could not hurry his crew with the dangerous work.

The tank filled, the crew stepped back while the sergeant in command opened the valve. Seconds later Jack saw a flutter run through the hose as it gradually expanded, hydrogen coursing through it toward his ship.

Jack finally motioned for Feyodor to join him.

"Signal just came in from Marcus. They've crossed the stream; the offensive is on," Feyodor announced.

"Anything from Keane?"

"Just the report of the rocket barrage. Smoke plumes indicate Ha'ark's moving his land ironclads north, though. They might be moving to cut Keane off."

"Damn all," Jack snapped. "We should have been up hours ago. Getting those damn wings attached held everything up." He motioned toward the wings jutting from either side of the airship. Nervously, he walked around the ship yet again, double-checking the anchor points where the bilevel wings were joined to the frame of the ship. The damn things had worked, but that was back at the base in Suzdal and not after a transport of a thousand miles. The ship should have at least half a dozen more test flights before they even thought about going into action, but the rumble of artillery fire to the east was argument enough against that.

He looked at the three red-painted boxes stacked beside his ship and the canvas bundles attached to them. When Vincent had first briefed him on the mission, he had thought it madness, but now, with the report from Feyodor that the assault was on, he knew with a grim certainty that they would have to go in.

He wanted to swear at his crew, to urge them on, but the simple laws of chemical reactions dictated the pace of things now, and he stood silent, watching as his ship slowly filled with gas.

"Are you certain you saw land cruisers?" Ha'ark asked, not even bothering to look at the courier who had just galloped up to his headquarters.

"Yes, my Qarth. It was coming out of the woods."

Ha'ark motioned for the messenger to leave, and he was again alone in the bunker, staring at the map spread out on the table.

Both of the moves he was facing were audacious, surprising. Keane had broken through and had advanced half a dozen miles, and now this, more than an umen of their infantry, with land cruisers coming out of the forest from the northwest, driving down to link up with the breakthrough.

So the attack on the center was a feint, a trick to draw his attention.

Gazing at the map, he struggled with the calculations. His reinforcements were coming up fast but had been ordered to move toward his position facing the human armies which had closed from the west. It was increasingly obvious, though, that the action here had simply been a masterful diversion. They were trying to link up with Keane by attacking out of the forest to the northwest. Studying the map, he extended the lines of advance. If his reinforcements moved quickly enough, there was still time to engage and cut Keane off.

Stepping out of his bunker he mounted his horse. The commanders of his land cruisers and the reserve umens watched him attentively. Raising his rifle high, he pointed toward the northeast and urged his mount into a gallop.

Chapter Twelve

"Andrew, I think you better come up here and look at this."

Following Pat's lead, Andrew urged Mercury across a narrow valley of waist-high grass and up a gentle slope to where a skirmish line of dismounted infantry were deployed in open order, every fourth man waiting just behind the ridge, each holding the mounts of his comrades who were on the firing line.

"Rather hot up there, so you better dismount," Pat announced. Weary after long hours in the saddle, Andrew was glad for the assistance of an orderly, who reached up to help him get down. To his surprise some of Pat's staff had started a fire of knotted-up hunks of dried grass and as he walked past them, one of the couriers offered up a cup of tea, which Andrew gladly took.

Crouching low, he went up to the edge of the crest and peered over.

A heavy line of Bantag skirmishers was in the valley below, concealed in the grass, popping up to fire a shot, ducking low, then reemerging again to fire another round after creeping several yards closer.

Once again he was amazed by the change in their tactics. There was no insane rush here. Rather, a steady, methodical pushing. Dark forms littered the valley and distant slope, the wreckage of their retreat, dozens of bodies of the men of the rear guard dotting the field, a broad swath of grass, several hundred yards across, trampled down from the passage of the troops, artillery batteries, and more than two hundred wagons bearing the wounded.

Looking to the northwest he could see wagons spread out across the open steppe, swaying white dots moving in a sea of green, surrounded by a disorganized trail of the walking wounded. Flanking columns protected the wagons, fire rippling along the lines where knots of Bantag warriors on foot harassed the retreat. The entire column was pushing toward a village nestled against the flank of a high conical hill. Advanced elements of Eleventh and First Corps were already approaching the town, where a firefight was brewing. Farther back toward the northwest horizon, three red rockets flashed then dropped away, the signal that was being sent up from the relief column, guiding him toward safety. The signals had started shortly after dawn, causing him to shift his retreat away from the west to the northwest. But they were too far away yet, at least six or seven miles distant from the head of his column.

A trooper came staggering off the firing line behind Andrew, clutching his chest, a comrade helping him into the saddle, mounting behind him, and leading the man away.

"Off to our right," Pat said, drawing Andrew's attention back to the fight. "Over there!"

Andrew put his cup of tea down and accepted Pat's field glasses. Raising them to his eyes, he focused where Pat was pointing, then looked back at his own retreating lines.

A bullet nicked past in the grass by his side, tracing a line through the green stalks, which popped into the air around him. A Bantag wagon was on the far ridge, and seconds later a puff of smoke appeared behind it.

"Damn mortars," Pat snarled, as the high, piercing shriek of an incoming whistled over their heads, the round detonating a hundred yards behind them.

Andrew continued to study the dark masses moving toward his flank. Land cruisers . . . it was hard to see how many, and he patiently tried to count the puffs of smoke, losing track after thirty when a gust of wind swirled the dark column together.

The cruisers were advancing in line, Bantag infantry deployed behind them in columns.

"Three miles, I'd make it," Pat said. "They'll hit the village just about the time our wagons push through. We've got about an hour at most before they hit us.

"Their rear guard's coming up fast." Pat pointed to the south and southeast. Andrew could see the dark columns of mounted warriors cresting the distant hills.

"They've got an airship up as well," Pat announced, tapping Andrew on the shoulder and pointing out the small dark cylinder moving up behind the column.

Sighing, Andrew handed the glasses back to Pat and slid down from the edge of the slope, curling up when a mortar round crumped down less than a dozen feet away, spraying him with dirt.

Startled, he looked over at Pat, who was grinning weakly as he brushed a spray of mud and grass off his uniform.

"Damn mortars. They can drop a round into a barrel."

The next shell detonated on the crest, and, seconds later, a shower of rounds exploded along the ridge. The last of the wounded were staggering off the crest, and Pat motioned for the skirmish line to start pulling back.

"They're going to get between us and the relief column," Andrew said, pointing to the south, where the first of the land cruisers was coming over the crest line, several miles away.

"I know, damn it. Andrew, you know what we might have to do."

Andrew looked at Pat and shook his head.

"We're talking about thousands of wounded, Pat, who can't move without help."

"We're also talking about the survivors of four corps."

"If they stay, I stay," Andrew snapped angrily. "I'll not have it said I left those boys behind to die, not with a relief column less than two hours away."

Another mortar round screamed in, and Pat fell forward, pushing Andrew to the ground, the concussion of the explosion lifting them up.

Pat stood back up, motioning for their staffs to get moving. Orderlies, leading their mounts, came up, and Andrew climbed back into the saddle, struggling to calm Mercury as two more rounds bracketed them.

Andrew beckoned for his staff to gather around him, the men looking up nervously as another mortar round shrieked overhead.

"We're stopping on the high ground," Andrew shouted, pointing to the conical, tree-clad hill across the valley. "We dig in there and hope that Vincent can break through. All of you ride, get to Schneid, tell him to abandon the attack on the village and get up onto the hill. Start digging in, and also try to push some couriers through to Vincent."

As he spoke he pointed beyond the hill, where, on the horizon, puffs of smoke still lingered from the signal rockets.

The last of the skirmishers came running down the slope, leaping to their mounts. "They're almost on us," one of them shouted. "You better get moving!"

His staff galloped off, only his personal orderly remaining, holding his guidon.

"Pat, see you on the hill," Andrew shouted, as he spurred his mount forward, galloping down the long slope, approaching the rear of the retreating column on the next ridge. Urging Mercury on, he weaved his way through the lines of wagons, which had backed up while negotiating their way down a steep embankment and across a swift-flowing stream. He tried to block out the screams of the wounded inside the wagons as they bounced down the slope.

"Andrew!"

Gaining the shore, Andrew leaned forward as Mercury bounded up the embankment and reined in next to Emil.

"We're getting cut off by the land cruisers," Emil announced. "Word just came back."

"I know." He pointed toward the conical hill. "Try and get the wounded into the woods up there. Get the horses unhitched from the teams and have the wagons upended as barricades."

"You know you could push on without us," Emil said.

"Us? Who the hell is *us?"*

Emil smiled.

"Keep them moving!" Andrew shouted.

Pushing on across the open fields, he passed columns of regiments, the front ranks breasting through the high grass, the men staggering forward at the double. Equipment littered the line of retreat, blanket rolls, backpacks, empty canteens, even bayonets and scabbards had been tossed aside, the troops stripped down to rifle, cartridge box, and their tar-covered haversacks which had been filled to overflowing with ammunition before the last of the ordnance wagons had been turned over to the wounded.

At the rear of the columns, exhausted and wounded soldiers struggled to keep up, comrades helping them along.

Spurring Mercury on, he started up the hill, pausing occasionally to glance back. The front of his column had already broken off the attack and was recoiling up the west and northwest slope of the hill. Pausing at a rocky outcropping, Andrew looked back along the line of retreat and saw his flanking units contracting, moving at the double. Pat's guidon stood out at the rear of the retreating column, positioned now by the stream, where the last of the wagons was crossing, a battery deployed by the guidon, firing at the line of Bantag infantry cresting the low ridge where he had been twenty minutes before.

Andrew urged Mercury farther up the slope where the ground began to steepen. He passed a clump of trees, a scattering of pines, with dozens of exhausted men sprawled under their shade. Edging his way around more toward the northern flank of the hill, he passed a rocky outcropping of boulders, some of them the size of small houses. A brigade of infantry streamed around him, the men deploying into the boulder field, Schneid galloping past below them, shouting directions, pointing out where the retreating brigades were to dig in. A battery of ten-pounders clattered up the slope, horses foaming, panting. The gunners swung their teams around, unlimbering the pieces directly forward of the boulders. The battery forge wagon came to a halt, exhausted gunners pulling picks and shovels from the back of the wagon and starting to dig in, while other gunners, armed with axes, attacked the nearest trees. A decimated infantry regiment came up the slope, their commander ordering the men to help with the building of the breastworks. Groans and curses echoed through the column, but the men set to work, knowing that a dug-in battery might very well decide whether they lived to see evening.

A wild shout erupted from the boulder field, followed by cursing and laughing as several of the men darted back out, followed by one of their comrades, who was holding a decapitated but still-writhing snake by its tail.

Andrew felt a shiver of horror. If there was one thing he was truly terrified of, it was snakes, and he suddenly realized that this rocky hill was most likely a haven for them. He stared at the soldier, who was teasing his comrades with his trophy. The soldier looked up at Andrew.

"Makes a great dinner, sir."

A ripple of laughter swept the regiment, and Andrew wondered if the terror he felt was evident.

Trying to smile, he turned his horse aside and continued on across the west flank of the hill. The column of land cruisers, which he had sighted from the last ridge and lost sight of crossing the valley, were again in view, far closer now, moving to the north, parallel to his line and just beyond artillery range. Dark columns of Bantag infantry moved with them, looking like some sort of living entity, a vast, threatening multilegged creature, the sunlight glistening off their weapons. Horse-drawn batteries, limber wagons, caissons, and mortar units all moved with the columns.

Angling around to the north side of the hill, he saw Schneid's guidon and rode up to join the corps commander, who was standing next to a battery watching as the gun crews maneuvered their pieces into place, caissons and ammunition wagons deploying into the tree line.

"How's it going here, Rick?"

"Don't have much time, Andrew." He pointed to where the line of land cruisers were deploying into open formation. Bantag skirmishers darted ahead of the lumbering machines, engaging the thin line of blue waiting for them at the base of the hill and in the village, which was now wrapped in flames.

"Any sign of Hawthorne?"

"Haven't you heard, sir?"

"What?"

"Vincent's down. A courier just come through."

"Oh God." Andrew sighed. "How bad?"

"The courier didn't know. He led a charge to fix Ha'ark's attention on the center, while Marcus moved into the forest with Sixth and Fourth Corps. The attack we saw last night. The courier said word was it was pretty bad, shot in the hip."

So that was the fight from last night, Andrew thought. And it'd be like Vincent to lead it, hoping Ha'ark would see him. Damn.

Schneid, taking the cigar from his mouth, pointed off to the northwest.

"At least six miles out, caught sight of a column engaged a few minutes ago."

Andrew accepted Rick's field glasses and saw the smoke, antlike figures moving on the distant hills.

"Two, three hours at least." Andrew sighed. "Damn, so close, so damn close."

"And they're fifteen minutes away," Rick interjected, pointing back down the hill.

The battery before the rocky outcropping opened up, even while their infantry assistants dragged freshly cut logs up and stacked them in front of the guns. The woods behind Andrew echoed with shouts, the ringing of axes, the men working feverishly to throw up some protection. Over in the rocky outcropping teams of ten and fifteen men struggled with boulders, stacking them into breastworks.

More guns opened up around the western slope of the hill and as the first rounds hit the columns, the Bantag, moving as if guided by a single hand, began to spread out. Andrew lowered his field glasses to watch, awed by the precision of the maneuver.

"Four umens, forty thousand warriors." Rick sighed. "They're moving slow, you can see that, even some straggling. They must have forced-marched through the night."

"Same as we did," Andrew replied.

"What's coming from behind us?" Schneid asked.

"At least six mounted moving up."

"The only ammunition we have is what we're carrying, Andrew. This is going to get tough."

Andrew nodded, saying nothing, judging the range, as half a dozen Bantag batteries darted forward at the gallop. The battery commander by the rocky outcropping ordered his four guns to cease fire on the advancing infantry and wait until the Bantag guns started to deploy.

The Bantag batteries continued forward, caissons and pieces bouncing over the rough terrain.

"Damn they're coming in close," Rick whispered.

Behind Andrew a regiment, moving in columns of four, ran past at the double, men gasping, staggering as they moved to the northeast side of the hill. Another regiment moved in behind the battery deployed to Andrew's right. In spite of their exhaustion the troops started to dig in, pile up rocks, drag dead tree limbs into the line. The few still with packs or blanket rolls threw them onto the barricade.

The enemy batteries below continued to advance, swinging around the burning village. The first of the Bantag batteries slowed, lead horses turning, guns swinging about.

"Case shot, six-second fuses! Range, thirteen hundred yards!" the battery commander to Andrew's left roared. "Remember, we're shooting downhill. Don't aim too high!"

Loaders sprinted down from the caissons, shells were slammed into breeches. The commander paced his line of four guns, stopping behind each to check on how the gun was laid.

Down below the first of the Bantag batteries was already unlimbered, crews swarming around their pieces, swinging them into position while the caissons were moved back.

"Battery . . . fire!"

The first gun next to Andrew kicked back, the other three firing less than a second later.

The first shell, an air burst, ignited just forward of one of the guns, knocking down the crew; the other three shells detonated behind the firing line. A caisson blew, the dozens of shells and more than two hundred pounds of powder inside exploding in a brilliant flash, the explosion causing a second caisson to go up an instant later. As the thump of the detonations washed up the hill, a cheer erupted from the weary defenders, the men coming to their feet, shouting their defiance.

Andrew looked over and nodded at the commander, who stood in front of his pieces, a childlike grin on his face, as if he had just accomplished something he hadn't been quite sure he could do. Seeing that he was under the eyes of the army commander, he immediately struck a pose of professional indifference, turning back to shout at one of the crews for firing too long.

The surviving crews of the enemy battery struggled back to their feet, and within seconds were at work once again, loaders running from the still-intact caissons. More and yet more batteries deployed into line, while the twenty guns Schneid had positioned along the northern slope of the hill opened up. Half a dozen of the Bantag guns never even fired a shot before they were smashed by the concentrated blows, but the surviving guns now came into play. The first shots ranged high overhead, plowing into the forest above and behind Andrew, treetops bursting, limbs raining down.

The Bantag gunners set to work, firing almost as rapidly as their human opponents, concentrating their fire on the battery on the rocky outcropping to Andrew's left. The air around Andrew seemed almost alive, quivering, shaking, as shells screamed in, explosions bursting in the trees, geysers of dirt fountaining upward.

"Think we better move," Rick shouted. "No sense getting killed when the game's just starting."

Andrew followed his corps commander up the

slope and into the trees, feeling guilty that he was leaving the gunners behind. Kneeling behind a fallen tree, he watched the uneven contest, as the guns seemed to be enveloped in a tornado of fire and slashing iron. The second gun in the line crashed on its side as a shot tore its left wheel off, while in the woods a caisson exploded, several trees toppling from the explosions.

A battery suddenly opened up to Andrew's right and, surprised, he stood up as the four guns cut loose, their position concealed in the woods.

"Brought the guns over the top of the hill."

Andrew looked up in surprise to see Pat coming through the trees from above.

"Two more batteries on the way over from Ninth Corps. Seemed like this is where Ha'ark was going to hit first," Pat announced.

"How's it back on the other side?" Andrew shouted, trying to be heard above the cannonade.

"Half hour or so the first of the buggers on horse will be up."

"Emil?"

"Last of the wagons are into the trees. Got two divisions of Ninth Corps digging in on the south slope, the other division and the boys left from Fifth Corps moving in to cover the east slope. What's left of Eleventh Corps is in reserve on top of the hill. Some Bantag with rifles are popping at us from long range, but all the action's up here. So I thought I'd come up for the show."

Andrew nodded in agreement and realized, that in many ways, he was almost superfluous to this fight. Schneid had done a masterful job of deploying on the north and western slopes, Pat, as usual, had handled the rear guard, and Emil had managed to get his wounded safely in.

Pat stood and started down the slope to where the beleaguered battery continued to fight, the commander pulling the men from his number two gun off to strengthen the ranks of his remaining three pieces.

"Pat, get the hell back here!" Andrew shouted.

"Now, Andrew me darlin', this is an artilleryman's fight, it is!" Pat roared, and, going over to the number one gun pitched in, shoving the gun sergeant aside to aim the piece himself.

Feeling as if some sort of challenge had been offered, Andrew stood and looked down the line. The infantry was deployed, men pressed low, enduring the bombardment. Motioning for his guidon bearer to follow, Andrew started to walk the length of the line, Rick falling in by his side.

"Sir, aren't these kinds of displays a little ridiculous in a modern war?" Rick asked, ducking low and pulling Andrew down with him as a shell burst directly overhead, clipping the top of a tree in half and sending the branches and severed trunk showering down around them.

Andrew forced a grin.

"The men expect it." Andrew could see the troops looking up at him. "And besides, there are times when an army commander's life no longer counts."

"Damn it, sir, you stole that line," Schneid said in English, laughing. "Hancock said that just before he got shot at Gettysburg."

Andrew, slightly embarrassed that his theft of a damn good line had been found out, was tempted to order Schneid to leave him alone.

A high-pitched shriek echoed up from the smoke,

which now obscured the valley where the Bantag were deploying. Andrew turned, gazing intently, and finally saw it. The first of the land cruisers was advancing, passing through the line of guns, swarms of Bantag infantry following.

"Press it in!" Ha'ark shouted.

"My Qar Qarth, their land cruisers are moving down on us from behind." One of his staff pointed to the swirling columns of black coal smoke.

Ha'ark turned about to look toward the northwest. The enemy relief column was clearly in view, a dozen land cruisers moving in line abreast, only a light screen of his troops falling back before their advance.

His own cruisers were deployed, nearly thirty machines. More than one was already falling behind. Looking back to the south, he could see the machines which had broken down in the advance, one of them exploding. If he turned about now, to face the threat, it would mean withdrawing, moving the machines yet again. How many more would break down?

"Pull five regiments of the Fourth Umen, three batteries of artillery," Ha'ark ordered. "Send them back to slow the advance. In two hours we can finish off Keane and his men trapped on the hill, then we shall turn and deal with the other threat."

Cursing, Marcus walked around the ironclad, the driver standing on top of the machine oblivious to the sniper rounds whipping past.

"Sir, the cylinder head's cracked. We have to shut it down, get a new cylinder from supply. I'm sorry."

"That's two machines down, and we haven't even gotten into the fight yet," Marcus roared.

The driver leapt down from the top of the machine and took off his helmet and chain-mail face guard which protected him from any flying splinters that would shard off on the inside of the machine when it was hit.

The driver watched with obvious envy as the iron-clad commanded by Timokin crept past, the exuberant major piloting the machine with the top hatch open. Timokin snapped off a smart salute to Marcus and joyfully pointed toward the battle ahead.

Marcus returned the boy's salute, then fixed his attention back toward Rocky Hill, which was now shrouded in smoke and a near-continual rain of bursting shells. Through breaks in the smoke he could see the first wave of Bantag land cruisers creeping up the slope, guns firing.

"God help Andrew now."

"I tell you this is going to be bad," Feyodor shouted.

"Just do the drop right. We're only going to get one pass."

Looking down from ten thousand feet, Jack Petracci watched as the line of Bantag land cruisers deployed in open line for the attack up the hill.

"Hang on and keep an eye open for their airships."

Pushing the stick forward, he started the airship into a dive, cutting throttles back and pulling the release valve to drain off a couple of hundred cubic feet of hydrogen.

Within seconds the airspeed climbed up to sixty, then seventy miles an hour. The stick felt taut in his hands, and a shudder ran through the airship as they were buffeted by the warm midday thermals rising from the open prairie.

Watching the smoke, he tried to gauge the wind speed near the surface, running calculations in his mind for drift, then nosed over even steeper. The height-indicator gauge continued to spin lower, dropping through five thousand feet, then four.

The enemy line was directly below; he could see the upturned faces of the Bantag, a quick glimpse of a rider on a white horse. A spray of splinters kicked up next to his feet, the rifle bullet passing between his legs and crashing through the top of the cockpit.

"Damn, they're hitting us!" Feyodor cried.

"Just hang on and get ready."

The smoke-wreathed hill was directly ahead, and he continued the dive, crossing through three thousand, then two, trying to remember that the hill most likely stood five hundred feet high.

"Get ready, get ready . . . now!"

He felt the weight drop away, and an instant later he yanked the stick back hard into his stomach. The nose of his ship started to rise, splinters kicking around him as first one, then half a dozen bullets crashed through the cab. Skimming low over the trees, the airship raced over the top of the hill, the ground finally dropping away as he pulled up and away. Focusing at last on the ground southwest of Rocky Hill, he saw where block formations of Bantag riders, tens of thousands of them, were steadily moving up, and a sense of futility tore into his soul, that all that he had risked to drop the three packages would be meaningless when the assault finally came in.

Andrew stepped out from the protection of the rough breastworks to watch as Petracci pulled up, skimming low over the top of the hill, while, behind him, three multicolored umbrellas opened, a red-lacquered box swinging under each of them.

The breeze carried the umbrellas across the face of the hill, both sides pausing in their desperate struggle to watch as the packages floated to earth, landing in a line two hundred yards in front of the humans' position.

Schneid was already past Andrew, shouting, pointing at the boxes, screaming for several companies to get up and rush forward to retrieve the drop. More than a hundred men spread out, racing down the hill, and within seconds the advancing Bantag resumed their fire, men dropping as they raced toward the boxes. As the first men reached a package a cheer went up as the rope attaching the box to the umbrella was cut loose. Four men grabbed the box and started back up the hill. A shell detonated above them, sweeping all four down. Others leapt forward, grabbed the box, and continued up the slope while a surge of Bantag skirmishers charged forward, racing for the third box, which had landed closest to their lines. A desperate battle flared around the red-painted crate as half a dozen Bantag reached the container and a vicious hand-to-hand struggle ensued. Humans and Bantag slashed at each other with bayonets; an officer leapt atop the crate and fired his revolver straight into the face of a Horde warrior, dropping him before being bayoneted in the back.

Another company dashed forward, charging through the high grass, the flag of the Third Suzdal in the lead. The flag bearer raced to the box and planted the colors next to it while his comrades swarmed around the container, hoisted it, and started to run back up the slope. A charge of Bantag leapt out of the grass, this time going for the colors, the flag bearer crumpling when struck by half a dozen bullets. A groan went up from the line, and the men of the Third Suzdal turned about, charging down the slope to retrieve their precious colors.

Schneid, screaming encouragement, started after them. Andrew found himself caught up in the passion of the moment as well. Drawing his revolver, he pressed down the hill toward the fight. A Bantag hoisted the colors high in triumph, just as a color guard sergeant leapt upon the Bantag's back and, grabbing his head, bared his opponent's throat and cut it.

Now a wild cry went up from the Bantag side as their champion fell, and, by the hundreds, skirmishers rose from the grass and began to rush forward. The sergeant tried to pick up the colors and was hit, dropping to the ground, the colors clutched in his hands.

Andrew could sense that the fight for the colors was out of control, that regimental and corps pride would bring on a hand-to-hand struggle forward of his position, and in such a fight humans were bound to lose against their eight- and nine-foot foes.

"Sound recall, damn it!" he roared, turning to a bugler. "Sound recall!"

The bugler began the call, but the passion of the Third and its brother regiments was up as men surged down the hill, colliding in the open field with the advanced lines of Bantag warriors. Bantag artillery now turned on the struggle, pouring in shells regardless of losses to their own side.

A drummer boy, casting aside his instrument, leapt forward, darting low through the grass, weaving his way through the struggle. Falling atop the sergeant who was lying atop the colors, the boy pulled out a knife and slashed the flag free from its staff. Turning, he sprinted back through the melee, stumbling as a rifle ball spun him around. Coming back up, the boy limped up the slope, holding the flag high over his head. At the sight of his triumph the troops in the melee broke off the struggle and streamed back up the slope, cheering the drummer boy as he paused atop the breastworks and defiantly waved the flag.

Pat, still in command of the battery, had already ordered his guns swung about, and, as the last of the troops withdrew, he sprayed the grass with canister. With the barrels of the guns depressed, the rounds cut through at knee height, so that it looked like a giant scythe had swept half an acre in an instant, the grass blown high in the air to swirl about, bodies of Horde warriors and the few Republic soldiers caught in the whirlwind, disintegrating under the spray of iron.

"It's nothing but damn artillery ammunition!" someone shouted, and, turning, Andrew saw a panting crowd of soldiers kneeling by one of the three boxes, a sergeant, using his bayonet like a crowbar, had torn the lid off.

Andrew went over and looked in the box and saw twenty wooden containers stacked inside, the standard shipping sheath for fixed rounds of powder charge and a ten-pound shell.

"We got cut to ribbons for this shit?" the sergeant roared with disgust.

Andrew started to turn away in confusion, wondering what madness drove Petracci to risk a precious airship simply to drop three boxes of shells when one of the soldiers stood up, holding a sheet of paper.

"This was inside the box, sir. Better look at it."

Andrew snatched the sheet of paper from the soldier, ducking as a mortar run crumped nearby. He scanned its contents—it was a handwritten note from Chuck Ferguson. Grinning, he stood again.

"Get that box up by those caissons. One of you men pull out a shell and come with me. Sergeant, find the other two boxes and get them over here. Now!"

Andrew darted across the slope to where Pat was still working his three guns. Andrew grabbed him by the shoulder and motioned for him to follow him into the boulders. Pat reluctantly followed. Reaching the boulders, Andrew ducked and showed Pat the sheet of paper.

"It's from Ferguson. He's had three boxes of artillery ammunition dropped in on us."

"What the hell for?" Pat roared. "Three boxes aren't worth ant piss to us compared to what we need."

"Look at this," Andrew shouted, and as he handed the paper to Pat, he motioned for him to uncase the shell.

Pat pulled off the lid of the shell container and let the round slide out. "Damn thing feels light; what the hell is this?" Then his voice trailed away as he held the round and looked back at the sheet of paper explaining its use.

"Son of a bitch! This will give us something to play with now!"

"You're going to have to wait," Andrew shouted. "It says three hundred yards is maximum range. Make it a 150. Let them get up in a group. I want this to hit all at once!"

Grinning, Pat nodded.

"How many rounds do we have?"

"Three boxes—I guess sixty—so you have to make them count."

"I'll pick out my best crews. It's going to be tough, Andrew. They'll be right on top of us."

"I know, but at least we have something."

A thunderclap ignited to their right as another caisson blew, the blast slashing through the woods, knocking down dozens of men.

Andrew looked over the boulder and saw the enemy land cruisers relentlessly pushing up the slope, now less than eight hundred yards away, swarms of infantry moving with them. The thirty land cruisers had stopped and were now bombarding the hill, while farther back on the plains and in the ruins of the village mortar crews were relentlessly at work.

The bombardment was beyond anything Andrew had ever endured, surpassing even Hispania for its intensity. These were not Merki firing cannons they barely understood; the enemy before him were disciplined and well trained, their fire coming in with frightful accuracy.

The tearing sound of a volley erupted behind Andrew, and he looked up the slope into the forest.

"Sounds like things are opening on the other side. Pat, you're in charge here. Get a messenger to me once those damn land cruisers start moving again. I'll be on the other side."

Andrew scrambled out of the boulder field, calling for his staff. Mounting, he started up the steep slope, weaving through the forest, flinching as shells crashed through the trees. Smoke was billowing where part of the woods, in spite of the driving rain of the previous days, had caught on fire. Wounded men were crawling up the slope, trying to get to the reverse side, and he could sense a growing demoralization. Reaching the pinnacle of the hill, he reined in for a moment, moving around an artillery crew who were busy felling trees to open up a field of fire, one of the guns already in play. Someone had ordered the lightly wounded and a reserve regiment to build breastworks around the pinnacle and they staggered about, ducking whenever a shell screamed in.

A medical officer came up to Andrew and saluted. "Their cavalry is pressing in, units armed with rifles; they're dismounting and pushing up the slope."

"Any artillery?"

"We saw a couple of batteries, but I don't think they're in play yet."

As if in challenge to the major's words a shell thundered in from the southeast and exploded in the treetops. The major looked up at Andrew and shrugged.

"Where's Emil?"

"Down there, sir. There's a ravine running down the east slope. That's where's he's putting the wounded."

Andrew saluted and rode off, picking his way through the forest, passing hundreds of wounded men who were hunkered low against the barrage.

The ground suddenly sloped off sharply, massive boulders blocking his way. He spotted the green-cross flag of the hospital corps and rode toward it. A makeshift operating theater had been erected under a canvas awning, and Andrew saw Emil at work. Unable to ride farther since every foot of ground was occupied by a wounded man, Andrew dismounted, making his way through the forlorn wreckage of battle. Orderlies moved through the press, passing out water, one crew operating on an anesthetized patient right on the ground. Horrified, Andrew realized they were cutting off the man's arm and he saw a pile of bloody limbs lying in a shallow pit.

Feeling light-headed, Andrew turned away, a sharp memory coming back of waking up in a barn, Emil sitting by his side, breaking the news that he had just taken off his arm. Again there was the strange sensation, the ghost arm, as Emil put it, that he could still feel his left arm, his hand. A blood-splattered stretcher bearer bumped against Andrew, not even bothering to look up, cursing as he shouldered Andrew out of the way.

"Andrew."

Emil, stepping away from the operating table, taking his surgical mask off, motioned for him to come over. Andrew hesitated until Emil stepped out from under the awning. Another shell rumbled overhead, smashing into the trees, exploding, screams erupting in the woods as a severed trunk crashed down into the hospital area.

"Damn it, Andrew. If we were fighting the Rebs, I'd tell you to surrender."

Andrew said nothing, looking around at the chaos, wondering how many of these men still might be able to fire a weapon. More shells arced overhead, most of them coming from the opposite side of the hill, the reverse slope and ravine at least offering some protection. But the batteries on the south side were starting to fire straight in.

"Can't you get some counterbattery down on those bastards?" Emil snapped.

"Pat threw nearly all our guns on the north and west sides—that's where the main attack is coming in. You're going to have to hang on."

"Colonel Keane!"

Andrew looked back to see one of Pat's orderlies at the edge of the ravine, standing next to his guidon bearer.

"General O'Donald said they're moving up!"

"I've got to go."

Emil nodded wearily.

"Last war I said I'd never touch a knife again; I can't take much more of this Andrew."

"None of us can take much more." Andrew sighed.

Patting Emil on the shoulder he scurried out of the ravine and, mounting, made his way back to the pinnacle. The artillery battery on top of the hill was now fully engaged. The slope directly below was blocked by the trees, but the open ground beyond was visible, and the crew was pouring its fire down on a mortar battery, which was shooting back at them, blanketing the top of the hill with fire.

A thunderous roar erupted below, smoke swirling up from the concentrated volleys of thousands of rifles firing at once. Andrew pressed down the slope, the woods around him alive with the hum of bullets, shells, and shot. As the trees began to thin out, he could see the embattled line, masked by smoke, men standing, kneeling, crouching behind shattered trees, casualties streaming back up the hill.

Dismounting, Andrew tossed Mercury's reins to Pat's messenger, ordering the boy to find a safe spot, and, drawing his revolver, he went down the slope, his guidon bearer dismounting and following in his wake.

Angling down to the field of boulders he pressed to the front of the line, dodging between the rocks, cursing when a bullet smacked into a boulder to spray his face with stinging splinters.

A high, piercing whistle sounded from the field below, picked up and echoed all along the line by dozens more. A deep booming roar, the death chants of the Bantag, reverberated, and from out of the shadows he saw the charge press in.

Ha'ark watched in silence as the bombardment smothered Rocky Hill, wondering if there would be any organized resistance left by the time his land cruisers reached the edge of the woods. A constant stream of couriers galloped up with dispatches and replies to orders.

Jurak was closing from the south. Lead elements of his mounted rifle units were already deploying, and within another hour thirty thousand more warriors would be up.

Looking down at the map he could see the crisis building. The dozen land cruisers of the humans were but three miles away, moving with an estimated twenty thousand men. Looking to the northwest he could see their columns advancing, land cruisers, puffing smoke, crawling down the distant slope.

He looked again at Rocky Hill. It would be best to let Jurak bring up more of his troops, yet to ease off on the pressure now would give Keane time to recover. In an hour he could strengthen his position, dig in. Already the Horde had expended more than ten thousand shells in the bombardment, more than half of all his artillery reserves.

No, the attack had to go forward. If there was a chance to annihilate Keane, it was now.

Chapter Thirteen

"They're at 250 yards!" Pat roared. "Damn it, Andrew, we can't stand out here like this any longer! Let me open fire!"

Crouched behind an upended fieldpiece, Andrew felt as if he would go mad if the barrage did not lift. The land cruisers had stopped, tantalizingly out of range. Lined twenty-five across on the slope, they poured in sprays of canister and explosive shell, sweeping the edge of the forest, while Bantag warriors lying in the grass poured in a devastating rifle fire. Andrew could sense his own rifle fire breaking down, men remaining crouched behind whatever protection they could find, no longer shooting back.

The roar of battle had swept around to the western slope of the hill, and in momentary lulls he could hear thunderous volleys from the south.

The number four gun in the battery collapsed in on itself as a mortar shell detonated directly on top of the weapon, the entire crew going down.

"Pat, put some solid-shot rounds on the ironclads. But hold the special shot."

"Andrew, it's a waste of powder. We know that."

"Do it. We've got to lure them in closer!"

Pat motioned for a messenger to pass the word to the other batteries. The boy had barely made half a dozen yards when he went down. Two more messengers went out, only one making it to the trees.

Pat passed the word to the two remaining gun crews, who trained their weapons on the nearest cruiser. Seconds later there was a spray of sparks from the front of the ironclad, and, along the line, Andrew heard the bell-like ring of shot hitting and ricocheting off.

With the change from shell and canister to solid shot on the part of the batteries, the Bantag infantry, which had been kept low by the artillery blasts, started to push in closer, some of them sweeping to where the brutal fight for the colors of the Third Suzdal had been fought out.

This time they controlled the field. No troops would dare to stand and oppose them now. A charge erupted from the Bantag line, a knot of warriors following a red standard, half a hundred of them reaching the woods and storming up over a battery before they were finally swept away by a battered regiment deployed around the guns.

Smoke from the intense rifle fire again obscured the field, and reports started to come in from brigade and division commanders, claiming that ammunition was fast running out.

"Pass the word to cease fire," Andrew shouted. "Hold fire until they're right on top of us. Hold fire!"

Fire started to drop off, and after several minutes, the rifle fire of the Bantag slackened as well.

The smoke, which hung so thick that Pat, who was standing only a dozen feet away, was nearly invisible, drifted and curled. From out of the gloom a lone narga horn sounded, followed an instant later by dozens more.

The sound of it chilled Andrew's blood. It was the

signal for the attack, the same in all the Hordes, an insistent braying, which started at the lowest note possible, then shifted quickly to a shrill, bloodcurdling wail.

A roaring erupted from the Bantag hidden in the smoke, a deep rhythmic chanting and then, piercing through the wild insane noise, there was the shriek of the steam whistles, followed by a low deep rumbling as the black land ironclads began their final attack up to the tree line.

"Bugler, sound the artillery signal to load!" Pat shouted.

The cry was picked up by the other batteries. Turning, Andrew shouted for the regiment concealed in the boulders above them to come down and deploy behind the barricade where the two shattered fieldpieces lay.

A loader ran past Andrew, carrying the precious bolts sent by Ferguson, and Pat personally took the round, gently sliding it into the breech, then stood behind the gun, waiting.

Rifle fire again erupted from the front, bullets slashing the air. Standing behind the number one gun, Andrew waited expectantly.

"Target to the right!" Pat shouted. "Number three gun, take the first in line. We got the second!"

Andrew could barely make out a dark form where Pat was pointing, and then it seemed to emerge in an instant out of the gloom, black iron dark and menacing, the human skulls arrayed across the top of the machine standing out stark white, obscene. Ebony smoke billowed from its stack, steam jetting from its sides.

Pat, screaming for his crew to work faster, stood behind his piece, sighting down the barrel as the crew shifted the prolonge, two men on each wheel helping to pivot the gun.

The machine they were aiming at shifted in its path, turning slightly to come straight on, and its forward gun port popped open.

"Down!" Andrew screamed. Even before he could duck the ironclad fired, canister slicing through the gun position, sparks exploding where the iron shot slashed against the barrel and iron-rimmed wheels of the gun, cutting down half the crew. The wind of the canister swirled around him, he felt a plucking, a pull which jerked him around.

"Lucky you had it cut off," Pat shouted, looking back anxiously at Andrew.

Andrew felt for his left side and then saw where his empty sleeve, which he usually wore pinned up just under the stump of his arm, had been torn open. The stump, nicked by the canister ball, was bleeding, the pain of the blow causing him to gasp.

Pat turned back to his piece, continuing to sight down the barrel, shouting for several infantrymen to get up and replace the casualties.

He suddenly held both hands high.

"Stand clear!"

Taking the lanyard up, he stepped back from the piece, turned halfway around, then jerked the rope taut and pulled.

A jet of flame snapped up from the touchhole, an instant later the ten-pound breechloader leapt back half a dozen feet.

In spite of the incessant roar of battle Andrew felt as if he could actually hear the bolt shrieking down-range, a slightly different sound, which, being unique, made it noticeable. A split second later a burst of steam erupted from the land cruiser's smokestack followed by a fierce detonation, the machine bursting asunder, a blowtorchlike jet of flame searing out of the still-open gun port.

Awestruck, Andrew looked down the line of advancing cruisers. Showers of sparks soared up from nearly half the machines, the high, piercing whine of some of the bolts ricocheting off the ironclads echoing over the thunder. For a few seconds Andrew wondered if Pat had just scored a lucky hit through the open gun port and that Ferguson's weapon was a failure. Then a second land cruiser exploded, followed a few seconds later by two more. Several of the machines had lurched to a stop, steam pouring out of their stacks and he saw a hatch open on one of them, a shrieking Bantag flinging himself out the open door.

Wild cheering erupted along the line, counterpointed by howls of dismay and confusion from the Bantag. But the majority of the machines continued to lurch forward. Pat shouted for another round.

Stunned, Ha'ark saw the first machine go up, explosions ripping down the line.

"Press in now!" he shrieked. "Press it in!'

Over the smoke Andrew saw the signal rockets soaring heavenward even as Pat fired the second bolt, destroying a cruiser at less than fifty yards range.

"Like shooting elephants!" Pat roared with delight as he called for a third round to be brought up.

"Here they come!"

The cry erupted from the infantry deployed around them and, looking up, Andrew saw the wall of Bantag warriors surging forward at the run, their long-legged strides consuming nearly a dozen yards a second.

The charge surged up over the low barricade in front of the battery. A Bantag, rifle held high, leapt atop the gun, only to collapse as Pat, jumping backwards, fired a revolver into his face.

The sound of the Bantag charge slamming into the line echoed across the hill. Rifles were fired at point-blank range, counterpointed by the dull, sickening thwack of clubbed muskets crushing in skulls, muffled reports of pistols cracking when pressed straight into the body of a hated foe.

Men went down, kicking, struggling on the ground, the fight around the battery degenerating into a mad brawl, giant-like Bantags laughing with wild hysteria, swinging their rifles like clubs, diminutive humans darting out of the way, stabbing bayonets into the legs, stomachs, groins of their opponents.

The impact of the charge hurled the line back from the guns. Andrew, pushed back by the crush, heard a hoarse cry, someone shouting his name, and saw a Bantag towering above him, looking down with triumphant glee. Raising his pistol, he fired, but the warrior kept on coming, rifle raised high, already arcing down. Clumsily, Andrew rolled to one side, striking the rocky ground face first, his glasses shattering. The blow struck the ground next to him, the metal of the gun's butt plate kicking up sparks.

Rolling over, he aimed straight up at his now hazy tormentor and fired, emptying off all five shots before the giant collapsed backwards. Staggering to his feet, he felt someone grab him by the shoulder, pulling him back out of the melee. It was his guidon bearer, the pennant gone.

Gasping for breath, Andrew allowed himself to be dragged out of the fight and into the protection of the boulders, where riflemen stood, firing down into the bitter hand-to-hand struggle.

"Your glasses, sir?"

Andrew nodded, fumbling to his breast pocket where he kept a spare pair, and the boy helped him pull them out and put them on.

Squinting, Andrew looked around, ducking low as a Bantag burst out of the swirling confusion, rushing straight at them. His guidon bearer calmly drew his revolver and put three shots into the warrior so that he crumpled up and collapsed at Andrew's feet.

A shrieking whistle sounded to Andrew's right, and he saw an ironclad lurching through the press, moving up to the edge of the trees, its cannon firing a burst of canister at point-blank range, sweeping a dozen men off the boulders above Andrew.

"The guns! We've got to take the guns back!" Andrew roared.

Tossing aside his revolver, he drew his sword and held it aloft.

"Who's with me?"

He started down the slope into the rear of the battery area, the men swarming around him.

"Keane to the rear!"

The cry erupted around him and Andrew was startled as soldiers swarmed about him, elbowing him out of the way of the charge, men stepping in front of him, turning about, pushing him back toward the boulder.

"I'll stop if you retake those guns!" Andrew cried.

Physically restrained by half a dozen soldiers, Andrew could only watch as the charge surged back around the guns. He caught a glimpse of Pat, standing by one of his precious pieces, holding a sponge staff, using it like a quarterstaff, roaring with delight as he crushed a Bantag's skull.

He's having a good time, Andrew realized. He's enjoying this madness.

The countercharge swept through the guns, pushing the last of the Bantag over the barricade, and in an instant Pat was back at the gun, screaming for the infantry to help him swing the piece around. In spite of the rifle fire still sweeping it, the crew stayed in position, pointing the gun straight at the land cruiser less than twenty yards away, which was slowly pivoting, while a charge of Bantag swept past the machine and pressed into the woods.

Pat screamed for the men to stand clear and jerked the lanyard. The bolt struck the side of the land cruiser, drilling a hole straight through and into the boiler, which exploded.

The Bantag, who had only been pushed back a few dozen yards, continued to pour fire in, dropping half the men who had helped swing the gun about.

"Nothing more to do here!" Pat shouted, and, pointing to the boulders, he led the way up the slope, pushing Andrew ahead of him.

"Hell of a fight, Andrew, damn hell of a fight!" Pat roared.

Andrew scrambled with him up into the boulder field. Looking to his right he saw where the enemy charge had pushed back his entire line, firing erupting in the woods farther up the slope. Where the battery stood, the Bantag infantry had regained the outer side of the barricade and were now trading fire with the survivors in the boulder field.

"At least we stopped their cruisers!" Pat shouted

with glee. "Must have killed fifteen, maybe twenty of 'em."

"But they're in the woods now," Andrew shouted, leaning against a rocky outcropping, gasping for breath. "If help doesn't break through, we're finished. Ammunition's almost gone."

"Then it'll be the bayonet," Pat said with a grin, his voice edged with the mad hysteria of someone who was intoxicated with fighting.

"Here they come again!" Through the smoke Andrew saw the charge swarming in once more.

"This is it!" Marcus shouted, reining his horse in by Timokin's ironclad.

Grinning, the young major saluted. "We'll see you at the top of the hill."

"Don't outrun your infantry support," Marcus cried. "Let the infantry clear the guns. Save our surprise for the hill beyond."

"Yes, sir!"

Marcus returned the salute and reined his horse about, galloping off to supervise the positioning of the batteries deploying along the hill.

Timokin leapt back into his machine, closed the hatch, and slammed the latch shut, locking it in place. Squeezing his way around the fireman, he looked at the pressure gauge, which was hovering near the red line as his ironclad, having labored over the top of the crest now began to roll down into the narrow valley. Watching the gauge, he saw it start to edge back down. The fireman, fire poker in hand, nodded and grinned.

"How's she holding up, Andrei?"

"Running like a clock she is, and still a quarter ton of coal left." He motioned to the bunker alongside the boiler. It was a suggestion Timokin had offered, and Ferguson had readily agreed to, mounting the coal bunkers from floor to ceiling on either side of the boiler, thus acting as additional armor. It also made it easier for the fireman to fuel the machine in the tight quarters. All he had to do was pull open a chute door and the coal spilled into the firebox. Closing the chute, he could then rake the coal out over the fire.

Tapping the gauge, Andrei opened a valve, letting more water into the boiler, the temperature dropping momentarily as half a dozen more gallons flooded in through the pipes. Seconds later the pressure gauge again began to climb as the water flashed to steam.

Timokin slapped him on the shoulder and edged forward to where the gun crew waited, their ten-pounder withdrawn from the port, which was slammed shut. Stepping up behind the engineer, he crouched to peer out the driver's open hatch.

"Little more to the right, Nikolai. Let's aim for that battery."

"Right it is, sir."

The engineer, grabbing hold of the wheel with both hands, slowly turned the wheel. Lining up on their target, Nikolai turned the wheel back.

"Streambed ahead!" Nikolai shouted. "Hang on."

The machine lurched into the narrow creek, Timokin grabbing hold of a hand strap bolted to the inside bulkhead, glad that he was wearing an iron helmet as he slammed against the side of his ironclad. Looking back, he saw his fireman cursing, rubbing his left arm where he had most likely banged it against the red-hot boiler.

The ironclad dug into the far bank, crept up the embankment, and surged forward. Popping open a side viewing port, Timokin saw that the rest of his line, save for one machine which appeared to be hung up on the creek bank, was pressing forward, infantry moving behind the ironclads, using their metal bulk as protection from the battery fire on the ridge.

"We'll give them canister at three hundred yards," Timokin announced, and his gun crew leapt to work. A high-pitched ping banged against the front of the ironclad, followed in seconds by dozens more, sounding to Timokin like hail striking against glass.

"Masks down!" he shouted, reaching up and pulling down his chain-mail mask, which he had pushed up over his helmet. A thunderclap boom echoed through the ironclad, staggering Timokin backwards. The head of a bolt ricocheted back and forth inside the ironclad, striking a glancing blow off Timokin's helmet.

Another boom slammed through the ironclad, tiny pieces of metal spraying off the right side, sweeping the inside of the machine, one of the gunners screaming a curse as he grasped his arm. For a second Timokin thought they'd been breached, until he looked over and saw the bulging dent just aft of the gun position, the metal shining brightly.

The pinging continued as bullets slammed against the ironclad from front, left, and right. A round singing through the open view port forward whistled past the engineer's head.

The engineer reached up, slamming the large view port shut, so that a narrow slit two inches wide and a foot across was now the only outside view offered.

Timokin stepped back, waiting, looking aft to where the fireman hovered over his gauges, feeding in more steam as they crept up the slope.

"Two hundred and fifty yards!" Nikolai shouted. "Open port, stop engine, run her out!"

The ironclad hissed to a stop as the forward gun port swung open and Timokin, squatting, bent over to sight along the barrel.

"Bit to the right, more, more." The two men on his left labored at the pulleys hooked to the naval gun carriage, the gun slowly swinging.

"Hold, stand clear!"

Timokin stepped back as the gun sergeant yanked the lanyard attached to an oversize gun trigger. The trigger snapped back, the hammer slamming down, driving a firing pin into the rear of the ten-pound brass cartridge.

With a roar the gun recoiled, the noise inside the ironclad deafening in spite of the wads of cotton stuffed into every man's ears.

Smoke filled the chamber, the men coughing and gasping as the four gun layers, set two each on the pulleys attached to each side of the carriage, ran the weapon forward as the sergeant yanked the breech open and pulled the shell casing out. He stepped back as a corporal slammed another round in. The sergeant stepped back, sighting down the barrel, and Timokin caught a glimpse of their target. Half the Bantag around the gun were down.

"Stand clear!"

The gun kicked back again, and then yet again, as a third round tore across the ridge.

Stepping back from the gun, Timokin climbed up the narrow ladder into the top turret. Resting on one elbow he reached overhead, pulled the latch for the opening to the topside, and pushed the lid open, a rush of steaming hot sulfurous air swirling up around him. Sticking his head out, he looked straight up the slope. The battery directly ahead was out of action, nearly every gunner down, horses piled up around a caisson.

Looking to his left he saw where several of his machines were already charging forward, infantry swarming up the slope, men dropping from mortar fire, and rifle fire crackling along the ridge.

Bullets zinged past. Ignoring them, he watched as his fourth round, aimed at the next battery to his left, tore in. Horses fell, screaming.

Stepping back down he braced himself on his elbows. Sticking his foot out he felt it brush against Nikolai's helmet. He kicked him three times between the shoulder blades, the signal to go forward. He heard the order shouted back to Andrei and, with a jarring lurch, *Saint Malady* rumbled into the attack.

Sticking his head out, he watched as his charging line crawled up the slope. Cheering erupted behind him and, looking back, he saw the column behind him deploying into open order line, the men breaking into a run, sweeping up the hill.

He was tempted to uncover his weapon but waited, watching as the charge rushed ahead, the men leaping through the high grass. A mounted battery galloped across the stream behind him, drivers lashing their horses as they struggled up out of the creek bed.

An explosion erupted on his right, and he looked over to see one of his ironclads, the *Iron Fist*, exploding. Stunned, he saw where a Bantag battery, partially concealed by its position on the reverse slope, had fired into the side of the ironclad at nearly point-blank range, tearing it open.

Stepping down, he put his foot on Nikolai's right shoulder and tapped him three times, the signal to turn. Even as his machine started to lurch into position, the Bantag gun fired again. His machine lurched back as the shot struck the front shield. A scream erupted from below and he held his breath, but they continued to push forward.

Even before he could line up on the gun, an infantry charge, following the regimental colors, swept up over the gun, bayonets flashing in the sun as they tore into the gun crew. Seconds later he saw an infantryman triumphally waving a sponge staff overhead, and, stepping down, he reached to tap Nikolai on the left shoulder. Something felt different, and, letting go of his hold up in the top turret, he slid down, his feet landing on a body.

Nikolai sprawled back in the cabin, at least what was left of him. The deflection shot, slashing across the face of his machine, had cut through the view port, fragments from the round nearly decapitating Nikolai. Blood was splattered across the inside; the gunnery corporal was still frantically trying to wipe it off his chest and arms. The gunnery sergeant was now in the driver's seat.

"Reload case shot, percussion fuse!" Timokin roared at the corporal, pointing at the open gun breech.

The gunner looked up at him and, fumbling, staggered back to the ammunition locker, pulling a round out.

Climbing back into his turret, Timokin again stuck his head out, gasping for breath, afraid he would vomit from the sight of Nikolai and the hot sticky stench of blood.

Regimental flags were cresting over the ridge and, for a brief instant, he saw Marcus, on horseback, galloping along the ridge, waving his sword, urging the attack forward.

A battery galloped past *Saint Malady,* reaching the crest, which was now less than fifty yards ahead, the drivers swinging the pieces around.

The ground ahead was covered with wounded and dead. Shouting, he motioned for men moving past him to clear a path. Soldiers, racing in front of his machine, dragged their fallen comrades out of the way, leaving the wounded Bantag to their fate. He blocked out the shrieks of agony as his machine rolled over more than one who was still alive.

The top of Rocky Hill was now in sight, covered in smoke and flame.

"Timokin, push in!"

Marcus was up by the side of his machine, hammering against it with the hilt of his sword.

"We're going as fast as we can, sir."

"Push it, damn it, push it!"

Lurching up over the crest, Timokin drew in his breath at the sight of the chaos ahead.

Swarms of Bantag were fighting at the edge of the woods, a dark column moving across the field to his right, storming up the west slope of the beleaguered hill. Dark burning masses littered the side of the hill, but he could see where at least ten of the Bantag machines were still in the fight, coming about, creeping back down the hill. Batteries from Sixth Corps were deploying along the ridge, taking up the positions occupied only minutes before by the Bantag. The surviving guns of the enemy and the wagons with the mortar crews were pulling back to the southwest, some of the guns already swinging around to protect the flank of the assaulting column. It was obvious Ha'ark was trying one final desperate rush, hoping to overrun the hill and then hold it. If he could gain the position, not only would it mean Andrew and his men were dead, but the relief column would be out in the open as well, with the full fury of Ha'ark's forces turning to smash them.

"Send your couriers to my other machines!" Timokin shouted, struggling with the Latin, trying to be heard above the roar of battle and the blasts of steam slashing out of his machine. "Tell first squadron to engage the surviving ironclads, second and third squadrons to follow me. Have Third Division on our right pivot and follow me, but make sure they don't get ahead!"

Startled at being ordered by a mere major, Marcus hesitated.

"I know what I'm doing, sir! First squadron has ten bolts per machine. They'll stay out of range and tear them apart. We need to break up that attack!" He gestured toward the column which was relentlessly pushing across the open field.

Marcus hesitated, then, pointing to his staff, he started to bark out orders. He looked back up at Timokin and nodded.

Sliding down into his turret, Timokin put his foot down on the sergeant's right shoulder, then slid down into the interior of the machine and looked at Andrei.

"Can you give us any more steam?"

"She's running red-hot," Andrei gasped, the fireman having stripped off his chain-mail shirt and apron, standing bare-chested next to his boiler.

Timokin felt a gradual increase in speed as his machine started to angle down the slope, momentum picking up so that his gunnery sergeant, now in the driver's seat, looked back nervously.

"Brakes?"

"Let her roll!" Timokin roared.

Saint Malady bounced and lurched down the slope, going faster than Timokin had ever dared attempt in the practice trials. Slapping one of the gun layers on the shoulder, he motioned to his turret.

"You remember how to do this?"

Grinning, the assistant gunner scrambled up the ladder and squeezed into the turret.

"Sergeant, just steer us straight at the nearest battery, go through it, then head for their attacking column."

Timokin climbed back up into his turret, finding the narrow confines impossibly crowded with the assistant gunner curled up beside him.

"Just remember to keep it flowing, that's all!"

The boy grinned.

"Can I shoot it, sir?"

There was no way Timokin was going to surrender that privilege, and he didn't even bother to reply.

Saint Malady lurched, bounced, and clattered through the high grass, Andrei giving long blasts on the whistle since there was no steam being wasted. Gravity alone was driving the heavy ironclad down the slope at breakneck speed.

Bracing himself, Timokin poked his head out of the turret. The infantry was deploying behind him, running, falling behind. Third squadron, on his right, was coming down in echelon formation, while the three surviving ironclads of second squadron, on his left, were lagging behind, moving in echelon behind him. One of the machines hit an outcropping of rock, surged up, seemed to hang suspended, then rolled over on its side, an explosion of steam blowing out through the top turret. He caught a brief glimpse of the ironclad commander struggling to get out as the machine continued to roll and then crushed him underneath.

The Bantag batteries forward, deployed in the open field, were firing, shells screaming in, explosions erupting on either side of Timokin. He realized it was time.

Slipping back into the turret, he pulled the canvas cover off his weapon, motioning for his assistant to pop the firing slit open. Reaching to his right, Timokin checked the steam-pipe gauge, turning the valve which opened the line into his gun. A swirl of steam erupted around him. Checking the traverse on his gun, he sighted it in on the battery which was less than two hundred yards away.

The Bantag guns kicked back. Another clanging boom echoed through his machine, screams and curses following as bolt heads, sheared off by the strike, bounced around the interior. A searing pain sliced through his leg, and, looking down, he saw where his right calf had been torn open.

Ignoring the pain, he looked back through his sights. The gun crews were frantically reloading; the next volley would be delivered at less than fifty yards, most likely close enough to punch through. He saw several gunners drop from rifle fire, but still the Bantag worked to reload.

"Get ready," Timokin cried.

He waited for *Saint Malady* to level out from its wild charge down the hill. Bracing himself, he wrapped his finger around the trigger, said a silent prayer to the blessed Saint Malady, and squeezed the trigger.

The steam-powered Gatling gun sprang to life, barrel spinning. Fifty-eight caliber rim-fired cartridges from the side hopper dumped into the breech and tore out at the rate of eight hundred rounds a minute.

The first spray went high. Timokin released the trigger for an instant, correcting his sights as they went up over a small hillock. A Bantag gun crew was centered in his sights, and he squeezed again. The one-ounce bullets shredded the crew, and, traversing his gun, he tore a stream of bullets down the line. Every sixth round had a powder charge drilled through its core and Timokin watched, amazed as the tracer rounds seemed like a near-continual stream of fire guiding him in. Two more gun crews went down, and, raising his sights, he stitched a caisson, which detonated in a thunderclap explosion that shook the ironclad.

Panic erupted on the gun line, Bantag turning about, running, as one of the ironclads from third squadron opened fire as well. Two of the enemy guns were still fighting, though, and Timokin could feel the concussion of one of the ironclads from second squadron exploding.

Crashing right through the wreckage of the guns, *Saint Malady* charged forward, Bantag artillery crews scattering, running in panic. Ceasing fire, he stuck his head out of the turret, gasping for breath. The cloud of smoke and steam inside was absolutely blinding. Coughing, he looked back and saw that only one machine of second squadron was left. Behind them, several hundred yards away, the dark blue lines of infantry were racing down the hill, a battery following in their wake.

Saint Malady shifted, and looking forward again, Timokin saw a mortar crew, set up in the open, looking up in wide-mouthed amazement as the ironclad shifted in its course, and came straight at them. The crew broke and ran, abandoning their weapon and ammunition limber.

The charging column going up the slope of Rocky Hill was now less than four hundred yards away and halfway to the tree line, while to his left, on the northern slope, he saw where the Bantag were already up over the boulders and into the trees.

Standing up in the turret, hoping to catch the attention of the ironclad commanders in third squadron, he pointed straight ahead, toward the column, then slipped back into the turret.

"Half-empty, sir."

Timokin, cursing, slapped the ammunition box strapped to the rear of the turret.

"Damn it, scoop some rounds out and reload the hopper, but don't get any in backwards!"

The boy pried the lid open and, reaching in, started to pull out handfuls of cartridges, laying them into the feed hopper.

Saint Malady slowed as they started to angle up the slope, the machine laboring and Timokin cursed as the battle on his flank continued to press into the woods. But straight ahead the attack column was beginning to waver as the Bantag, seeing the ironclads approaching out of the smoke, realized that they were flanked. Mounted riders rode about them, waving battle standards, pointing up the slope, and for an instant he saw one mounted on a white horse.

"Ha'ark?" Timokin hissed.

The range was down to less than three hundred yards. Still a bit too far for his liking, but swinging his gun around he aimed at the rider and squeezed the trigger.

* * *

Stunned, Ha'ark saw the tracers walking up through the grass, coming toward him, as the enemy gunner raised his sights. The attacking host, who but moments before were surging forward to victory, slowed, looking in wide-eyed amazement at the machines closing in on their flank, many of them, at first, mistaking them for their own.

The staccato chatter of the Gatling gun reached Ha'ark, and he cursed, something that he had troubled over for so long and not been able to make, the humans had created. They had machine guns.

The tracers closed in, and, kicking his left foot out of the stirrup, he flung himself off his mount. Just as he hit the ground the horse reared up, shrieking in agony, and fell over, Ha'ark scrambling to get away from the dying animal's thrashing hooves.

"The Redeemer!"

The cry went up, an agonized wail, and looking up he saw his pennant falling, its bearer cut nearly in half.

He tried to struggle to his feet, but ducked back down as the bullets tore up the ground around him.

Timokin held the trigger down, sensing that keeping Ha'ark down was perhaps even more important than killing Bantag. A machine gun from third squadron joined in, followed within seconds by the other three, along with the one gun on his left from second squadron. It looked to Timokin like six hoses of fire spraying into the packed mass, and in that instant he sensed that what they were doing was yet again changing how war was to be fought upon this world.

His gun suddenly ceased firing and he looked over at his assistant who was struggling to reload, unable to keep up with the demand. Steam was venting out from the water casing that encircled the barrel mount, and he realized that he had come close to melting down the barrels. The gun would have to cool for a moment.

"Fill the hopper and get some more water into the barrel casing!" Timokin shouted. Letting go of the trigger, he stuck his head out of the turret.

The entire column was breaking apart, surging back to the south, running in mad panic, while the arcing lines of tracers pursued them. He could hear cheering and, looking back, saw where Third Division, Sixth Corps was finally catching up, the swiftest pushing ahead, leaping through the high grass past his machine. One of the ironclads from third squadron was already turning, swinging its Gatling fire up onto the northern slope of Rocky Hill, sweeping the Bantag advance clambering up through the boulders, tearing it apart.

He could hear artillery fire to the northeast, and through the smoke he saw flashes of light as first squadron, sitting at the bottom of the hill, fought it out with the surviving enemy ironclads, which were racing down the hill. Two of his machines were going into reverse, backing up to keep the range open. Explosions detonated along the open slope as several of the enemy machines exploded.

Turning his attention forward, Timokin slid down into the turret.

"Loaded, and the barrels are cooling!" his assistant shouted, pointing to the temperature gauge, which had drifted down out of the red.

Aiming high to avoid striking the charging line which was now ahead of him, Timokin arced a burst of fire into the retreating mob of Bantag, spurring the panic along. Remembering to pace his fire, Timokin fired a burst, waited a few seconds, then fired again.

Slowly they crept around the western side of the hill, catching a glimpse of the broad open plain to the south. Columns of horse riders were deployed nearly a mile away, but they were stopped already, drawing back. Raising his gun to maximum elevation, he squeezed off a hundred rounds, the shots arcing up high, then plunging down, the demonstration of fire more than enough to check any riders who were still considering pressing the attack.

Timokin looked over at his loader and finally nodded.

"Just tap it. Hold it for just a heartbeat or two, and aim high!"

Grinning, the boy slipped behind the gun, as Timokin dropped back down below. In the excitement he was unaware of the fact that his main gun had been pouring in fire as well, now firing shot at long range.

"Sergeant, steer her around so that we're guarding the southern approach."

"Major, we're damn near out of coal!" Andrei shouted. "You've been blowing steam like mad up there!"

"Just another minute or two, Andrei."

Watching through the open gun port, he guided the sergeant to a spur of land projecting off the side of Rocky Hill. Cresting it, he signaled Andrei to disengage the engine.

Blue-clad infantry, deployed in open order, were already several hundred yards ahead, the Bantag infantry streaming southward, the mounted warriors retreating out of range as well.

A hammering echoed on the side of his machine

and, going aft Timokin pulled the hatch open, Andrei moaning with delight as the outside air, which seemed as cold as a January blizzard, swirled in. As he stepped out of his ironclad, the cold air caused Timokin to reel, feeling as if he would faint, and he leaned wearily against the side of his machine, looking up at Marcus.

"Hell of a fight!" Marcus roared.

Unable to speak, Timokin could only nod. Behind Marcus he saw two of his ironclads deploying farther down the slope, a battery of twenty-pounders swinging in beside them, the lead gun already tossing shells at long range.

"We're damn near out of fuel, water, and ammunition, sir," Timokin finally was able to gasp.

"I'll have them brought up. Hold here. You picked a good spot, but I think the fight's knocked out of those bastards for today."

Taking off his helmet, Timokin let it fall to the ground as he looked across the field. Hundreds of bodies, nearly all of them Bantag, littered the slope. The roar of battle still sounded from the north side of the hill.

"Marcus!"

Timokin was startled to see Colonel Keane coming around the side of his cruiser. Marcus, grinning, snapped off a salute.

"Damn good to see you, Marcus," Andrew said, leaning over in the saddle to shake hands. Timokin looked up wide-eyed at the legendary commander. The attention of the entire Republic had been focused on getting Keane and his lost units out. Now that it was accomplished, Timokin stared at the two generals. He sensed there would most likely be a print of this scene in Gates's paper; perhaps he would even be in it as well, but at the moment he'd trade all of it for an ice-cold bottle of vodka.

"Andrew, you're wounded," Marcus cried, pointing at Andrew's bloody sleeve.

"Well, like Pat said, lucky the arm was already cut off. I'll live."

Andrew looked down at Timonkin and extended his hand.

"Your leg, son, it needs attention."

Timokin nodded, touched that his commander had noticed.

"Once things calm down, sir, I'll have someone see to it."

"Never really thought these damn things would work, Major. You charged like cavalry with them. Damndest thing. You could hear the Bantag howling in panic."

"Thank you, sir," Timokin whispered.

"How is it over there?" Marcus asked, pointing toward the north slope.

"They're breaking, streaming off to the east. You got here just in time. We're damn near pushed back to the summit; there was no place left to go."

Andrew, shading his eyes, looked southward.

"Can you keep those warriors back, Marcus?"

"The fight's out of them, sir."

"We've got ten thousand or more casualties to get out," Andrew announced, and to Timokin it seemed like all life had suddenly drained from his commander. "We've lost nearly all our wagons and horses when they pushed us back up the slope."

Marcus nodded toward the field.

"I'll get men upending their caissons, there's hundreds of horses loose out here. We've got a couple of hundred wagons at the rear of the advance as well."

"Fine." Andrew sighed wearily. "I just want to get the hell out of here."

Andrew turned his mount about and rode off, Marcus following. Timokin watched as they rode up the slope.

"Sir?"

It was the gunnery sergeant, sticking his head out of the hatch and watching in awe as Keane rode off.

"Can we grab some air for a few minutes? The boys are damn near dead in there."

"Fine, Sergeant."

Another burst of Gatling gun fire erupted from the top turret, the rounds soaring high into the air before plunging into the open steppe.

"Tell that damn fool up there to cease fire."

Picking up his helmet, Timokin walked around *Saint Malady*, examining the dozens of pockmarks, dents, and buckled plates. A wagon, loaded with sacks of coal and barrels of water, lumbered up, the teamster shouting for some infantry to help him unload. Behind it a limber wagon arrived, carrying boxes of cartridges and shells.

Timokin sagged against the front armor, gladly accepting a canteen of water offered by his sergeant. Uncorking it, he upended the canteen, pouring half of it over his head, then took a long drink.

"We sure beat the hell out of them," the sergeant announced, sliding to the ground beside him.

Timokin, remembering Keane's expression, looked across the field at the dark host on the distant ridge.

"It's only just started," Timokin sighed.

"Ship oars."

Admiral Bullfinch, not waiting for the launch to reach the dock and tie off, leapt for the gunnel, and up onto the wharf. A shell, slicing the air high overhead, shrieked out into the bay, a geyser of water mushrooming off the bow of his ironclad. He didn't even bother to look back. It was nothing but light field artillery, its threat like that of an insect attacking an elephant.

"So, Bullfinch, you finally decided to show up."

Bullfinch looked into the eyes of Sergeant Major Hans Schuder, not sure if the opening comment was a reprimand or not. In the twilight he could see that Schuder was exhausted, features drawn, eyes red-rimmed. He waited for the blow, ready to accept the blame.

"You're here, that's all I wanted Bullfinch, you're here." Hans extended his hand. "You got me out last time; I knew you'd do it again."

"Sir, I'm sorry, I . . ." His voice trailed off and he lowered his head.

"We've all lost fights, Bullfinch. Lord knows I've lost my share."

Bullfinch looked out across the bay, where one of his steam transport ships was dropping anchor, and then back to the city. In the shadows he could see armed patrols in the streets.

"The Cartha?" Bullfinch asked.

"I think I just started a war with them." Hans sighed. "I asked permission for us simply to evacuate through here. They refused and barred the city gates."

He chuckled softly.

"Funny what a battery of twenty-pounders can do as a persuasive tool. A dozen shots and they threw in the towel, but the half dozen ships that were here hightailed it out. I guess they've run back to Cartha with the report."

"Kal was worried about that, but my orders were if this was where you were heading, I was ordered to blow down the walls if need be to get you out."

Hans exhaled noisily.

"Relief hearing that, but there was no place else to go."

Bullfinch wanted to ask, but was afraid to. There was something about the look in his eyes.

"Miraculous, sir," Bullfinch finally ventured. "I mean 150 miles, no line of supplies, fighting all the way through. Sherman's march through Georgia was a romp in comparison to what you did, sir. Coming down the coast we picked up some of your men from Bates's command. They said you had up to fifteen umens on you."

"We counted eighteen all total."

Bullfinch hesitated.

"How bad is it, sir."

"I've got thirty-one thousand men with me, Bullfinch, nine thousand of them wounded. I started with nearly fifty."

"Merciful God."

Hans turned away, and Bullfinch could see that the sergeant was struggling to control his emotions.

"I thought they had us yesterday. They completely broke the square of Seventh Corps, overran it. God, it was a damned nightmare, the screaming, men panic-stricken, trying to get into our square, chopped down, swept by our own rifle fire and canister. We had to fire into them, had to."

His voice trailed off, and he spit over the side of the dock.

"We finally cut our way through; I left close to ten thousand men back there." He nodded toward the open steppe.

"Walk or die," he said, sighing. "Walk or die."

Hans stepped away from Bullfinch, his gaze fixed on the western horizon as twilight drifted in around him.

"I'll have fifty ships up by morning," Bullfinch announced. "We can start pulling you out then."

"Evacuate?" Hans asked.

"I thought that was the idea."

Hans spit again and shook his head.

"We've got this town—it's ours. The Cartha are in the war now, like it or not."

"What the hell are you talking about, sir?"

"Bullfinch, we're keeping this town."

"Sir?"

Hans forced a smile. "We hold this town, it'll force the Bantag to stay here, too, covering their flank. It's the jumping-off place for a second front for us. Hell, Ha'ark flanked us. Now let's threaten to flank him. We have the sea and this port to cover the flank of Roum. You keep the supplies up, and we'll hold this place till hell freezes. Get my wounded off, but the rest of us stay.

"I paid for this place with blood, and this is where we'll finally make our comeback, damn it."

Chapter Fourteen

Ready to collapse from exhaustion, Andrew hesitated by the door into the hospital railroad car, braced himself, then opened it and stepped in. Kathleen looked up with a start and silently slipped down the corridor, all but collapsing into his arms. He winced as her arms swept around him, and she drew back.

"You're hurt," she gasped.

He pulled her back into his embrace.

"Scratch. I've had worse."

In spite of his feeble protests she forced him into a chair and, kneeling before him, unbuttoned his tunic. He was suddenly embarrassed. It'd been weeks since he had bathed, and now nearly three days without sleep.

"I stink; I'm covered with lice."

"I'm a doctor, remember." As his jacket came off she held it between thumb and forefinger and tossed it toward the door of the car. Next came the tattered shirt, and, motioning for a nurse to bring a basin of water, she started to wash the stump of his arm, which had been torn open by the shell fragment.

"It's infected, but I think we got it in time," she whispered, and Andrew suppressed a groan as she washed the wound with disinfectant.

"It's going to need stitches."

"Not now. Things to do, but I wanted to see you first."

He looked back up the corridor.

"How is he?"

"Not good. Running a high fever."

"I want to see him."

"So, Dr. Keane, how's our wounded hero?"

Andrew looked up to see Emil come through the door, followed by Pat.

"Emil, how the hell could you let him wander around like this," Kathleen snapped.

"Well, Kathleen darling," Pat interjected, coming to the protection of his friend. "It's been rather hard pinning the colonel down long enough, what with fighting a withdrawal from the Shenandoah, attacking the Bantag, holding out on Rocky Hill, then directing the retreat back to here."

"Let me see Vincent," Andrew said.

Kathleen looked back up the corridor as if ready to argue with him, then nodded. Taking a blanket, she draped it over Andrew's shoulders and motioned for him to follow quietly. Pat and Emil fell in behind, and though she started to raise an objection, Emil's gesture for her not to debate the point silenced her.

Stretchers lined both sides of the car, and Andrew moved slowly, reaching out, taking hands as he passed.

"Licked 'em good, didn't we, sir . . . the old First Corps didn't let you down did it, sir . . . don't worry, sir, we'll win this yet."

Andrew nodded, unable to speak, slowly moving to the back of the car, following Kathleen as she opened the door into a private room, then stepped out a minute later.

Andrew stepped in and, at the first sight of Vincent, he felt his throat tighten. The diminutive general seemed to have shrunk, looking like a wasted child. Father Casmar was by his side.

"Sir, how are you?" Vincent whispered.

Andrew drew up a chair and sat down by the bunk.

"Damn all, Vincent." Andrew sighed. "Marcus told me about the charge. Why, son? Why did you do that?"

"It was the only way, sir. Had to fix Ha'ark's attention, make him think we were coming straight in. Would you have ordered the charge and then stayed behind?"

Andrew shook his head, unable to reply.

"And you said I was a dumb mick," Pat interjected. "Vincent Hawthorne, I think you're madder than I am."

"How you doing, Pat?"

"Hell of a fight." He looked over at Casmar. "Sorry, Your Holiness."

Casmar smiled. "Damn it; heard a lot worse since I joined the army."

Pat smiled and relaxed. "Well, damn me, Vincent, you should have seen my guns tear 'em apart. And them ironclads of that boy Timokin. Lord, what a charge."

"Wish I'd been there."

Andrew reached out and took Vincent's hand, surprised at how frail it seemed.

"You did well, son. I knew I could count on you. It was worth it, Vincent. Not for me, for Pat, or Emil. We got four corps out of the trap. It wasn't the Potomac this time."

"And Hans?"

"Wire just came in from Roum; Bullfinch got to him, they're on the coast."

Vincent sighed and laid his head back on his pillow, his features tightening.

"Kathleen?" Emil hissed.

"Gentlemen, please leave," Kathleen ordered.

Vincent started to tremble, struggling to sit up. Kathleen reached out with firm hands, forcing him back down.

"Don't leave me," he gasped.

"I'm here, son," Andrew whispered.

"Sir, I'm scared."

Andrew put his hand on Vincent's forehead, pushing back a lock of sweat-soaked hair.

Vincent's gaze locked on Kathleen.

"Mama?"

Andrew closed his eyes. How many times had he heard that cry. The wounded, who in daylight would stoically hold on, not crying, not struggling, but in the night, would call for their mothers, the oldest of soldiers, and the youngest boys, in their fear, their pain, dreaming of a soothing hand, the gentle touch in the night.

"Here, son," Kathleen whispered.

She took his hands in hers and, leaning over, softly began to pray.

"Now I lay me down to sleep, I pray the Lord . . ."

Andrew drew back, tears streaming down his face, stunned by the anguish he felt for the boy he had used up, the frightened young Quaker who had become the coldest of killers and was now a frightened boy again.

He was stunned as well by this other side of Kathleen. In his eyes she was, and always would be, the beautiful young Irish lass, red hair, sparkling green eyes, the lilt of a brogue when anger or passion flashed.

And now, she seemed almost Madonna-like, the soothing mother, not just of their children but of so many frightened boys who stood upon the final threshold.

A hand touched him on the shoulder. It was Emil, and Andrew withdrew. Walking the length of the car, he stepped out onto the rear platform, breathing deeply of the cold night air. There was still a war on, artillery fire flashing along the ridge, Marcus directing the bombardment that was covering their final loading up. An hour before dawn the remaining guns would be spiked, the crews loading onto the last train, and then the pullback to where new lines were being prepared, two hundred miles to the rear.

Ferguson had even thought of how to manage that. The last locomotive to back down the track would pull a hooked plow behind it, tearing up the track, twisting the rails so that Ha'ark would be forced to advance slowly, repairing the track if he ever hoped to keep his army supplied.

In the darkness he could see the last of the wounded being loaded on the cars in front of him while on the siding a battered ironclad, the name *Saint Malady* stenciled on its side, edged up a ramp onto a flatcar, the ironclad's commander standing anxiously by his machine, shouting orders. On the other side of the train he could barely see Petracci and his copilot, supervising the loading of their airship's wings, all that could be salvaged of their ruined machine, which had crash-landed after dropping a Bantag airship.

"Smoke?"

Andrew nodded, accepting the cigar Pat offered. Sitting down on the steps of the car platform, Andrew was grateful as Pat gently readjusted the blanket draped over his shoulders.

"It's all so different now." Andrew sighed. "Perpetual

war, no end in sight, new machines and yet newer machines." He pointed toward Timokin and his ironclad.

"No more cavalry charges, no more volley lines shoulder to shoulder," Pat replied sadly. "At least not against those damn smoke-eating monsters."

"It saved our asses, though," Andrew said. "Hell, another half hour and they'd have overrun us."

He shuddered at the memory of it . . . the Bantag bursting into the forest, falling back up the hill, trees crashing down around him, the high, ululating screams of the enemy slashing forward with the bayonet, driving toward the pinnacle of Rocky Hill, and the huddled wounded on the east slope, then the charge of the ironclads breaking into the rear of the Bantag host.

"You two sound like you'll miss the old way of killing," Emil snapped. "It's just killing to me."

"No alternatives anymore," Andrew replied. "We have to keep on going. The retreat buys time yet again, trade space for time. God willing, the weather will help, autumn rains, winter snow, maybe the fighting won't start up again till next spring, give us time to build a new army yet again."

"And he'll build a new one as well," Emil replied.

"The way of things back home, and here," Pat said. "Keeps us employed, it does."

"Sometimes I think you really are one sick son of a bitch," Emil snapped angrily.

Pat laughed sadly.

"Keeps me from going crazy with all of this, dear doctor."

Emil nodded, embarrassed over his outburst and, reaching into his jacket pocket, pulled out a flask and handed it to Pat.

"We might call this a defeat, but you two fought like avenging angels, you did."

Pat raised the flask, looking to the east, as if offering a salute to the fallen, and took a long drink.

"Andrew."

Frightened, he looked up at Kathleen. Sighing, she stepped down from the platform and, taking the flask from Pat's hand, took a long drink and sat down.

"Vincent?"

"Asleep."

"Thank God," Emil sighed.

"Fever's breaking, but oh, Andrew, that boy's torn up terribly. I don't know if he'll ever walk again."

"At least he'll live," Andrew said.

She nodded, unable to speak.

"Sir."

Andrew looked up and saw a messenger standing, holding a telegram. Somehow he could sense that the news was bad, and, reaching up, he took the slip of paper. Opening it, he fumbled in his pocket for a match. A light flared beside him as Pat held a sputtering match so he could read.

"Merciful God," Andrew whispered.

He looked over at his friends, tears in his eyes.

"Chuck Ferguson's dead. He passed away in his sleep an hour ago."

"Oh God, no." Pat sighed and, lowering his head, walked off into the darkness.

Kathleen stood up, shaking, her arms going around Andrew.

"What are we going to do now?" she whispered. "Without him, what are we going to do?"

"We'll live, we'll find a way to live through this," Andrew whispered. Holding Kathleen tight, he looked to the east and the glow of fire on the horizon.

* * *

"One hour," Ha'ark snarled bitterly. "One hour difference and we would have had him."

Jurak stood before his commander, defiant in spite of the burst of outrage.

"Eight of their umens should have been destroyed, and yet now word comes that even Hans will most likely escape. We should have crushed Keane and been marching on Roum, following their panic-stricken retreat. We should have ended this campaign before winter in Roum, perhaps even Rus itself. Now winter will stop us, all because you could not come up fast enough."

"You ask too much, Ha'ark," Jurak snapped. "You've taken a damn mob of illiterate barbarians and raised them through a thousand years of change. Six months will give you the time to finish that change. Come spring another dozen umens will be armed, there'll be a hundred land cruisers, with rails connected all the way back to our factories. You yourself said this war started too early."

"But now they know," Ha'ark said bitterly. "Keane now knows what he faces. In six months, what will he do as well? You should have killed him; then it would be different."

"Four of their umens are shattered, Ha'ark. They cannot replace that. We love eleven, but we can replace them. We will grind them down and win."

Ha'ark finally nodded and, leaving his lieutenant, stepped out of the command bunker and looked to the west.

He could sense they were pulling back, that come dawn the line would be empty.

You can run, but I will follow, he thought coldly. *And in the end, there will be no place to run to, and then I will finish it, finish it as I should have finished it yesterday. As I will finish it tomorrow.*

Organizational Structures of the Army of the Republic At the Start of the Bantag Wars

It should be noted that prior to the beginning of hostilities the Army of the Republic had been organized into two separate "armies"—the First and Second. The First, made up of 1st–6th Corps, was primarily of units from Rus, while 7th–12th Corps were recruited from Roum. This initial organization was due in large part to the language difficulty, along with the usual political considerations. The decision was reached to abandon this structure and fully integrate the two "armies." This did create certain command difficulties, even though it had been agreed that the language of Rus would be the official language of the army.

COMMANDER OF THE ARMIES—
COLONEL ANDREW LAWRENCE KEANE

(Note—Andrew Keane has always maintained the official rank of Colonel, even after the rapid expansion of the army, refusing any attempt to confer upon him a high ranking appropriate to the level of command. The same is true of Sergeant Major Hans Schuder.)

ARMY OF THE SHENANDOAH
(EASTERN FRONT)

Major General Patrick O'Donald
1st, 3rd, 9th, & 11th Corps

ARMY OF THE SOUTH

Sergeant Major Hans Schuder
2nd, 7th, & 8th Corps

RESERVE CORPS

Major General Vincent Hawthorne

At Fort Lincoln	5th Corps
At Suzdal	4th Corps
At Roum	10th Corps

WESTERN FRONT

(Deployed to the west of Suzdal on the old Potomac Line to block possible action by the scattered remnants of the Merki Horde.)

Major General Vincent Hawthorne
6th & 12th Corps

NOTES ON ARMY ORGANIZATION

Corps Organization

- Three Divisions per Corps
- Two Brigades per Division
- Five Regiments per Brigade

Average strength of a regiment at the start of the Bantag Wars: four hundred and thirty men, though certain units in 1st–3rd Corps had as little as two hundred men under arms. 1st through 6th Corps bore the brunt of fighting during the Merki Wars and as such had the strongest contingent of veterans. 7th through 12th Corps was recruited primarily from Roum.

A battalion of artillery is attached to each Corps. Four to eight batteries of four guns each comprise a battalion. Approximately two thirds of the artillery batteries assigned to field operations are equipped with ten-pound breechloaders converted from Parrott Guns. Rocket batteries, part of the overall artillery reserves, are assigned to Corps as needed.

Additional units attached at the Corps level—one regiment of engineering troops, a light brigade of cavalry, pontoon bridging unit, one company of sharpshooters armed with either Sharps long rifles or Whitworth sniper guns, various supply, transport, medical, and signals units.

Military Railroad of the Republic

Railroad transport had been reorganized as well, recognized now as a separate branch of service answering directly to the Commander of the Armies. During the Tugar and Merki Wars, men serving on the military railroad were also part of field infantry units, usually from the 1st Corps. With the increasing needs of railroads to support far-flung operations, men were assigned to the military railroad system on a permanent basis. A fair percentage of personnel are veterans of the earlier wars, discharged from field service due to disabilities.

Naval Units

The Navy is divided into two fleets; the First Fleet based in the Inland Sea, the Second Fleet in the Great

Sea. Given the relatively small size of the Fleets, both are under the direct command of Admiral Bullfinch, who answers directly to Colonel Keane. Plans were underway at the start of the war to form a separate Marine Brigade.

Additional Units

The air force, fortification units, heavy artillery, artillery reserves, the headquarters and training regiment (the old 35th Maine & 44th New York) all answer to the office of the Commander of the Armies.

UNION FOREVER

SPLIT IN THE RANKS
ON A CRACKED-MIRROR WORLD

Colonel Andrew Keane and his blue-coated soldiers were not the first humans time-space-warped to a world so familiar yet not so foreign. Humans abounded on the perverse planet—humans treated like cattle by the alien warrior overlords. Keane's Civil War weaponry defeated the swords, spears, and crossbows of his monstrous adversaries. And part of the human population was freed, but the other part became puppets of the overlords in a vast counterattack. Now it was human vs. human, gun vs. gun, ironclad against ironclad, as the empires of Roum and Cartha clashed in gut-wrenching, soul-stirring struggle for the future of a world beyond time. . . .

"One of the more interesting writers today in the field of historical and military science fiction."

—Harry Turtledove

TERRIBLE SWIFT SWORD

THE 35TH MAINE HAS LOOSED THE VENGEANCE OF THE HORDES

After four years of fighting the Rebs, Keane's battle-hardened boys discovered that the creature's crossbows, swords, and spears were no match for Union rifles. But it didn't take long for the odds to even up. The humans fought hard and bravely, and after defeating their adversaries on land and on sea, Keane and his troops had hoped to live in peace. But it was not to be.

Thanks to a human traitor, the aliens acquired a decisive edge—air power. And in their bloodthirsty quest for vengeance, they plotted to crush the humans once and for all—and forever reinstate their bloody reign of terror. . . .

"A wonderful world where Civil War-era Yankees have been tossed in with Medieval Russian peasants, Roman legionnaires, English pirates, Cathaginians . . . as well as a race of nine-foot-tall, flesh-eating aliens whose hordes make Ghengis Khan's mongols look like party guests."

—Raymond G. Feist

FATEFUL LIGHTNING

A WORLD DRENCHED IN BLOOD

Andrew Keane was now leading a mixed force of humans snatched from assorted periods in history on a desperate flight from an enemy more horrific than any nightmare. The alien Merki hordes, to whom all the humans brought to this distant world were cattle to be harvested at will, were mobilizing to destroy the humans in payment for the assassination of their revered warlord. And, his own military lines overextended, Andrew saw no alternative except to retreat, burning the land behind him as he went.

But retreat would offer only a temporary respite. For when the thirty days of mourning their leader were at an end, the Merki slaughterers would sweep forth to conquer, under a bold new warlord—the ruthless, ambitious Tamuka, who had sworn to leave no human alive on the face of the planet!

"The *Lost Regiment* series moves like a bullet. . . . An excellent read!"
—LOCUS

BATTLE HYMN

THE PRICE OF FREEDOM IS BLOOD

Hans Schuder, mentor and longtime friend of the 35th commander, Andrew Keane, now lives a nightmare as the captive of Ha'ark, the charismatic new leader of the alien Bantag Horde. Escape is impossible—but the courageous old Yankee has no other option. He must warn Andrew of this new foe, with his formidable plans and advanced weaponry.

If Hans and his ragtag group can make their way through the hundreds of miles of enemy territory, there might be enough time to save the fledgling human Republic from a terrible onslaught. But if they are caught, Hans and his fellow soldiers face a ritual death as horrific as Ha'ark's alien imagination can conjure—and a planet's only chance for freedom will fall to the Bantag sword. . . .

"Rousing good adventure . . . military SF fanciers will love it."

—*Painted Rock Reviews*